COLONY WAR

THE COMPLETE ALIEN™ LIBRARY FROM TITAN BOOKS

The Official Movie Novelizations
by Alan Dean Foster
*Alien, Aliens™, Alien 3, Alien: Covenant,
Alien: Covenant Origins*

Alien: Resurrection by A.C. Crispin

Alien 3: The Unproduced Screenplay
by William Gibson & Pat Cadigan

Alien
Out of the Shadows by Tim Lebbon
Sea of Sorrows by James A. Moore
River of Pain by Christopher Golden
The Cold Forge by Alex White
Isolation by Keith R.A. DeCandido
Prototype by Tim Waggoner
Into Charybdis by Alex White
Colony War by David Barnett
Inferno's Fall by Philippa Ballantine
Enemy of My Enemy by Mary SanGiovanni

The Rage War
by Tim Lebbon
*Predator™: Incursion, Alien: Invasion
Alien vs. Predator™: Armageddon*

Aliens
Bug Hunt edited by Jonathan Maberry
Phalanx by Scott Sigler
Infiltrator by Weston Ochse
Vasquez by V. Castro

The Complete Aliens Omnibus
Volumes 1–7

Aliens vs. Predators
Ultimate Prey edited by Jonathan Maberry
& Bryan Thomas Schmidt
Rift War by Weston Ochse & Yvonne Navarro

The Complete Aliens vs. Predator Omnibus
by Steve Perry & S.D. Perry

Predator
If It Bleeds edited by Bryan Thomas Schmidt
The Predator by Christopher Golden
& Mark Morris
The Predator: Hunters and Hunted
by James A. Moore
Stalking Shadows by James A. Moore
& Mark Morris
Eyes of the Demon edited by
Bryan Thomas Schmidt

The Complete Predator Omnibus
by Nathan Archer & Sandy Scofield

Non-Fiction
AVP: Alien vs. Predator
by Alec Gillis & Tom Woodruff, Jr.
*Aliens vs. Predator Requiem:
Inside The Monster Shop*
by Alec Gillis & Tom Woodruff, Jr.
Alien: The Illustrated Story
by Archie Goodwin & Walter Simonson
The Art of Alien: Isolation by Andy McVittie
Alien: The Archive
Alien: The Weyland-Yutani Report
by S.D. Perry
Aliens: The Set Photography
by Simon Ward
Alien: The Coloring Book
The Art and Making of Alien: Covenant
by Simon Ward
Alien Covenant: David's Drawings
by Dane Hallett & Matt Hatton
*The Predator: The Art and Making
of the Film* by James Nolan
The Making of Alien by J.W. Rinzler
Alien: The Blueprints by Graham Langridge
Alien: 40 Years 40 Artists
Alien: The Official Cookbook
by Chris-Rachael Oseland
Aliens: Artbook by Printed In Blood

ALIEN™
COLONY WAR

A NOVEL BY

DAVID BARNETT

TITAN BOOKS

ALIEN ™ : COLONY WAR

Print edition ISBN: 9781789098891
E-book edition ISBN: 9781789098907

Published by Titan Books
A division of Titan Publishing Group Ltd
144 Southwark St, London SE1 0UP

First edition: April 2022
10 9 8 7 6 5 4 3 2

A CIP catalogue record for this title is available from the British Library.

Printed and bound by CPI Group (UK) Ltd, Croydon, CR0 4YY

Did you enjoy this book?
We love to hear from our readers. Please email us at readerfeedback@titanmail.com or write to us at Reader Feedback at the above address.
www.titanbooks.com

To Mum. I promised myself I'd dedicate the next book to you. Sorry it's all monsters and killing.

1

```
Private Towing and Salvage Vessel: Clara
Crew: Five
Cargo: 300,000 tonnes of mineral ore plus
unidentified bio-material samples
Course: The Hub
```

The first thing Gambell thought was that the new diet Kathryn had him on was working, because he'd never before come out of cryosleep not feeling like he'd gone ten rounds with a particularly malicious heavyweight who took great delight in punching him in the gut until his insides turned to water.

As he sat up in the pod, rubbing his eyes and pulling off his monitors and catheter, he actually felt great. No cryo-hangover meant no lost, achy, blurry days when they made planetfall, and maybe he could actually take Kathryn out for their wedding anniversary tomorrow night for the first time in he couldn't remember how long.

The other pods radiating out from the central life-support hub weren't yet hissing and opening. Gambell's always opened first—captain's prerogative. His daddy always said that the skipper should be up first to welcome the crew in good times, and to protect them in bad. Well, it was good times at last for the crew of the STSV *Clara*, and for Gambell Reclamations.

The lights on the cryodeck were at full strength already. Gambell could hear them buzzing and flickering to life in the corridors that led off to the communal areas, quarters, and flight deck. Seemed like the *Clara* was recovering more quickly, as well. Gambell gingerly stepped out of his pod to test the strength of his legs—surprisingly good—and wondered if Kathryn had the old girl on a diet as well.

Gambell yawned and stretched and reached for the stew of post-sleep nutrients that was already gushing into the paper cup in the vending hatch at the front of his tube. He needed to pee, which he knew was totally a psychological thing, because the cryotube had been draining his bladder for the best part of the past three months. Then a shower, and a shave, and get out of these sleep shorts and vest… He sniffed at the front of his vest, suspiciously. Had Kathryn's diet stopped him sweating?

There was something else, as well.

Was it too quiet?

"Mother?" Gambell called, his voice croaky and his throat dry. "Where's my wake-up song?"

There was a hum and a pause, and then it started. "The Lark Ascending" by Ralph Vaughan Williams. Gambell's daddy had always come out of cryosleep to it, and so did he after taking over the family business. MU/TH/UR said nothing, though. Gambell's frown deepened. Was she sulking about something?

She'd always been a bit temperamental, that old computer. For a crazy moment, he wondered if Mother was jealous, then barked a laugh out loud that surprised even him. Computers didn't have feelings—but she would have seen on the bioscans what Gambell saw after finishing the last planet-side job, before they all went into the chambers. He was glad to have his skipper's hour before the rest of the crew woke up, to think about it, and decide whether he should tell Kathryn.

"Coffee in my quarters, Mother," Gambell called, his legs now steady enough to take him out of the sleep deck. "I'm going to freshen up. Start waking the others in fifteen minutes."

To be honest, the job had come as a godsend for Gambell Reclamations. They'd been cruising around the Frontier for the best part of five years, picking up bits and pieces of legit work, acting on rumors and tip-offs. Sometimes they were the first to the sites of salvage opportunities, more often than not second or third. It had been a pretty hand-to-mouth existence.

Gambell wasn't even sure why they'd been approached to do the job on the tiny little satellite at the ass-end of nowhere. It had come through a third-party commissioner, and he neither knew nor cared who was the prime client. It was a lucrative little number, retrieving a cargo of oil-rich minerals from a crashed freighter. They were being paid handsomely, but not a fraction of the worth of the stuff sloshing about in the containers they were towing. After the Oil Wars had cooled off, the old black gold had been in great demand all over the colonies, as well as on Earth. Those that had it were keeping hold of it, and selling it for top dollar.

More than once since they'd done the straightforward salvage job, Gambell had flirted with the idea of just going dark and selling it themselves. But he guessed that whoever was behind the contract had the kind of influence and muscle to make things very, very difficult for them if that happened. Best to stay aboveboard.

Plus, there was the matter of the unexpected bonus they'd picked up on that barren rock.

Gambell toweled off and inspected his face in the mirror. He had the space-farer's pallor, accentuating the lines on his face and the bags under his eyes. When was the last time he'd seen some sun, other than filtered through the viewing screens? Five years was a long time to be zipping about the frontier. He wondered if he should shave his beard, then decided to leave it. They were all due a break, and after what he'd seen when he put the others into cryosleep—"*Be the last man to sleep and the first man to wake,*" he heard his daddy's voice say—there were some serious talks to be had.

Question was, what was the protocol on this? It felt only right that it should be Kathryn to tell *him* she was pregnant, not the other way round, but when you knew something like that, what were you meant to do? Wait another month or however long it took her body to tell her what was going on, and then act surprised when she told him?

He dressed in his fatigues and buckled on his watch. Mother should have started the wake-up for the crew thirty minutes ago. They'd be emerging from cryosleep now.

"Mother, get some coffee on in the mess."

Gambell felt that dry, electric pause again, that hum of almost... uncertainty? Which was ridiculous. MU/TH/UR was an old AI, nothing like the sophisticated ones they had now—and which Gambell could never afford. He'd grown up with her. She was attuned to his ways, and knew more about him than even Kathryn. Even so, she was still just a—

The lights dimmed and switched to a slowly pulsing red, just as an alarm began to sound in a low, insistent, *whoop-whoop-whoop*.

"Mother? What the hell?" Gambell said, pulling on his boots. But it wasn't Mother that answered. The intercom crackled into life and it was Currie's deep, Southern voice that rumbled out.

"Skipper? You dressed? Either way, you better get your ass to the flight deck pronto."

* * *

"And where the hell is *that*?" DJ said, running a hand through her close-cropped hair and glaring at the viewing window as though the planet filling it was some kind of personal affront.

"Sure as hell not where we're supposed to be," Simpson said, his thin, pale hands cupped around his coffee.

DJ turned her gaze on him. "No shit," she said witheringly. "Why is it you're on this crew again? It ain't for your incisive insights or your sparkling personality or your—"

"Shut the fuck up," Currie said, hunched over a monitor and saving Gambell the job of intervening in the endless, infinite squabble-fest that Paul Simpson and DJ Roberts had been carrying on as long as they'd been on the crew.

"David, where are we?" Gambell said to Currie. He glanced at Kathryn, standing with her arms folded over her stomach, silhouetted in front of the big viewing window, against the yellow orb of the planet that was most decidedly not the Hub.

"LV-593," Currie said, looking up at him. "Weyland Isles System."

"The fuck?" DJ said. "That means we're… what, six fucking weeks out from the Hub?"

"Eight, more like," Simpson said. He turned his thin face to Gambell. "Why'd you wake us up, skip?"

It was a damn good question. Gambell felt Kathryn looking at him. They'd not had much chance to talk since she woke, but she had mentioned that she'd been throwing up. She put it down to a bad cryosleep, yet Gambell thought he knew better. Now wasn't the time, of course, but he felt more disquiet than usual that things weren't following the ordained path.

"Mother," he said measuredly. "Why'd you wake me early?"

That pause again. Like she wanted to tell him something, but didn't know how. He pushed the thought away. At least he knew why he hadn't got the usual cryo-hangover now. He'd only been under for a little over a fortnight.

"*I had an overriding… directive*," Mother said.

Gambell frowned. "From?"

"*I… cannot say.*"

"The fuck?" DJ spat.

Gambell suddenly had a very bad feeling. "DJ, Simpson, go and check the cargo."

"I checked it," Currie said. "We're still towing."

"Not *that* cargo."

DJ nodded, hauled the thin frame of Simpson off his stool, and dragged him off the flight deck.

"Mother," Gambell said evenly. "Who did the override come from?"

"*I… cannot say*," Mother repeated. "*I'm sorry, Jamie.*"

Jamie. Mother hadn't called him that since he was a kid. Did she sound… sad?

"There's something wrong," Kathryn murmured, sliding on to the stool Simpson had vacated. "Something doesn't feel right."

"It's fine," Gambell whispered. "As soon as we get to the Hub, I'll get Mother looked at and—"

"I don't mean that, Jamie," Kathryn said. She still had her arms wrapped around her waist. "I mean something feels different… inside. Inside me."

Gambell opened his mouth to say he had no idea what. Then the intercom spluttered.

"*Skip*," DJ crackled. "*We have one fuck of a problem.*"

In the cargo bay there was a bank of mini-cryotubes, mainly for the transportation of small animals. Sometimes the colonies traded livestock, and one time the *Clara* had been paid a ridiculous amount of money to take a rich old lady and her five Chihuahuas to Earth. They'd used twenty-seven of them for the unexpected little bonus cargo they'd found in that crashed freighter.

All of them were now empty, the plasteel fronts smashed.

Gambell stared wordlessly for a moment at the carnage. The planet where they'd salvaged the freighter had a sub-Earth atmosphere, but they'd suited up fully anyway, given the storm that had been raging and the marked acidity of the precipitation. Which was fortunate, because in the hold of the freighter, which they'd given a cursory sweep after attaching the towing containers filled with ore, they'd found… well, he didn't know what they were.

Which was the whole point.

Eggs, had been his first thought. Soft and organic. Pulsing slightly. About as tall as his waist. Not hugely pleasant to handle, even with their thick gloves. There were twenty-seven of them in total, and both Currie and Kathryn had wanted to leave them, but Gambell had a hunch. Whatever these things were, they were going to be worth something to somebody. Biotech was quite the thing at the moment. Everybody had heard the tales of black goo raining down on frontier worlds, even if nobody really knew what it was or what happened afterward. But the word in the bars and on the salvage chatter streams was that everybody was looking for bioweapons.

True, these egg things didn't appear particularly dangerous, but what was he, an expert in this kind of shit? Never look a gift horse in the mouth, his daddy always said. So Gambell had had the crew load them up into the mini-cryos for the journey to the Hub. Once he'd delivered the ore he'd start putting the feelers out to find a buyer for whatever the hell these things were.

Or at least, that had been the plan. Now there were twenty-seven busted mini-cryos, and no eggs.

"Maybe they hatched," Simpson said, looking around warily. As though he expected to see… Gambell had no idea what sort of thing would come out of an egg like that, if they were indeed eggs. A bird seemed doubtful. He got a mental image of something spider-like, which he brushed away.

"Mother!" Gambell yelled. "What am I looking at, here?"

It seemed as if there was a trembling in the air, but Mother said nothing. Gambell felt Kathryn's heavy stare on him, and did his best to ignore it.

"The fucking things hatched and broke out and they're running around somewhere," Simpson said, his eyes wide.

"Dick." DJ sighed. "If they were eggs there'd still be eggs wouldn't there? Even if they'd hatched. Or… eggshells."

"What fucking things?" Currie said, an undertone of menace in the big man's voice. "What do you know, Simpson?"

"I hear stuff," Simpson said, his Adam's apple bobbing. "We all hear stuff, right?"

Kathryn was standing by one of the empty mini-cryos, fingering the glass shards in the broken panel. Gambell wanted to yell to her to put it down. God knows what those things were, and what… what chemicals were on them. She had to be careful now. In her condition.

"Jamie," she said, turning to him and frowning. "Most of the glass is on the inside. Nothing broke *out* of these cryos. Someone smashed them from the outside."

"Mother!" Gambell roared, looking around as though he could see the presence of the invisible AI in the air around him. "Who has been on my ship? Were we boarded?"

"*Override forbids—*"

"Mother!"

They all looked at him, head thrown back, fists clenched, the scream dying on his lips.

"Jamie, I'm scared," Kathryn whispered.

"*I'm sorry,*" Mother said, and Gambell couldn't deny sensing a sadness in her electronic voice. "*I'm sorry. You should make your peace with your gods and say your goodbyes.*"

The *Clara* had been bought by Gambell's father Dennis when his wife died and he sold up every inch of property they had on Earth, ploughing his last cent into setting up Gambell Reclamations. Dennis had left his only son with his sister until Jamie was nine, and then took him out into space and taught him the ropes of the business he would inherit when the old man died—which happened ten years ago.

Gambell could barely remember his mother, and couldn't recall their life on Earth much at all. He'd been brought up on the ship, he'd spent most of his life in space. The *Clara* was his home.

Whump!

The charges clamped to the drive at the rear of the ship exploded, setting off a chain reaction that caused the *Clara* to list sharply to starboard, ripping a hole in the hull. The ship went into a spin toward the planet below them, a series of smaller explosions bursting through the vessel, taking all the major networks and life-support systems off-line.

When the lights went out in the cargo bay, Gambell drew Kathryn close to him and told her he loved her, and would always love her, and that he was sorry for what had happened to her, to him, and to the life that grew in her belly. And he held her tight as she fought and wailed until it was all over, and the *Clara* was no more.

2

Everyone told her to leave it alone, which of course only made her more determined not to.

Even her daddy, weary and grieving and with the stuffing knocked out of him, sighed when she told him what she was planning and rubbed his eyes.

"Cher, honey, just let things lie."

It took four commissioning editors saying no before one said, "Yes, well, maybe, let's just see what you turn up. I can't give you a commission, but I can promise to look at what you get. You know you're poking a hornet's nest here, right?"

She wasn't at all surprised to find a handwritten note under her windshield wiper two days before she left Earth, written in solid block capitals.

SMART MONEY
SAYS DROP IT

It was like nobody really knew Cher Hunt at all.

One person who would like to know her better was the guy with the beer belly and triple chin who'd been casting lascivious glances at her as they climbed into the cryosleep pods, just after leaving Earth's atmosphere. Not for the first time did she wish she had enough money to fly business class instead of coach. At least then she'd get a private cryo chamber and not have to feel self-conscious in the stupid grey vest and pants they made you wear on the communal sleep deck. It was only three weeks out to the Weyland Isles anyway. She'd have been happy to sit that out awake.

But RyanSpace ran its vessels on a shoestring and didn't have the crew or on-board infrastructure to deal with non-sleeping passengers. So here she was, waking up with her usual cryo hangover and the first person she sees is Mr. Beer Belly, staring at her from the tube opposite hers, rearranging himself in his shorts. She knew "cryo-wood" was a thing for guys, which is why they always usually stalled a bit getting out of their tubes until the women had cleared out. She swore to God that if the guy didn't stop rummaging around in his shorts and staring at her, she was going to go over and kick his ass.

While she stood in line for the showers, Cher scrolled through the news feeds, more hungry for updates than her stomach was for food. They said a week was a long time in politics; three weeks was a lifetime in journalism. Another reason she hated cryosleep. Yes, her body was only minutes older than when she'd set off from Earth, but the political situation back home and across the colonies hadn't been frozen in the same way.

There was a joint-agency effort underway to reclaim the outer suburbs of Canberra and rid them of radiation poisoning, three years after the end of the Australia Wars. A Globe Corporation whistleblower who claimed that her former employer was locked in a "silent war" with rivals Weyland-Yutani had been found dead in a New York alleyway.

Nothing about her sister Shy.

Nothing about Hasanova. Not that there was any reason there should be. It had been six months since the hearing at The Hague concluded that Captain Kylie Duncan of the Colonial Marines had nothing to answer for in the wake of the widespread deaths on the Iranian colony, including those of Shy Hunt and the rest of her colleagues at McAllen Integrations, who were only on Hasanova to set up environmental systems for the massive data storage facility there.

Well, they would say that, wouldn't they? The whole thing had been a total whitewash, and while nobody was talking about the actual events on Hasanova, the ripples were still spreading out through the colonies. The Independent Core Systems Colonies had declared war on the United Americas over the desultory inquiry, and while it had been more of a war of words than all-out Armageddon, as some had feared, the political crisis was rumbling on, and showing no signs of reaching any kind of resolution.

On Earth, at least. There was news filtering in from the outer colonies that things were a lot less diplomatic there. Raiding missions, ships being shot down, and the endless third-, fourth- and fifth-hand tales of bioweaponry being deployed, the black goo raining down on remote colony worlds. Nobody knew what it was or who was supposed to be throwing this shit around, or even what it did. There were no direct reports of what was happening.

Just rumors.

Often being a journalist was like holding up a set of weighing scales and trying to achieve some kind of balance between the conspiracy nuts on one side, who believed and talked about anything, and on the other side the stuff that was actually happening but which was being suppressed.

But black goo wasn't Cher Hunt's responsibility, or even of any interest to her, at least not right now. What *was* her responsibility was finding out exactly why her sister had died on Hasanova. The official line was "collateral damage during a covert Colonial Marines operation." That might do for the final report, to be filed away and never looked at again, but for Cher it raised more questions than it answered.

What happened on Hasanova wasn't just the latest salvo in an age-old spat between America and Iran. It was something else. And, after the final day of the hearing in the Hague, she had vowed to find out what.

* * *

They were six hours out of LV-593, which filled the monitor screen in the passenger liner's cramped arrival deck. Remarkably Earth-like in appearance, though a tenth of the size of home. It had been a dream of a find for the Three World Empire, located square in the habitable zone of a yellow sun. She could see why the British loved it. As if on cue, the image of the approaching planet fizzed out on the big screen and was replaced by a promotional video for their destination.

"Welcome to New Albion!" a voice declared in a plummy, upper-class English accent. The seat-belt sign above her flashed on and Cher fastened up for the descent. *"You are imminently about to arrive on the jewel of the Weyland Isles colony world network, a temperate paradise that's just like home!"*

The camera swooped through a very polished but very obvious artificial representation of the New Albion colony. There was a wide river flowing right through the middle of a green, lush park, surrounded by ordered avenues lined with trees, and streets full of widely spaced townhouses. There was even a recreation of Big Ben set against the blue sky, and in the hazy distance a ring of high-rise apartment blocks surrounded the city center. Cher was reminded of New Delhi back on Earth, where the British raj had tried to recreate an idealized vision of London in the stifling heat of a land that was not theirs to claim.

"Throughout its long and illustrious history, Britain has had

a reputation of expanding throughout all possible territories, bringing peace, technology and our great sense of fair play to people and lands at first on Earth, and now across the galaxy. The British pioneering spirit has been forged into a relentless drive to colonize space and disseminate our values far beyond the limits of the home planet over which we once held sway with a benign and magnanimous rule."

Jeez, Cher thought. She knew that New Albion had been basically colonized by a clutch of the richest Old Money families from Britain, but not that they were buying so much into the old British Empire bullshit. Cher knew her history. Far from being a "benign and magnanimous rule," the British Empire of the eighteenth and nineteenth centuries had been essentially a mass invasion of pretty much every country on Earth outside of Europe, wherever they could get boots on the ground.

The footage changed to a procession of faces smiling at the camera and trotting out platitudes about how wonderful it was to live and work on New Albion. A lot more diverse than the old British Empire, Cher guessed. There, the black and brown faces would have been either crushed underfoot in their homelands or put to work, actually or practically slaves, to feed the money-sucking beast of London.

"I work in data analysis," an Indian woman said.

"I work in transport," a black man said.

"I work in the coal mines," a young white man said with a cheeky grin.

"We work for New Albion," the three said in unison, and the camera pulled back to reveal a huge crowd of them, waving and cheering. *"We all work for New Albion!"* the whole group of them chorused, and the picture cut to an animation of the breeze rippling through the trees in an idyllic park.

"They work for New Albion... Why not join them, and make New Albion work for you?" the plummy voice said. *"Immigration applications are now open. And the best of British to you!"*

The monitor switched back to the planetary image, now filling the screen. Cher would have to endure that promo film at least another half dozen times before they made planetfall. Flying coach with RyanSpace meant she was crushed up against passengers on either side of her, both of whom had resolutely laid claim to the armrests with their elbows. Across the aisle she saw Mr. Beer Belly hollering in a southern English accent to one of the hosts, demanding that they bring him a gin and tonic.

Cher dug into her pocket and pulled out a sleep mask.

This was going to be a long six hours.

Cher didn't know exactly what she was going to find on New Albion, but she *did* know she had to be there. Four weeks earlier, a postcard had arrived at her home in New York—an actual paper postcard, sent by actual post across the galaxy. Three questions had occurred to Cher when she received it and looked on the front image of the raging whirlpool known as Charybdis.

How long had this taken to get from Hasanova?

Why the hell did Hasanova even have postcards, which suggested an actual goddam *gift shop*, in a data storage facility?

And, of course, who the hell had sent it?

On the back, in the space to the left opposite Cher's address, it simply said "NEW ALBION" in blocky handwritten capital letters.

From that point it had taken her a week to get the commission—and arrange funding that would allow her to book passage to LV-593—and now here she was, waking from an uneasy doze as the trademark tooting horn recording of RyanSpace announced that they had landed at the terminus.

"This is your captain speaking, thank you for flying RyanSpace to New Albion, where the local time is 10:23 AM and the weather is rain with an outside temperature of 16 degrees Celsius. We hope you enjoyed your flight and wish you well on your onward journey."

Cher filed off the ship with the rest of the passengers, putting space and bodies between her and Mr. Beer Belly, who—with six hours' worth of gin and tonic inside him—was weaving unsteadily and bouncing off the walls. Through the windows of the tube that led from the ship to the terminus, she tried to get a glimpse of her destination, but saw only rain sluicing the windows and the indistinct, grey shapes of squat buildings on the perimeter of the transport hub.

As the passengers were conveyed by escalator down toward immigration, wall-mounted screens sparked to life, each one with an attractive young person in the red, white, and blue livery of the Union flag welcoming them to the colony, each message finishing off with a resounding, *"Best of British!"*

"Jesus fucking Christ, save me from this," Cher muttered, getting ready to approach the biometric station that would read all her documentation from her thumbprint and retinal scan.

"You're American!" a voice boomed right in her ear, making her at first jump, and then her heart sink. Mr. Beer Belly.

"Excellent deduction, Dr. Watson," Cher said, sighing.

"Barry," Mr. Beer Belly said, holding out a sweating hand. Cher ignored it, turning her face away from his alcoholic breath. "You here for a holiday? Business? Moving here? I reckon we could do with a few more beauties like you to liven the place up."

"Give me fucking strength," Cher breathed. It was her turn at the immigration station, and she held her head still while she was scanned, then placed her thumb on the keypad.

"You need a guide, give me a shout," he pressed. "Here, let me ping you my comms details."

"No thanks," Cher said curtly as the gateway turned green and the barrier swung back to let her through.

"Frigid cow," Mr. Beer Belly said behind her as she followed the signs for the baggage reclamation. "You might change your mind once you've seen New Albion, mind. It's nothing like they show on the videos."

For all his many faults, Mr. Beer Belly wasn't a liar, at least not about New Albion. It was nothing like the promo video suggested.

Cher stood on the apron of the terminus with her suitcase, peering out from under the verandah at the rain-soaked panorama of the colony's capital city. No Big Ben, no parks, not even a river, though there was a wide ditch in the process of being dug right through the colony center. No townhouses bathed in golden sunlight, just a series of low concrete buildings flanking a network of wide roads, all made indistinct by the precipitation pouring from leaden clouds.

"Not what you were expecting?" a voice said, and Cher blinked and looked around to see a man standing by a flyer. It had a round, black chassis and an illuminated yellow sign over the cockpit that said TAXI.

"Not what I'd been led to believe it was, no," Cher said, allowing the driver to take her case and put it in the trunk of the cab.

"New Albion's what you might call a work in progress,"

the cabbie said, opening the door so Cher could scoot into the back and avoid the rain. He let himself into the front. "It's the big vision, innit? Ambitious plans. We're good at that, us Brits. Ambitious plans. Bold ideas." The flyer whined into life and jerked forward and up. "It's putting them into practice that gets us a bit tangled up sometime. Where can I take you?"

"I'm staying at the Ritz," Cher said.

The driver guffawed. "You ever seen the Ritz in London?"

Cher nodded. "Never stayed there, though. Out of my price range. Was surprised it was so cheap here."

"That's because it's sod all to do with the Ritz back home," the driver laughed. "Lawsuit waiting to happen." He wheeled the cab over the heavy plant digging out the ditch in the middle of the colony. "That's going to be the Thames when they ever get it finished." He pointed into the rain-soaked distance. "That'll be where Big Ben is. Except did you know it's not called Big Ben really? That's actually the name of the bell. Just called it the Clock Tower, didn't they?"

From the window Cher could see utilitarian housing blocks and, in the distance, the blocky shapes of what she presumed were factories and processing plants.

"We got coal mines, tin mines, oil mines, the works," the cabbie said, as if reading her mind. "Most of it in the north. Some nice farmland up in the Midlands. Good trade deals going on top of that."

"But no rivers or parks or Big Ben or townhouses," Cher said. "What exactly do you do for fun on New Albion?"

The cabbie grinned over his shoulder at her. "We might not have all the bells and whistles they show on those promotional films yet, but we got our priorities right. Pubs and chip shops. Them we got in spades."

The cabbie had been right. The Ritz was, in the local parlance that Cher was picking up very quickly, a right shit-hole. Little more than a concrete box filled with other concrete boxes.

"Bit of a joke, love," the stout woman said from behind the reception desk. "The Ritz, innit? Enjoy your stay." As Cher headed for the elevator the woman called after her. "Oh, something came for you." She handed over a letter-sized envelope with a hand-addressed label.

CHER HUNT
℅ THE RITZ HOTEL
NEW ALBION

She recognized the handwriting, the same blocky capitals as on her Hasanova postcard.

Cher stuck the envelope between her teeth and got into the elevator to the seventh floor, then negotiated the gloomy corridor to the equally gloomy and claustrophobic room. She found a bed that might not have been made out of concrete, but was just as hard. A sink and toilet, the tiniest possible shower cubicle, and no window. There was barely room to slide her case between the bed and the wall. Once she had, she sat on the bed and ripped open the envelope.

A small handprinted note fell out first.

THIS IS WHY
YOUR SISTER DIED.

Cher felt her breath catch in her chest, and reached into the envelope, feeling the glossy surface of a printed photograph. She slid it out and stared at it for a long time, not quite sure what she was looking at.

"Sweet holy fuck."

3

"What did the men want, Mama?"

From the observation deck window in the canteen, Merrilyn Hambleton watched the shape of the departing ship disappear into the relentless, raging storm. Her daughter's hand was held tightly in her own.

"I don't know, Little Flower," she said, watching until the vessel was completely gone from sight. She glanced down at Therese, only five years old, her Pinky Ponk dangling from her hand. The soft toy was filthy with grime and oil stains. Everything on this planet was filthy with grime and oil, but Merrilyn had to try to stem the rising tide of filth. To not try was to surrender. She would put Pinky Ponk through the wash. "And speak in French, now the men have gone."

"Yes, Mama," Therese said, switching back to her native tongue. She paused and said, "I wish I could go with the men. I don't like it here very much."

It broke Merrilyn's heart to hear that, but it was true. LV-187 was no place to bring up a child. It was so small nobody had even bothered to give it a name. A storm raged perpetually, days pale and pitiful, with the light from the wan sun barely penetrating the thick, roiling clouds that unleashed rain, hail, and sometimes shards of ice like knife-blades. Yet what LV-187 lacked in comfort and pleasantness it made up in something else: oil.

The Independent Core Systems Colonies had been on an aggressive oil hunt for decades, and that had been only accelerated by the Oil Wars. Thank God, LV-187's supplies had not been tainted by the sabotage she had heard about on other colony worlds, where entire stocks had been destroyed by a bacterial agent that broke down the petroleum's composition. And now the Oil Wars were effectively over. With the ICSC brokering major trade deals in return for plentiful supplies, her work here was more important than ever.

TotalEnergies had been one of the first Big Oil corporations to invest heavily in off-world mining, and as one of their leading petroleum geologists Merrilyn had known it was only a matter of time before she was asked to head up a colony operation. She'd have liked her first major posting to be a little more hospitable than LV-187, but it was only for a year. And at least she could bring Therese.

"Where did you get the lollipop?" Merrilyn said suddenly, noticing for the first time the candy in her daughter's hand.

"The man gave it to me," Therese said. "He was nice."

"You shouldn't take things from strangers without asking Mama first," Merrilyn chided, but the visitors had been pleasant. An ad hoc trade mission, on their way to somewhere else, calling at LV-187 to take a little bit of rest time and to inquire about the chances of some business between their colonies. This was not uncommon these days on oil-producing worlds. Plenty of smaller settlements wanted to strike under-the-counter deals to get them the oil they needed.

But the mission had been told to go through the proper channels and contact the ICSC. They had taken it in good humor and left. Even such a small kindness as a lollipop for a child was something to cling to in these dark days.

Merrilyn turned from the window, the memory of that day—the last day—aching in her chest. Now the canteen was empty, no drilling crews just come off their shift enjoying steak and frites. No hubbub of conversation, no clanging of cutlery, no music.

No Therese.

She looked down at Pinky Ponk in her hands. She always brought the toy out on a foraging mission. It gave her luck. She'd secured the canteen three days ago, and in that time there had been no incursions. But the supplies were running low, even though she'd been eking them out as best she could. Power systems were on minimal, the canteen—the entire colony—dark but for emergency strip-lights. The big freezers had failed and the food spoiled, though the smaller refrigerators were still working.

With a churning gut, Merrilyn knew that soon she was going to have to venture out of the safety of the canteen and her little hideaway in the store cupboard, not just for food but to get to the comms center and send out an SOS. The next supply vessel wasn't due for a month. She would not last that long, and not just through lack of food.

Merrilyn turned back to the window. The last time she'd been here she'd been watching that ship leave, with Therese. Now she was alone, scanning the storm-ravaged sky for a sign of a vessel, someone coming to help. Surely by now someone must have noticed that there had been no contact from LV-187.

Surely help was on its way, even without a formal distress call.

The worst thing was the silence.

Well, not the *worst* thing, obviously, but after the colony had been so alive with people, so full of noise and chatter and the clanking of the wells and the music and laughter—because the French could make any place vibrant and vital, even such a cold, barren rock as this—the quiet gloom was eerie. Conducive to nightmares, both sleeping and waking.

More than once Merrilyn had stopped dead, certain she'd heard a skittering or scrabbling of claws above or below her, and she'd stood statue-still for long seconds, stretching into minutes, until she was sure the sound had either been in her imagination, or the source of it had moved on.

She didn't know still what put her in danger. Sound? Movement? Scent? Just the act of being alive, and therefore in danger of being dead? Once, while rifling through the kitchens, she'd simultaneously thought she heard something in the roof space above and dropped a big Le Creuset pot, which smashed to the tiles and sent a reverberating, discordant note echoing around the space. Yet nothing came for her. So, she had started to risk making a little bit of noise, specifically by using one of the big video screens in the canteen to access the security camera feeds.

It took a lot of juice and she didn't know when it would run out for good. But she told herself that it was necessary, to keep a close eye on the rest of the colony's hub. Most of the time she saw nothing. Sometimes there'd be a darting shadow or a swift movement too fast for the eye to catch, and when she'd swept the remaining working cameras, she often scrolled back to watch some archive footage.

Which, she knew, was the real reason she was sitting there now, eating from a can of cold soup, surprised still at the time-stamp on the shot of an empty corridor. It was dated just seven days earlier. Was that all it had been? It felt like a lifetime.

The footage wasn't empty for long. A figure moved into the shot, and the camera started tracking. Small, swaddled in a big coat and woolly hat. As the camera swiveled to follow the figure—who had absolutely no right to be in this service corridor on the east flank of the colony— something else came into view in the bottom left corner.

Merrilyn could only think of it as an *egg*, but this was soft and pliable, pulsating almost imperceptibly, as if it was breathing through the vaguely obscene puckered opening on its top.

There was a sound coming from the figure as it moved inexorably toward the egg, which was about the height of an adult's waist. A tuneless, high-pitched singing. An old tune that was imprinted on Merrilyn's cortex, the mother of all earworms. "Joe Le Taxi." She'd always found it hilarious how Therese had sung the song, got her to stand up on the table in the canteen once and perform it to the raucous cheers and roaring applause of the drillers joyfully drunk on pastis.

Now it turned her stomach and chilled her heart. "Joe Le Taxi." Prelude to apocalypse. The song cut off as Therese, on the screen, stopped dead, suddenly seeing the egg thing for the first time. She pulled off her hat as though to see it better, frowning as she peered at it.

"*Hello,*" she said clearly on the tape. "*What are you? Are you lost?*"

Merrilyn's chest fluttered. So caring, that girl. So thoughtful. She knew what was coming next, but she couldn't tear her eyes away as Therese dropped her hat on to the floor and walked cautiously over to the egg.

"Don't do it, Little Flower," Merrilyn whispered again, as if she could reach back in time through the video screen by some act of magic, and alter the course of events, like when she used to pile rocks in the stream near her home on the hillside of Ramatuelle and divert the flow of the water. But time was not water. It could not be dammed or diverted, stopped or frozen or boiled. It simply went on, and left in its wake things that could never be changed.

On the screen, Therese was standing by the egg, almost as tall as her. She was concentrating hard, Merrilyn knew, trying to work out if she knew what this thing was. She was pulling her thinking face, with her eyes screwed up and her tongue stuck out and her top teeth exposed like a rabbit. *You can sometimes be very ugly for a pretty girl*, Merrilyn used to say to her, which always made her laugh.

She found she was gripping her seat as the puckered lips of the egg started to quiver and open when Therese leaned in for a closer look, her face illuminated by the faintest of sickly, pallid glows emerging from inside the object.

There was a frozen moment then, Therese looking into the egg with a curious, perplexed expression, and the egg—pod?—seeming to shiver slightly.

Then it happened.

And Merrilyn killed the feed.

After that, things had happened pretty quickly. The first day, people started to be reported absent from their stations or not returning to their quarters after their shifts. Just two or three at first, then more and more over the next two days, an exponential growth until the missing started to outnumber those left. And then…

Hell was visited upon LV-187.

By accident or design, the comms tower seemed to be the source of a major... infestation, Merrilyn supposed was the right word. She didn't know if a *m'aidez* call had been put out. Even if it had been, a week may have been too little time to expect help. If an SOS *hadn't* been sent... then it was a long time until the next supply run. LV-187 was quite literally off anyone's radar. So long as it continued producing oil, no one gave them much thought. Maybe when the ICSC didn't get their next shipment of black gold as expected, they might investigate.

She was certain she wouldn't survive that long.

Merrilyn went back into the kitchens to get some bottled water for her inner sanctum and to use the toilet. She sat down in the end stall, listening for any tell-tale scratching in the spaces above and below. There was nothing, but she frowned. She couldn't see anything or hear anything, or smell anything. Early on they'd discovered that while the things could be hurt, even in death they were deadly, with acrid, violent blood that stank and burned through anything and everything

Something hovered on the periphery of her non-physical senses. As though she wasn't alone in the bathroom stall. It had to be her imagination. She'd bolted the door to the bathroom, and all the ceiling and floor panels were intact. She'd done a sweep of all the other stalls.

There was nothing—

Outside the stall, one of the bottles of water slapped to the tiled floor and rolled across the gap of the open door.

She jumped, then leapt up, dragging up her fatigues, and was just about to pull the serrated kitchen knife from her belt when something closed around her ankle, and she screamed.

"Little Flower!" Merrilyn said sternly. "How many times have I told you not to go wandering on your own! I thought we were beyond this by now."

"I'm sorry, Mama." Therese held her hands behind her back, staring at her feet and the floor of the canteen. "I woke up and I didn't know where you were and I wanted Pinky Ponk."

Merrilyn sighed and handed over the toy. "I suppose you thought it was funny, sneaking your hand under the bathroom stall and grabbing me like that?" Therese smiled her little girl smile, the one that melted everyone's heart.

"Did you think it was a—"

"Hush." Merrilyn marveled at the child's ability to take all this… this horror in her stride. The adaptability of the young never failed to astound her. Therese had blindly accepted Merrilyn's instructions that they had to leave their comfortable—by LV-187 standards—quarters and now had to sleep in a nest of blankets inside a storeroom just off the canteen. The girl was basically programmed to trust her mother, which made Merrilyn's insides turn to water. How long could she protect her? What would happen to her if Merrilyn was taken?

"Mama?"

"Yes, Little Flower?"

"I had a dream. About the egg."

Merrilyn grunted noncommittally and started to stack the water bottles in a plastic carry-box. She didn't like the girl dwelling on that too much.

"Mama, if I hadn't found the egg, would everyone else still be here?"

Therese was learning guilt. Merrilyn didn't want that to happen. She wanted her daughter to realize that actions had consequences, but not to have regrets. It was true that the service corridor into which Therese had wandered was pretty much unused most of the time, and if she hadn't found the egg, then reported it to Merrilyn who sent a maintenance team to investigate… well, things might perhaps have been different. But only if that egg had been the only one on the colony.

As it turned out, it wasn't. It was just the one that had been found first. What had happened on LV-187 was inevitable.

"Therese, don't think like that." Merrilyn squatted down in front of her. "You did exactly the right thing by coming to your mama about the egg. You were very clever and very brave, and that's why you're still here with your mama today. OK? Now what shall we have for dinner?"

"Trout!"

"No trout."

"Steak!"

"No steak."

"Ham!"

"No ham."

Therese smiled slyly. "Elephant!"

It was a game they played every mealtime, with Therese finishing off with whatever exotic or extinct Earth creature she could think of. Merrilyn said, "Elephant it is."

"You mean canned beans again, don't you?" Therese giggled.

"I do," Merrilyn replied. "Now you go and stand by the big window while I get our canned *elephant* and some more gas for the cooker. I'll be two minutes. Have some water."

She hadn't even got to the swinging kitchen doors when Therese called her frantically. Merrilyn had the knife drawn from her belt before she had spun round, but it wasn't her worst fear. Instead, Therese was jumping up and down and pointing out of the observation window, shouting.

"Mama! Mama! Mama!"

Merrilyn joined her and peered through the clouds, thick with rain and marbled with lightning. Then she saw what Therese's keen eyes had already discerned, breaking through the storm.

"It's a ship, Mama!"

Merrilyn felt the strength sap out of her, as though she was suddenly as weak and pliable as Pinky Ponk. Therese was right.

It was a ship.

4

"What's your business in the Shires?" the soldier said, frowning at Chad McClaren from beneath his polished metal helmet. His uniform was serge green and there was a patch over one breast that proclaimed him to be a junior officer in the New Albion First Duke of Wellington's Regiment. Over his shoulder was slung a standard issue projectile rifle, and two other guards, watching the interaction, bore the same weapons.

Chad's flyer had been pinged on the flight over the rough, mountainous scrubland just about half a world away from the New Albion colony, and as requested, he'd put down on the checkpoint—just a wide landing platform and guard hut, really. There'd been a cursory search of the flyer, though Chad had made sure there was nothing to find anyway, and those on board had been requested to disembark. Which amounted to Chad and the dog.

The soldier looked curiously at the dog as Chad said, "I'm on a scientific research mission. Looking at possible ore deposits in the Shires."

"What sort of dog is it?" the soldier said, giving the electronic permissions and papers a cursory glance on his tablet screen. Chad was glad of that, considering they were forged. Expertly forged, of course, but ultimately fake nonetheless.

"Cockapoo," Chad said, leaning forward to ruffle the dog's head. It growled warningly at him.

"You're American," the soldier said with that way the British seemed to have of pointing out the blindingly obvious. "Cockapoo. Funny old name. Sounds more like a bird."

The other two soldiers laughed. Chad looked around the wind-whipped platform, at the low mountain range they'd called the Pennines. Aside from this checkpoint, New Albion had done nothing here, and had no other presence. Which was good news for him.

"Cross between a cocker spaniel and a poodle," he said. "Used to be popular a couple of hundred years ago."

"Well, have a good trip, sir." Apparently satisfied, the soldier tapped at his tablet and Chad felt his comms unit shiver, the green-light approval for onward travel registering on it. "Hope you find something useful out there for the furtherance of the glory of New Albion. Stay safe."

"To say nothing of the dog," Chad said.

"To say nothing of the dog," the soldier agreed. "What's his name, anyway?"

"Scooby," Chad said, ushering the dog up the steps into the flyer and climbing up behind him.

"Best of British to you both!" the soldier said, standing back and waving as Chad fired up the flyer and lifted off with a whine of engines, pointing the nose toward the grey shale of the hills.

"I understood both of those references," the dog said once the checkpoint was far behind them. "*To Say Nothing of the Dog*; a 1997 novel by Connie Willis which deals with the concept of time travel. And *Scooby-Doo*, a mid-twentieth century originating animation series for children in which the titular dog and a group of teenage humans investigate paranormal activity which generally turns out to be the work of villainous adults who are invariably unmasked at the close of each installment."

"Of course you get the references, Davis," Chad said, glancing down at the map on his comms screen. "You're a synthetic with an artificial intelligence brain that can access the sum of human knowledge."

Davis cocked his furry head on one side and regarded Chad, who caught the dog staring at him and glared back.

"A dog can't out-stare a human," Chad said. "So don't try. What's up, anyway?"

"I'm not quite sure I like being a Cockapoo," Davis said. It wasn't strictly necessary for Davis to move the dog's jaws to ape the physical act of speech; he could simply transmit his voice through the speakers in the dog's collar. But Davis seemed to enjoy doing it. Maybe he didn't mind sharing a body with the AI of a dog, at least not as much as he claimed.

"It's good cover," Chad said. By his estimations, they had about an hour's flying into the depths of the wasteland New Albion called, rather romantically, the Shires. Everything they'd done to this planet was with some kind of pastoral, idealistic, rose-tinted vision of an England that had been lost, or more likely never existed except in the fevered imaginations of latter-day patriots. "Nobody suspects a dog."

The dog raised one eyebrow at him. "I am a Weyland-Yutani corporate security drone," Davis said. "Being a dog feels somewhat... beneath me."

"You *were* a Weyland-Yutani corporate security drone," Chad corrected. "Then you went and developed free will and a conscience and the ability to transfer your AI into practically any network or system. Now you're... well, I don't know what you are, really. Something new."

"Something new with an age-old problem," Davis said, looking out of the window at the landscape unfolding ahead of them with dreary monotony. Could a dog look wistful? Davis certainly seemed to pull it off, Chad thought.

"Davis... don't," he said. "I don't want to think about it right now. We have to concentrate on the job at hand."

"Two buddies on the road without their womenfolk." Davis sighed. He lifted a brown paw and held it out. "But you're right. Let's not talk about them. 'Pals before gals,' eh, Chad?"

"If you say so, Davis." Chad fist-bumped the dog's paw. They sat quietly for a while, each of them in a bucket seat in the cockpit.

"Funny how entertainment in the twentieth and twenty-first centuries was so concerned with impossible things," David said. "They were in the midst of a white-hot explosion of technology, yet they dreamed about time travel and monsters, as though the wonders they were creating were never quite enough."

"Well, they were right about one thing," Chad said. "Monsters do exist."

Neither of them said anything else, until Davis jumped off the bucket seat. "I am going to let this synthetic's programming be dominant for a while. It is important to do that to stop it becoming permanently corrupted."

"Why do you care?" Chad asked. "At some point, you'll have no further use for it."

"I just do." Davis looked back at him. "Like you said, I'm something new. I will be resting for the remainder of the journey. In accordance with this synthetic's directives, I may shortly lick my genitals and simulate the appearance of sleep. See you soon, Chad."

"Why wouldn't he like being a dog?" Chad muttered quietly. "Sounds like the dream life, to me."

The crash site was located in a wooded valley overhung by a large rock outcropping on the western side of the mountain range, which was both a blessing and a curse. It was good because providence had put the ship down in a place that was practically invisible from above, save for the damage to the landscape as it had made violent planetfall, so it hadn't been picked up by anyone who wasn't specifically looking for it.

Perhaps because nobody was looking for it, Chad thought... at least not on LV-593. Its location was bad, however, because the area was completely inaccessible for his flyer due to the dense foliage, which meant they'd had to land several kilometers away on the edge of the forest and hike through woods where no human had trod before.

The flora wasn't too dissimilar from what was found on Earth, and so far they hadn't encountered any problems with the fauna. A few small mammals that had skittered out of their way, some dull-plumed birds that Davis had run at, barking. He seemed to delight in them flapping noisily away. Sometimes it was hard to tell if Davis's AI was in charge, or the dog's.

Trust the British to find a temperate world that was ineffably safe and dull, he mused. Much like the tiny rain-soaked island from which they'd orchestrated their domination-seeking affairs for generations, back on the home planet.

"Is the dog still dominant?" Chad asked as Davis chased yet another grey bird away, then cocked his leg against the trunk of the nearest tree.

"No," Davis said, "but I am getting a certain satisfaction from the things in which it finds joy."

The dog didn't find joy in anything, really, or at least, nothing that wasn't included in its programming. It was a synthetic, of course—a very nice little job from what Chad was certain wasn't a strictly legal operation. Once synthetic capabilities had been developed for research and military use, it was inevitable that it would be repurposed for other things. The sex industry, always an early adopter in any new tech, had jumped on it, of course, but there was also a little grey-market economy in replicating—for those who could pay the eye-wateringly high prices, of course—formerly living creatures.

The Cockapoo had been the faithful companion of a grand old dame who was the head of an organized crime family, and when the critter had died she had been inconsolable. Until she found a synthetic technician to bring poor Fido back to life with a nearly perfect synthetic AI personality. For those with enough money, word was there were no limits to what could be remade in synthetic form.

As a result Fido—or whatever the mutt's name had been—had come to be the repository for the weird misfit of the AI world that was Davis. Her loss had become a unique asset—and besides, at the time it had been their only viable option.

The dense woodland broke suddenly, and their path was crossed by a wide avenue of scorched earth where the ship had come down and careened through. Chad looked to the right and saw a tangled mess in the lee of the overhanging rocks, a kilometer distant. They'd found it.

"Lovely place, this," Davis said, trotting to heel beside Chad. "We should bring the ladies when everything is sorted." He scampered ahead, saying loudly, "For now it's just us couple of swells, out on the town."

Chad frowned as he picked up the pace, following the dog. Davis wasn't exactly what you'd call a normal synthetic—he was in that uncharted, fuzzy, grey zone somewhere between AI and human, a synthetic with free will and agency and, yes, emotions. Or something very much approaching them. In the time that Chad had known him, however, Davis had become more... erratic, he supposed. Quirky, at best. Disturbingly unpredictable at worst. It was as though... Chad didn't really know.

As though Davis was trying a little too hard to be human, perhaps.

Not that Chad could blame him for going a little off the rails after what had happened to him. After his synthetic body was destroyed, he—by accident or by design of his own—had managed to live on as an invisible cloud of AI technology, inhabiting and controlling other tech systems, even spaceships. He'd been destroyed and cheated whatever passed for synthetic *death* many times.

Oh, and he was in love.

Lost in thought, Chad almost tripped over his stationary companion. They were at the crash site, the ship folded up into a crumpled wreck against the foot of a steep cliff.

"I wish Zula and Amanda could see us now."

"Davis, will you shut up?" Chad glared at him. "Can we just get on with the job?"

The dog looked at him with a mournfulness that made Chad think that somewhere along the line rogue animators must have been involved in designing the goddamned synthetic.

"Sorry, Chad. I know. It hurts us both."

Stop trying so hard, Chad thought, then immediately regretted his harshness, unspoken as it was. Instead he said, "Come on, let's get inside."

The STSV *Clara* had been a private towing and salvage vessel, licensed to a small family-run business called Gambell Reclamations. It had run into difficulties close to New Albion when one of the engines blew. The ore they had been towing had been cut free by the explosion and presumably still drifted in space, or had been picked up by opportunistic salvagers or pirates. The ship had crashed planetside. No distress call had been sent out. The crew of five had died before impact.

This was all in the *Clara*'s black box, accessed by Davis as they stood in the tangled mess of what had once been the bridge.

"What does Mother say?" Chad asked, looking around the twisted metal of the flight deck. "About what *really* happened?"

"Mother is being unusually quiet on the subject," Davis said. The dog looked at Chad. "You could say she is keeping mu—"

"No." Chad put up a hand. "Enough. What exactly do you mean? Mother is refusing to speak to you? It's been destroyed?"

"It… deactivated itself before impact. As far as I can tell from the files. Due to a manual override."

"From the crew of the *Clara*?"

"No." Davis looked up at Chad. "They were boarded. While the crew were in hypersleep."

Chad nodded. "Makes sense. Do the files or the manifests mention anything about their cargo?"

"Just the 300,000 tonnes of mineral ore they were towing."

Well, he knew for a fact they'd been carrying more than that. "Let's search the ship. Did they have cryo storage facilities for cargo?"

Davis scanned for a moment. "In the hold."

They picked their way through the folded *Clara* and climbed up into the hold. There wasn't much left of it, but enough for Chad to see the remains of the rows of cryotubes. A few had survived the crash, and all had their plasteel fronts shattered.

"Did you locate any human remains?"

"Most were obliterated in the explosion or the crash. Only one of any substance is left."

"And it's *just* human?" Chad said.

"Yes." Davis nodded, an action that Chad still found it difficult to get used to. "There was no infestation on the *Clara*. There were by my reckoning twenty-seven of these cryotubes used for storage of Ovomorphs. I don't think any of them hatched."

"So someone boarded the *Clara* while the crew were asleep, took the eggs, planted explosives to destroy the ship, and reprogrammed Mother to cover their tracks."

"It appears to be the case."

"The question is, who?"

"Isn't that obvious?" Davis said. "Weyland-Yutani."

As a scientist, Chad McClaren had to agree with him. Very often the most obvious answer *was* the most obvious answer because it was the right answer. Yet as a human being, he'd learned—sometimes the hard way—that nothing was as it seemed. Especially once you dipped a toe into the murky pantomime that was being played out behind the scenes of real life.

When it came to dealing with Xenomorphs, and the human agencies that would control them, nothing at all was certain. It was a situation Weyland-Yutani had controlled for decades, but it was getting more and more difficult for them to keep a lid on it. And everybody seemed to have dollar signs in their eyes.

"Maybe you're right," Chad said, letting himself

down from the wrecked hold and clambering back to the burned earth in the shadow of the ruined ship. He helped Davis down and added, "But something doesn't quite add up here."

Chad had never seen a dog shrug before.

"Weyland-Yutani commissioned Gambell Reclamations —through several partners—to recover the eggs from the crash site out on the frontier," Davis said. "That much we know. Then, to distance themselves completely from the operation, they boarded the *Clara* before it reached its destination, took their cargo, and destroyed the ship." Davis walked on and looked back at Chad. "So the question isn't who did this, but how we can prove it?"

Chad's comms unit pinged. He glanced at it.

"Well, we might have some help on that score. Cher Hunt is on New Albion. She received the package. She says she's ready to meet us."

5

Cher was eight years old, and Shy had just turned ten. Cher was the bookish sister, the one happy with her own company, the girl who could contentedly sit indoors lost in made-up worlds while her older sibling Shy tore her jeans and scuffed her knees and muddied her face in the stream and woods back of the Hunt place in Oregon.

Different as chalk and cheese. Cher was darker, her hair and eyes and olive skin. Shy was a shade or two paler, and prettier, at least everyone said, but they had one thing in common: a voracious appetite for news. That was their daddy Ken's doing. Every day at six o'clock he would stand on the porch and call out to them.

"Cheyenne! Cherokee! Time to come in!"

Not for dinner, though that would be served up soon after, but for the six o'clock news. It didn't matter that breaking news was served up 24/7 on every single screen they might carry or in their house or office or car or flyer. Ken Hunt always insisted that they sit down together as a family—or what was left of their family—to watch the news on the live-stream TV at six o'clock. Then they would talk about what they'd seen, and discuss the politics behind it all.

Some people thought politics were boring, Ken Hunt said, but those folks didn't realize that politics were everything. They were behind everything and in front of everything and under everything and over everything. Politics put food on your table, or not. They gave you a job, or not. Need a highway running past your town? That would be a political decision by somebody.

Everything was a political decision. Choosing what to wear when you got out of bed was a political decision. Deciding what to eat for your dinner. Calling your children Cheyenne and Cherokee, even if they shortened those names to Shy and Cher, that had definitely been a political decision on Ken Hunt's part. They had First Nations blood flowing in their veins and they had to honor that every day—because wiping out the Native Americans? That was sure as shit a political decision.

Even Momma's death had been a political decision. Sure, nobody actually decided she should get cancer and take to her bed and wither away like a little sparrow, but maybe if there had been better healthcare and cancer drugs were cheaper and Ken Hunt hadn't lost his job two years before and, and, and…

Yeah, everything was politics.

Even Cher standing in the shadow of the massive grain silo on the edge of Old Man Nesbitt's farm, shielding her eyes from the sun and looking up at Shy, gripping a narrow steel bar that ran around the silo top, her feet perched on a narrow ledge, fifteen meters up. Cher hadn't wanted to go play on Nesbitt's Farm. She was halfway through a new book she'd got from the library and desired nothing more to sit aside and finish it, but it was a glorious summer day and Shy had threatened to try to flush her book down the toilet if Cher didn't go with her.

"Where are we going?" Cher had whined, listlessly following her sister over the fields. "And why?"

"We're going for an adventure," Shy said. "You gotta stop reading about them, and start having them." Which was all well and good until Shy's adventuring got her into a place that she couldn't come down from.

"You've got to come up, Cher," Shy hollered, her voice shaking. Cher watched her sister with interest. She'd never seen Shy look scared before. It was a new thing. She liked new things. So she said nothing and just stared up at her.

"Cher, I'm not screwing around! Just climb up the goddam ladder!"

"Why?" Cher said.

Shy seemed to do a little dance, her tippytoes scrabbling for purchase on the narrow ledge. She took a deep breath.

"Because I can't go any further, and I can't go back unless you reach out and grab my hand and pull me round."

"I still don't know why you went up there, Shy."

"Because I wanted to see if I could get all the way 'round the silo, dummy."

Cher thought about it. "But why, Shy?"

Shy said a bad word, one Cher had never heard Daddy say but had heard sometimes on movies or videos. She added, "Because it was there and I wanted to find out. Jesus, Cher, come on!"

Cher considered it a bit more and went to the foot of the ladder that was bolted on to the side of the silo. She looked up and could see that Shy had gone up the ladder and stepped out on to the tiny ledge, but handholds had run out about two meters along.

"And you want me to climb up there and hold out my hand and pull you back to the ladder?"

"Yes, baby girl," Shy said tremulously. "Come on, you can do it."

"OK." Cher put a foot on the ladder and gripped it with both hands.

The first three or four rungs were fine. Then she started to get a tingling feeling in the soles of her feet. Her hands felt sweaty and slippery. She went up a few more rungs and looked down. She was twice her own height already. She looked up. Shy seemed impossibly high.

"I can't do it."

"Sure you can!" Shy said. "Just a little further."

Cher tried, but she started to feel sick, like she was going to throw up. She looked up at where Shy, her face contorted in what looked like pain, gazed down at her, and shook her head.

"I can't," she said. "I'll go get Daddy."

"There's no time, Cher! I can't hold on…"

Cher started to steadily descend the ladder, her mouth dry, tears pricking her eyes. She couldn't do it. Her sister would just have to hold on a bit longer.

There was a scream and a sudden rush of moving air past Cher's face, and Shy reached the ground before Cher did.

"You let me down," Cher muttered to herself, blinking in the strip-lighting of the concrete room in the Ritz, reaching for her watch to see what time it was.

That was what Shy had said to her in hospital, after they'd plastered up both her broken legs. She missed a whole summer of adventures because of that fall, and never really forgave Cher. The memory still stung, crying by her sister's hospital bed, promising never to let her down again.

Cher sat on the edge of the hard bed, rubbing her face. She couldn't spend many more nights in this horrible, airless box. The dream had knocked her sideways.

You let me down.

She always had bad dreams for a couple of days after hypersleep. She'd be happy if she never had to go through it again. There was a movement on Earth called "Real-Lifers," who refused to ever undertake faster-than-light travel. They just wanted to live out normal lifespans, their three-score years and ten or whatever, and believed it was wrong for humans to indulge in the longevity granted by the cryotubes. They were mainly cranks, but Cher had a little sympathy for their general position. Every time she went into hypersleep she could only think of those horror stories of things going wrong and people sleeping for centuries, lost out in space.

Cher pushed the thought away. She had more concrete things to concern her today. She reached for the envelope that had been left for her, the note on top of it.

THIS IS WHY
YOUR SISTER DIED.

It was time to shower and go and find out exactly what that meant.

There had been an encrypted comms tag scrawled on the back of the photograph. She sent a curt message, and a response had come back with a time and a place. Noon at the Queen's Head. Cher got there half an hour early, walking through the rain for ten minutes from the Ritz, stopping to buy an umbrella from a woman selling them from a rickety stall set out in front of a convenience store.

Along the way there were screens set into the concrete walls, promising a glorious future for New Albion, a return to the greatness of Empire, and seemingly endless sunshine. Cher, huddling under her umbrella, wondered if they were going to terraform the climate to be more like the idyll on the simulations than the reality of the planet.

Like the cabbie said, they'd had their priorities straight. Even on the short walk, Cher had passed two takeout shops selling battered fish and chunky fries, the hot, greasy air emanating from their open doors making her stomach rumble.

They'd made a bit more effort with the Queen's Head, which was clad with dark wood and had overflowing flower baskets on the windowsills. A sign hanging over the door bore a painting that Cher recognized to be Queen Victoria. The pub was well-lit inside, a polished wooden bar with mirrors behind it reflecting the open space filled with round tables and short stools, about half of them occupied by small groups of mainly men. Most of them glanced up at her as she walked in, shaking her umbrella, and scoped the place out. Along the side wall were a series of booths, and she spotted an unoccupied one that gave her a good view of the main doors.

Behind the bar, a young man in a white shirt and a black apron around his waist appraised her as she walked up. "What'll it be for the lady? Half of lager with a dash of lime? G and T?" He glanced at his wristwatch. "Or is it Prosecco o'clock?"

"Just a coffee, black, no sugar," Cher said, pointing to the empty booth. "I'll take it over there."

She had almost finished her coffee when, on the stroke of twelve, the doors opened and a man walked in, with a small, fluffy brown hound that shook the rain off its fur, causing a volley of complaints from the men around the nearest table. Could this be him? He was tall, with dark, thinning hair, sturdy looking. Cher watched him slough off his raincoat and walk to the bar. Both he and the barman—and the dog, Cher noted—looked in her direction. She tensed a little on the wooden seat. Yes, this was him. She concentrated on her coffee cup as the man walked over and stood by the table.

"Mad dogs and Englishmen go out in the midday rain?" she said, glancing up at him. The dog stuck its nose over the top of the table.

"I'm American, like you," the man said, and he slid into the booth across from her. "I took the liberty of ordering you another coffee."

"Who are you?" Cher said.

"I need to know I can trust you before I tell you that." The dog jumped up on to the bench beside the man and sat down, regarding her with an unnerving stare.

"Why did you send a postcard from Hasanova?"

"So you'd know that I know what happened to your sister."

"Why drag me halfway across the galaxy to this godforsaken place?"

The man shrugged. "I had to come here. I thought it would be a good place for us to meet."

Cher paused as the barman brought them both coffees. When he walked away she took the envelope out of her bag and pushed it across the table toward the man. "And what the actual fuck is this meant to be?"

He sipped his hot coffee carefully, never taking his eyes off Cher.

"Let me tell you a story," he said eventually, "from a little over sixty years ago. It's about a ship, a commercial towing vessel called the USCSS *Nostromo*, and a signal it received from LV-426, later known as Acheron, a moon orbiting Calpamos in the Zeta Reticuli system…"

Cher listened to him for thirty minutes, then stood up and started unfurling her umbrella.

"What are you doing?" said the man.

"Leaving," Cher said. "Going to book passage on the next available ship back to Earth. Where I'll continue my search for the truth about what happened to my sister without being hindered by some fucking maniac peddling horror stories for what I can only guess is his own sick amusement."

"It's all true," the man said quietly. "Sit down. Please."

Cher leaned over the table toward him. "You really expect me to believe these… these…"

"Xenomorphs."

"These *Xenomorphs* exist, and that Weyland-Yutani, one of the biggest and most successful corporations in the entire universe, has been covertly conducting experiments to create the ultimate bioweapon and has managed to keep this completely quiet?" Cher could feel her anger rising. "And furthermore you want me to believe that my sister died because there was an infestation of these things on Hasanova, and Captain Kylie Duncan was actually heading up a secret squad called the Midnighters deployed to collect specimens of them, and leave no witnesses alive to tell the tale?"

"It's all true," the man again said, and her anger didn't seem to phase him. "Look. My name is Chad McClaren. I worked for Weyland-Yutani. I... saw the things they did. To both Xenomorphs and humans. They've got no conscience, Cher. No boundaries. They'll stop at nothing."

Cher sat down again. "Why did you come to me? Philanthropy? Just wanted to do a good deed by letting me know how my sister died?"

"Not quite," Chad said. "You're a journalist. You have connections. We need to get this out there. Are you really going to walk out on the biggest story of your career? The biggest story in history?"

Cher thought about it. "Why not just go to the media yourself?"

"Because I'm a dead man walking," Chad said quietly. "I tried to turn whistleblower. Weyland-Yutani wants me terminated. I know too much. I break cover for even a second, and I'm gone like I never existed."

"You said *we*, earlier. 'We need to get this out there.' Who's we?"

Did the dog sigh? *Can dogs even sigh*, Cher thought, then she turned her attention back to Chad.

"There's a bacterial research facility," he said. "The Tark-Weyland Station. I've got a few other scientists there, thinking of coming over to our side. That's why I'm here on New Albion, trying to find some proof to get them fully committed to the cause. And there's Amanda and Zula…"

Again with the dog. Cher glared.

"Is your mutt really sighing? What's this some party trick you've trained him for?" She looked back to Chad. "Amanda and Zula who?"

"Amanda is the daughter of Ellen Ripley, who was the only survivor of the *Nostromo* incident. She's devoted her life to blowing open Weyland-Yutani's Xenomorph research. Zula Hendricks is a former Colonial Marine who… worked with Amanda to destroy the Company's Xenomorph experimental facilities."

"Maybe I should be talking to them, then," Cher said. "Mr. McClaren, I appreciate you coming to me, but your story is just bullshit, and I can't let myself get sidetracked. I'm… I'm sorry."

Everything was politics. So Cher made herself a political decision, and stood up again. She tossed a few New Albion shillings on the table for the coffee and walked toward the doors, without looking back.

Thankfully the rain had stopped, so she left the umbrella folded and headed back to the Ritz, where she would make arrangements for the next ship off this dump. Her emotions see-sawed between fury and despair. She'd barely gone a dozen meters.

"Ms. Hunt!"

Cher turned but there was no one there. No one except Chad McClaren's dog, sitting on the wet sidewalk, wagging its tail. Cher frowned and looked around. There were some people walking along the sidewalk on the other side, but nobody near who could know her or would have said her name.

"Ms. Hunt," the dog said. "Please. Just listen to us."

"You have to be shitting me," Cher said, glancing around. "What is this, ventriloquism? You guys should be doing children's parties, not peddling bullshit monster stories. Where are you, McClaren?"

"He's still in the pub," the dog said. "Come back. Please. My name is Davis, and I'm a Weyland-Yutani security drone. Well, I was. I just currently inhabit this synthetic... Cockapoo. It's a long story. Everything to do with this is a long story, but we need you, Ms. Hunt, and you need us. To help prove why Shy died, and to get justice for her."

"You let me down," Cher heard Shy say again from her hospital bed.

"It's really all true?" Cher said suspiciously.

The dog—Davis—nodded. "We can show you more. Pictures. Video. We've got it all. Just listen to us."

If she'd had a single other lead to go on, Cher would have kept on walking. But she didn't. There was something about that horror on the picture, that shiny, black, skeletal grotesquerie, saliva dripping from its maw, crouched like a coiled nightmare, something that spoke to her deeply, and made her shudder. She *wanted* it to not exist, but her soul seemed to tap into some other, stronger truth, and screamed to her that it did.

"OK," Cher said. "I'll come back. I'll listen." As Davis began to lead her back to the Queen's Head, she muttered, "But you start humping my leg, and all bets are off."

6

The landing platform was on the other side of the main colony hub. The ship wheeled toward it and then was lost out of sight in the clouds. Getting there from here would be a mad, dangerous dash... could Merrilyn risk it, especially with Therese? It would take only one of those things to confront them along the two kilometers of corridors, and they would be lost—just when salvation was so close.

"Mama, are they soldiers? Are they coming to help us?"

"Yes, I hope so, Little Flower," Merrilyn said, thinking furiously. She hadn't been able to tell what sort of ship it was or who it belonged to in the glimpse she'd had from the observation window. Somebody must have managed to get a distress call out. It didn't matter who it was, all that mattered was that they were here now.

"Mama, what if... what if *they* get to them first?"

"I'm thinking, Therese." Her daughter was right. The entire crew could be wiped out before they could be any help at all. She had to warn them somehow.

Merrilyn switched on the monitors that showed the security camera feeds and cycled through rapidly until she got to the landing platform camera. Thank God it was still working. There was a tannoy system connected to the cameras, and Merrilyn could use it to both warn them and tell them where she and Therese were located. The storm was making the feed grainy with interference, but she could see the ship coming into view, buffeted by the strong winds and, after three attempts, coming to rest on the wide platform.

She couldn't make out the designation numbers or name of the vessel, but it looked like a small commercial vehicle rather than a military ship. Merrilyn felt a pang and hoped they had guns. For a long while nothing happened, and then a hatch opened in the front of the ship and a set of steps was lowered.

Merrilyn counted five crew who disembarked and stood in the shelter of their ship, looking around at the deserted colony. They wore ordinary spacer fatigues. A merchant or trading ship. It didn't matter. They were saved. Merrilyn took manual control of the camera and zoomed in a little, making out the Union Jack on the side of the ship. Three World Empire, then. No beef with the ICSC. But even if they had been United Americas marines, Merrilyn was sure they wouldn't have abandoned a mother and child, even with the war.

It took a while for her to work out how to patch into the tannoy from the remote control, and she pressed the button just as the five crew began walking toward the access door leading to the colony hub. She needed to warn them to get back, or at least to take care. There must have been a burst of static from the speaker, because they all looked up. Merrilyn was about to introduce herself when it happened.

Behind the five figures, a black shape flitted across the landing platform. Merrilyn's breath caught in her throat.

No. Don't say it's too late. Don't say their saviors were dead before they even entered the colony.

But it wasn't one of the creatures.

It was a human.

Merrilyn frowned and zoomed in, then her eyes widened in surprise. She recognized him. One of the miners. She didn't know his name, only knew him by sight, but he'd survived, too. He must have been hiding out at the far end of the colony. How many other survivors were there? She had assumed only her and Therese. At least he would warn them about the—

Merrilyn's hand flew to her mouth at what she saw on the screen. The man—François, she suddenly remembered—had come up behind the crew, and they turned. He waved his hands and pointed toward the colony buildings. One of the crew pulled out a handgun. At first Merrilyn thought, *Thank God, they have weapons*.

Until the woman turned it on François and shot him in the chest.

Very slowly, Merrilyn disconnected the link to the tannoy system.

"Mama?" Therese said, staring at the screen. "What happened? What does that mean?"

"It means, Little Flower," Merrilyn said, "that we are going to have to hide again and be very, very quiet while Mama works out what to do."

"What the *fuck* did you do that for?" Tom Moran bellowed over the raging storm, staring at the twitching body of the Frenchie colonist on the landing platform. Amina Mir looked at the gun in her hand and then at Moran.

"Sorry, guv. I thought he was going to go for us. He looked as mad as a bag of snakes. Banging on about monsters, and that."

Moran shook his head. "You trigger-happy cow, Mir. Probably going to get us in a pile of shit, that. Well done."

"I'm not exactly sure it will," Boffin said. His real name was Jerry Bough, but everybody called him Boffin on account of him being the cleverest one of the crew when it came to science. "That distress call was sent out nearly a week ago. I just had Mother scan the colony mainframe. There's been almost no activity since then." He looked at Moran, then at the dead Frenchie. "I think just about everybody's gone already. He must've been the last of them."

Moran thought about it. "Sling him over the side. We never saw him, right?" The others murmured assent and began to roll the body to the edge of the landing platform.

It was a long way down. Nobody would ever find him. When it was done, Moran said, "What do you mean, Boffin? All gone? Gone where?"

Boffin shrugged. "I don't know. Weather's a problem, too. Hard to get solid readings. I can get Mother patched into the colony network, but it'll take a bit of time. She's old, and we're not used to hacking something so big."

"Do it," Moran said. "Rest of you, let's get inside out of this bloody storm. See if we can work out what the hell happened here."

If it had been up to Moran, he'd have ignored the distress call. They were a trade mission, not a rescue outfit, but base had suggested it would be good form to check it out anyway. They'd off-loaded a load of iron ore at a very nice little Chinese colony about a week out, and it was just his bad luck to be passing LV-187, the nearest colony to home, when they picked up the transmission.

Still, it would only hold them up for a day or so. The wife could wait that long to see him. Though, to be fair, she was only really interested in his pay-packet these days. Not that Moran was bothered. They'd had a nice little brothel on that Chinese colony, and he'd spent a little more than he should have of his bonus while they were there.

Once inside the French colony, though, he really, really wished somebody else had picked this up.

"You got your body-cam on, Mir?" he said as they picked their way through the corridor. It was fucking carnage. There were at least ten corpses, and none of them pretty. It was like a pack of rampaging wild animals had torn through the place. "Rest of you, weapons out."

Priestley squatted down and turned over a prone corpse. The front of the woman's torso had been ripped out, like something had exploded out of her from the inside. Frank Priestley was a tough old Yorkshireman and Moran had known him for donkey's years. He'd never seen the old boy look as white as this. Looked like he was going to faint.

"What happened here, guv?" Priestley said, suddenly choking back a mouthful of bile. "It's like a slaughterhouse."

"I think we should get back on the *Victory* and get the fuck off here," Bromley said, running a hand through her dreadlocks. "Whatever shit went down here, we don't want to be next." Moran was inclined to agree, but now they were hampered by regulations. Until there was a material threat to their lives, they were duty-bound to stay here and call it in. A sign on the wall, smeared with dried blood, said the comms tower was a quarter of a click ahead.

"Let's call it in and get orders," Moran said. "The colony comms is going to be a lot stronger than the ship system." He thought about it for a moment. "They're going to tell us to sweep the whole colony. Let's save time. Priestley, Mir, you do a full circuit. This place isn't that massive. Two kilometers end to end. Circle back and meet Bromley and me in the comms tower. Quicker we do this, quicker we can be on our way home."

Amina and Priestley looked doubtful, but they moved off along the corridor. Then the Yorkshireman paused and turned back to them.

"What if we find survivors, guv?"

Moran scratched his beard. That would complicate things, he was sure, because he had an inkling about what sort of orders he was going to get back once he'd reached the comms tower. Moran was ex-military, and he could see the way the wind was blowing out here in the colonies. Survivors would mean a fully accountable rescue mission, and depending on how many of them there were, they might have to wait for an official response from the ICSC.

Then there was the Frenchie who Mir had shot. It was a long way down in a storm, for sure, but a full-scale investigation here—which there obviously would be—might turn up a something that was all a bit bloody awkward.

He walked over to them and flicked off Amina's body-cam.

"There are no survivors," he said quietly. "They're all dead. Looks like they went crazy and killed each other. Understood." Priestley nodded, and Moran switched Amina's body-cam back on.

Then he said loudly, "Go now, and for God's sake I hope you find somebody alive in this hell-hole." When Amina turned to walk slowly up the corridor, he winked at Priestley and beckoned for Bromley to follow him in the opposite direction.

"Pinky Ponk!" Therese said.

"He's here," Merrilyn said, handing the toy to her daughter. "Now remember what I said, Little Flower. As soon as we are outside the canteen, we are playing the Quiet Game. You like the Quiet Game, don't you?"

Therese nodded, pulled an imaginary zipper over her mouth, and nodded seriously.

"Good girl. Now just let Mama pack her bag, and we can go."

She had been watching the newcomers on the security cameras, and had seen them split up. Two were heading this way, and would inevitably come into the canteen. Shooting François might have been a terrible mistake, but could she take the risk? They were going to have to leave the relative safety of the canteen and avoid, not just the things, but the people, too.

Monsters everywhere you look, Merrilyn sadly thought. Not for the first time she wished she'd never set eyes on LV-187, never brought Therese within a hundred light years of it.

With as many bottles of water, tins of food, and makeshift weapons that she could carry, Merrilyn hefted the rucksack onto her back and carefully opened the canteen door a tiny crack. She peered out, then turned and took Therese's hand. Merrilyn put a finger to her lips and then mimed pulling a zipper over her closed mouth, nodding as Therese did the same. Then, taking a deep breath, she opened the door wide and led her daughter by the hand, out into the dim corridor.

"Well, what the fuck am I looking at here, then?" Moran said, tugging on his beard. They'd regrouped, and got Amina's cam footage up on a monitor in the comms tower, where the storm was lashing the windows with rain as night started to fall over LV-187.

"I've never seen shit like that before in all my years," Priestley said. "They were soft to the touch. Organic."

"Kind of like big seed pods," Amina said. "That had burst open."

"Seed pods," Moran said, staring at the paused image on the screen. "Frenchies growing some weird-arse shit here, then? I thought this was an oil operation."

Priestley shook his head. "If that was the case, surely they'd have them in some kind of… nursery or something. These were sort of scattered around. Hidden in corridors. Access hatches. Storage cupboards. Weirdest thing I ever saw."

"How many?" Moran said.

"Ten that we counted. Not saying there aren't more—we didn't get into every single service conduit or anything like that."

"You know what this is," Bromley said slowly. They all turned to look at her. "Black goo, innit?"

Moran sighed as Priestley said, "What's that? Some shit you people put on your hair?"

"Racist twat." Amina sighed, looking away.

"Fuck off," Bromley said. "You know what I'm talking about."

"We all know what you're talking about, but we don't know anything about that shit," Moran said. "It's rumor and conjecture."

"Yeah, well, I know somebody who had family in one of the colonies out in the Kruger 60 system," Bromley said, frowning. "You tell *them* it's just conjecture, that whole worlds being wiped out by black bombers pouring shit into the atmosphere."

"I heard it was the Union of Progressive Peoples," Amina said.

"I heard the United Americas," Bromley said.

"I heard it was Ronald McFucking Donald," Priestley said. "Black goo. What a load of shite. You see any black goo here?"

"Priestley's right," Moran said, trying to take control. "Whatever's going on with these border bombings isn't anything to do with LV-187. This is some whole other shit." He looked at Amina. "Any survivors?"

"No."

"Really no survivors, or no survivors *now*?"

"No. Nothing. The canteen looked like someone had lived in it for a little while, but there was nobody in the vicinity."

"Probably that poor sod who Deadeye Mir here blew away," Priestley said, making a gun from his fingers and thumb and pretending to fire it at her with a *pew-pew* sound. Suddenly there was a buzzing sound from the comms console. Moran went over to check and turned to his team.

"Orders from our masters on New Albion."

"Well?" Bromley said.

"Do we still have that Union Jack in the *Victory*? We're going to need it, boys and girls, because we're about to make history," Moran said with a grin.

"I'll buzz Boffin, tell him to get up here," Priestley said, firing up his wrist comms. "And it's the Union *Flag*, guv. It's only the Union Jack when it's flown from a ship."

"History how?" Amina said.

"Shit's going down," Moran said. "Top-level shit, and we're going to be part of it."

Priestley killed the comms link and frowned at Moran. "Boffin's on his way up. With the flag. He's got Mother patched into the colony mainframe, but he thinks the readings are all fucked up."

"How do you mean?" Moran said.

"He reckons the scan is showing lifeforms."

"Well, duh. We're here," Bromley snorted.

Priestley flipped her two fingers. "Apart from us."

"How *many* lifeforms readings apart from us?" Moran said.

"Seventeen," Priestley said.

7

"Tell me one more time."

Chad sighed. It was almost midnight and they'd been talking for nearly twelve hours now. At least they had managed to secure a couple of rooms in an apartment block close to where the heavy plant machinery was digging out the trench for the fabled recreation of the River Thames that was to be the New Albion centerpiece. Chad wasn't sure he could have spent a night in that horrible concrete edifice called The Ritz.

"OK," he said, pinching the bridge of his nose. "So we start with what we call the Ovomorph—"

"Egg," Cher said, writing it down on a big legal pad for the umpteenth time. "And these are laid by the Queen, and these things can stay inanimate for... how long?"

"Generally until a potential host approaches. At which point the egg's four lobes at the top will open..."

"And out comes the face-hugger." Cher nodded and made more notes. "And this thing attaches itself to its host, sticks a breathing tube down its throat, and impregnates it."

"Right," Chad said. "And this is why we get variations in the Xenomorphs. The relationship is more symbiotic than just parasitical. There's an adoption of the host's DNA to help the creature grow. You can't get the face-hugger off without killing the host, but once it's done its job it'll detach itself and die."

"Like a bee after it stings you."

Chad watched Cher's face wrinkle up as she made notes. He was so used to living his life with Xenomorphs, he'd forgotten what it was like when people discovered them for the first time. Usually that was very quickly followed up by running and screaming and death, so it was refreshing to be able to sit down and talk almost calmly about the creatures.

Cher was just the first step... if everything went according to plan, the entire human race would be hearing about the Xenomorphs through her journalism. They would no longer be the dirty little secret in the shadows. They would be in the full glare of a thousand suns, and instead of fighting its petty little wars and skirmishes, humanity would have something against which to unite...

The aliens, and those who would exploit them.

"And how long does the next stage take?" Cher asked. "The... chestburster?" She paused. "I must say, for scientists you've given these things *very* media-friendly names."

"Anything from an hour to a day to a week," Chad said. "It varies considerably depending on the host and the Queen that laid the Ovomorph, and other factors related to environment and the DNA reflex process."

"But eventually…" Cher put her hands to her chest and aped an explosion with them. "*Boom*."

"Boom," Chad agreed. "And then the fun really starts, and by fun I mean killing."

Davis was sitting on the rug, watching the video screen with interest. The New Albion Broadcasting Company had hours and hours of ancient British television footage, going back to the mid-twentieth century. Davis had tuned in to the comedy channel. Chad had been trying to teach him about humor, something Davis felt he sorely lacked, but it was so subjective… Davis was trying to understand, but Chad realized he simply couldn't understand why something was meant to be funny.

Maybe it was that, and not love, that was the gulf between AI and human. One that was just too wide to ever be bridged.

"Can I interrupt?" Davis said.

Chad and Cher both looked at him. "Sure," Cher said. "You have something to add about the chestburster stage?"

"No. I am curious about something." He turned back toward the screen. "Why is this funny?"

They all looked. There was a man gesticulating at another man in a shop that sold animals. The first man was complaining that a parrot he had bought from the second man was dead. Chad vaguely knew what this was, in the same way he had a vague understanding of Shakespeare's plays and Beethoven. Something from long ago that people thought was classic, but which nobody really had any frame of reference for anymore.

"The parrot is dead," Davis said. "Why is that a source of humor? Is it not tragic? And how did the man purchase a bird and only discover it was not alive when he got it home? I'm not seeing the logic here."

"Don't ask me." Cher shrugged. "I never got British comedy ever."

Chad thought about it. "I think it might be more about the delivery than the content. This stuff was meant to be absurdist anyway, as far as I can tell."

Davis nodded, licked his nose, and turned back to the program.

"So," Cher said, picking up her pen again. "*Boom*."

"The Xenomorph is at its most vulnerable then. Most killable. It's only maybe a foot tall. Weak. It'll immediately take itself off to hide, and grow."

"And this takes…?"

"Hours to reach maturity, and an adult Xenomorph can be anything from two meters tall when fully extended. That's for a drone. The most common type. Depending on the DNA reflex, it might be a Praetorian, twice as big and twice as nasty. You draw a Queen from the genetic deck, then you're really talking. Six meters tall, more than double that from tail to pharyngeal—"

"Spell that, please," she said. "And that is…?"

Chad did, and then made a fist and put it near his mouth, as though kissing the top of his wrist. Then he snaked his arm forward, his hand opening and closing like a claw in Cher's face.

"A secondary mouth that extends from the first. The primary weapon," he said. "Along with their prehensile tail, their claws, and the acidic blood."

Cher put her pad and pen down and rubbed her face. "You do, of course, realize how batshit crazy this all sounds?"

There'd been many a time over the past few years Chad had wished he was crazy, and all this was some kind of fever dream. It was a lot to take in.

"Let's leave it for tonight," he said. "It's late. We can talk some more tomorrow."

"You'll tell me about Amanda Ripley?" she replied. "And Zula Hendricks?"

Chad caught Davis looking over his shoulder. He said carefully, "Their stories need to be told—they're a big part of this whole thing—but we have to be careful. Zula's in a lot of danger out there. She's made a lot of enemies. We have to tread lightly to avoid putting her in the crosshairs, any more than she already is."

"And Amanda? She's in danger too?"

"Tomorrow." Chad stood up and yawned, and stretched. "You take the bedroom. I'll have the couch. There's still a lot to go over before you write your story."

Cher stood also and grabbed her bag. "There's more than going over old stories that needs to be done before I write a single word," she said.

"Such as?"

"You seem genuine, Chad, and you're very convincing, but you could still just be a crazy guy with an agenda." She dragged her case over to the door of the small bedroom, off the lounge. "You know what needs to happen. I need to see one of these things. With my own eyes." Then she continued through. "Goodnight, Chad. Goodnight, Davis."

When the door closed behind her, Davis rolled onto his back and looked for a long time at Chad.

"Obviously you knew this was going to happen."

Chad nodded. "I was hoping it wouldn't, though. Cher Hunt obviously has balls of steel, but she's not going to be much use to us dead, is she?"

Cher knew she wasn't going to get much sleep. Not after all that. She lay in the uncomfortable bed, listening to the sounds of construction on the Thames ditch. It seemed like they were going to work all through the night.

Chad McClaren's story sounded just too incredible to even consider believing, but she'd made him go over the details four, five, six times. Not a word or fact out of place, even when she'd tried to catch him out by playing dumb and repeating something back to him with slight variations an hour after he'd said it.

He corrected her every time. Either the guy was a consummate actor, or an actual psychopath, or…

Or he was telling the truth. In which case these things, these Xenomorphs, were the real reason the inquiry into the Hasanova incident had been such a whitewash. Captain Kylie Duncan hadn't just gone rogue, she'd been working to another agenda. And Shy had died for it.

To keep it quiet. To cover it all up.

If it was true, then her sister had seen these things. Up close. Even now, and hating herself deeply for it, Cher felt a pang of jealousy. Shy had seen these monsters. These aliens. Shy was always the bold one, the adventurous one, the get-things-done one. Cher wrote about people who were bold and adventurous and got things done. That was the difference between them. Shy was a doer. Cher was a spectator.

"You fucking bitch," she said out loud, to herself. "Your sister is dead, and you still can't let this thing go." Cher closed her eyes, willing sleep to come. Listening to the sounds of New Albion. And something else. Something hard and brittle and skittering. She sat bolt upright in bed, her mind filled with face-huggers and chestbursters and—

Davis. The dog was pawing at the door until it swung open, and stood there, framed in a square of light from a street lamp thrown through the undraped window in the living room.

"Do you mind if I sleep in here?" Davis said. "Chad snores awfully, and I can't get comfortable on that rug."

"Sure," Cher said uncertainly. She patted the bed, then felt a little stupid and self-conscious. *It's a talking robot dog.* "Jump on."

Davis leapt up on to the bed and padded in a circle then curled up beside Cher. They lay there in silence for a moment.

"You know," Cher said, "I'm not sure how comfortable I am with this. I mean, you're basically a man in a dog's body, right?"

"I'm flattered that you think that. I was created as a combat synthetic. My purpose was to fight, but I was made with a flaw... free will. Self-autonomy, and with that came a desire to be more than what I was born to be." There was a moment of quiet, then Davis said quietly, "Ms. Hunt—"

"Cher. Please."

"Cher. What do you think makes humans *human*?"

She thought about it for a long while, listening to the rumble from the construction site. "Well, it's not an appreciation of comedy, I think we've established that. Maybe love?"

"I have loved," Davis said, his dog jaws suddenly yawning. "I *do* love."

"Zula Hendricks?" Cher guessed.

"It is perhaps not conventional love," Davis said, "but it is what I understand love to be. A need to nurture and protect that overrides all else. A desire to be with her above anyone."

"You're lucky, then," Cher whispered. "I've never felt like that. Maybe you are human after all, Davis."

"No. I'm not. Not yet. There's something missing, some vital ingredient lacking. It is as though… as though I am a perfect forgery of the Mona Lisa, but the smile is slightly off."

Cher thought about Shy, about the reason she was here in the first place. About that day on the grain silo. Something changed between them at that very moment, something broke and snapped. *"You let me down."* It was awfully heavy shit to lay on an eight-year-old, and Cher knew that Shy hadn't ever seemed to really think about it afterward, certainly never mentioned it. But it stuck with Cher.

"Perhaps…" she said slowly in the dark. "Perhaps what makes us human is the willingness to sacrifice ourselves for those we love. And if we have the chance and don't, to be haunted by it forever."

"I have made sacrifices, Cher. I have been a nuclear bomb. I have been a spaceship. I have been lost in the depths of the ocean. All for her. And always I found her again."

Cher felt sleepy, suddenly. "Is it real sacrifice, though, if you know you aren't going to die?"

Davis was quiet for so long that Cher thought he'd gone to sleep, or whatever synthetics did. Put himself in stand-by mode. Begun to recharge. She realized she didn't know much about synthetics at all. She'd met one or two, but never for any great length of time. She'd assumed them to be just machines, no more aware than her watch or phone, but in human form. There was something disquieting about Davis's almost-humanity, more so because he was currently a damned dog.

"I never knew I would survive any of the incidents," Davis said slowly. "I... hoped I would."

"Hope," Cher murmured. "There's your humanity right there." She rolled over to face the wall. "Maybe you're asking the wrong person, Davis. I've spent my life watching, interviewing, writing about and reporting on humans, and I'm no closer to knowing what makes us tick. What separates us from animals, really? What separates us from the goddam Xenomorphs?"

"Xenomorphs exist only to reproduce, kill anything that threatens them, and spread themselves across the universe."

"So," Cher said, yawning. "Nothing really separates us at all, then."

She must have fallen asleep because she woke up with a start, a warm, round patch of flattened blankets on the bed beside her where Davis had slept and recently vacated. So synthetics—synthetic dogs, at least—had body heat.

Then it registered.

Chad was hammering on her door and calling for her to come quick.

"What's up?" she said, yawning and stretching in her vest and shorts as she walked into the living space. "Coffee. We have coffee, right? I need coffee."

Chad led her to the big monitor in front of which Davis was already stationed, sitting up, alert, his tail wagging.

"Who's that?" Cher said, pointing at the figure on the screen, a stout, ruddy man wearing an ill-fitting suit and looking seriously out from under a shock of blond hair.

"Maurice Pepper. The prime minister of New Albion. He's making an emergency broadcast."

Pepper shuffled some papers at the lectern which bore the crest of the colony, and coughed. Cher looked at Chad.

"And this affects us how?"

"I don't know," Chad said. "I just have a very bad feeling about it."

"*Citizens of New Albion,*" Pepper boomed. "*It is my great honor to inform you that this glorious colony is, as of this moment, on a war footing.*"

8

Transcription: The full address of Prime Minister
Maurice Pepper
New Albion
July 17, 2186 (Earth standard)

In three short years, it will be a century since the United Kingdom joined forces with Japan to form the political, commercial, and military alliance that would become known as the Three World Empire—named for the first three planets to be controlled by humanity: Earth, Mars, and Titan.

For many on Earth and the widespread colonies to which mankind has spread in the last hundred years, this will be a cause for celebration, a revelry of pomp and circumstance, an opportunity to unfurl the flags of our nations and let them flutter in the breeze of continued co-operation and mutual benefit.

So you would think here on New Albion. This colony is home to some of the most venerable and wealthiest families who helped to build Britain's rich and illustrious history, the legacy on which the Three World Empire was built.

Yes, much has come out of that alliance, notably the formation of the Weyland-Yutani Corporation which was created through the efforts of two of each country's greatest minds. But while the trumpets blare and the drums roll on Earth in commemoration of this successful alliance, there is less cause for festivities on New Albion—and, I'll warrant, on many other colonies under the sway of the 3WE.

Despite the obvious benefits that arose from the coupling of Britain and Japan, in 2088 there were many misgivings among the influential families and corporations that called this sceptre'd isle home. Why? Because Britain has never been a "joiner." We have always worked best as a leader, not as a follower. A little under seven decades before the formation of the Three World Empire, Britain voted resoundingly to leave the confines of Europe and go it alone, with remarkably successful results that assuaged any doubts that Britain was just as much of a force to be reckoned with as when it was at the head of an Empire that spanned the entire world.

They called it the Age of Discovery in the fifteenth and sixteenth centuries when Britain, along with the other dominant European powers, began to expand across Earth and declare dominion over the lesser nations.

By the eighteenth century, we held sway in India and, despite the loss of the American colonies thanks to the treachery of the rebels, Britain went on to slap down its greatest rival France and become the dominant military and trade force in the world. For almost a century, the world enjoyed the safety and security of what they called *Pax Britannia*. Britain bought peace to the planet, until the First World War in the early part of the twentieth century changed the political landscape forever.

Why the history lesson? Because it is time for *Pax Britannia* once more. Thanks to the warmongering of the Independent Core Systems Colonies and the United Americas, sparked by the Hasanova incident, the universe is on the brink of chaos that brings to mind the horrors of what the world faced in 1914. But Earth was just one planet. Now the diaspora of humanity may plunge into war on an even more massive scale as colonies become disenfranchised with their ruling blocs, treated merely as resources to feed the ever-growing hunger for oil, minerals, and food back on Earth. To them we are out of sight, out of mind.

This unsettled political landscape, coupled with the so-called border bombings which have seen unexplained "black goo" raining down on innocent communities, and which seem obscured behind a fog of willful misinformation by the authorities, reveals that New Albion has only one path forward.

As of today, we are formally seceding from the control of both Britain and the Three World Empire. The United Kingdom has lost its way; this once-mighty lion is now little more than a neutered house cat, and Britannia herself weeps with sadness and frustration at what they have let us become.

Yet all is not lost. New Albion shall be the new face of Britain, here among the stars. We shall become what Britain has forgotten it used to be. We have wealth and resources and the desire to expand our borders, creating a new British Empire even more glorious than the first. We are entering into what might be called an Age of Re-Discovery—both of the principles and spirit which made our nation great, and of the galaxy around us, rich with untapped resources ready for the taking.

To that end, I am pleased to inform you that New Albion has already made its first foray into widening our sphere of influence. The valiant crew of one of our trade ships, the *Victory*, just yesterday responded to a distress call from our nearest planetary neighbor, LV-187, a small, inhospitable satellite under the control of the ICSC.

Our brave men and women found the colony utterly deserted, for reasons unknown. We are not ones to look a gift horse in the mouth here on New Albion, and for that reason—as you can see from this footage transmitted to us last night—the Union flag now flies over the abandoned colony. We have claimed salvage rights on LV-187 and its rich resources of crude oil.

Citizens, this is a glorious day, but merely the first one of the rest of our lives. New Albion is ascendant, and the sun shall never set upon the new British Empire. We fully expect bleating and threats from the interstellar community. We are prepared to meet them full on, with the bulldog spirit that has lain dormant in us for so long but has now come growling back with a vengeance.

New Albion must protect itself and its burgeoning collection of territories. New Albion *will* protect itself, and it will protect you, our people.

There may be dark days ahead for all of us, but we will rise to the challenge and the light will triumph. Today is a day for celebration, people of New Albion. If our enemies want war, they shall get it, but for today I am declaring a national holiday. You must see it as your right, nay, your *duty*, to raise a glass and toast our magnificent future, which starts right now.

The very best of British to you all.

"They didn't need telling twice," Davis said, paws up on the windowsill. "Everyone is on the streets. Waving flags. And drinking. There appears to be a lot of drinking."

Cher scrolled through her phone. "They're already calling it 3WExit," she said, looking up. "There's a Reuters stringer here on New Albion. I should go find her, pool our resources."

Chad looked away from the video screen, which was again showing the footage of the crew of the *Victory* raising the Union flag on the rain-swept landing platform of the LV-187 colony. He froze the image.

"What?"

Cher looked up at him. "I'm a journalist, Chad. This is a major breaking story, and I'm right here at ground zero. A colony with the influence of New Albion, breaking away from the Three World Empire, is big news."

"Bigger than the Xenomorphs?"

Cher said nothing, so Chad pressed. "I thought you were here for your sister. Not just for your own benefit."

She scowled at him and he wondered if he'd pushed too far.

"Chad, I'm a journalist... it's in my blood. I can't ignore a story like this. Besides, I told you I wanted to see these things first-hand before I could even think about doing anything. How were you planning to make that happen? Do you know where we can even find these Xenomorphs?"

"If I was a betting man," Chad said, pointing to the frozen image of the Union Flag at the LV-187 colony, "I'd put my money on *there*."

Cher stared at the screen for a long time.

Chad was right, of course. She was here to get justice for Shy, and getting evidence of the Xenomorphs seemed to be the only way to blow this whole conspiracy wide open. But she was a journalist, and driven by needs and hungers normal people didn't understand. A story was like a barrel of chum thrown into the path of a starving great white shark. When you got that scent as a journalist, your eyes rolled back and you clamped on, and literally nothing else mattered.

"How can you be sure there are Xenomorphs on LV-187?" she said.

Chad shrugged. "People don't suddenly abandon lucrative, oil-rich colonies *en masse*," he said. "So, they send out a distress call and by the time help arrives they've all... what? Been picked up by someone else? Gone home for a vacation? Disappeared into thin air?" He nodded at the dog. "Davis and me, we've seen this too many times."

"Which also blows open the whole question of what happened to the *Clara*?" Davis said as he trotted up and sat on the rug in front of the screen.

"*Clara*?" Cher said, looking at them both.

"The reason we're here on New Albion," Chad said, getting up to pour her a coffee from the cafetière he'd had brewing. "Back on the Tark-Weyland Station, we deciphered a load of random communications that pointed to a stock of Ovomorphs—"

"Eggs," Cher said.

"Eggs," Chad agreed. "On a remote, uncolonized world. A private salvage company was sent to collect some ore from a crashed ship. They brought the eggs back with them—unofficially. Except they never made it home. Someone boarded the *Clara* and crashed it out in the sticks on New Albion. The eggs were gone." He pointed to the screen. "I think that's where."

Cher pointed at Davis. "You said this blew your theories open. What did you mean?"

"Our initial thought was that the *Clara* had been commissioned via a pyramid of fake front companies to salvage the crashed ship, knowing they'd get the Ovomorphs too," Davis said. "We thought Weyland-Yutani was behind it."

"*You* thought that," Chad grumbled. Cher ignored him

"Isn't it a lot of trouble to go to?" she said. "For Weyland-Yutani? Why not just go and get the eggs themselves?"

"Because although they have big muscles and deep pockets, and can make problems go away..."

Problems like Amanda Ripley? Cher thought.

"...they still have to keep a relatively clean profile where the Xenomorphs are concerned," he finished. "They have to be indirect and covert, especially in heavily-populated systems like this."

"But now you've changed your minds?" Cher said.

Davis did his doggy-shrug again. "It's still on the table, but I suspect Chad is looking at the possibility that it was New Albion who boarded the *Clara* all along. And it was them who planted the Ovomorphs on LV-187. Maybe not yesterday. Maybe some weeks ago."

"Then it's not a salvage operation," Cher said. "It's an invasion."

"Only one way to find out," Chad said. "We go to LV-187. If we find there's been a Xenomorph infestation, and

New Albion is responsible for it, then lucky you. Two scoops for the price of one. More coffee?"

"Yeah," Cher said, as the strains of "Land of Hope and Glory" rose up from the crowds massing in the street outside. "Lots of it."

"You have a ship?" Cher said.

"The *Elvik*," Chad said. "Docked at the terminal. LV-187 is close, so we don't even need to hypersleep."

"Good. I'll go and get ready." When she'd disappeared back into her room, Chad felt Davis staring at him.

"What?" he said, glaring at the dog. "You still can't outstare me, you know."

"I like her," Davis said haltingly. "She's a good person."

Chad shrugged. "She's going to be a good ally. If we can get the proof we need from LV-187, then we can start to really think about taking Weyland-Yutani down."

"She's a good person," Davis said again. "I think we owe it to her to tell her."

"Tell me what?" Cher said suddenly, standing in the doorway, wearing a pair of combat trousers and a vest, a shirt wrapped around her waist.

Chad sighed. "How dangerous this is going to be," Davis said.

"I get it," Cher said. "Hurty-hurty killy-killy alien monsters with acid for blood. Running along corridors, screaming, dying. I pretty much got the picture from all your stories last night. Look, we're not going to LV-187 to have a picnic with these things. I just want to see them for myself, hopefully after they're already dead. Maybe grab some video and photographic evidence, then we can get the hell out of Dodge."

"Davis is right." Chad bit his lip. "It's not just the Xenomorphs. Assuming we survive LV-187—and that's a very big if, I'm sorry to have to tell you—then it's what comes afterward that's going to be the real problem."

Cher raised an eyebrow. "How so?"

"Weyland-Yutani has been conducting its Xenomorph program for decades," Chad said. "There have been untold trillions of dollars poured into it—likely more. They're not going to take too kindly to what we're about to do, to put it mildly."

"You mean my life will be in danger?"

"Yes," he said. "I should have laid this out from the get-go."

Cher seemed to think about it for a moment. She walked to the window and looked out at the singing crowds.

"Sometimes you have to climb the silo even when you don't want to."

"I don't know what that means," Chad said, frowning.

"It doesn't matter," Cher said. "I'm in."

Chad started to organize the necessary take-off clearances, watching with one eye as Davis padded over to Cher.

"Last night," the dog commented, "you said that maybe

what makes people human is the willingness to sacrifice themselves for those they love."

Cher nodded, and look down at Davis. "But as we established, you sacrificed yourself for Zula many times."

"Perhaps…" Davis said slowly. "Perhaps what actually makes us human is the willingness to sacrifice ourselves, not just for those we love, but for everyone. For the greater good."

"You think that's what I'm doing by agreeing to go to LV-187?"

"Maybe. I hope it doesn't come to that, but just the fact you're going to do it…" Davis trailed off. "This requires further analysis."

What were those two talking about last night? Chad was about to say something when his attention was drawn back to his screen by a volley of pings and vibrations. He read the notifications, then read them again, and looked up. "Shit," he said. "We have a problem."

Cher and Davis looked at him.

"In anticipation of Three World Empire retaliation following this morning's announcement, New Albion has closed its airspace to both arriving and outgoing traffic." He looked at both of them. "We're trapped here. New Albion is on lockdown."

9

Even the rain had stopped for New Albion's glorious "ascendence."

Cher followed Chad through the packed crowds thronging the wide concrete avenues, Davis trotting at her heels. She wondered just how the news was being taken back on Earth, and suspected that it wasn't with as much gravity as the New Albion government imagined. Maurice Pepper had been right about one thing: out of sight, out of mind.

New Albion was a corner of a foreign field that was forever—or so everyone had assumed—England, but it was a long way from home, and outside of the main cut and thrust of diplomatic life. Was it even a very great consideration for most people on Earth?

Most likely not.

That said, the New Albion secession wasn't an isolated incident. There might be many on Earth worrying about how it would fit into the colonial unrest on the Frontier worlds, where the Union of Progressive Peoples had started an aggressive expansion program and had, quite naturally, come up against the aggressive United Americas. There was even talk that the UA was going to instigate a draft on the Frontier worlds, which would signal an all-out war.

How would what was conducted out on space be mirrored on Earth? For most people on the homeworld, what happened out on the Frontier was so distant that it was abstract. But if that conflict spilled over to war on Earth...

"Do you always get that look on your face when you're lost in thought?"

Cher blinked. "What look?"

He shrugged as they stood on a corner of two wide intersecting avenues. "Kind of like..." He screwed his face into a frown, nose wrinkled, biting his bottom lip.

"That's my 'resting journalist face.'" She looked up and down the intersection, crowds spilling into the roads, cheering and waving bottles. "What are we doing, anyway?"

"Getting a cab to the terminus." Chad waved his hand as a black taxi negotiated the throng, pulling in beside them.

"You didn't stay long," the cabbie said, putting Cher's bag into the trunk. It was the same guy who'd brought her from the port two days ago.

"You the only cabbie in New Albion?"

"Nah, just the hardest working," the driver said, opening the doors for them to get into the back. "Where we going?"

"Terminus," Chad said.

"You know the airspace is closed?" the driver said, pulling away from the curb and nosing through the revelers. "Big mistake if you ask me. Where we gonna get our stuff from? We're not self-sufficient here. And what we going to do when the ICSC warships turn up? Shoot 'em down with pulse rifles?" He snorted at that as the taxi cleared the central crowds and turned on to a pitted concrete highway, the buildings and control tower of the terminus ahead of them at the end of the straight road.

"I mean, it's not like we got a military to speak of. Not really. All these tin soldiers with Duke of Wellington patches. What we need is ships. Big ships! With big guns!"

Cher looked out of the window at the grey scrubland that passed by the window.

"Well, there's the Royal Marines, right?" Chad said.

The cabbie laughed. "Bunch of toothless old dogs." Davis growled from between Chad and Cher. "Sorry, Fido. No offense, but the Three World Empire ain't exactly what you call aggressive, is it? Runs from a fight like a mangy cur with its tail between its legs." Davis growled again. The cabbie laughed. "It's like he really understands me. Anyway, Royal Marines. They forgot how to have a scrap, that's their problem. Besides, they ain't ours, are they? New Albion's I mean. They're 3WE. We see a Royal Marine Dreadnought in the sky, it'll be getting in line behind the ICSC to kick our arses."

The cab rolled smoothly to the outside of the terminus departure building.

"What you doing here, then?" the cabbie pressed. "You heard what I said, right? Nothing coming in and out without permission."

"We heard," Cher said. "I've got to say, you're very… philosophical about the whole thing. It almost seems like you find it funny."

"Well, you have to laugh, don't you? Or you'd cry. It's what we do here, innit? Only happy when it rains." There was a crack of thunder high above them. "Which is a good job on this bloody planet." He helped Cher get her case out of the trunk and gave Davis a hearty ruffle of his head. "Well, whatever you're up to, best of British to you. Ta-ra!"

The three of them stood at a wire fence topped with razor wire, to the side of the departures terminal, looking out on to a broad concrete expanse dotted with ships of all sizes. Chad pointed through the fence to a small, tidy Level II cruiser on the east side.

"There she is. The *Elvik*."

"Nice," Cher said. "Must have cost you a pretty penny."

"He won her in a card game. Same way he won me," Davis said, sitting between them. "That's our Chad. Lucky at cards, unlucky in love." Chad shot the dog a warning look. He was trying far too hard with this *being human* business. Cher looked at them both.

"So, what's your plan?"

They'd already tried to get through the terminus via the proper channels, but been told by two armed Duke of Wellingtons that there was no chance they were getting to their ship—even when Cher broke down in tears and told them that her mother's medication was on the vessel and without it she would surely die. Chad was quietly impressed. If the journalism business was ever a bust for her, she could definitely make it as an actress.

"One less mouth to feed then," one of the soldiers said, grinning viciously. "You think I was born yesterday? You don't have a sick mother. Clear off, the lot of you, and take that dog before it does a shit."

Chad couldn't help but smile as Davis cocked his leg and peed on the animatronic Beefeater by the door, imploring the empty terminal to come back to New Albion soon, adding a resounding, "Best of British!"

"I didn't even know you could pee," Cher said.

"When the occasion demands," Davis said as they hastily left the terminal, the soldier bellowing at them. "The woman from whom we procured this body must have demanded thorough authenticity."

Chad peered through the fence. "I see one guard hut for this whole section, though there may be more behind those other ships," he said. "They're really not expecting anyone to want to leave."

"Where would they go?" Davis said. "I mean, New Albion is a glorious paradise, isn't it? Best of British?"

Chad and Cher exchanged a glance then both looked down at Davis.

"You know," she said, "you're getting better at this humor thing. Which gives me an idea. Brits love dogs, don't they?" Then she added, "How's your dexterity?"

"The problem with this place, see, is—"

"The rain."

Corporal Terry Smith shot Corporal Bob Jones a withering look. "No, *Robert*, the problem with this place isn't the fucking rain. The problem with this place—"

"The noise, innit? All the construction."

"Robert." Corporal Smith stood up in the metal cargo container that had been repurposed into a guard hut on the main departure apron of the New Albion terminus, and went to put the kettle on. "Let me finish. Please."

"Do go on, Terrence."

"I will, Robert. As I was saying, the problem with this place is—"

"A dog."

Smith slammed the tin containing their teabags onto the work surface.

"Flaming bloody Nora, Robert, did I not just—"

"No," Jones said. "There's a dog. Here."

Smith turned round to see Jones pointing his pulse rifle at a brown, fluffy hound standing in the doorway, head cocked on one side, tongue lolling out happily.

"Hello, boy," Smith said, crouching down. He looked at Jones. "Robert, put your bloody gun away. You're going to shoot a dog?"

"We were told nobody comes on or off the site," Jones said doubtfully. "Orders is orders, innit?"

"It's. A. Dog," Smith replied flatly. "Gordon Bennett, Robert, you are as thick as two short planks sometimes." He looked to the dog and patted his knees. "Hello, boy. What you doing here? Lost?"

"He doesn't look like a stray," Jones said doubtfully as the dog padded over to Smith and started to lick his outstretched hand. Then the animal turned to him, and started to sniff his gun.

"What a good boy," Smith said. "Here, he wants to play with your gun. Look, he's trying to grab it."

"Ow!" Jones said suddenly, pulling his hand back. "The fucking thing bit me!"

Smith laughed uproariously as the dog bounced back to the door, Jones's gun in its mouth.

"You idiot, Robert. You lost your bloody gun." He grinned at his colleague as the dog, stopped, sat down, and positioned the weapon between its front paws, looking intently at it as if for all the world it was trying to work out what it did. Then Smith said, "Here boy, better give me that. Could be nasty if it went off by accident."

"Oh, it won't be an accident if it goes off," the canine said. Jones and Smith froze, and their jaws went slack as a man appeared from around the corner of the hut, grabbing up the gun and pointing it at them.

"Terrence…"

"Yes, Robert, the dog just fucking *talked*."

"Hand over your weapon," the dog said. "Or he will, to employ your colorful vernacular, blow your bloody bollocks off."

Smith started toward the new intruder, but Jones grabbed him by the arm. So Smith carefully and deliberately slid his gun across the floor, and stepped back.

"You're not going to shoot us, are you?" he said, still talking to the dog. "You're a good boy, right?"

When Chad had finished ripping the guards' shirts into strips, then tying and gagging them, he went to join Davis and Cher at the computer terminal in the cargo container. Abruptly, there was a cacophonous drumming as rain started to batter down on to the metal roof.

"Well?" he said.

"Two more guard huts within a hundred meters of the *Elvik*," Davis said as Cher operated the terminal. "We'll be in both their sightlines when we head for the ship. There's no avoiding it."

"Can we get there before they can get to us?"

"Only if they're as stupid as these two, and the law of averages would suggest that it's very unlikely," Davis said, to a volley of muffled grunts of objection from the bound guards. Chad looked back at them in their vests and shorts.

"But not impossible," he said slowly. "I've got an idea."

They were within fifty meters of the *Elvik* when four guards—two from either side—began to run at them, weapons out, hollering for them to stop. They stopped on the concrete, the rain pounding down around them.

"State your business!" the first soldier to reach them said.

"Isn't it bleedin' obvious?" Cher said, glowering at each of the men as they surrounded them, guns out. "I'm taking this bloody trespasser for questioning."

The men turned their attention to Chad, his hands tied behind his back, then looked back to Cher. The first man said, "Who are you? Haven't see you around."

"New, ain't I?" Cher said. "Corporal... Poppins."

The guard raised an eyebrow. "Poppins?"

"Wanna make something of it, friend?"

"Not at all," the man said, standing back a little doubtfully. "Get on with it, Corporal."

"Hang on," another soldier said, looking narrow-eyed at Cher and the case she was pulling behind her. "Where did you say you were garrisoned?"

"I didn't," Cher said. "You trying to tap me up for a date, soldier?"

The others guffawed, but the man wouldn't be put off.

"Where are you stationed, Corporal?"

"I've just transferred from…" Cher desperately tried to think of something, anything, that sounded vaguely British. "… from Apples and Pears Station." The men looked at each other, then frowned and started to move in.

Cher groaned, and said, "Davis, sic 'em," just as Chad pulled his hands free from his loose bonds and aimed a punch at the nearest soldier.

Cher followed suit with a swinging hammer-blow to the head of the guard that had questioned her, while the poor sap who'd been first on the scene got Davis closing his jaws around the man's crotch with a muscle-rending crunch that momentarily sickened Cher.

"Go!" Chad yelled, whipping out one of the weapons they'd taken from the guards and firing a series of haphazard shots over the heads of the four soldiers, who dove to the ground in disarray. Cher didn't need to be told twice. With Davis at her heels, she pounded the wet concrete toward Chad's ship, dragging her case and yelling as a pulse blast hit the ground just a meter away from her.

As she reached the cruiser, she risked a look behind her to see one of the guards down on the ground, and another holding an injured arm, while the other two traded pulse blasts with Chad. He was running for the ship and firing over his shoulder.

"They're getting close!" Chad shouted, dodging a blast as he reached Cher. They sheltered behind the cruiser's stubby engine, and he pulled a small object out of his pocket, tapping in a command. The ship vibrated, and a hatch opened in the side of the squat vessel. Chad didn't wait for the access steps to descend but threw Davis and Cher's bag up into the ship then leapt up behind, holding out his hand for her.

She grabbed for it but screamed and pulled back as a pulse blast bounced off the ship's hull.

"Come on!" Chad urged. The ship was already starting to tremble and she could feel heat from the engine block. Chad must have initiated the take-off procedures remotely.

"Halt, or we shoot!" one of the two guards shouted as they bore down on them. The ramp was almost down. Cher grabbed Chad's hand and he hauled her up, then slapped the door control and pulled her back as the ramp reversed and the hatch closed. One well-aimed pulse beam made it through the tightening gap and exploded beside Cher's head.

"This is your captain speaking," Cher heard Davis's voice say over the internal comms as the ship shuddered and bucked and started to lift off. *"Welcome aboard this Air Davis flight to LV-187. We will shortly be leaving New Albion airspace, providing we don't get shot down for gross infringement of local laws. At our next stop we will be welcomed by murderous living weapons who wish us only the most gruesome deaths imaginable. Don't forget to fasten your seatbelts."* The *Elvik* angled up sharply and accelerated quickly to enter New Albion's upper atmosphere

"We really shouldn't let the dog watch so much TV, you know," Cher muttered.

1 0

"So I guess we're heroes now," Boffin said, killing the sound as the broadcast looped back to the beginning and started to replay Prime Minister Pepper's rousing address to New Albion.

Tom Moran looked out of the comms tower window at the Union Flag, soaked by rain and wrapped around the antenna they'd flown it from. Not exactly fluttering in the breeze of a new dawn, but he supposed the rhetoric was more important than the reality.

"How long are we going to have to stay on this rock?" Teesha Bromley said, using a fork to dig into a can of peaches. "We're traders, not soldiers. It's not up to us to hold a whole goddamn colony."

"That's not our main concern," Moran said, and he called up the schematic map of the colony on the central hub. "What's bothering me right now is Boffin's seventeen life forms. That means a clutch of people survived whatever happened here, and they are hidden away somewhere. Which could cause us lots of problems."

"Especially if they're the ones responsible for those corpses," Mir said. "What happened here? Did half of them go insane and slaughter the rest? The way those bodies were mutilated…" She shuddered visibly.

"The army will be on its way from New Albion," Moran replied. "Then it won't be our problem. We can get the hell off here."

"The Duke of Wellingtons," Mir said in disgust. "Bunch of weekend warriors. You'd have thought New Albion might have developed a proper military before, oh, you know, declaring war on the rest of the bloody universe."

"That's certainly unpatriotic," Priestley said, joining Moran at the control hub. "Our boys are as good as anyone's. The Duke of Wellingtons are a fine body of men and women."

Ignoring them, Moran pointed to the map. "So we're here, on the east side. There's the landing platform. Under here is the fusion reactor that keeps this place going. There's two klicks of corridors, labs, recreation facilities and living quarters between here and the west side, where the canteen, stores and command deck are." He moved his finger south. "These must be the oil and ore storage tanks. How are they accessible? Tunnels?"

"I think you have to go overground," Priestley said. "You thinking that's where the last colonists are, guv?"

Moran nodded. "Want to go check it out? See what the situation is? Not to the actual tanks, just to this area here… looks like it might be a dispatch point. There are probably buggies, or maybe fliers. Take the pulse rifle."

"And what if I find anyone?" Priestley said.

Moran looked at the others, then at the Yorkshireman. They'd already killed one survivor, albeit by accident. Seventeen more *accidents*... that would take a bit more explaining. But the Prime Minister had already declared LV-187 deserted and claimed by New Albion. Moran held Priestley's gaze for a long time.

"Best of British to you, Frank."

Priestley set off along the corridor that connected the comms tower to the main colony buildings, the pulse rifle slung over his shoulder. Boffin was working on getting the power back up to full capacity, which couldn't happen soon enough. The metal and glass thoroughfare was lit by dull striplights in the ceiling, which barely illuminated the scattered corpses splayed out in his path.

The majority of the dead were at this end of the colony. God knew what had happened here. Frenchies. Priestley shook his head. Who could tell what they'd got up to? Probably had some bad frogs' legs or something, and all went crazy.

Priestley whistled tunelessly as he rounded a bend that took him past a series of research labs. He stopped and peered through one of the glass doors at the benches and computers. They'd lucked out with this place, the

Frenchies. Little old turd of a planet, but must be ninety bloody percent oil below the surface.

Something caught his eye in the room and he tried the door, which easily swung open. In the middle of the tiled floor was what looked like… He squatted down in front of it. Looked like a burn hole, like something had gone straight through into the warren of maintenance conduits below. He poked at the hole with his finger; it was hard, like lava that had set. Priestley glanced up and saw that directly above him was another hole. Whatever had made it had burned through the ceiling and straight through this floor.

Some kind of… acid?

There was a sudden clatter, and Priestley jumped up and whirled round, the pulse rifle off his shoulder and in his hands. He scanned the gloomy lab. On one of the benches a plastic beaker was rolling gently, as though it had been knocked over.

"Who's there?" he said loudly. "Come on out, it's alright, I won't hurt you."

There was no sound. Priestley moved cautiously forward. Unlike the others, he relished this. He'd already applied to join the Duke of Wellingtons, and was waiting for the call for an interview so he could sack off all this trader malarkey and do some proper work for the glory of New Albion. With him being a bona fide hero and all, he might even get a commission straight off the bat. "Sergeant Priestley" had a nice ring to it.

A sudden flash of movement at the periphery of his vision had Priestley whirling around and letting loose a short, sharp blast from the rifle. A computer terminal exploded in a shower of sparks and plastic. He shielded his eyes and peered at the smoking wreckage, but there was nothing. He hadn't imagined it, though. Frank Priestley wasn't given over to imagination and fancy. Something had moved.

"Come out now," he said firmly. "Or it'll be bad for you. You've seen I'm no slouch with this thing. Next shot'll be between your eyes."

Apart from the faint fizzing of the striplights above him, there was silence. Priestley pivoted on his heel, doing a full three-sixty survey of the lab. Then he noticed the big glass tank on the far wall, fractured at one end, revealing a gaping hole in the glass.

He went over to investigate. Straw was scattered on the bottom and drinks tubes attached to the sides. In the middle were two very dead white rats. Lab rodents. These had died of starvation, probably. The glass had been broken somehow, and one or more had got out. He sighed and relaxed.

Just a bloody rat. There was a skittering sound behind him. Priestley turned and smiled into the empty gloom. "As you were, Ratty. I'll not waste rifle charges on you. I've got bigger game to hunt."

He let himself out of the lab and continued along the corridor, then stopped dead. There was something ahead of him, close to the intersection of another corridor that ran across his. Something he'd been pretty sure hadn't been there before he went into the lab.

Priestley raised his rifle, and advanced.

Merrilyn had not slept a wink during the night. When the ship had arrived, she'd led Therese cautiously and silently along the dim corridors to the garage where the colony's vehicles were housed. She had no idea how the creatures operated, whether they were nocturnal or active during the day, whether they even slept at all. She didn't know if they could smell her or hear her or sensed her brainwaves or her heart beating. All she knew was that if they met one of them—and she had no idea how many they actually numbered—then they were dead.

The canteen wasn't viable because she knew the newcomers would make their way to it eventually, probably in search of supplies. The death of François might have been an accident, but she couldn't take the risk— not until she knew more about these people. Not with Therese to think about.

In the garage bay there was an array of vehicles, including some big old armored trucks with huge solid rubber wheels which were used for negotiating the rocky landscape in search of new oil and ore deposits. At first Merrilyn had an idea that they might get out of the hub altogether, escape to the far side of the planet, and wait it out there. But she hadn't taken enough supplies, so when she crept into the garage and located one of the big trucks, she decided that they would spend the night in the cab— surely it would offer protection—and then if the coast was clear, head back to the canteen to grab as much food and water as she could.

She'd probably have to wait until the night again, when the crew of that ship were hopefully asleep, before rolling out of the hub and heading off into the wilderness.

Surely somebody else was on their way. Surely the ICSC was sending someone to find out why LV-187 had gone dark. Surely help must come soon.

They just had to survive long enough.

These were the thoughts that occupied her mind all night as Therese snuggled against her under a pile of blankets in the cab of the truck. Merrilyn constantly scanned the dark garage, looking for a telltale movement, the whipping of a tail, the reflection of the dim striplight off a shining black carapace. There was nothing, but every time she tried to close her eyes she saw images of the things, their rapacious slaughter of the colonists in a melee of blood and screams. So she didn't really try to sleep, just held Therese close.

She didn't know why—there was no logic to it, and she was a scientist, so she chided herself for the thought—but she felt that the daylight hours, such as they were on LV-187, were safer from the creatures. At least she hoped so. Of course, now she had the humans to deal with, but if the worst came to the worst, at least she could try to negotiate with the ship's crew, bargaining for their lives. The monsters didn't have a better nature to which she could appeal. She had seen the colony's pastor try, as though they were just another type of God's creatures.

She would never forget seeing Father Henry's face ripped off.

Merrilyn wanted to leave Therese in the cab of the truck while she went for supplies, but the child refused point blank, and she didn't have the heart to insist. If something *did* happen to her out there, the thought of her Little Flower sitting there alone, waiting for her mama to return when she never would, broke her heart.

So. Cautiously. Quietly. Slowly.

Retracing their steps from the garage to the canteen, where she saw evidence that the crew had already been rifling through the cupboards and fridges. Merrilyn filled her bag with the remaining tins and bottles and then led Therese back toward the garage. They were almost there when Therese suddenly gasped and pulled her hand free of Merrilyn's.

"Pinky Ponk!" Therese whispered, pointing back to the intersection of two corridors, where the soft toy lay. She must have dropped it.

"No!" Merrilyn whispered fiercely as Therese set off at a run for the toy, but it was too late. Merrilyn swore, hitched her bag higher on her back, and ran after her.

It was some kind of child's toy, Priestley realized as he walked toward it, and it had definitely not been there when he was walking down the corridor before. Which meant...

And then the child it belonged to, a small, dark-haired girl of about six, he estimated, skidded from the corridor branching off to the left, looking first at her toy and then, wide-eyed, at Priestley.

She was followed by a slim, long-haired woman in her thirties, wearing fatigues and a vest, with a stuffed pack on her back. The woman gaped at him.

"S'il vous plaît, ne blessez ma fille!"

"You'll have to speak English, love," Priestley said calmly, though he got the idea of what she was on about. "Name's Frank Priestley of the New Albion trade ship *Victory*." He paused, and then lied, "I'm not going to hurt you."

"Thank you," the woman said in English. "My name is Merrilyn Hambleton and this is my daughter Therese. We must get off the colony at once. You are all in grave danger."

"No can do, love." Frank smiled and shook his head. "We've claimed it for New Albion, you see. We're just waiting for the military to arrive to relieve us."

The woman, Merrilyn, frowned. She was quite fetching when she did that. Little button nose.

"Claimed? This is an ICSC colony. But that doesn't matter now. Your ship is flight-worthy? We need to leave. Now."

"What exactly went on here?" Priestley said. "Why did you lot kill each other like that? Did you all go bonkers? That famous Gallic hot-headedness?" He had to admit, she was a bit of a looker, this Merrilyn. The guv hadn't said anything about not having a bit of *fun* before he took care of any survivors he might meet. He'd have to off the kiddie first, though. He wasn't going to make her watch.

It wasn't as if Frank Priestley was some kind of monster.

"Oh, *mon Dieu*..." Merrilyn whispered, pulling the child close to her.

"I said English, love," Priestley said, wondering whether he should just do it in the corridor or find a nice quiet room, when he suddenly felt a chill. The hairs on his neck stood up.

Something wet and viscous dripped on to his shoulder and he turned his head, looking right into the face of a demon.

It was suspended from the roof-space above the corridor, held there by a thick, prehensile tail. It was like a black, skeletal insect, but would have been taller than him if it stood on its muscular legs. Its head was a distended, shining dome with a gaping mouth and rows of vicious, dripping teeth.

"What. The. Fuck?" Priestley said slowly. He felt a warmth in his pants and dimly realized he had pissed himself. Vaguely aware of the woman and child fleeing back the way they'd come, he couldn't think of what he should say or do. All he could manage was to gaze into that gaping maw like an animal entranced by a cobra.

Then something emerged from the mouth, a muscular, thick... tongue? Limb? His mind failed to cope with what he was seeing. It was shedding words and thoughts and memories and just filling his head with one single thought.

Run.

But it was too late. The thick tongue had a mouth of its own on the end, which opened and hissed, as strong, clawed hands gripped his shoulders and he felt himself hauled off his feet. Needle-sharp teeth sank into his face and with his final breath Frank Priestley began to beg for a quick death.

1 1

"There's LV-187 ahead," Chad said.

Cher peered at the grey speck dead center in the cockpit windshield. Davis sat upright between her and Chad.

"How long?" she asked.

"Six hours and twenty-three minutes," Davis said. "We'll be in hailing distance in three hours."

Suddenly she was nervous. All the talk of Xenomorphs and face-huggers and chestbursters had seemed abstract and distant on New Albion. Following the frantic flight from the terminus, she hadn't had much time to think about where they were actually going and what they were going to do when they got there.

"What if the New Albion military doesn't let us land?"

"They haven't even been deployed yet," Chad said. "I've been monitoring for military transmissions in this sector—there aren't any. Besides," he added. "you saw those soldiers. New Albion is a colony ruled by a buffoon with an army of idiots under his command."

"Hmmm," Cher said, not convinced. "In my experience,

the politicians who pretend to be buffoons can ultimately the most dangerous. As much as it looks like it, Maurice Pepper isn't winging this. He's got a plan, all right, and if that doesn't involve sending his army to LV-187, then we've got to assume there's something even more dangerous going on."

"Anyway, we're not here to interfere in whatever New Albion does or doesn't have planned," Chad said. "We're there to gather evidence."

"And what if you're wrong?" she countered. "What if there isn't a 'Xenomorph infestation'?"

"There is." Chad stared ahead at the gradually growing sphere of LV-187. "I know it. You spend as long fighting these things as I have, you develop a kind of sixth sense about them. I can smell them, even from here."

"In space no one can detect your scent," Davis put in.

She looked at the dog, then up at Chad, who shrugged.

"Cher, why don't you go grab some sleep?" he said. "There won't be much opportunity for rest, once we get down there."

"He seems sad," Cher said as she pulled a blanket over her on the narrow bunk in the sleeping quarters. Davis had followed her and was lying down beside the bunk. "And more than a little angry."

"He's seen a lot," Davis said.

Cher stared at the low ceiling for a while.

"Because of Amanda? What happened to her?"

Davis seemed to chew on that. "To understand that," he said, "you must first understand Chad a little better. He went into biomedical research because he wanted to help people. To cure diseases, to eradicate illnesses. His career led him to work with the most brilliant biomedical scientists in the Weyland-Yutani Corporation. They were very close to several major breakthroughs with regards to a host of conditions, including many cancers."

Cher sat up in the bunk. "What happened?"

"Chad discovered that the research was not entirely... ethical. One of his collaborators even had experienced direct contact with Xenomorphs. In fact, he had been held captive in a hive and survived. He was convinced that the answer to his work lay in the symbiotic relationship between Xenomorphs and their human hosts, and what changes were wrought inside the human body when a host was impregnated with a Xenomorph."

Cher stroked her chin. "So what you are saying is... these creatures could actually be a force for good? In research terms? But this is huge. They could actually hold the answer to curing cancer?"

"Theoretically, but it depends on how far you are prepared to go to test that theory." Davis licked his paws for a while, then continued. "Chad's collaborator was... changed by his time in the Xenomorph hive. Not physically, as far as I know, but mentally. He lost his humanity. His experiments on both Xenomorphs and humans were without the constraints of scientific ethics. He was cruel. Indifferent to suffering.

"Chad was conflicted. On the one hand, their work was important. On the other…"

"On the other," Cher guessed, "he couldn't condone what he was witnessing. So he… what?"

"He turned whistleblower. Tried to tell the world what was happening at the Weyland-Yutani research labs, and that's when he realized his life was in danger. That the company would go to any lengths to cover up the work they were doing with Xenomorphs. Fortunately, that's when he met Amanda. She saved his life, in more ways than one."

"She worked for Weyland-Yutani as well?"

Davis nodded. "She was an engineer, but always looking for answers about what happened to her mother." He looked at Cher. "A little like you with your sister. Anyone who comes into contact with Xenomorphs falls into a black hole of Weyland-Yutani's making. It is a conspiracy that spans the stars. Sometimes it seems like the biggest secret in the universe."

"The world should know," Cher said. "All the worlds. They all should know. This is the greatest threat humanity has ever faced."

"*Cui bono*," Davis said.

Cher pulled a face.

"Latin," he explained. "It means, *to whose benefit*? There is no profit for Weyland-Yutani in having humanity unite against an alien threat, but there *is* profit in revolutionizing the pharmacological industry through the research. Or weaponizing the Xenomorphs."

"But all these wars… they're all pointless in the face of the threat of these monsters."

"Pointless, but still profitable," Davis said. "Wars require weapons. The Xenomorphs are worth more as potential combatants than as a common foe." He paused, and added, "Imagine an army of them dropped onto an enemy world. Just imagine."

Cher thought about it. She really hadn't considered the enormity of this, about what they were going to do. She remembered the handwritten note stuck on her windshield back home. *"SMART MONEY SAYS DROP IT."* The Weyland-Yutani tentacles stretched far and deep. Shy's death had been sucked into that corporate black hole, and people were already watching her, warning her not to try to reach in and pull anything out. Or she'd go the same way, get trapped there as well.

SMART MONEY SAYS DROP IT.

Here she was, going up against murderous alien killing machines, and if she survived she was going up against the might of the military-industrial-pharma complex that ran a good portion of the universe. Question was, which one was most dangerous?

"Where is Amanda Ripley now?"

"Amanda *McClaren* was cremated and interred at Westlake Repository, Little Chute, Wisconsin, following her death from cancer on December 23, 2178," Davis said.

"Oh," Cher said. "I didn't… No wonder he's so sad."

"At least," Davis said after a while, "that's the official story."

"You mean she's still alive?"

"She's in hypersleep. At a secret location. If she wakes, she will die, but that will not happen. Not until Chad has the means to wake her free from cancer."

"He wants to… what? Restart the experiments on Xenomorphs to cure his wife's cancer? But surely he could have done that by staying to work with Weyland-Yutani, instead of deciding to fight them?"

"That is what drives Chad McClaren, and divides him, and pushes him on, and beats him down," Davis said quietly. "Every single day of his life. In one hand he has his principles, in the other he has the life of Amanda."

One life against potentially billions, Cher thought. From what she had heard of the Xenomorphs, it would take one egg—just one—to make it to Earth, and then… It didn't bear thinking about. They had to be eradicated.

Weyland-Yutani had to be stopped.

But she knew if she could bring back Shy, even at the cost of blowing this whole Xenomorph conspiracy wide open, then she'd do it. Without even thinking. No contest.

"What Chad told me, about the way the Xenomorphs work," Cher said. "Growing in the body, co-opting their host's DNA… they're like a cancer, really, aren't they?"

"It is perhaps more of a journalistic analogy than a scientific one, but it stands," Davis conceded.

"Maybe Chad's focus has shifted," Cher mused. "Maybe, with this mission to wipe out the Xenomorphs wherever he finds them, he's not trying to cure Amanda's cancer anymore. Maybe he just wants to eradicate it."

Davis appeared to think about it. "I think I understand you, even if it does not make a huge amount of logical sense." He cocked his head and looked at her. "It's a very human thing to say, I think."

"Thank you," Cher said, and turned on to her side to face the wall, hoping to try to get a little sleep.

"LV-187, come in. This is the *Elvik*, private cruiser registered to New York Port Authority, United Americas, Earth. Permission to land requested, over."

There was a static hiss, then Chad heard a voice with a British accent say, "Permission denied, *Elvik*. LV-187 has been claimed under interstellar law by the colony of New Albion. In light of the impending conflict between New Albion and the Three World Empire, this is not an appropriate place for you to visit right now. Repeat, permission denied. Over and out."

"We have an emergency," Chad said into the comms link. "Repeat, we have an emergency. We require immediate landing permission. We won't make it anywhere else, over."

There was a long pause, then the British voice came back. "Sorry to hear that, *Elvik*. However, I cannot grant you permission to land. If you want take up an orbital position around LV-187, we are expecting imminent aid from New Albion, who may be able to assist. But to be quite honest, mate, the military might have a bit more on its plate, what with a colony war on the horizon. Best to take your chances and move on, I'd say. Over and out."

"Not an option, LV-187," Chad insisted. "This is a code red emergency. Interstellar law compels you to offer a safe harbor for any ship in distress, no matter what the political situation is, over."

"Look, mate, you enter our airspace and we'll blow you out of the sky. Can't make it much clearer than that. Now, piss off. Over and fucking out, all right?"

"So, what do we do now?" Cher said.

"It's a drilling colony, not a military base," Chad said. "They don't have any weaponry to shoot us down. We're going in."

"Is it possible they were trying to put us off because of the Xenomorphs?" Cher said. "To protect us because of the infestation?"

"It didn't sound like it—I doubt they even know about it yet," Davis said. "The creatures are consummate hunters. They can stay hidden for a long time, even in great numbers. Until it's time to show themselves."

"And if that had happened," Chad said, punching a landing program into the *Elvik*'s flight computer, "they'd already all be dead down there."

* * *

"Fucking space tourists." Moran killed the comms link and turned to Bromley. "They'd better not try to land."

"It sounded like they really might be in trouble," Bromley said doubtfully.

"They bloody will be if they try to put down here. Last thing we need is more witnesses." Moran looked up and frowned. "Where the hell is Priestley? He's been gone hours."

"Lifeforms have dropped by one." Boffin looked up from where he was scanning the colony, monitoring the *Victory*'s MU/TH/UR patched into the colony mainframe. "Either Frank has offed somebody, or he's found a store of whisky and has managed to shoot himself."

"Fuck." Moran rubbed his eyes. "We'd better send someone to find him. Mir, you want to take a look?"

"Sure," Amina said, checking her pulse rifle. "He's probably found a stash of Frenchie porn and is holed up in a toilet somewhere."

Bromley pulled a face. "Ewww, though can you imagine?" Both she and Amina mimed sticking their fingers into their mouths and throwing up.

"Calm it down, you two," Moran said. "He could be in trouble. We don't really know why all those colonists died, and what these bloody lifeforms are on Boffin's scans."

"On my way, guv," Amina said, and she opened up the door from the comms tower. She immediately shrieked and let loose a blast from her handgun as the others all whirled around.

"Dirty fucking thing!" Amina yelled. Moran sighed at the smoking, almost obliterated corpse of a fat white rat on the floor of the corridor outside.

"Lifeforms down to fifteen," Boffin said from his screen.

Moran stared at him. "You're telling me those readings could just be escaped lab rats?"

"It's possible." Boffin shrugged. "Or cats. They might have a chicken farm here, for all I know."

Moran felt himself relax. Maybe there weren't any rogue colonists to dispose of, after all. They could sit this out with just a few animals to pick off for target practice until the Duke of Wellingtons arrived.

"Priestley probably fucked a chicken to death," Bromley said, high-fiving Mir by the door. "Go and find the old pervert and drag his arse back here."

Amina turned to Boffin before she left. "You any closer to getting the lights back on?"

"Scared of the dark?" he said.

"No, but I really do hate rats," Amina said, sidestepping the rodent's smoking corpse and heading out down the corridor. She decided to head for the dispatch deck where Priestley was supposed to be going, singing loudly and kicking open doors as she went. She really *did* hate rats. Always had, ever since she was a kid in Lancashire.

She'd once been playing in the alley behind her family's ancient terraced house in Blackburn and come across one of the things sitting on top of a garbage skip. A malevolent, grey creature as big as a dog. She'd stood there in front of it, almost hypnotized by its red eyes, which regarded her with a baleful stare. She only snapped back to reality when she heard the other kids laughing, and realized there was a warm trickle of pee running down her leg.

She'd run all the way home, crying.

At least there were no rats on New Albion. She'd been quite particular about finding out about that when her father, an engineer, had announced ten years ago that he wanted to apply for immigration status for the whole family. It was cold and wet and ugly—just like home—but there were no rats.

"You in here, Priestley?" Amina called, kicking open the door to a bathroom, a row of stalls set against the far wall. "It's time to stop wanking and start working."

Silence. Amina pushed open each of the stall doors and then turned back to the door, and stopped. What was that puddle of goo on the tiled floor? She was certain she hadn't stepped over it when she came in. She leaned forward to inspect it. Soap from one of the dispensers? It looked thick and gloopy—she didn't want to touch it. She hopped over it and let herself out of the bathroom.

Further along a set of double doors opened to a wide, dark space filled with vehicles—jeeps, trucks, flyers, and buggies. The dispatch deck. At the far end was a closed retractable exit. Damn Boffin. Why couldn't he get the lights on? She took her flashlight from her pocket and walked slowly between the rows of armored trucks, calling out.

"Priestley?"

At the end of the row was a stack of fuel barrels, before the next row of jeeps began. Amina jumped at a sudden movement behind them, what sounded like the scratching of claws on concrete. She shivered. She really, really hated rats.

Holding up her gun she cautiously sidled around the side of the stack of barrels, training her flashlight on the ground.

"OK, you furry little shit," she muttered. "Do you want some of what your little pal got back at the—"

The words died on her lips as the flashlight beam travelled over something on the ground. She raised the beam up, up and up, taking in the full height of the impossible thing that stood there, hissing, its jaws dripping with drool.

It was no rat.

1 2

Merrilyn held Therese tightly to her in the cab of the truck and slumped down as far as she could in the seats, below the windshield. The woman with the gun walked noisily between the rows of vehicles, shouting out the name of the man who they had seen so gruesomely taken by the creature.

She wouldn't find him in one piece, and if she kept shouting like that, she was going to suffer the same fate. Merrilyn bit her lip, torn between the desire to warn the woman, and protection for herself and her daughter from the murderous newcomers.

Therese whimpered.

"Sssshhh, Little Flower," Merrilyn said, pushing the little girl further down into the footwell. She chanced a look through the windscreen. She had lost sight of the woman, and lifted herself a little higher to scan the garage.

Wham!

She screamed as something slammed against the glass. It was the woman, blood pumping from her mouth, eyes glassy, a gaping mess of bone, muscle, and flesh where her stomach should have been, spreadeagled on the windshield like a Daliesque crucifixion canvas.

"Mama…" Therese said tremulously.

Merrilyn turned to tell her to be quiet and then her blood turned to ice in her veins. Behind the girl, framed in the side window, was the monster, its face frozen in an almost rictus-grin, drool dripping from its teeth, its bulbous black head dully reflecting the dim strip-lights far above in the ceiling. It lifted a skeletal hand and tapped on the glass with one vicious black claw.

Little pig, little pig, let me in, or I'll blow your house down, Merrilyn thought crazily. Then the beast shrieked like a tormented soul from the depths of hell, leaned back, and slammed its head against the side window.

The toughened glass warped but held. The creature repeated the move as Merrilyn hauled Therese out of the footwell and backed up against the other door. A third time, and a hairline fracture appeared in the glass.

"Mama…"

"Hush, Little Flower."

The monster head-butted the window once more and a spider-web of cracks rippled out. It would only take one more blow. Merrilyn wrapped her arm around Therese.

"When I say so, Little Flower, push backward, OK?"

The creature slammed into the glass and it shattered inward, the beast howling a cry of triumph. It held onto the window with both clawed hands, pushed itself back with its feet, then launched forward, jaws wide open, screeching.

Merrilyn's fingers closed around the door handle and she pulled, pushing herself back.

"Now!"

The door flung open and they tumbled backward as the monster folded itself into the cab, occupying the space they had just vacated. Merrilyn leapt to her feet and slammed the door closed, then grabbed Therese's arm and pulled her down onto the floor, rolling them both under the adjacent truck and then out the other side, repeating the maneuver until there were two rows of vehicles between them and the creature.

She heard the monster howling and put a finger to her lips. Therese nodded solemnly. What was best? Try to make it back to the main colony buildings, or make a run for the retractable door to the outside? The creature howled again, louder this time. It was out of the vehicle. She beckoned for Therese to follow and crawled on her hands and knees to the end of the row of trucks, where there was a stack of fuel drums. Could she perhaps trap the monster under them? Cause them to explode? With what?

Then she saw something by the drums. The rifle that the woman had carried. It was maybe six meters away, across open ground. Could she make it in time? She looked at Therese, put her finger to her lips again, and patted the concrete floor, indicating that the girl should stay put.

Therese hugged Pinky Ponk and nodded, but Merrilyn could see the terror in her eyes.

She kissed the top of her daughter's head and then crouched by the wheel of the truck, eyes on the gun. Run or crawl? She decided speed was more important than stealth, took a deep breath and launched herself forward.

Merrilyn had just closed her hand around the gun when Therese screamed. Merrilyn's strength deserted her as she turned to see the creature crouched over her daughter, one of its claws wrapped around her throat. She felt as though she couldn't move, that she could almost sleep. Her mind was shutting down. Her body was deserting her.

No, thought Merrilyn. *No. Not today.* Letting loose a howl to match the creature's own, one torn from a deeper, more damned circle of Hades, she raised the gun and set off at a run toward it as it looked up at her. Letting her momentum carry her forward, she slid down to her ass and alongside her daughter, ramming the barrel of the gun into the secondary dripping mouth that was emerging from the monster's gaping jaws.

"Fuck you, you piece of shit," Merrilyn said through gritted teeth, and she pulled the trigger. The pulse blast momentarily illuminated the black and red interior of the creature's mouth before it blew off the back of its helmet-like head. It issued a gargling shriek, then toppled backward in a pool of sizzling ichor that started to bubble and smoke and eat through the concrete of the garage floor.

"Mama," Therese said. "Mama, you killed the monster for me."

Merrilyn finally allowed herself to breathe and hugged her daughter tight. The tears finally came, ripped out of her by the horror and relief and realization of what she had just done.

"That's all right, Little Flower," Merrilyn sobbed into Therese's hair. "That's exactly what mamas are for."

Ten minutes later, having transferred their bags to another truck, Merrilyn drove the vehicle up to the big retractable doorway that opened on to the outside. She headed toward where the huge storage tanks for the oil and ore were located, half a kilometer out from the main colony buildings. She didn't know what her plans were, other than to get out of here and buy herself time to think.

They had maybe enough food for three or four days. Perhaps in that time proper help might come. All she had to do was stay put out there on the edge of the terraformed sector, and hope to God those monsters didn't decide to go walkabout outside the colony buildings.

"Don't leave me, Mama," Therese said as Merrilyn put the vehicle in neutral and opened the door.

"It's OK," she said. "I'm just opening the doors to let us out. Then we're going on an adventure, all right, Little Flower?"

Therese nodded doubtfully, and Merrilyn let herself down on to the concrete, scanning around for any more creatures, the gun in her hand. She ran over to the wall and slapped the big button that worked the door. As it started to trundle up, letting in a blast of cold air and rain from the outside, Merrilyn started to head back to the truck, only to see Therese in the window, waving frantically at her.

Her heart pounding, Merrilyn spun around, her gun up, as the door rolled up to reveal a figure standing framed in the dim late afternoon light. It was a woman, tall, with long dreadlocks falling over the shoulders of her jacket. She had a pulse rifle trained on Merrilyn.

"OK, sister, drop the gun," the woman said. "You're coming with me."

"Monsters," Tom Moran said doubtfully.

"I fucking saw it," Bromley said. "It ripped Amina to pieces." She nodded toward the French woman, huddled with her daughter in the corner of the comms tower. "She blew its fucking brains out. "

"We need to get off this planet," the woman—Merrilyn something?— said in perfect English. "These things are all over the colony."

"And that's what killed all the colonists?" Moran said. "And Frank?"

"Your friend, the man? Yes," Merrilyn said. "Your ship is working, yes? We can leave?"

He thought about it for a bit. "We have orders to stay. LV-187 has been claimed for New Albion. We're just waiting for relief."

"That's what your friend said," Merrilyn replied sourly. "Just before he died."

"If we're going to go, then we should think about it soon." Boffin was standing by the big observation window, watching the dusk fall. Rain was battering against the glass. "There's a storm coming in. A big one. It'll be impossible to fly soon."

"It'll take the comms out, too," Merrilyn said. "We get big storms here. Bad ones. So we go now, yes?"

"Guv," Bromley said, seeing his hesitation. "It was a fucking *monster*. It killed Amina. And Priestley."

"Maybe not the same one," Merrilyn said.

Moran looked at her. "How many of these things are there?"

"I don't know. Maybe a dozen? Maybe more. They were difficult to count when they were slaughtering us all."

"Yet you survived," Moran said. "And you killed one. So maybe they're not that big a deal after all?"

"I'm a fucking scientist," the woman spat. "Do not underestimate me."

Boffin chuckled behind Moran. "Maybe I should call this in," he said.

"We won't get an answer back before the storm hits," Boffin said. "Look, guv, if what they're saying is true... we're no good to New Albion as dead heroes, are we?

Should I go and at least prep the *Victory* for take-off?"

"OK," Moran decided that couldn't do any harm. "I'll call it in anyway. The military needs to know about this shit."

"Thank God," the woman said, holding her small child close. "And thank you."

Walking through the hanger that led to the landing platform, Boffin found a rack of waterproof coats and wrapped himself in one before stepping out into the failing daylight. The sky was roiling with black clouds, marbled with snakes of lightning. The temperature had dropped a good eight or nine degrees since he was last outside.

The *Victory* sat squatly on the landing platform, the access steps down as he'd left them. He should have closed them up when he came up last time. The inside would be soaked. The wind almost took him off his feet as he ran across the slick platform toward the ship.

Careful, now, he thought. *Don't want to end up like that dead Frenchie we shot when we first arrived. It's a long way down off the platform.*

Monsters, though. He was burning to see that corpse in the garage for himself. Maybe they could grab a quick look before taking off. He'd heard the stories, of course, about the border bombings, this black goo raining down on the distant, remote colonies. One guy had told him that if this black goo hit you, it turned you inside out. And if you were downwind of it… then it changed you. Mutated you. Made you into something else. Monsters, maybe. Is that what had happened here?

Boffin hauled himself up the steps and closed the access hatch behind him. Water pooled on the floor of the deck. He'd have to mop that up, but later. He'd better get the *Victory* prepped for take-off. He was with Bromley on this—they'd done their bit. Flying flags was one thing, fighting monsters was something entirely different.

Boffin settled himself in the cockpit and began the preliminary checks. Rain battered the windshield; the storm was coming in a lot faster than the computers had predicted. They were really going to have to get off this rock very quickly. He opened a comms channel to the colony but got only static. He wondered if Moran had managed to get a message off-world.

Everything looked in order, which was no surprise because the *Victory* was a good little ship. They could be ready for take-off in minutes. He tried the comms link again but there was still nothing—in fact the static hiss was worse. He'd have to go out and brave the storm again to get the rest of them down here.

Boffin flipped off the comms link. There was still a faint hissing sound. He frowned. It wasn't coming from the comms deck.

It was coming from behind him.

Boffin slowly turned his head, and screamed.

* * *

"Anything?" That was Bromley, the woman who'd captured them at the garage.

"Nothing," her boss Moran replied in disgust. "Storm's totally knocked out the comms."

"It always happens," Merrilyn said. "Storm might last all night, maybe even all of tomorrow." It was one of the many pleasures of living on LV-187, one of the reasons they were pretty much forgotten by everyone else until it was time to send a nice big shipment of oil off for use on the other ICSC colony worlds.

Moran turned to her. "You think we're going to be able to take off?"

She looked out through the window. Visibility was practically zero now. Under normal circumstances she'd say no, it wasn't safe at all, but they had this very small, rapidly narrowing window of opportunity to get the hell off LV-187, and she wasn't sure she could bear to pass it up.

Moran was already on the comms again.

"Boffin? Come in, Boffin. We prepped for take-off yet?" He swore as he got nothing but a static hiss. "OK, maybe we should just go."

"Guv," Bromley said. "Incoming."

He joined her at the window, and Merrilyn went over to look, as well. Just emerging from the black clouds was a bank of lights. It was a ship.

"Your New Albion military?" she said.

Moran squinted into the growing darkness. "It looks a bit small for an army vehicle... Teesha, try hailing them."

Bromley stood at the comms hub and after a couple of minutes shouted, "Nothing, guv."

As it got closer, the ship revealed itself to be a small personal cruiser, swinging and buffeting in the high winds as it entered a landing program, swooping and ducking as it tried to align itself with the platform. With a sinking heart, Merrilyn knew that the weather was too bad to even attempt a take-off. She didn't even know if this ship, whoever was in it, was going to be able to land.

"Ah, bollocks," Moran said. "You know who it is? Those idiots who requested landing permission earlier. What was the ship called? The *Elvik*?"

"That's a skilled pilot," Bromley said admiringly as the ship rolled, then straightened, then swung in the wind and rain, positioning itself over the landing platform. The *Elvik* hovered just ten meters above the platform, and started its reverse thrusters, slowly descending. Moran had been right, Merrilyn thought. They were idiots for coming here. Now they were going to be trapped until the storm cleared as well. More people to die.

Just three meters from touching down, the *Elvik* was suddenly slammed by a gale-force burst of wind that twisted it, flinging it to one side, bringing it crashing down the final two meters. Its starboard flank and engine smashed hard into the landing platform with a shriek of rending metal and an explosion of fuel.

1 3

"Thank you for flying Air Davis, we apologize for the rough landing and the damage to our craft that has apparently trapped us on a Xenomorph-infested planet in the middle of a raging storm. The time on LV-187 is 6 PM GMT and local conditions are murderous with approaching slaughter."

"Still not fucking funny," Chad said, picking himself up off the cockpit floor. "Starboard engine sitrep?"

"Not irreparable." The dog stared for a while at the mainframe display. "Fuel burn wasn't critical, but we're not leaving any time soon."

Chad helped Cher up to her feet. "You OK?"

"Yeah." She nodded, then winced. "Ow. Think I bruised my ass, but still alive."

Chad looked out of the cockpit at the colony buildings, grey against the black sky. They were all dark apart from a slim needle on the east side, not far from the landing pad. Probably the comms tower, where there were lights blazing in the top stories. "Best guess, that's where they're holed up," he said. "I wonder if it's started yet?"

"Hey," Cher said. "There's another ship over there."

"The *Victory*," Davis responded. "The New Albion trade ship that put down here and claimed LV-187. At least there's a way off here if things really deteriorate."

"So, what do we do now?" Cher said. "We go in there and get a good look at these things? Confirm what happened here?"

She's still treating this like some kind of safari, Chad thought. Nobody could understand the Xenomorphs until they saw them for themselves. Not really—and most people who did see them, didn't survive to tell the tale. That couldn't happen with Cher Hunt. She had to do what Chad couldn't—tell everyone else about them, and Weyland-Yutani's complicity in their existence.

So what they *wouldn't* be doing was heading off all gung-ho into the colony and offer themselves up as a Xenomorph buffet.

"Nope, we wait," Chad said. "Until someone from inside comes out to get us. Then we'll know it's safe—or at least that there's a safe harbor somewhere inside."

"In that case, what are we going to do in the meantime?" Cher said, sounding exasperated.

"Gather round the campfire and tell tall tales," Davis declared.

Chad frowned. Davis was getting increasingly… erratic, maybe. Ever since he'd decided he needed a sense of humor, it was as if he'd devoted too much processing power to the task. *That AI has been a dog for far too long*, he thought. *He's never going to achieve this Holy Grail of humanity he craves while he's padding around on all fours.*

"Well, if we're doing story-time," Cher said, settling into the cockpit seat and spinning it around to face Chad. "Let's have the one about how you won a spaceship and a robot dog in a game of cards."

Previously…

Some thought that the LV designation given to colony worlds meant "Life Viable," but to the conglomeration of businesses, entrepreneurs, and organized crime families who set up LV-222 out on the fringes it was a revenue stream. Pretty soon after they'd established the first freeport—not under the authority of the United Americas, the Three World Empire, the Union of Progressive Peoples, the Independent Core Systems Colonies or, in fact, anyone—everybody started calling the place "Las Vegas."

Chad McClaren found himself there on the trail of the crew of a trading ship that—so rumor on gossip on hearsay had it—possessed the corpse of a Xenomorph. They were offering it for sale, along with the Weyland-Yutani go-between who had been very keen to take it off their hands.

By the time he got there the trail was cold, or it had been a red herring all along. He was carrying Davis around in little more than a portable hard drive, which was entirely frustrating for the AI.

"Chad," Davis would whisper into his earphones, "can you imagine being stuck in a dark, black, infinite box? I was made as a combat synthetic. I could touch, and see, and smell, and hear. This is torture. Please, get me a body. Somehow, get me a body."

The fact was, carrying Davis around in his pocket made it a damned sight easier for him to get around. Weyland-Yutani had placed a price on his head, and he'd had more than one narrow escape them that would have been an awful lot more difficult had he been teamed up with a humanoid synthetic.

Still, he sympathized with Davis. They'd been through a lot together, and were united not just in their war on Xenomorphs and Weyland-Yutani, but also in loss. Chad had lost Amanda, and Davis had lost Zula Hendricks. Or at least, they were parted, and no one knew where Zula was, so it was the same thing.

On Las Vegas, while he didn't find a pirate crew with a Xenomorph corpse to sell, Weyland-Yutani found him. Las Vegas was policed by crooks and populated by cheats, liars, and thieves, so he wasn't hugely surprised when he returned to the port on the day he wanted to leave to find that his ship had been impounded. He didn't wait around long enough to find out who or why, but he knew

Weyland-Yutani would be behind it. So he ducked into the nearest casino and considered his next move.

His next move was, it turned out, finding out to his surprise that he was very, very good at poker. It was a matter of assessing all of the variables and determining the best way to proceed.

Either that, or he was very, very lucky.

Over the course of six hours he'd built up enough of a pot to force the brash young scion of a crime family that ran three colony worlds in the sector to put his neat little cruiser up as collateral for a hand the kid was sure was unbeatable.

It wasn't.

Chad was just about to walk away with the keys when the casino fell into a hush and a stately old woman with a high beehive hairdo and a grand cocktail dress was pushed in on a wheelchair by a brace of tuxedo-wearing gorillas, a cute brown dog by her side.

"My grandson wants his toy back," the woman drawled in a dry, Southern American accent. "You know boys and their toys."

"I won it, fair and square," Chad protested. His way off Las Vegas about to be taken away from him, probably with a few punches to the gut for good measure.

"That you did," the grand old dame agreed. "And I intend to win it back from you, fair and square." She was wheeled to the table and said, "What would you have me stake against the *Elvik*?"

"Chad," Davis whispered in his ear. "The dog… it's a synthetic. Very good work. Black market wet job. Never seen anything like it."

Dorothea Whittaker had with her three goons packing weapons beneath their suit jackets, and a thin, bespectacled man with a sheen of sweat on his forehead and bloodless lips he was constantly licking. He noticed Chad inspecting the dog.

"You are admiring my handiwork."

Chad disliked the man immediately.

Dorothea tutted benignly. "Mr. Higgs here takes every opportunity to boast about his craft. He is one of the finest synthetic technicians in this sector." She glanced at him mildly. "He could have been the finest in any sector, save for certain unsavory proclivities. Fortunately, my… operation is a very broad-minded one."

"Separate the art from the artist, Chad," Davis cautioned.

"This is an exact replica of my beloved Jasper," Dorothea continued, looking with love at the dog. It fulfilled its programming by returning her gaze with adoring, big eyes. "He died three years ago. I was quite distraught. Mr. Higgs here gave Jasper back to me."

Synthetic production and deployment was carefully controlled by the authorities, but the fact remained that any legitimate technology would, sooner or later, be co-opted by the underground. The sex industry led the charge, of course—and no doubt Mr. Higgs had experience with that—but a surprisingly popular by-product of that was facsimile pets created for the very, very wealthy.

"I'll stake the *Elvik* against your dog," Chad said.

The old woman bristled. Higgs seemed unaccountably delighted that his work was the focus of such fierce competition.

"I can make you another one if you lose," he said through his thin, wet lips.

Dorothea narrowed her eyes. "I won't lose."

One hand of cards later, Chad walked out of the casino with the keys to the *Elvik* in one hand and a leash in the other, on the end of which trotted Davis's brand-new synthetic body. Neither of them hung around Las Vegas long enough to find out what would happen if the Georgia Mafia decided to up the stakes and demand a rematch.

"That was a lot funnier than I was expecting," Cher said. "You didn't strike me as the sort of guy who tells shaggy dog stories."

"Life can't all be running around trying to not get killed," Chad said, and he shrugged. "Were you hoping for something more appropriate to a dark and stormy night?" As if on cue, a strong wind buffeted the *Elvik*.

Cher looked out of the window. "Some storm, all right. What do you think they're doing in there?"

"Probably wondering what we're doing in here," Chad said. "Davis, any chatter on the comms?"

"Nothing," the synthetic replied, accessing the system through the tech that allowed him to speak. "The storm's knocked everything out. Even short-range."

"I wouldn't worry about that," Cher said, squinting through the rain lashing the windscreen. "I think things are about to get up close and personal."

"What the fuck are they doing out there?" Moran said, shielding his eyes from his own reflection against the observation window in the comms tower.

"Maybe they didn't survive the landing," Bromley suggested. "They came down pretty heavily."

"Maybe good for them if they didn't," Merrilyn said.

Moran ignored her. "And where the fuck is Boffin? He's been in the ship forever." He made a decision. "Right. I'm going out there to see what's going on with him, and I'll bring whoever's in that ship back up here."

Proceeding to the hanger, he dragged on one of the waterproof coats and let himself out onto the landing platform. Moran immediately threw himself back into the building, unprepared for the ferocity of the winds and the driving rain. Christ, it was like a bloody hurricane. And he'd thought the weather on New Albion was crap. He pitied the poor sods who had to come and live here permanently when all this was over.

Bracing himself against the howling wind, he tried again, leaning in toward the gale and pushing forward through the almost horizontal rain. The *Victory* was dark, aside from the faint glow of the instrument panel in the cockpit. Had Boffin decided to take a nap, in the middle of all this? A faint part of him hoped that was the case.

There was absolutely no chance anyone was taking off in this weather, so Moran wanted everyone inside where he could see them. First he'd find out who was in this new ship, then he'd get Boffin. Wiping the rain from his face, he peered toward the *Elvik*. Two figures in the cockpit window, as far as he could tell. He waved his pulse rifle at them, so they knew he'd seen them, but also so they knew he was armed.

Moran moved around to the side of the ship and watched the hatch slide open. The two figures emerged to the lip of the entrance. It was a man, tall and stocky, and a woman, with dark hair and olive skin.

"I told you not to land," Moran shouted.

The man replied, but the wind whipped his words away. "*What?*"

"How many dead?" the man shouted.

"What?" Moran called back. "The entire fucking colony is dead."

"How many…" the man began, but the storm swallowed his last word.

"How many *what*?"

"Xenomorphs. *Aliens.*"

"What?"

"Monsters!" the man shouted.

Moran wiped the rain from his face. "I think you'd better come down."

Chad gave Cher a padded coat then unlocked a cabinet on the flight deck and handed her a pistol. "Can you hide this anywhere? This guy's going to try to take them off us, I'm sure, but I'm not going on there without weapons."

Cher slid it into the back of her trousers and watched as Chad did the same. Rather than the ramp, they extended the disembarkation ladders and carefully descended into the howling storm, Chad with Davis in his arms.

"You brought a fucking dog?" the man said, waiting for them on the rainswept landing platform. He held out his hand. "Tom Moran, of the New Albion trade ship *Victory*."

"We saw you on TV," Cher said, taking the hand. "I'm Cher Hunt, this is Chad McClaren, and the dog is Davis."

"What was that word you said before?" Moran said to Chad, loudly enough to be heard clearly. "That thing you called the... them?"

"Xenomorphs," Chad shouted. "Have you got a secure area inside? We should get in."

Moran nodded and pointed to the other ship. "I just need to get my crew member. He was prepping the *Victory* for take-off, but nobody's going anywhere in this storm." Moran pushed against the wind to the ship, and was just about to hit the panel on the outside to open the door and bring down the steps when Chad put a hand on his arm.

"Wait," he said. "Look."

Cher followed Chad's outstretched arm and peered at the cockpit window. There was indeed something strange about it. Half of the windshield darker than the rest. The closer she looked, the more it looked like...

"Blood," she said. Moran was pulling away from Chad's grip and going for the control panel again. "Blood!" Cher shouted. "Don't open it!"

"Boffin's in there!" Moran said. He began to yell. "Boffin! Boffin! Jerry! You OK in there?"

Something else appeared at the window.

"Holy fuck," Cher whispered to the storm.

She had seen the photographs. She had made notes—endless, relentless notes, recording every single detail as described by Chad and Davis. She knew the life cycle inside out and back to front, knew the heights to which they grew, and the radius of their mouths and the potency of their acid blood. Like all journalists, Cher had become an instant expert in her subject through immersion and obsession. She had pushed less important things out of her head and filled those spaces with Xenomorph facts and figures and lore.

When her story was written, the details would be discarded, room made for the next topic, but for now, she knew everything she needed to know about them.

Or so she had thought.

No amount of research, of questioning, of interviewing, of assimilation of the facts, could have prepared her for what appeared at the window of the *Victory*. She'd had an idea it was some kind of animal. An alien, unknown, deadly animal, but a creature born of some kind of logic and evolution.

That wasn't what she was looking at.

This was a nightmare.

A haunting, a thing carved from night and drenched in death. It had been dragged from Hell and clothed in armor, its sinews taut like the strings of a musical instrument on which only overtures of pain could be played. It was a demon, a djinn, a spirit, a fury. It was *horror*, from the tip of its segmented tail to the drool-dripping point of its sharpest tooth.

It was a Xenomorph.

"I had no fucking idea."

Chad was dragging Moran away from the ship. "Leave it," he shouted. "Leave it! If your friend was in there, he's dead. We need to get inside or we're going to end up the same way."

Moran looked from Chad to Cher and back again. "Who are you people?" he said.

"Your best chance of getting off this rock alive," Chad said, and the four of them hurried against the raging storm toward the dark colony buildings.

1 4

The storm raged, and redoubled its efforts, and raged all the more. Merrilyn could swear that she felt the solid concrete comms tower sway in the wind of knives that assaulted the colony. She had never known a storm this bad in all her time on LV-187. It was as if the planet knew it harbored death of the most final sort, and wanted to mark the occasion with all that it could muster.

There were seven of them now, including the dog. Her and Therese, Moran and Bromley, and the newcomers—Chad McClaren, Cher Hunt, and Davis, who was sitting patiently while Therese petted him and whispered to him in the corner. At least the animal gave her daughter some respite from the horror, distracted her from what the grown-ups were talking about.

"Tell me again," Moran said.

Chad took a breath and repeated his story for the entire group. They had a name, the monsters. Xenomorphs. They existed merely to kill and to reproduce. The longer any humans stayed on LV-187, the more Xenomorphs there would be. They would eventually be overwhelmed; either slaughtered outright, or worse, become breeding vessels for the beasts.

"Where are they from?" Bromley demanded.

Chad shrugged. "Extraterrestrial in origin. We think. We don't know where their homeworld is. We also don't know what part, and to what extent, Weyland-Yutani has had in their development and evolution."

"They've killed three of my crew," Moran said, "and all the colonists, apart from her and her kid." He pointed at Merrilyn. "But they're not indestructible, are they? She killed one."

Chad looked at Merrilyn with interest. "You did? How?"

"I put a gun in its mouth and blew its head off."

He nodded, visibly impressed. "That takes guts."

"My daughter was in danger," Merrilyn said with a shrug. She looked over to Therese, who was whispering in the dog's ear.

"You won't tell, will you? It will be our secret?" Merrilyn wanted to ask, but held back. The girl had seen so much. So many things no child should see. If—when—they got off here, she was going to need to have therapy, counselling, to get over what she had been through. So was Merrilyn. She was keeping it together for the sake of her child, and because to fall apart would mean certain death.

"So, what do we do now?" Moran said. "Your ship is a bust. Mine's got a bloody Xenomorph in it. Not that we can take off in this storm, and we've no idea how long it's going to last. Help is on its way from New Albion, but if we can't get off, then they can't get down."

"I don't think help is on its way," Chad said, and Moran and Bromley stared at him.

"What are you talking about?" the woman said. "Of course they're sending someone."

Chad looked at his companion, Cher.

"We think it's possible this whole thing was orchestrated by New Albion," she explained. "These things hatch from eggs. A trader ship carrying such eggs was recently boarded in the planet's vicinity. Everyone on board was killed, and the vessel crashed in a remote area of New Albion. The Ovomorphs—eggs—were taken. We think New Albion deliberately placed them here to kill all the colonists, so that they could claim the deserted colony for themselves."

"Is this true?" Merrilyn glared at Moran. "Is this why you are here? Is this why everyone is dead?"

Moran held up his hands. "Lady, look, three-fifths of my crew is dead, too. You think I'd come down here if this was true? Which, incidentally, I don't think it is."

Merrilyn believed him, at least about the part of him not knowing about it. She was quite certain that New Albion was more than capable of such a plot, was sure that *any* government would be.

"Thing is, I don't really think New Albion knew what they were playing with," Chad said. "They might have heard whispers about Xenomorphs, and put two and two together with the rumors about the border bombings, and come up with the notion that they had some kind of bioweapon on their hands. But I don't believe they knew the full extent of what they were unleashing on LV-187. They'll be keeping a watching brief to see exactly what happens here."

"But they sent us down…" Bromley said doubtfully.

Chad shrugged. "They needed to raise the flag. You got the job. You'll be remembered as heroes of the new British Empire. Probably posthumously, I'm afraid."

"Chad," Cher said quietly, motioning to Therese.

"It's fine," Merrilyn said. "She's seen what everyone else has seen. She needs to know the facts about what we're facing, as much as everyone else does." She looked at Cher, who had said she was a journalist on Earth. "So you do not think anyone will come to our aid? Nobody cares about what happens here?"

"Everybody cares about what happens here," Cher said. "According to the news feeds just before we made planetfall, LV-187 is at the center of a major interstellar incident. Since New Albion announced its secession, the Three World Empire has formally cut all diplomatic and defense ties with the colony. That goes for any colonies that support it, too. According to unsubstantiated reports, there are a number of them in the Weyland Isles—with a variety of allegiances—who are sympathetic with New Albion's move.

"The ICSC is being more aggressive. They've made a

formal declaration of war against New Albion over what it says is the invasion of LV-187. That said, the ICSC declared war on the United Americas after the Hasanova incident. Whether they have the balls to follow it through remains to be seen. They *haven't* with the UA."

"And what are the United Americas doing?" Moran said.

"Like New Albion, keeping a watching brief," Cher said. "There were some who thought they might move against the ICSC, given their state of war, and support New Albion. But they're twitchy about some of their own colonies who are making noise about secession in the wake of Maurice Pepper's announcement."

"So the best we can hope for is that the ICSC sends a ship to retake LV-187," Chad said. "And that they can get us off-world before we all get killed." There was silence while they all thought about it for a moment, as the storm howled outside.

"So what do we do in the meantime?" Moran said.

"Try to stay alive," Chad said. He looked at Merrilyn. "Are we sure there aren't any more surviving colonists?"

"There was one, but they shot him," Merrilyn said, gesturing toward Moran.

"Hey, that was an accident!"

Chad looked around the comms room. "This isn't a bad defensive position. Minimal roof space above us, which is good. We need to secure every single hatch and duct vent in the room. What about supplies? And weapons?"

They all put down their guns and rifles on the central counter. Merrilyn hesitated, then laid down her kitchen knife.

"We have supplies in the ship," Moran said, "but that's off limits unless we can kill that critter."

"We have some," Chad said. "Kitchen and food stores?"

"Far side of the colony," Merrilyn said. "We were holed up there before the New Albion ship came. There are tinned goods and water."

Chad nodded. "Let's try to avoid leaving here unless we have to."

"These things," Merrilyn said. "These… Xenomorphs. What will they be doing now?"

Chad glanced at Therese, then back at her mother. "They've probably formed a hive. There might well be a queen. There's a very good chance not all of your fellow colonists are dead… yet. Some of them might be incubating Xenomorph embryos. But don't get up any hope; if they're not dead, they soon will be."

"They'll be coming for us?" Bromley said, picking up the pulse rifle.

Chad nodded. "They'll be coming for us. We have to be ready."

A crack of thunder sounded right above them, shaking the comms tower, and the lights flickered. Merrilyn beckoned Therese over to her and held her very tightly.

* * *

Frank Priestley wasn't dead. For the first six hours he'd wished he was, but not now.

His body was a symphony of agony, every nerve ending singing a torturer's lament. He could only see through one eye and his face was raw and stinging, his throat as dry as a desert. He was in darkness, save for the thinnest of lights emanating from he didn't know where. Suspended, trapped against the wall by a resinous spider-web of hardened fibers crisscrossing him like scar tissue. He didn't know where he was, other than it was hot, unbearably hot, and he didn't care anymore.

He had been chosen.

When the creature had taken him in the corridor, he had thought he was in the presence of the very devil himself. But as it dragged him along the access tunnels in the ceiling, he realized that it wasn't the devil, it was merely one of the foot soldiers of Hell. The true devil was waiting for him in the hive.

She was magnificent.

He had lost consciousness for a long time, and when he awoke there was something covering his face, something soft and pliable yet hard and skeletal at the same time. It had put something down his throat, which allowed him to breathe in a raspy, labored way, and he felt something happening to him, deep inside. While he was unconscious the thing covering his face must have fallen away. It was gone when he awoke.

There were others, too—other humans, spider-webbed

to the walls just like he was, covered in a goo of cells and protein and bile from the guts of the monsters themselves. At first it made him retch, but then he realized what it was, and why it covered him.

It was mucus, it was meconium, it was the slime of rebirth. Frank Priestley was being changed, he was shedding his old self. He was being remade. He was being reborn.

He had been chosen.

Some of the other people moaned faintly or, in more lucid moments, screamed and begged. Frank Priestley did not beg. He was not weak like them. He recognized that whatever was inside him was changing him. Altering him. Improving him.

All his life Frank Priestley had longed to be a part of something bigger. That was why he had emigrated to New Albion. That was why he had signed up with the trade corps. That was why he had applied to join the Duke of Wellingtons. Frank Priestley felt safety in numbers, preferred it when he was part of a consensus, liked it when he didn't have to think for himself.

This was better than any army or brotherhood. Frank Priestley felt a part of something, felt it growing within him. He hadn't had to beg to join them, he had been chosen.

Through his one good eye he saw movement in the wide, subterranean space. There were moans of fear from those still alive around him, the stench of terror, but Frank was not afraid. He rejoiced. His heart sang. He felt joy flood his very being as the shape rose, rose, rose, filling the cavernous space.

No, more than joy. Love.

She was a thing of beauty, a goddess, a being of ineffable purity and truth. She was a queen, and a queen deserved pomp and circumstance when she chose to move among her subjects. Huge and magnificent she shone blackly, moving fluidly like the River Styx flowing through Hades. She drew herself up to her full height and turned her huge dome of a head, inspecting those that belonged to her. A snatch of poetry from his school days flitted through his head.

She walks in beauty like the night
Of cloudless climes and starry skies;
And all that's best of dark and bright
Meet in her aspect and her eyes

She seemed to test the air, the very pheromones on the still, hot, heavy breaths of her subjects. She deserved more than this mewling and moaning. She deserved music and song.

Frank opened his mouth and gasped, then tried to maneuver saliva around his sand-dry mouth. Eventually he began to croak a paean of honor to her.

"God save our gracious Queen," he grunted. "Long live our noble Queen. God save the Queen! Send her victorious, happy and glorious, long to reign over us, God save the Queen."

Her huge, bulbous head paused in its sweeping of the hive, cocked to one side, as if considering him. She drew closer, her fetid breath anointing him with foul spittle. He reveled in her attention.

The queen lifted up a massive claw and drew its sharp point down the raw, ragged flesh of his ruined face. He gasped in agony and ecstasy at her touch. Then she presented her hand to him, and he leaned forward as best he could, and kissed it.

She hissed and screeched, and drew back.

At first he thought he had offended her, and awaited her righteous rage. Her claws outstretched, she paused in front of his face for a moment, then slashed at either side of him. He felt the resinous bonds weaken and stretch, and then snap as she raked her claws over him. His helpless body sagged, and then fell to the floor at her feet.

Frank looked up at her. Was she about to deliver a fatal blow? No. She regarded him silently, waiting. He realized what was happening. She had a design for him, a plan. He was to do her bidding for the glory of the hive. Among all the chosen, Frank had been elevated, had been doubly chosen.

"Thank you," he gasped. She hissed at him. She did not want his gratitude. That was a human thing, a failing, a weakness, and there was no place for that in the hive. She merely needed his complete and total obedience.

A colonist stuck to the wall beside him opened her eyes.

"*Aidez-moi, s'il vous plaît*," she whispered. "*Aidez-moi.*"

Frank could not help her. Could not help anyone. Could not even help himself. He was in thrall to his queen, and he could do no more or no less than what she demanded. As if to prove his point, the queen bent low, hissing at the colonist who had spoken, and raked her claws viciously across the woman's face, silencing her with finality. Then she brought her head close to Frank's, and bared her teeth.

"Yes," Frank hoarsely said. "I understand. I won't fail you."

Then, adrenaline flooding his ruined, battered body, he spun around and half crawled, half ran away from the charnel house of the hive and back to the land of the living.

1 5

Cher sat silently in the corner of the comms deck and watched the others going around every inch of the walls and floors, duct-taping over vents and service hatches. They'd found a set of welding tools and bolt-guns in a cabinet, and were securing pieces of metal stripped from around the comms console to anything that might allow even the slightest ingress to the circular room.

She was beginning to feel claustrophobic, desirous not just of air but the specific sweet-smelling, honey-golden, late fall air of an Oregon dusk, where the land seemed to roll on forever into the encroaching darkness and the sun blinked below the horizon with the promise that it would be back in the morning.

Thinking of that made her think of Old Man Nesbitt's grain silo, and Shy dangling fifteen meters up, and the sick feeling in the pit of Cher's stomach and the tingling in the soles of her feet as she knew with a sinking heart that she couldn't go up to help her sister.

"You are not the story," one of her journalism tutors,

Professor Schmidt, had said to them time and time again. *"You are not the story."* Cher had made a mantra of it, too, and always reported the news from a respectful distance, letting events unfold at their own pace and giving other people their voices. She never went up the grain silo, *any* grain silo. It wasn't her place to do so. All she wanted to know was how the people were feeling who were hanging by the tips of their fingers, fifteen meters up.

"You are not the story." And yet, here she was. The story.

How are you feeling? she asked herself. That was what she'd asked a thousand times in her career, of people who were bereaved or dispossessed or injured or lost. *How are you feeling?* It was a stupid question because it was obvious to anyone watching how this person or that person was feeling in the midst of tragedy and horror. And yet, unless the question was asked, very often the answer wasn't forthcoming. People didn't usually say, without prompting, how they were feeling. So you had to ask the stupid question to get the right answer.

Cher pulled her knees up and hugged them, and asked herself again.

How are you feeling?

Scared, she told herself. *Numb.* Like it all wasn't really happening, and she was watching it with a detached air on some entertainment channel. Then scared again. *Terrified*, and, in a little corner of herself, somewhat elated. Excited. With that shiver of hairs on the back of her neck that always signaled being at the heart of a really big story.

How are you feeling?

Like I'm the fucking story. Suck on that, Professor Schmidt.

"Are you all right?" a voice said in her ear. It was Davis, sitting upright, head tilted to one side.

"Mama! Mama!" the little French girl said. Therese, who had stopped what she was doing piling up a pyramid of duct tape rolls, to stare at Davis. "The doggo talked!"

"Hush, Little Flower," Merrilyn said, crouched down by an air vent and shooting big bolts into the corners of a square of aluminum. Cher wished she was being as useful as the colonist. "Doggos don't talk."

"This one does," Cher said, smiling as best she could. She liked this Merrilyn. She was tough and no-nonsense, yet tender and loving, too. She wanted to be her. "He's a synthetic carrying a rather special AI called Davis."

Merrilyn stared at her, and stood up, frowning. She beckoned Therese over.

"Do not bother the lady and the… dog, Little Flower," the woman said to her daughter, pretty coldly, in Cher's opinion. "Stay by me."

"Maybe she doesn't like synthetics," Cher murmured to Davis.

"Many people don't," Davis said quietly back. "Sometimes we went wrong, in the early days. People are still a little scared of what they don't fully understand, because what they don't really understand they can't properly trust."

"Perhaps that's why humans are always fighting

goddamn wars," Cher said. "Nobody seems to understand anybody else, ever."

"This will cheer you up," Davis said.

"Have you learned a new joke?"

"No, I just calculated our chances of survival."

Cher pulled a face. "Maybe not, huh? I'd rather this not be a numbers game."

"Fair enough."

Davis trotted over to the big observation window and jumped up, putting his front paws on the sill so he could look out at the relentless storm. Cher climbed to her feet and joined him, looking at their reflections in the dark glass.

"I wish Zula were here," Davis said.

"Kick-ass broad, right?" Cher said.

"Definitely. I've never seen a braver woman. A braver human. She has done things that a synthetic's programming would rail against, because of the apparent stupidity of it. But she did it for others."

"Fearless," Cher said, half to herself. "I wish I was like that."

She saw Davis's reflection look up at her. "Fearless? No. Only an idiot has no fear," he said. "It's how you conquer it that makes you brave."

"Mama, why can't I play with the talking doggo?" Therese whined.

"Hush, Little Flower, just stay by me," Merrilyn said.

"Is it because he's not a real doggo?"

Merrilyn hesitated. This wasn't a conversation she really wanted to have. "Why don't you go and get mama a big roll of duct tape so we can wrap it around this vent?" she said.

Therese toddled off and Merrilyn became aware of someone else standing behind her. It was the journalist, Cher. She gave her a tight smile. Cher crouched down beside her.

"Your daughter is beautiful."

"Thank you," Merrilyn said.

"Unusual for a girl of… what is she? Five? Six?"

Merrilyn shot her a look. "She is six. Why do you say unusual?"

Cher waved a hand vaguely in the air. "All this. All this stuff. She's taking it in her stride so much. At that age I'd have been a quivering wreck, hiding behind my daddy."

Merrilyn relaxed a little. The woman was just being friendly. "Kids are resilient though, aren't they?" she said. "I bet you'd have been stronger than you think you would have been." She paused, and added, "Could you hold this plate into place while I bolt the corners?"

Cher smiled quickly, seemingly keen to be of use. She held the metal with the flats of her hands and said, "Davis is no danger to your daughter, or anyone else. He's a very unusual AI. As far as I can gather, he's got free will."

Merrilyn looked at her, frowning. "How is that possible?"

Cher shrugged. "I don't know. He's an anomaly." She lowered her voice. "He's in love. With a human woman. How crazy is that?"

"And does she love him back? This synthetic dog?"

"I think so." Cher moved her hands away as Merrilyn finished bolting the panel. "I'm not quite sure where she is. I don't think anyone knows. But Davis wasn't always a dog. That's a fairly recent turn of events. He started off as a combat droid, in humanoid form. Then he was kind of… a floating bunch of AI. Or something."

"You're not a scientist, are you?" Merrilyn smiled..

"No." Cher laughed. "I'm not. Are you?"

"Petroleum geologist. That's why I'm here on LV-187. It was meant to be a three-year posting." She looked at Cher. "I'll be asking for one fuck of a bonus when we get back to Earth."

Therese brought over a roll of tape and Merrilyn used it to secure the edges of the hatch. That was all the vents done, now. She stood up stiffly and surveyed the room, where the others were finishing off their jobs.

"No children yourself, I presume?"

"No," Cher said. "Too busy with work, and never met anyone I liked enough to have children with."

They watched as Therese, glancing at her mother, sidled off toward where Davis was still looking out of the window. Merrilyn raised an eyebrow at her, but gave her the slightest of nods.

"Neither did I," Merrilyn said, "but I knew I wanted children. I used a donor." She gazed at Therese across the room. "In a way, I wish I'd chosen more wisely." She felt Cher's curious stare on her, and shook her head. "Ignore me. Come on, let's find out what is supposed to happen next."

The Chosen walked with impunity along the corridors of death. That was how he thought of himself now. Not Frank Priestley, but the Chosen. It was as if he could barely remember Priestley, could hardly understand his life before. That had been empty and meaningless and without purpose or structure. Now he had a mission, a holy crusade for his Queen.

Emerging from the bowels of the hive he assumed an air of his old mortality, but it was merely a flag of convenience, a cloak of deceit. He knew what he was now, as did his Queen. As did this drone, crouched in the corridor in front of him, hissing and smelling the air as he approached.

The Chosen felt a pang of jealousy when he saw the creature. It was a perfect living machine, not an ounce of its being wasted, every beautiful glistening inch of it devoted to its reasons for being: to kill its enemies and protect its Queen and propagate its kind.

He pushed the thought away. Jealousy was an emotion for lesser men, lesser beings than he. This drone might have been blessed with the appearance of their dark mistress, but it was just a soldier when all was said and done. He was the Chosen. He walked carefully toward it, hands outstretched.

"You know me," he murmured. "You know who I am."

The drone crouched lower, as though getting ready to attack. The Chosen showed no fear. He continued to walk as it put its head first this way, then that, its tail whipping behind it. When he was just a meter away, he bowed his head. The drone bared its teeth and let loose a long, sibilant exhalation. It took a step forward on its skeletal legs, crouched low. A silent agreement passed between them, and the Chosen could sense the heartbeats inside him.

He raised his head again.

"I have work to do," he murmured.

"Anything?" Chad McClaren said.

"Nothing," Moran responded, turning off the comms desk. "The storm's getting worse, and more importantly, we're on back-up systems here. Every time we try to make contact, we're using juice that isn't being replenished." He looked at the others, busying themselves with pointless but diverting tasks. He dropped his voice to a low whisper. "You want us to be seeing the night with absolutely no power? No lights? Imagine if one of those things got in here."

"Fair enough," Chad conceded.

Moran leaned in. "You've fought these things... what? How many times?"

"More than I care to remember or count."

"But you always survived, is my point."

"I did. A lot of people didn't."

"But these things aren't unstoppable. They're not unkillable. They're just very, very tough, right?"

"I suppose," Chad said doubtfully, "but you shouldn't underestimate them."

"I'm not," Moran said. "I'm just determined to get off this rock alive. It's all about perspective, innit, McClaren? All depends on where you see yourself in the pecking order. You and me, we're the same. We're main characters. Protagonists. That's why you always come out on top, and so do I." He looked over to the others. "These guys, they're supporting cast. You get what I'm saying?"

Chad looked at him and shook his head slowly. "That sort of thinking is a very quick shortcut to getting yourself killed when dealing with Xenomorphs, Moran. There are no heroes in these situations. Just survivors. It's the best you can hope for."

Moran shrugged. "That's not how winners think, McClaren, but, hey. It's your funeral. I'll say a prayer for you when I'm back on New Albion. Say what you like, out of the seven of us left in this shithole, I think I'm best placed to be your survivor-type—"

A sudden hammering on the doors to the comms deck made everyone jump.

"Fuck!" Moran said.

"Mama, it's a monster," Therese said, leaping into her mother's embrace. The hammering continued, followed by an indistinct, but very human, shouting. Moran flipped on the monitor that showed the security camera feed outside the room and stepped back, swearing.

"Fuck! It's Priestley. He's alive!"

Chad joined him at the screen where a man with a mangled, bloody face was hammering at the door, screaming into the camera. Chad hit the unmute key and the man's voice filled the room.

"—in! Let me in! The fucking thing is going to kill me!"

"Impossible!" Merrilyn said, holding Therese close. "I saw the Xenomorph kill him."

"Obviously fucking not," Moran said through gritted teeth. He reached for the door control but Chad stopped him with a hand on his arm. "What are you doing?" Moran asked.

"Look," Chad said, and he pointed. Behind Priestley, there was a figure moving in the dull strip-lighting, a thin, hunched, almost ape-like creature that eventually moved into focus behind the man's bobbing, screaming head.

"Xenomorph," Chad said.

"Well get your guns and let me open the fucking door!" Moran shouted. "On my count of five. One…"

Bromley, Chad, Merrilyn, and Cher grabbed their weapons and assembled in front of the door.

"Two…"

"Please!" Priestley's voice came over the monitor. "It's coming!"

"Hit the deck when the doors open, Frank," Moran said into a microphone. "Three…"

"Cut to the fucking chase, guv!" Priestley screamed.

"Fuck," Moran said. "Five. Go!" He hit the doors and they slid open, and Priestley dove forward on to the deck, the Xenomorph growling and hissing two meters behind him. Moran grabbed a gun, leapt forward, and started firing. "Don't just stare at it, kill it!" he yelled as the others opened fire.

The Xenomorph jerked and twitched in the hail of pulse blasts, thrown back to the floor. As it tried to get to its feet it took a shot straight in the face, screamed, and fell in a smoking heap. Its acid blood started to bubble and smoke and burn its way down through the floor and to the story below.

"Close the doors!" Chad shouted as Moran ran forward and dragged Priestley's prone body into the comms room.

"Thank you, thank you," Priestley gasped as Moran turned him over in his arms. "I thought I was a goner there, guv."

1 6

They'd wrapped Priestley in a blanket and Bromley, who had some medical training, tried to do something with the razored tatters of his face. "You're not going to be winning Olympic Gold at archery, mate," she said tenderly. "You've lost the left eye."

Pumping him full of painkillers she wrapped half of his head in bandages after cleaning the raw wound as best she could.

"We'll get you fixed up properly when we get back to New Albion. You're going to need skin grafts." She took a step back to appraise her handiwork, and added, "Neither will you be getting first prize in any beauty contests. That said, you always were an ugly bugger."

Priestley seemed to be processing the words she was saying and responding a beat or two too late, forcing a laugh. Chad frowned. The guy had been through a lot, and could be excused for not being in top form, but there was still something strange. He had a deep mistrust of anyone who came up close to Xenomorphs, and didn't die without killing them.

"So, it just… left you?" Chad said again.

"Jesus Christ, mate, can you lay off him?" Moran said. "You can see what he's been through. What are you getting at?"

"It's OK, guv," Priestley said. "When that thing dragged me up into the crawlspace in the roof I thought I was dead meat. I was in shock. I couldn't move. I don't know what happened. It just scarpered. I suppose something might have scared it off, maybe?"

"Xenomorphs don't scare easily," Chad said. "Priestley, you're sure you didn't lose consciousness? While you were with the alien? What about eggs? Did you see any eggs?" He held up his hand. "About this tall. Did you see any of those? Might you have blacked out for a while?"

Priestley shook his head, gratefully accepting a mug of tea from Merrilyn.

"Thanks, love." He turned to Chad, and even that movement seemed painful. "I knew if I lost consciousness, I was dead. I waited until the thing had gone, then I dropped back down to the corridor. It took forever, but I crawled to the canteen and found this little nest of blankets in a storeroom. Shot myself full of morphine from my belt and zoned out, but I never blacked out anywhere near those things, and never saw any eggs.

"When I came to, I made my way back here, and came across another one of those monsters. If I hadn't been so

close to the comms room, I'd have been dead for sure."
Priestley looked around the room. "Boffin still at the ship?
And where's Amina? She shouldn't be out there on her
own. Not with those things."

"Both dead," Moran said quietly. "Like we thought
you were."

Priestley rubbed a hand over his good eye. "Fuck. Fuck.
We getting off this place, guv?"

"Soon as the storm clears. Look, we've made you a bed
of blankets in the corner. Why don't you get some rest?
We're going to try to cobble together a meal in a couple
of hours."

Chad watched Moran and Bromley help their colleague
over to the pile of blankets. They might be glad to see their
crew member back with them, but for some reason, he
wasn't quite as convinced as he'd like to be.

"I don't like that man, Mama," Therese said.

"Hush, Little Flower, Merrilyn said, glancing over to
where Priestley was sleeping at the far end of the comms
room. The big observation window was rattling in the
wind, as though it was coming loose in its fittings. She
had never known a storm like it.

She had to agree with Therese, remembered the way
Priestley looked at her when he had confronted them in
the corridor. There was something mean and… hungry
about him. She had to admit she had felt a little dismayed

when he had turned up alive, and she hated herself for the uncharitable thought.

Cher came, squatted down by them, and picked up a can of beef stew, peeling the top off it and adding it to the pot with the others. Merrilyn had rigged up a makeshift electric ring on which to heat the food, the pot a repurposed casing unscrewed from one of the comms banks.

"We'll eat well tonight," Merrilyn said, "but we're going to have to get more supplies from the canteen tomorrow."

"I don't relish going out there," Cher said, stirring the stew with a broken length of antenna. "Not after what happened to him." They both looked over to Priestley.

"Can I go and talk to the doggo, Mama?"

"I suppose," Merrilyn said, still a bit uncertainly.

When Therese had gone, Cher said, "Can I ask why you don't like Davis? Have you had a bad experience with synthetics?"

Merrilyn shook her head. She was starting to like this American woman, but how could she tell her the truth? It could put Therese in danger, and she would never countenance anything happening to her. She had already told her daughter that it was her mama's job to kill monsters. That went for human monsters, too, and she knew that people were capable of as much evil as Xenomorphs. Given the right push.

"Just an overprotective mama, I suppose," Merrilyn said, with a tight smile. "It's nothing. Davis seems nice." By way of changing the subject, she added in a low voice,

"Chad seems to be disquieted by Priestley's return." Cher nodded, opening some sachets of salt and emptying them into the bubbling stew.

"He does, and I don't really know why. It's like he doesn't believe the guy, but how do you lie about something like that? One of those things grabs you, you're either dead or you get away. Surely there's no in-between. You should know. You've seen them in action."

Merrilyn blinked and she saw the Xenomorph in the garage again, holding Therese in its claws like a rag doll, about to deliver the killer blow.

"How is it nobody knows about these things?" she asked. "Why aren't we all warned about them? Why aren't we at war with them, instead of each other?"

"That's why I'm here," Cher said. "Chad and Davis contacted me to try to get the word out. There has been a war against the Xenomorphs, but it's been fought in the shadows. Chad wants it out in the open." Cher sighed and rolled her eyes. "Stupid old me demanded to see the evidence with my own eyes, though. Wish I'd just taken their word for it, now."

Suddenly, and without warning even to herself, Merrilyn leaned over and gave Cher a hug. "Well, I for one am glad that you came, if you won't take that the wrong way. I fear that without your arrival, Therese and myself would not be alive right now."

Cher hugged her back. It was good. Nice. She felt safe, for the first time in more than a week. Somewhere deep inside of her a spark lit up the darkness she had carried around for so long. She began to think—to hope—that things might just turn out all right.

The Chosen lay with his eye closed, but he did not sleep.

He communed.

His Queen's tendrils reached out, up from the hive, snaking through the dim corridors, tapping and feeling around the doors and taped-up vents until they could worm their way inside and plunge, almost making him gasp with orgasmic delight, into his mind.

He felt her in all her black, dark glory, her own mind a pure, focused whirlpool of forged rage. She was a *chok-chok-chok* of slicing blades, a crunch of bone between steel teeth, a rippling of vertebrae, a pungent perfume of acid musk that drove him almost insane with the need to abase himself in front of her, to beg to be made her slave, to serve her unto death and beyond.

The Chosen lay still and imperceptibly shivered as she plunged her mind into his again and again, like a violent paramour whose hatred was as sweet as her love.

I'm here, my Queen, he thought as she stabbed his soul with her own. *I am yours. I have done your bidding. Love me. Hate me. Nourish me. Hurt me.*

On the periphery of his beautifully violated being he sensed a gathering. His Queen was drawing her forces together, marshalling her troops, gathering her storm. She was making him shine like a beacon, his agony radiating through the colony, attracting the skittering, crouching, crawling beasts under her command like moths to the flame of his exquisite pain.

Come to me, the Chosen sang in his head, the song reverberating around the darkened colony. *Come to me. Come to me.*

From the tunnels and storerooms and maintenance shafts and air ducts and from all the secret, hidden places where they had been lurking and waiting, they started to move as one.

"You're getting on well with the kid," Chad said as Therese toddled off toward her mother. "You need to be careful, Davis. You're going to end up more dog than…"

"Than what, Chad?"

Chad shrugged. "I was going to say human."

"I'm flattered," Davis said, "but I'm not human—not yet. There's something eluding me and I don't yet know what it is." He paused to lick his paw, then said, "Cher thought it might be sacrifice that makes one human."

"You've sacrificed yourself a dozen times," Chad said, looking out of the window. He was worried about that glass and the punishment it was taking.

"Always for Zula," Davis mused. "Cher thought… maybe a more selfless sacrifice is what is needed. The willingness to sacrifice one's self not just for those we love, but for those we've never even met."

"In that case, I don't know many humans."

Chad looked beyond Moran and Bromley, deep in quiet conversation, and to where Priestley was lying stock still in his makeshift bed of blankets.

"You don't trust him, do you?" David murmured.

"I don't trust any of the New Albion contingent," Chad said quietly. "We only have their word that they weren't involved in planting the Ovomorphs on LV-187. *Someone* took those eggs from the *Clara* and brought them here. It seems awfully convenient that the *Victory* was passing just at the right time."

"The infestation had occurred long before they were in LV-187 airspace, Chad."

Chad looked down at Davis. "Yeah, but they got the distress call on the way back to New Albion, didn't they? How long before had they passed this way on the outward leg of their trade mission? A week, maybe? Perhaps we should ask them."

"Maybe later," Davis said, getting to his feet and sniffing the air. "I think the food's ready."

Chad smiled crookedly at him. "You really are becoming more dog, Davis, you know that?"

Moran had Bromley rouse Priestley and they all gathered around the comms hub for dishes of stew. The control desk wasn't much use for anything other than a dining table at the moment.

The power was dropping in the colony, and Moran was worried. There was meant to be a goddamn baby fusion reactor, somewhere in the bowels of the place. The connections to it must have been goosed, either by the storm or by the infestation. Either way, they weren't getting the power they should be. He didn't want to think about what might happen if the lights went out before whatever dawn the storm allowed to break on this place.

"Feeling any better?" he said as Bromley helped Priestley to the table.

"My face is sore, guv, but I think that's the painkillers wearing off. Other than that, I'm feeling pretty chipper." He looked up at Bromley as she helped him sit. "Thank you, Teesha. You're a good friend."

Bromley cast a look at Moran, raising an eyebrow. He shared her vague disquiet. Where were all the off-color jokes and casual sexism they were used to? Could a near-death experience have that much of an effect on a man? Moran decided he didn't want to find out for himself. He was happy being who he was, and didn't want to change—especially not if it meant going through what Priestley had endured.

Moran clapped his hands. "OK. Let's eat, and for the next half hour or so, we talk about anything other than you-know-what. Let's give ourselves a bit of a break, people, all right?"

"Given that the majority of the group is British, now, I guess that means we have to talk about the weather?" Chad said. As if on cue, there was a sudden flash of lightning right outside the window, followed by a rumble of thunder that lasted ten seconds. Everyone gasped, and then laughed with a sudden and welcome release of the tension that had been building since they'd arrived.

The stew was gloopy and thick and not particularly hot, but Moran thought it might have been the best meal he'd ever had. The group fell into easy conversation in their twos and threes, and he half-listened to Bromley giving him her considered opinion on West Ham's chances in the forthcoming season. The other half of his attention was on Priestley, wrapped in a blanket and pushing his food around his plate without really eating any.

"You OK, mate?" he said as Priestley suddenly started to bang his fist against his chest. "Bit of heartburn? Want some water?"

Priestley gave him a tight smile.

"Not heartburn. It's time."

"Time for what?" Moran frowned. "You want some more sleep?"

"Time for the nativity," Priestley said. "Time for me to fulfil my glorious purpose for my dark monarch, who walks in beauty like the night." Then he lurched forward, his head slamming hard on the control desk.

One of the women screamed.

Moran leapt up, yelling, "Priestley? Jesus Christ! What the fuck?"

Priestley threw his head backward and arched his spine, as though he was a puppet possessed by an invisible demon.

"Oh, no," Moran heard McClaren say. "No, no, no…"

"His stomach!" Bromley shouted. "The fuck?"

Priestley's stomach was rippling and distending, as though something inside him was trying to punch its way out. Then he screamed, and bent almost backward, his arms flailing around, knocking the plates and drinks over as he twisted in his seat.

Moran was dimly aware of McClaren scrabbling for a handgun beside him as Priestley's wide, rabid eyes met his. His crewman smiled at him, a horrible, grotesque, rictus grin.

"Don't feel sorry for me, Tom. I am the Chosen."

Then Priestley's chest exploded outward in a shower of flesh, bone, blood… and something that should not have been there.

1 7

TURNING POINT
Editorial Opinion
The Times
London, July 20, 2186

There will be much hand-wringing in the corridors of
power about the news filtering in from the Weyland
Isles Sector of deep space and the New Albion colony
which has found itself at the center of a diplomatic row
which could see ripples spreading out across the entirety
of known space.

It is quite possible that many ordinary people in
Britain had not even heard of New Albion—just another
distant colony among the stars, one of many operating
under the auspices of the Three World Empire, sending
back resources to be used on Earth.

However, New Albion was never just one of those
utilitarian colonies on an inhospitable rock circling a
distant sun. It always had grander ambitions than that.

Over the past decade many influential British families, who can trace their roots back to the glorious high points of our illustrious history, have been quietly investing in the colony, as have some of our most profitable and successful corporations and businesses.

New Albion is not just a means to an end. It is, it appears, an opportunity to recreate everything that is best about Britain without the shackles and chains this country has heaped upon itself for more than a century.

So it should come as no surprise to anyone that Maurice Pepper, the elected Prime Minister of New Albion, has—with the support of his cabinet—declared full independence from the Three World Empire.

As a news organization with Britain's best interests at heart, we should perhaps be decrying this move that potentially threatens the stability of the socio-economic bloc of which we are a part. But this country—and this newspaper—has a more venerable history and a longer memory than our relatively recent association with the Three World Empire.

So like many people reading this, we find it difficult to not sympathise with Maurice Pepper and the people of New Albion, and to wonder what effects this situation might have on the politics of Earth, and Britain, and our sometimes uncomfortable place in a world we might no longer recognize as the one we had a major role in building.

HOP OFF, SPACE FROGS!
The *Sun*
July 20, 2186

The Union Flag was flying over a former French colony in the Weyland Isles Sector today as a plucky band of Brits claimed the oil-rich planet for breakaway settlement New Albion.

One government source said that there wasn't a Frenchie to be seen on LV-187 when the brave crew of the *Victory* put down to answer a distress call, adding, "It was like Dunkirk all over again. Whatever trouble the French had been in, they'd all turned tail and run by the time help arrived." Sounds familiar, eh?

While the Independent Core Systems Colonies conglomerate said that it would retake LV-187 by force, New Albion's Prime Minister Maurice Pepper showed true bulldog spirit by telling them in no uncertain terms to "Hop off!"

BLUSTER AND BUFFOONERY
New Albion could signal the greatest crisis
in the history of the Colonies
The *Guardian*
July 20, 2186

At any given time, somewhere in the world—or

beyond—there is a leader who is a figure of fun. A buffoon. A blusterer who even their political enemies find somehow endearing, despite themselves.

These are the most dangerous people of all.

People like Maurice Pepper do not get to the office of Prime Minister of a colony such as New Albion— named last year by the Dow Jones as one of the top one hundred most potentially economically and politically influential off-world colonies—without exercising a razor-sharp ruthlessness somewhere along the line.

And when that is dressed up in clownish behavior, sly winks to the camera, ruffled hair and shabby suits, it is usually no accident at all.

The secession of New Albion from the Three World Empire might appear to be the hollow posturing of an empty vessel, but make no mistake. This Weyland Isles Sector world has suddenly become the sounding board for the entire colony network, and from the United Americas to the Union of Progressive Peoples, everyone is nervously eyeing Pepper's administration to see what happens next on New Albion... and what might happen elsewhere.

"Would you like to see any more?" Maurice Pepper's press secretary asked.

"*Are* there any more?" Pepper responded, leaning back in his chair in the cabinet office of the huge concrete edifice called the Mother of Parliaments, the window behind him looking out onto what would be the River Thames when construction work was eventually completed.

"Lots," the secretary said. "The *Washington Post* has a piece headlined 'Assault On Pepper'"—everyone in the cabinet groaned—"which is actually very supportive, the *Colonies Free News Network* says that New Albion is about to be, and I quote, 'a force to be reckoned with in the Weyland Isles, and beyond,' and one online site has even posted a quiz entitled 'How Maurice Pepper are you?'"

The prime minster ran a hand through his unruly straw-colored hair and guffawed. "I should take that."

"I already took the liberty of filling it in for you," the press secretary said. "You are thirty-eight percent Maurice Pepper, apparently."

Everyone laughed again and someone threw a screwed-up ball of paper at Pepper, which bounced off his head. He stuck up two fingers at the perpetrator, the secretary for trade and industry.

"Pipe down, you lot," he bellowed indignantly. "We've got serious business to discuss."

"At last," the defense secretary muttered.

Pepper looked at him. "Yes, quite, Roger. We'll get to you in a minute. First I want to hear from Charlotte, if she's quite finished throwing balls at my head."

The secretary for trade and industry coughed and called up some graphs on the big screen on the wall of the room.

"Early signs are very encouraging indeed," she said. "Aside from hardcore ICSC worlds which have been instructed in no uncertain terms not to deal with us, we're getting very positive responses from a lot of very big players in the Weyland Isles, who are keen to open up trade negotiations. Our stockpiles of oil and metal ores are looking like very attractive propositions, and prices on the former are rocketing as the markets took a major plunge the day after we announced our secession."

Pepper beamed broadly around the room. "We did that!"

The secretary for trade and industry nodded to the foreign secretary. "Karen and I have been working closely, because we're getting a lot of early suggestions that people might be willing to enter into deeper alliances than merely for trade."

"Yes," the foreign secretary agreed. "So far we've had semi-formal communications from New Amsterdam, Constantinople, New Kemet…"

Pepper held up his hand. "Be polite, but firm. I don't want us entering into alliances. Not yet. New Albion isn't swapping one confederation of worlds for another. We are not being subsumed in a faceless mass of colonies. The entire point of this exercise, dear Karen, was for New Albion to go it alone. To lead. To stand proud. We do not want partners in this enterprise. We want *acquisitions*."

There was a volley of cheers and fists banging on the table and Pepper turned to the defense secretary. "Which brings us to you, Roger. Pipe down, you lot! So.

We currently have a rag-tag band of highly unreliable trader types holding our first acquisition as an independent power. What are we doing to beef up our forces on LV-187?"

"We have two transports ready for flight, each able to carry thirty troops, and we've cancelled all leave for the Duke of Wellingtons for the foreseeable future, so we're ready to go when able."

Pepper put his elbows on the table and steepled his fingers. "And why, dear Roger, are our troops still sitting on their arses on New Albion, rather than about to touch down on LV-187?"

The defense secretary tapped on his tablet and the image on the big screen changed to an image of deep space, the grey ball of LV-187 filling the monitor.

"We've got a drone out there sending back footage." The defense secretary tapped his screen again and the image updated. "This is why we haven't got any boots on the ground yet." Everyone stared at the huge cruiser hanging in space in high orbit around LV-187.

"That's the USC *Cronulla*," the defense secretary continued. "A Bougainville Class Attack Transport. The United States Colonial Marine Corps are in a holding pattern above LV-187 as of three hours ago."

Pepper narrowed his eyes. "I thought the United Americas were keeping out of this?"

"They are," the defense secretary acknowledged. "The USCMC is essentially a private military service. Working mainly for the United Americas, yes, but also in the service of Weyland-Yutani Corporation."

Pepper sat back in his chair and swiveled it so he could look out of the window. "Why is Weyland-Yutani interested in LV-187? It's never been one of their worlds. It's ICSC. I could see the Three World Empire sending a warship, but not Weyland-Yutani. Have they attempted planetfall yet? Any dropships?"

"That's the other thing, Maurice," the defense secretary said. "There's an incredible storm raging over the colony. No fliers are going to get in or out until it's over, and it's completely knocked out all communications."

"So this is why we haven't sent the Duke of Wellingtons yet," Pepper said. "We're not going to get past the Weyland-Yutani blockade."

"Not in one piece," Roger said. "I mean, I've been asking you for years for funding for a proper air force, Maurice. For God's sake, we've closed our airspace and we don't have the ships to even enforce that, let alone escort a troop drop to LV-187, where we might get involved in an exchange of fire." The defense secretary shook his head. "It's not as if there isn't any money on New Albion. We could have instituted a proper military expansion program a decade ago. Instead we throw it all at recreating Big Ben and the Thames."

"Roger, don't ever underestimate the power of symbolism." Pepper stood up and walked to the window, surveying the colony spread out below him. "Symbols are a standard for people to rally around. They are a shield to offer protection. Symbols shine like a beacon, giving hope and confidence to the people in even the darkest times." He turned to face the entire cabinet. "Symbols give hope and succor and comfort. In the shadow of a symbol, people will come together to fight a common enemy. In the light of a symbol, they will surrender their freedoms for the greater good, and when it comes to it, in the embrace of a symbol they will die for it, should that be required."

There was a smattering of applause, and the defense secretary sighed. "Symbols don't win wars, Maurice."

"Are you sure about that?" Pepper said. "King Arthur's Excalibur? Boudicca's chariot? HMS *Victory*? The Spitfire? HMS *Ark Royal*? Symbols do win wars, Roger. They do."

"And you have a symbol for New Albion that is going to win *this* war?" Roger countered. "Not a river or a clock tower?"

Pepper smiled. "That I do." He leaned forward to the table and pressed a button on the intercom. "Send him in."

The doors opened and in marched a tall man wearing a royal blue dress uniform with a wide white belt and a black-peaked cap, a red band around the white cover. He stood to attention and saluted the cabinet. Then when Pepper nodded to him he stood at ease, legs parted, hands clasped behind his back. He had a lined, chiseled face, one scar running from his right temple to his jaw.

"The Royal Marines," the defense secretary said, looking at Pepper. "What's this? You've already entered into some kind of negotiations with the Three World Empire? Why weren't we told?"

"Ladies and gentlemen, this is Captain Augustus Trent," Pepper said. "There is no negotiation. No surrender. No accord. Captain Trent—"

"I know that name," the defense secretary said, half standing.

Pepper smiled. "I should expect so. He is one of the most decorated officers of the Royal Marines, and a veteran of some of the bloodiest fighting in the past thirty years. He is the skipper of one of the most famous ships in the Three World Empire fleet." Pepper leaned on his fists on the table. "Or rather, that *was* in the Three World Empire fleet. Ladies and gentlemen, *God's Hammer* and her crew now fight for New Albion.

"And the best of bloody British to them."

18

It's like a foot-tall lizard, Cher thought. Or a fat worm. Pink and bloody like raw flesh, its tail wrapped around it like an umbilical cord. It swiveled its head and regarded them all, standing shocked and still around the ravaged corpse of Frank Priestley.

Then it opened its tiny mouth filled with pin-sharp teeth and screeched, suddenly skittering from Priestley's exploded chest cavity and across the makeshift table, scattering plates and cups, as everyone leapt backward and away from it.

The chestburster. She'd never expected to see it. Now she had, and she'd never forget it. A whine sounded close to her ear and the table shook, crockery flying as a shot slammed into it just where the thing had been only a second before.

"Kill it!" Chad shouted, taking aim again as the thing skidded off the table, Moran leaping away from its trajectory. "It's at its most vulnerable now! We can't let it get away!"

Bromley was the first to react, grabbing her pulse rifle and taking aim as the creature—*baby?* Cher thought crazily—skittered along the floor, heading toward one of the taped up ducts and then veering off to the right. Finally Moran got his shit together and pulled out his handgun, firing off a volley of pulse bursts, always just a second behind the careening horror.

Cher backed away, bumping into Merrilyn and turning quickly, grabbing her and Therese and pulling them away, toward the door. Chad saw her and yelled over his shoulder.

"Don't open those doors! We have to contain the thing!"

"We're getting it cornered," Moran said, he and Bromley letting loose pulse bursts and herding it toward the flat space beneath the window. "McClaren, take the fucking thing out."

The chestburster chattered and then dove forward. Cher realized what it was doing at the same time as Chad, as it headed directly for where one of the panels had been unscrewed from the central comms desk to cover up the vents. If it got into the innards of the comms hub they'd never find it.

"Got it in my sights," Chad said, taking aim. He squeezed the trigger just as a sudden, howling gale buffeted the comms tower.

All the lights went off.

Cher stood stock still, barely daring to breathe. It wasn't

completely black, the luminous storm clouds outside offering a faint, preternatural glow against which she could see the silhouettes of the others. She closed her eyes to blot it all out, and suddenly thought about her daddy, being told that he'd lost another daughter, and not knowing why. If there was anyone to ever tell him, of course.

She was going to die here on this distant planet, at the claws or teeth of a Xenomorph, and they might never find her or know who she was. Even if they did, her father would never know the truth. Two daughters killed because of a conspiracy of darkness surrounding the existence of something that everyone denied.

No. No, she would not die here. She had too much to do. Too important a job to finish. Cher opened her eyes— she would not look away. Too many people had done that already, and that was why Shy was dead.

Why Cher would live. To tell this story.

"Fuck. Fuck." Somebody turned on a flashlight, and then another. Chad shone his underneath the comms hub. "It's in there somewhere. We're not safe."

"I thought you said it wasn't dangerous," Moran said, shining his flashlight into the gap beneath the comms desk.

"It will be," Chad said. "In a matter of hours. It's down there somewhere, growing as we speak." He shook his head. "We're not going to last the night in here."

"Please," Merrilyn said, hugging Therese to her. "You're scaring my daughter!"

"I'm all right, Mama."

"She *should* be scared." Chad looked at them both. "It's the only way she's going to survive this."

Merrilyn had a flashlight in her bag, the *Victory* crew each had one, and Chad found two more, giving them one each—aside from Therese and, of course, Davis. He handed Cher a handgun.

"You ever used one of these before?"

"I'm American," she said.

"So, what are we going to do?" Moran said. "If we can't stay here, where are we going to go? With no power, we can't even get the schematics of the colony."

"I know the layout well enough," Merrilyn said. "We were safe in the canteen. Before you arrived."

"Far end of the complex," Moran said. "Two klicks. How many of these things are out there?"

"I found evidence of twenty-seven eggs on the wreck of the *Clara*," Chad said. "Assuming they've all implanted embryos…"

"Fuck," Bromley said. "That's an army."

"And if there's a queen, there could be more already," Chad said. "I think we can certainly say that there's a hive operating." They all looked at the dark shape of Priestley on the comms desk. Moran shone the flashlight on him for a second, then swung the beam away.

"Chad," Cher said. "He was acting weird, like… I don't know. Can these Xenomorphs, like, *mind-control* people?"

"Not that we know of, but people who spend time in a hive and survive… it changes them. I don't just mean becoming a host. I worked with a scientist… He spent time in a hive, and it messed with his head."

"It would," Moran said. "Poor Frank. God knows what he was put through in there." He shone his beam at the doors. "So, we're going to make a run for it? To the canteen?"

They all looked at each other in the dancing lights.

Cher felt sick. This seemed like suicide to her. Surely they should stay here, and try to kill that baby one. At least the comms room was secure. And they could call for help when the storm lifted.

"What about your ship?" she said.

"There's a goddamned monster in it," Moran said.

"Maybe we could kill it. Hide out in there."

"We can't take off yet, anyway," Chad said, going to the window. "And if they decided to attack *en masse*… we'd be sitting ducks in a very confined space."

"How do these things hunt, anyway?" Moran said. "Scent? Sight? Movement?"

"We don't know for sure," Chad said. "There's even a theory they can locate and zero in on human brainwaves, but it's far from proven, and I'm more than a little skeptical."

"Sounds like you don't really know shit about these things," Bromley said, checking her rifle for the umpteenth time. There was accusation in her voice. "They can die, that's all I really need to know. We should move out."

"Is that really…" Cher said. "I mean, all of us? Two kilometers of corridors? In the pitch black?"

"I'm inclined to agree with Cher," Chad said.

"You stay if you want," Moran said. He looked at Chad. "Like I said, McClaren. I'm a main character in this thing. I thought you were, too, but I guess there's only room for one in any story." He walked to the doors and his hand paused over the keypad. "Anybody wants to come with me, fall in now. Anybody wants to stay…" He shrugged. "I'll make sure you get a mention when I give my report."

Moran slammed his hand on to the keypad and the double doors whispered open. He shone his torch into the corridor and screamed as the Xenomorph barreled at him, its jaws clamping down on the forearm that he threw up to protect his face. Man and monster tumbled backward into the comms room, Moran's flashlight hitting the floor and spinning around, picking out the vicious attack like an ancient stroboscopic movie show.

It picked out something else as well. Cher gaped in horror as she glanced away from the Xenomorph and through the doors, into the corridor, shining her flashlight to reveal the darkness bubbling and boiling as though a black sea… a black sea that was a horde of Xenomorphs, advancing on them.

"Close the doors!" she screamed, running forward. Merrilyn blinked at her, then at Moran underneath the wiry attacker. She seemed to debate the wisdom of shutting themselves in with the creature.

"Now!" Cher screamed.

Merrilyn complied and hit the pad, and the doors hissed shut—but not before a long, bulbous head forced its way through the gap, screeching and baring its rows of cruel teeth.

"Chad!" Cher cried as the Xenomorph got its hands to either side of its slick head, and began to force the doors open. Chad looked at her, then at Moran, then at the alien leaning in.

"Fuck," he said.

There was a volley of pulse fire and the Xenomorph on top of Moran writhed and twisted as Bromley's rifle punched burst after burst into it. Chad aimed a shot at the alien in the doorway and hit it on its armored head, causing it to loosen its grip on the closing doors but not forcing it back far enough.

"Cher!" Merrilyn said. "In the mouth!"

She looked at the gun in her hand. She'd exaggerated her street smarts when Chad had asked her if she'd ever used a gun. She had, but only for shooting rats on the farm.

The Xenomorph began forcing the doors further open. She glanced around desperately. Moran was on his back, not moving. Chad and Bromley were emptying their pulse rifles into the twitching Xenomorph beside him.

It was up to her. Except she was frozen. She couldn't move a muscle. She was going to die here.

I'll go get Daddy, she remembered saying to Shy, stuck up the grain silo. *I'll go get someone else to help.* Just before Shy plunged to the ground. Now Cher was going to die here, and so was everyone else. Because she couldn't do anything.

"*Merde!*" Merrilyn said, leaving Therese cowering by the wall and running over, grabbing the gun from Cher's hands and stuffing it into the gaping jaws of the alien. She pumped the trigger several times and the Xenomorph was thrown backward. The doors slammed shut.

Cher sank to her haunches, back to the door, and began to sob uncontrollably.

"That sure is some powerful shit," Moran said, watching the acidic blood bubbling and burning through the floor underneath the corpse of the Xenomorph. He'd taken a nasty bite to his forearm and his face was slashed with claw marks, as was his chest. His jacket hung in tatters.

Once he'd been assured by Chad that he wasn't going to turn into a monster, that Xenomorph bites didn't work like that, he'd allowed Bromley to wash his wounds with alcohol and bandage him up. Moran looked over to where Cher was still sitting hunched against the door, hugging her knees.

"Hey, how many of those things did you say were out there?"

Cher said nothing.

Moran shouted, "Hey! I'm talking to you! How many Xenomorphs?"

"Leave her alone!" Merrilyn shouted back. "She's been through a lot."

"Duh." Moran held up his bandaged arm. "I was fucking wrestling with one of 'em. How many, Hunt?"

"I don't know." She looked up at him, eyes red and puffy from crying, mascara running down her face. "All of them. All the monsters."

"Great," Moran muttered. Just what he needed. A hysterical woman along with a kid and a dog. These were *not* the sort of people for this kind of movie. He squatted down by the dead Xenomorph. "Ugly fucking thing."

"So, what do we do now, guv?" Bromley paced up and down in front of the window. "We can't stay here. We got a dead alien and a dead Priestley and this place is starting to stink. Plus that little bugger growing up under the comms desk somewhere, and we can't go outside because there's a horde of the bastards waiting to rip our heads off. So, what do we *do*, guv?"

Moran wished he knew. He stood up and scratched his beard, then became aware that everyone was looking at him. Well, he supposed he was a natural leader.

"I wish the power was on. Then we could see the camera footage from outside, in case those things have gone."

"If they've gone, it won't be far," McClaren said. "Not now that they know we're in here."

"If only there was some other way out," Moran said. He looked at Bromley as a blast of wind rattled the big observation window. "Wait a minute," he said slowly, and he reached for his gun.

"You're fucking crazy!" Chad yelled over the howling wind that roared in through the big open space where the toughened glass of the observation window used to be. Moran had taken his gun and shot it out at the four corners. Its already weakened housings had given and the glass had blown inward, shattering all over the comms room floor.

Chad leaned over into the gale and looked down. It was fifty meters, at least. A smooth, metal surface with no handholds. Icy rain and winds like a battering ram.

"You got any better ideas, McClaren?" Moran shouted. "We get down there, we can get to the landing platform and into the colony buildings away from the Xenomorphs. Make our way to the canteen, or even to the garage and get some of those trucks Hambleton was talking about— just drive the fuck out of the storm."

Chad looked at Cher, then Merrilyn. The Frenchwoman shrugged. Cher gave him a wide-eyed stare and shook her head. He sighed. Much as he hated to admit it, Moran was right. There was no other way off the comms deck.

"How are we going to get down?"

Moran pulled his head back in and looked around the room. "We need to make some kind of rope. Like they used to do in the cartoons, right? Tie bedsheets together."

He pointed with his good arm. "We can start with those blankets that Priestley was sleeping on. Everybody, go through every cupboard and see what else there is in this place."

Chad thought for a moment that they should have done this *before* Moran shot out the window, but decided this was no time for regrets.

They all started to search the room, using their flashlights—all except for Cher, who just stood there in her own pool of darkness, numbly looking at the rest of them. Chad had seen this before. A form of trauma. The human mind could barely cope with the idea of the aliens, let alone seeing them up close. Let alone almost dying at their hands. In some ways, those who were killed by Xenomorphs were the lucky ones. The survivors… they were the ones who had to live with the knowledge of their existence. Who woke up screaming every night, drenched in sweat. Who jumped at every shadow and came to view the darkness with unholy, unbridled terror.

"Cher," he said, as gently as he could. "I get it. I honestly do, but you're going to have to pull yourself together. I know it's hard, but you have to do it. You have to survive."

"Survive," she said flatly. She looked at him. "We're all dead, Chad. We're already all dead."

"*Survive*," he said fiercely. "You have to. We have a job to do. We have to stop this happening to anyone else."

"The story," she said quietly. "I was going to write a story." She laughed, humorlessly. "Who's going to believe this?"

"They'll believe you, Cher," he said. "They will. That's why we need you. Do it for all those people, so they never have to see what you've seen." He paused. "Do it for your sister. Do it for Shy. She saw what you've seen. She didn't survive. You have to."

"For Shy," Cher said, then she shook her head, as though clearing it. When she looked at Chad again, whatever had been lacking in her eyes before seemed to be creeping back. "Yes. For Shy. And for everyone else. Come on. What do I have to do?"

As she went off to help in the search, Chad noticed Davis looking after her.

1 9

Between the blankets, several lengths of plastic ducting, and a coil of flexible steel cable, they'd managed to assemble a serviceable rope that, once secured to the main comms desk, fell only about two meters short of the distance between the tower and the landing platform—though it was difficult to estimate as the wind whipped it around.

Moran leaned forward through the window and looked down.

"I'll go first," he said. "I can probably hold it taut at the bottom so it's easier for everyone else."

"I'd have thought a leading man would have been wanting to go last, make sure everyone was safe," Chad said mildly.

Moran straightened and squared up with him. "Well, we're the biggest fellas here, so it'll have to be one of us first. Be my guest if you want to test the strength of the rope."

"Jesus fucking Christ," Cher said. "Can we all get

our dicks off the table and start getting ourselves out of here?"

Moran and Chad stared each other down for a moment, then the Brit shrugged and gave the rope a tug. He swung himself over the lip of the window. The wind buffeted him and the rain soaked him, and he gripped the length of cable with both hands.

"See you on the ground floor."

They all leaned over to watch his careful descent, feet against the slick surface of the tower, letting himself down gradually, hand over hand. It was a hell of a drop, Cher thought. The blankets seemed to stretch and tighten as he passed over them, the knots pulling at each other.

"I think we're going to have to go down one by one," Chad said. "I don't trust it to hold more than that at any one time."

Merrilyn held Therese close. "I am not going down without my daughter."

"I'm not sure if anyone has taken this into account," Davis said, "but I have a marked lack of fingers and opposable thumbs."

"I'll strap you to me." Chad found some strips of plastic that were left over, but too short to be used for the escape line. "Therese, do you think you could climb down that rope if your mama was right below you?"

The girl nodded bravely.

"I think we get as many people on the ground as we can before Merrilyn and Therese come down," he said.

"That way, if the worst happens... well, there's a chance of catching them." Merrilyn made a moaning sound. Bromley nodded and slung her rifle over her shoulder.

"I'll go next."

There was a tug on the makeshift rope and Cher looked over the edge. "Moran's down. He can barely grip the rope."

Bromley took hold and swung over the sill, then started to let herself down. Still at the window, she turned to Merrilyn.

"You sure you don't want to go next?"

"I am sure," the Frenchwoman said. "Chad is right. If the rope should break with Therese and I on it... at least you can catch her, or break her fall."

There was another sharp tug on the rope. Cher swallowed.

"I guess it's my turn." She looked over the edge. Moran and Bromley seemed so far below. The wind was howling around the comms tower, and when she took hold of the cable it slipped in her hands. She was just about to turn to say she couldn't do this, that there must be some other way, when she saw Therese's face.

"OK," she said, taking a deep breath. She held onto the lip of the window. How was she supposed to do this? Bromley and Moran had literally thrown themselves over as though it was just three meters off the ground—not nearer fifty.

Merrilyn put her hand on Cher's arm. "It's all right. One hand over the other. Brace yourself with your feet against the tower. The wind is fierce so it's going to throw you around a bit. Just keep tight hold. Don't look down."

Cher nodded and gripped the rope with both hands, then awkwardly and with little grace rolled herself over the edge, her feet swinging in space and her stomach flipping. She gave a little scream and hugged the cable to her chest, her feet scrabbling for purchase on the wet surface. Everything spun off its axis for a moment, then stabilized.

Chad and Merrilyn nodded to her, and Therese gave her a thumbs up. Slowly, Cher began to inch downward into the driving rain and gale-force winds.

"Doggo looks like a baba," Therese said with a little laugh as Chad wound strips of plastic around him, forming a kind of papoose on his chest to which Davis was strapped, facing outward.

"Not my most dignified moment, to be sure." the synthetic said.

"You go next," Merrilyn said. "Therese and I will bring up the rear."

"If you're sure—" Chad began. Then he stopped, and cocked his head. "What was that?"

They all went silent for a moment, and then there it was. Audible, even over the storm. A distinct thud noise. And again. Chad frowned and looked toward the doors. Was it coming from the corridor? Then there was a violent smack into them, and they shook.

"The Xenomorphs," he said. "They're trying to get in by force of numbers." There was another volley of thumps, and this time one of the doors buckled slightly, a dent appearing in the center. "I'm guessing the doors aren't military-grade hardware."

"We never expected them to have to hold off an army of monsters," Merrilyn said, grabbing Therese close.

"It would be prudent to let Merrilyn and Therese go down next," Davis suggested. "That way we can hold them off, if they get through."

Easy for you to say, Chad thought, but he nodded, getting out his gun. "Yes. Go. Now. No time to wait for Cher to get to the bottom. Merrilyn first, and Therese following." He squatted down in front of the girl. "This is just going to be like climbing rope in gym class, OK, Therese."

"OK," she said, "but I never climbed rope in gym class."

"It's fine," Merrilyn said. "Just do what I do, Little Flower."

She climbed over the edge, pausing to get used to the wind and rain, then took firm hold of the rope and started to let herself down. Chad lifted Therese, a little awkwardly with Davis on his chest, and hefted her over the sill facing him.

"Don't look down," he instructed her.

"Why?" Therese said, frowning. "Mama always said focus on what you want and you'll get there. I want to be on the ground. So I'll focus on that."

"Little Flower, just this once, listen to the man and not

Mama," Merrilyn said. "But just this once, OK? Now come on. Let's move."

Chad watched them making painfully slow progress down the rope in the raging storm, until he heard a volley of thuds and the sound of something metal rending and twisting.

As he stared at the door, Davis said to him, "Chad… we've got company."

You really want to take your daughter to a mining and drilling colony in the ass end of nowhere?

Won't she be bored, no other kids, nothing to do?

Isn't it a little… dangerous for a child, a place like that?

Merrilyn had heard it all, from friends and colleagues and well-meaning strangers, and she'd batted away every single objection. There was nothing to worry about on LV-187. Merrilyn would take care of her education. She'd make sure the girl wasn't bored.

She'd keep Therese safe.

Now, thirty meters up in a storm that lashed her with rain and rocked her with winds, her hands slipping on a length of cable, her feet struggling to maintain a grip on the walls of the comms tower, her daughter inching down the same way just a meter or two above her, she seriously wished she'd listened to them all.

You can do this, she told herself. *You have to do this. And you have to survive.* For Therese. *You cannot die and leave her alone in this place. Come on, Merrilyn. One hand in front of the other. One step, then another. You can do this.*

She moved as quickly as she could, urging the little girl to hurry. Another three meters. Then another. And another. Then she could risk looking down, seeing Moran holding the end of the cable, Bromley and Cher calling to her to hurry, to keep moving.

They were more than halfway now, moving in swift, smooth progress. Therese was being so brave. Merrilyn was so proud of her Little Flower. Not far to go, only the height of a house.

That's it, she thought. *Think of something else.* She envisaged a house, pretty, made of wood and brick, somewhere in the Loire Valley, nestled in the hillside, bathed in sunlight, a fragrant garden at the back and—

The rope jerked, and went slack, and Merrilyn lost her grip. Her feet scrabbled for traction but there was nothing to hold her up, and with a scream that was more for Therese than for her, she felt herself launched into the cold, dark wind.

"Company?" Chad said, turning with his flashlight to see what Davis had already spotted. Crawling out of the gap at the base of the comms desk was a Xenomorph. A small one, no bigger than the dog body Davis inhabited. Not fully formed, but emerging, inner jaw extending in Chad's flashlight.

"Priestley's chestburster," Chad said. He wondered if it had been attracted by the Xenomorphs still throwing themselves at the doors, if there was some link between the creatures that went beyond the normal human senses, some way of communicating.

The infant Xenomorph regarded them for a moment, as if weighing them up. Then it turned toward the window. The length of cable and blanket was still secured to the comms desk and the creature tilted its head on one side.

"Shit," Chad said. He lifted his handgun, taking aim at the thing's head. His shot was on target, slamming into the creature's head and throwing it backward in a gouting spray of acid blood. Its carapace wasn't yet full hardened, and the shot was fatal, but the damage was done. Chad heard a distant scream from Merrilyn, carried on the wind as acid caused the rope to break, and it snaked toward the window.

He dropped the gun and dove for it, grabbing it with both hands and feeling himself dragged along toward the opening. He twisted around, Davis heavy on his chest, and planted his feet against the wall under the window, the rope suddenly going taut.

"You did it," Davis said.

There was still tension in the rope, still weight on it. *Thank God.*

"Secure it to the comms desk again," Davis said.

Chad dragged it back with him, sweating under the effort. He wound it around the base of the desk, careful to avoid the bubbling acidic blood around the Xenomorph's corpse, then fell on to his back, breathing hard.

"I think it would be a good time for us to get out of here," Davis suggested.

"I'm inclined to agree."

Then the doors exploded inward.

Merrilyn fell, drenched by rain, tossed by the winds that didn't care what happened to her. Her eyes were fixed on Therese, hanging on the rope, her head buried in her arms. It couldn't come to this. Not after everything they had been through. This wasn't how the story ended. She wouldn't let it.

Blood pounded in her ears, drowning out the sounds of the storm and the noise of people shouting and screaming. It was as if she was listening to everything underwater—and then everything twanged back into place, like the flicking of an elastic band. The sound roared back into her, and she felt herself hit something soft and yielding that was definitely *not* the surface of the landing platform.

"Good catch, guv," she heard Bromley say.

"Best wicket keeper in my school," Moran gasped from underneath her. They were a tangle of limbs, and while the breath had been knocked out of them both and they'd both have bruises, if not fractures, Merrilyn was alive. He'd caught her.

Her relief lasted only a millisecond, and she hauled herself to her feet to where Cher was standing by the swaying rope, calling for Therese, still fifteen meters up.

"Little Flower!" Merrilyn yelled above the torrential rain pounding all around them. "Keep climbing, Baba! Keep coming down!"

From high above them, there was a sudden volley of pulse rifle shots. She turned to Bromley, who was helping Moran to his feet.

"This does not sound good at all," Moran said.

"Therese!" she shouted again, even more forcefully. Her daughter was frozen, head buried in her arms, dangling from the rope. "Come down at once, young lady! Now!"

"Oh my God," Bromley said behind her. "What is *that*?"

Chad had never seen so many adult Xenomorphs in one space. At last he understood what Weyland-Yutani was trying to do with their endless experimentation, their boundless desire to possess them, their relentless desire to weaponize them.

This was what an army of Xenomorphs would look like. This was what enemy combatants would be presented with—a cadre of killing machines, a death squadron, a phalanx of dark angels who would fight to the bitter end and who, even in defeat, could spray deadly acid blood on their enemies. Any fight where Xenomorph shock troops were deployed would be over before it had even begun.

"Magnificent, aren't they?" Davis said. "I mean, you have to admire them. In a way."

"I'd rather kill them," Chad said, raising his gun and letting off a volley of shots toward the first three of the creatures that hissed and screeched in the broken doorway.

"I suspect the feeling is very much mutual," Davis said as, *en masse*, the Xenomorphs launched themselves into the room.

2 0

Cher followed Bromley's outstretched hand to the dark square of the window, lit by sudden bursts of pulse fire. Illuminated by Chad's gunshots—he was still alive, thank God, but for how long?—there was a black shape, leaning over the sill. Then in a fluid movement it crawled over the edge.

It was joined by another. And another. More, until Cher counted six of them. Six Xenomorphs, clinging to the exterior of the comms tower like black beetles. They began to crawl downward, inexorably zeroing in on the tiny figure of Therese, still dangling from the rope.

"No," Merrilyn breathed beside her. "No no no." Then she raised her gun and took aim, letting loose a pulse blast at the first Xenomorph, her shot pinging off the wall just a foot from its crouched form. "NO!" she screamed. "Leave my daughter alone, you fucking bastards!"

Behind Cher, Bromley opened fire with her rifle as well, laying a line of fire between the advancing Xenomorphs and the terrified child, causing them to screech, even above the howling wind… and retreat a little.

"Therese!" Cher yelled. "Let go of the line, baby! Jump! We'll catch you!"

High up, Therese shook her head.

"Teesha," Moran said in a low, urgent whisper.

Bromley glanced over her shoulder. "Guv, what are you doing? Use your fucking gun."

"Teesha," he said again. "The Xenomorphs have breached the comms room."

"Duh, *yeah*. On account of they're crawling all over the outside of the fucking tower." She put her rifle to her shoulder and opened fire again, shouting, "Yessss!" as a Xenomorph squealed and fell from the height, plunging into the ravine beside the landing platform.

"That means the corridors will be clear," Moran said. "We could make a run for it. You and me. Get one of the trucks and get the hell out of here. Until the storm's cleared."

Bromley looked at him, dumbfounded. "You're really suggesting we leave them? When that kid's hanging up there?"

Moran couldn't meet her eyes.

She shook her head. "I thought you were the leading man of this movie, not the bad guy."

"I just thought—"

"Yeah, well, maybe stop thinking and start fucking shooting."

Bromley turned away from him and picked out another Xenomorph in the sights of her rifle.

"I'm going up there," Merrilyn said, tugging at the rope. "If she's not coming down."

"No," Moran said. "You can shoot. She can't." He nodded at Cher. "She's going up."

Another Xenomorph hit the landing platform, twitching but not quite dead. Moran ran over and emptied thirty seconds of pulse bursts into it until it was a smoking mess of black chitin, sinews, and acid blood.

"I... can't..." Cher said, refusing to meet Merrilyn's stare. High above, two more Xenomorphs crawled over the lip of the window, replacing those that had been brought down. Bromley paused from her shooting to glare at Cher.

"Why the hell not?"

"You got to come up, Cher," Shy hollered, her voice shaking. Cher watched her sister with interest. She'd never seen Shy look scared before. It was a new thing. She liked new things. So she said nothing and just stared up at her.

"Cher, I'm not screwing around! Just climb up the goddam ladder!"

"Why?" Cher said.

Shy seemed to do a little dance, her tippytoes scrabbling for purchase on the narrow ledge. She took a deep breath.

"Because I can't go any further and I can't go back unless you reach out and grab my hand and pull me round."

"I still don't know why you went up there, Shy?"

"Because I wanted to see if I could get all the way 'round the silo, dummy."

Cher thought about it. "But why, Shy?"

"Because it was there and I wanted to find out. Jesus, Cher, come on!"

Cher went to the foot of the ladder. She looked up.

"You want me to climb up there and hold out my hand and pull you back?"

"Yes, baby girl," Shy said. "Come on, you can do it."

Cher put a foot on the ladder and gripped it with both hands. "OK."

The first three or four rungs were fine. Then she started to get a tingling feeling in the soles of her feet. Her hands felt sweaty and slippery.

"I can't do it."

"Sure you can! Just a little further."

"I can't. I'll go get Daddy."

"There's no time, Cher! I can't hold on…"

"I let you down," Cher said quietly. Her breath was coming short and shallow. "I let you down." Her heart was beating ten to the dozen. "I let you down."

"We don't have time for this," Merrilyn snapped, and she grabbed the bottom of the rope, pulling it tight.

"I can't do it," Cher said.

She paused. She closed her eyes.

"I *can* do it."

Cher took the rope from Merrilyn's hands and pulled on it hard.

"I can do it," she said. "I will do it. I won't let you down again." Then she braced herself against the rain-slick wall, and began to haul herself upward.

"I guess this is goodbye, Chad," Davis said. "I know I never achieved my dream of becoming human, but I have known love, and I have known comradeship, and I am honored that I can call you my friend."

"Shut the fuck up, Scooby," Chad said through gritted teeth, pumping a volley of pulse bursts into the gaping jaws of a Xenomorph, throwing it backward into two more behind it. That made his kill tally three. At least eight had gone over the edge. There were another ten fighting their way into the comms room. "Neither of us is dying here today."

Chad set off running, as best he could, with Davis strapped to him like a baby. "Is this what makes you human, Chad?" the dog said. "The continual clinging to the belief you will survive, even in the face of unsurmountable odds and overwhelming evidence to the contrary?"

"No," Chad said, picking up speed as he barreled across the room, three Xenomorphs hissing and shrieking as they leapt after him, their claws cleaving the air he left in his wake. "*This* is what makes you human."

He launched himself into the air, his momentum and the added weight of Davis carrying him forward. "*Rank fucking stupidity!*" he bellowed as they both catapulted through the open window, fifty meters up in the raging storm.

Pulse fire bursting around her, Cher made it to where Therese hugged the rope, sodden with rain.

"Hey," she said.

Therese looked at her over an arm. "Hi, Cher."

"Your mama is worried about you."

Therese flinched as, just meters away, a Xenomorph howled and fell past them. Far below, Bromley cheered.

"You came to get me."

"Yeah. Your mama asked me to. She's busy killing monsters."

Therese thought about it as the wind whipped her hair, plastering it to her face.

"OK," she said.

Cher braced herself as Therese wrapped first one arm around her, then the other. She looked up. Xenomorphs were swarming toward them, driving their claws into the exterior of the tower, dragging themselves down, their heads glistening in the light from the pulse fire, drool falling from their teeth, mingling with the rain.

"Hold tight, Little Flower," Cher said. "That's what Mama calls you, right?"

Therese nodded. "I'm scared."

"Me too," Cher said, the child wrapped firmly around her. "But I'm not going to let you down." She said, "You ever been to an amusement park?"

"One near Paris," Therese said. "Before we came here. As a treat, but I was too little to go on the big rollercoasters."

"Well, you're a big girl now," Cher said. "Get set for the ride of your life, Therese." Then she pushed her feet against the tower, loosened her grip on the rope, and the pair of them started to slide down, screaming half in terror, half from the thrill.

"Little Flower!" Merrilyn said, hugging Therese. "Are you hurt?"

Cher had tightened her grip on the rope as they neared ground, burning her hands as she slowed their fall, and they landed in a wet heap at the bottom.

"I'm fine, Mama! *Wheeee!* That was a good ride! Can we do it again?"

"Can we save the family reunion for later?" Moran said through gritted teeth. "Let's fall back. Those things are still coming. They'll be at ground level in no time."

"There's something else coming as well," Bromley said, lowering her rifle and shielding her eyes against the rain as she peered up toward the window.

Chad made a grab for the rope, feeding it through his hand as they flew out into the storm. There were Xenomorphs clinging to the outside of the tower like black flies, crawling down to the landing platform where he could see the figures of the rest of them, apparently all safe.

For the moment.

Three meters out he gripped the rope tightly and started to swing back to the tower. His outstretched feet connected with the wall, hard, and he pushed off again, feeding the rope through his hands, rappelling out and down another few meters, past a pair of Xenomorphs that screeched and reached out for him.

"This is rather exhilarating," Davis said as Chad repeated the maneuver, again and again, gaining more and more distance and putting more and more space between him and Davis and the advancing aliens.

"Couple more and we'll—" he shouted, then there was a sound like snapping elastic bands and the rope gave, sending them out into space, everything spinning dizzily until he connected, hard and heavy with the rain-slick landing platform. He landed on his back.

"Looks like the gang's all here," Moran said, helping

him up and firing his gun. "Now we can decide what the hell we do next."

Chad ripped the plastic strips away, letting Davis fall to his feet. His body was bruised and battered and he suspected he'd fractured a rib or two, but he was alive. They all were. But as he looked up at the Xenomorphs, too many of them to count as they picked up speed, he wondered how long that would last.

"Fall back!" Moran shouted above the howling gale. "Everyone, back along the landing platform. We can't make it to the colony buildings now. We're going to have to regroup and rethink."

They all ran, past the *Victory* and its deadly occupant, and toward the crippled *Elvik*.

"In our ship?" Cher said. "It'll give us some protection."

Chad shook his head. "For a while, but we'll be sitting ducks. They'll tear it apart, eventually."

They cleared the parked ships and ran the length of the platform, until they ran out of places to go. The darkness of the ravine and mountains on which the colony was built reared up ahead of them, the force of the wind intensifying as they neared the open wilderness that stretched out for kilometers.

"End of the road, guys," Moran said, breathing heavily.

They all turned to face the buildings. The Xenomorphs had reached the platform, and were moving like a single mass of black, flowing toward them like a dark, shining river. A crack of thunder sounded, accompanied by a flash of sheet lightning that painted the advancing black tide with silver. Bromley dropped to one knee and took sight, opening fire at the advancing horde. Merrilyn pushed Therese behind her and began to pump the trigger of her pulse rifle.

"Give me a weapon," Cher demanded. She might not be able to hit a barn door at ten paces, but the law of averages meant she'd at least get one of the damn things if she fired in the right direction long enough.

Illuminated by the flashing bolts of the pulse rifles, the Xenomorphs dropped in ones and twos, but infrequently and not always permanently.

This is hopeless, Cher thought. They were going to be overwhelmed. There was nowhere to run and nothing they could do. She had wanted evidence of the Xenomorphs' existence, and she'd got it in spades. She just wished she'd been able to write the story before she died.

"It was all a waste of time," Moran said. "We might as well have just stayed in the comms room and died there."

"No!" Merrilyn cried fiercely, firing into the Xenomorphs. "Never say that! You have to try to live, or what's the point of being alive at all?"

"Mama?" Therese said. "Are we going to die now?"

The nearest creature was so close that Cher could see its needle-sharp teeth. She wondered what it would be like, to fall under those cruel jaws and slashing claws. Wondered how long it would take her to die.

"None of us are dying here today," Davis said suddenly.

Moran looked at him. "What have you got, Davis?"

"Rank fucking stupidity!" he announced, and launched himself, growling at the Xenomorph just feet away from them.

"Doggo!" Therese screamed as Davis's jaws clamped around the creature's forearm. The creature howled and snapped at the dog with its jaws, flinging its arm out and sending Davis, yelping, tumbling to one side.

This is it, thought Cher, bracing herself for the onslaught, for the carnage. *At least I didn't let anyone down.*

"Wait," Chad said. "What's that?"

There was a sound below the raging storm, and then suddenly above it. A protesting mechanical whine that was accompanied by a sudden hot wind. Not a natural gale, but one produced by a machine, laced with fuel and metal. Suddenly, the entire landing platform was bathed in blinding white light. The Xenomorphs screeched and howled and paused in their advance.

The whine became deafening and Cher turned, the hot air blasting her face as something rose from the darkness of the ravine. Blinking into the arc lights she could make out the indistinct but unmistakable shape of a dropship, rising up behind them.

2 1

They scattered as the dropship put its nose down and moved forward, hovering and rocking in the driving winds before settling on the landing pad with a whine of protesting engines.

The forward hatch opened and spewed five Colonial Marines in their distinctive body armor and helmets, two pairs of them each carrying a squat cannon which they swiftly set up on tripod stands. In the bright lights cast by the ship, the fifth marine gave a signal and the soldiers began to fire indiscriminately at the confused, milling Xenomorphs on the platform.

Not pulse bursts or bullets, Chad noted. The cannons fired tight parcels with hydraulic *whump* sounds which unfolded in the air into Kevlar netting weighted with metal balls. As the first two Xenomorphs became entangled in the nets and fell, writhing, he realized that the marines weren't here to kill the aliens.

They were here to capture them.

Another two Xenomorphs were hit by the Kevlar

netting, and one of the soldiers punched a hand-held box about the size of a radio, which activated a sparking, snaking lightshow of electrical pulses that sputtered over the captured creatures, causing them to screech and howl.

When a third pair of Xenomorphs fell, the rest of them began to back off. They would kill what threatened them, but they also would retreat if the battle was going badly, would regroup and find another way to continue the assault. The black shapes turned and ran—crouching, tails whipping—into the driving rain and back toward the comms tower.

The marine who had directed the quick operation pulled off his helmet, revealing a craggy, battle-worn face under a blond buzz-cut.

"Six piggies," he drawled in a Mid-West American accent. "Tag 'em, bag 'em, and let's roll out." As the marines started to drag the unconscious Xenomorphs into the dropship, Therese stepped forward from behind Merrilyn.

"Mr. Lollipop!"

The marine wiped rain from his face and glanced down at her. "Oh, hi, kid. You're still alive. Well done."

Chad looked at Merrilyn. "You know these guys?"

"They were here a week or so ago," Merrilyn said frostily, glaring at the soldier. "Except they said they were a trade mission."

"Yeah, sorry about that, ma'am." The marine smiled crookedly. "Means to an end."

"Where are you taking those Xenomorphs?" Chad demanded. "You can't just transport them off-world. You need to kill the rest of them. You can't leave."

The marine sighed. "Corporal Barrington B. Jones III of the United States Colonial Marine Corps," he said, "and I'm very much afraid I can do what I like."

"Actually, you can't, mate." Moran stepped forward. "This planet is under the jurisdiction of New Albion. You can't just waltz in here and…" He looked back to the darkened comms tower. "…and nick our bloody monsters."

Jones grinned. "Your pissant little colony with no military to speak of has already got the Three World Empire and the ICSC on its ass. But, sure, go ahead, declare war on the United Americas too, why don't you." He turned to his marines, standing by the lowered hatch. "OK, let's get off this rock."

Chad grabbed his arm. "You have to take us with you," he said, and the marine gave him a long, menacing look. "And you have to tell me where you're taking those Xenomorphs."

"Those bio-samples are the property of Weyland-Yutani," Jones said. Then he frowned. "Hey. Wait. I *know* you." Jones took out his pistol and pointed it straight at Chad's head. "Chad McClaren. I'm placing you under corporate arrest for crimes against Weyland-Yutani. Get in the ship."

"Whoa, Barry the Bastard." Moran interjected himself between them. "You're taking all of us."

"No, Limey, I'm not."

"For God's sake, man," Moran said. "Therese... the girl, she's a *child*... If you leave them here with those things, it's murder."

"No," Jones said, turning the pistol on Moran. "*This* is murder."

Then he shot him in the face.

Cher watched helplessly as the Cheyenne dropship rose up, engines screaming, and then turned, buffeting them with hot exhaust air. It headed out into the storm-lashed darkness. She looked back at Bromley and Merrilyn crouched by the corpse of Moran, blood pooling out from the wound in the back of his head where the marine had blown his brains out.

"I thought they were here to save us," she said numbly. "They killed Moran. They took Chad."

Bromley looked up at her, tears in her eyes mingling with the rain washing her face.

"Nobody's here to save us. Nobody's coming for us. We're on our own." She stood up, surveying the darkened colony buildings. "We need to get off here before those munters come back." Cher wasn't sure if she was talking about the Xenomorphs or the Colonial Marines. Bromley looked at Merrilyn. "You know this place, right?"

Merrilyn nodded. Bromley pointed to the doors at the far end of the platform. "Then let's get inside, and hope to fuck those things aren't waiting for us."

Merrilyn held tight onto Therese's right hand, and Cher took the child's left as they ran to the doors. Davis caught up to them, shaking off his limp.

"Hey, does it feel like the storm's slackening off a bit?" she said.

"Dawn's breaking, behind the clouds." Merrilyn looked up. "If the weather improves, it might mean communications are back up."

Bromley, holding up her rifle, peered through the open doors. There were dim striplights glowing weakly in the foyer that led to the corridors.

"All clear," she said. "We're getting a bit of juice back, as well."

"If we can get to a safe place, we might be able to patch into the colony mainframe," Davis said, shaking the rain off his fur as he padded through the doors. "We might not have to risk getting into the comms tower again to send out a signal." They all paused at the next set of doors.

"I'm sorry about Moran," Cher said.

Bromley shrugged. "He was a dick, at times." She looked at Cher. "He wanted to leave, you know. When Therese was trapped up the rope. Just him and me."

"But he didn't," Cher said. "That's got to count for something."

"Yeah," Bromley said, hefting up her pulse rifle and hitting the door control. "Even the slightest act of goodness means a lot in Hell."

* * *

"You're making a big mistake," Chad said, sitting in a chair on the Cheyenne's cramped troop deck, sipping a bottle of water one of the Colonial Marines had handed to him once they'd hustled him on board. "You can't deliver those things to Weyland-Yutani."

"That's precisely what we're going to do," Jones said, biting the end off a cigar and lighting it with a Zippo. "So I'd say we're making the exact opposite of a mistake."

"So you're not here on United Americas business?"

"Basically, the USCMC is a private military contractor these days, you know that. We follow the money, and Weyland-Yutani has lots of sweet, sweet money when it comes to Xenomorphs." The Cheyenne was buffeted and rocked by the winds, and the pilot kept it low over the mountainous terrain.

Chad looked out of the window. "You've got a cruiser in orbit? We're not going to dock?"

"Not until the storm's blown itself out," Jones said, taking a seat across from him and resting a pistol lightly on his knee. "We'll never make escape velocity, but we've got plenty of time. Unlike your friends."

"You've given them a death sentence," Chad said quietly. "There's a child with them."

"I know. Met her when we were here last. Cute little thing."

Chad shook his head. "You're one cold bastard."

The pilot put the Cheyenne, rocking and rolling in the

wind, down in what looked like a narrow valley between two high, jagged peaks.

"This'll do to sit out the storm," Jones said, puffing on his cigar and regarding Chad coolly. "I reckon we'll be on our way in a couple of hours. The Company's going to be awfully pleased to see you. Should be a nice, fat bonus in it for us. Good thing I keep up to date with all the briefing notes, right?"

"Lucky me," Chad said. He stroked his chin. "It was you, wasn't it? You planted the Ovomorphs on LV-187. You boarded the *Clara* and took them, crashed the ship on New Albion, and brought them here."

"All part of the service." Jones took his cigar out of his mouth and did a little theatrical bow.

"You sentenced an entire colony to death," Chad said, trying to keep his voice calm and level. "Why?"

"Just following orders."

"Where have I heard that one before?"

"We're soldiers, McClaren." Jones sneered at him. "We do as we're told. End of sentence. Weyland-Yutani wanted LV-187 to be their little petri dish, right? Dump a load of eggs here, infect the colonists, and then we take the Xenomorphs back for them to do all their little experiments on, see what kind of DNA shenanigans are going on inside those ugly bastards."

"You're putting yourself out of a job—you know that, don't you, Jones? Weyland-Yutani wants to make itself an army of these things. The sort of army that doesn't demand payment and bonuses." He leaned forward. "You know a lot about the Xenomorphs, Corporal. That's dangerous knowledge to have. Weyland-Yutani isn't going to want you running around with it. That's how they work. Your days are numbered."

Was there a moment of doubt in Jones's eyes? If there was, the marine blinked it away, and gave Chad a humorous look.

"If I was you, McClaren, I'd worry more about myself." He nodded to the closed doors of the cargo bay. "Who knows what Weyland-Yutani's scientists are planning for this bunch? Maybe you'll be part of their experiments, too. Nice future for you as a hybrid soldier, maybe?"

As the dropship's engines powered down, one of the marines lifted his head from the comms unit. "Sir, still no contact with the *Cronulla*. We'll have to wait until the storm clears a little more."

Jones shrugged. "In that case, put Mr. McClaren in the hold with our other guests. About time he got acquainted with his future. I'm going to grab myself a nap."

They moved slowly along the dim corridor, Bromley taking the lead with her rifle, Merrilyn and Therese following behind, and Cher, armed with a pistol, walking backward at the rear, scanning behind them for any sign of the Xenomorphs. Ahead, Davis padded along, sniffing at the still air.

"Where are we going?" Cher asked in a hissed whisper.

"The canteen," Merrilyn said quietly. "There's still some food and water there, and it's relatively secure."

"Maybe not against those things," Bromley said, sweeping her rifle from side to side, peering into the gloom. "Once we get supplies, I think we should get back to that garage where I found you two, and follow your original plan to get off the base."

"There's also Chad to think about," Davis called from the front. "Shouldn't we be trying to effect some kind of rescue?"

Bromley barked a laugh. "From a squadron of Colonial Marines, armed to the teeth and with zero compunction about killing? Forget McClaren, Davis. We're on our own."

Davis looked as if he was about to say something else when he stopped, sniffed, and bent down, growling. Bromley held up her hand for the others to stop.

"What is it?"

Cher turned to look, peering over Bromley's shoulder. There was a dark shape huddled in the corridor ahead, right in the center of the floor. Bromley lifted her rifle.

Suddenly, the lights above fizzed and sparked and shone a little brighter, revealing the shape to be a rotting, twisted Xenomorph corpse. Then they dimmed again.

"From the fighting when they first emerged," Merrilyn said. "We weren't completely helpless. We managed to defeat two of them, I think, but they overwhelmed us."

The group edged around the dead monster, Merrilyn directing them where to go in the warren of corridors. They passed a set of heavy-duty double steel doors marked with yellow and black radiation warning triangles.

"What's down there?" Cher said

"It leads down to the fusion reactor that powers the colony," Merrilyn said.

"Great," Bromley said. "So this place could go nuclear, as well?"

"Doubtful. Unless it has manual safety codes punched in every day, it goes into a standby mode. That's why we're on minimal power in the main colony buildings," Merrilyn said, then she gestured. "Take a left here."

A few minutes later Merrilyn signaled for them to stop. They had arrived at the canteen. Bromley led them in and swept through it, rifle up. Then she breathed a ragged sigh.

"It's clean. Let's get everything we can carry, and move out."

"Therese is exhausted," Merrilyn protested. "As am I. As are we all. Can we not rest for a while? It will be fully daylight soon and the storm is abating. The creatures seem to be less active in the day, and it will be easier to negotiate the landscape in a truck if we can see what we're actually doing."

Bromley made to say no, then shrugged. "We all had quite a night of it. Yeah, makes sense. Let's take a few hours, but we'll have to do shifts on watch."

"I'll take the first hour," Cher said. She didn't feel sleepy at all. She was jittery, in fact, as if she'd been mainlining coffee, or something stronger.

Bromley handed her the rifle. "Anything moves that isn't one of us, blow its arse off." Then Merrilyn led the others to the storerooms where she and Therese had been hiding out for a week, and where there were blankets and pillows.

Cher spent the first twenty minutes patrolling the canteen and kitchen, peering under units, cautiously flicking open cabinets with the rifle barrel. Then she got some water and a couple of protein bars, and began to relax a bit. There was a monitor on the canteen wall, and she fiddled with the controls, seeing if it could pick something up.

An image formed on the screen, and to Cher's surprise it was Therese. The date stamp placed it nine days ago. Security camera footage, she guessed. She sat back to watch, munching on the protein bar, smiling at Therese's rendition of an old song.

Then something came into focus that chilled her blood. An Ovomorph. The alien egg. She sat forward on her seat as Therese approached it, murmuring to it in French.

"Oh, no," Cher whispered. "Don't do it."

The egg seemed to pulsate and quiver as Therese leaned over it. Then it opened up like a flower, and Cher squinted, but was unable to tear her eyes away. This is what Chad and Davis had told her about. She gasped as the spidery, bony creature—the face-hugger—leapt out.

She watched for a while longer, not sure what she was exactly seeing, and then skipped back the video and watched it again from the beginning.

2 2

Chad McClaren just wanted to help people.

That was why he had spent seven years in college on Earth, then entered the field of biomedical research. That was why he took a position with Weyland-Yutani. That was why he had been thrilled to be given the chance to work with some of their most brilliant researchers.

That was why, after he'd seen what he'd seen on the Weyland-Yutani research station, he turned whistleblower, and put his own life at risk to try to blow the activities of his former employer wide open.

From a purely scientific point of view, the Xenomorph—just the existence of it—was something akin to the Holy Grail. Such a complex species, such a triumph of evolution, such a fascinating, terrible creature. And, yes, Davis had been right. Taking a pragmatic view of them, the monsters were magnificent. They were the apex predator, the top of the evolutionary tree, the very definition of survival of the fittest. If they had been able to think beyond their base instincts to survive, to propagate, to kill, then they could have ruled the universe.

Chad didn't hate the Xenomorphs, not really.

Not in the way people hated something they didn't understand, or feared without reason, just because it was different from them and what they knew. However, Chad hated what they had become—pawns in the very human quest for profit, control, and triumph over others. The more he had dealings with them, the less he thought of them as living things, and more as weapons. Weapons that were too dangerous for humanity to wield. Weapons that could not, *must* not, remain secret, hidden in the shadows, for any longer.

Those who would control the Xenomorphs, Weyland-Yutani chief among them, were playing God—that most unscientific of games. Were they playing the right sort of God, then perhaps Chad might have been more uneasily complicit in their dabbling. The Xenomorphs had so much to offer science—with their DNA appropriation methods, they could help human beings evolve to be more adaptable and durable. They could hold the secrets to curing illnesses, diseases, cancers... but Weyland-Yutani weren't playing the benign gods of medicine and goodwill.

They were playing at being the gods of war.

So Chad had run from them, and fought them, and made it his personal crusade to wipe out the Xenomorphs, to prevent them becoming the soldiers of the apocalypse, the agents of Armageddon, the army of Ragnarök, bringing to an end humanity's mastery among the stars. And yes, he'd become inured to the reality of them, immune to the primal terror they dragged from the depths of the human subconscious, numb to the sheer impossible horror of them.

Chad McClaren had forgotten just how *frightening* Xenomorphs were.

Until now.

Curled up like a fetus, he kept his eyes tightly closed and muttered to himself, hands over his ears, piss warming and spreading around his crotch. He wasn't sure what he was saying. Prayers, perhaps, or scientific formulae, something to ward off the terror.

The six Xenomorphs rendered unconscious by the Colonial Marines had been chained to the walls of the Cheyenne's cargo hold and, over the course of the last three hours they had slowly wakened, rattling their bonds with fury, spitting and drooling and reaching out with their claws, opening and closing their sets of jaws, hissing and screeching and howling.

Chad lay in the middle of them, rediscovering his fear over and over again every time one of the creatures strained at its chains and edged a centimeter closer. He should not have forgotten. Should have remembered how magnificent and terrible and impossible and deadly the Xenomorphs were. There, in the darkness, trapped with them, the weight of the last few days pressing heavily on him, he had been reminded starkly and quickly just what the Xenomorphs really were.

Fear incarnate.

Chad McClaren had just wanted to help people.

But who was going to help him?

Chad finally managed to sleep, fitfully and haunted by terrors; for how long he didn't know. When he woke, he was still in the near semidarkness with the six bound Xenomorphs rattling their chains like ancient ghosts, hissing and chattering and regarding him with unbridled hatred. They sat in judgement on him.

A parliament of monsters.

A jury of death.

Chad pushed himself to a sitting position, crossed his legs, and watched them watching him. "You could help me, you know," he said. "If I could unlock your secrets. How you adopt the characteristics of your hosts. How you appropriate their DNA. How you effect changes on a cellular level. You could help me. Help me to help… her."

He thought of Amanda, his wife, his partner in the never-ending war on Weyland-Yutani. Thought of her lying, on the very edge of the abyss, on the brink of death, the cancer ravaging her body but not quite claiming her. Amanda, frozen in hypersleep, neither dead nor alive, one foot over the threshold of whatever—if anything— lay beyond mortal existence.

"Help me," he said fiercely. The Xenomorphs rattled their chains and howled and spat. Chad shook his head. "You don't want to help me. You don't even know what that means. You can't help me."

He swiveled around to look at the ones behind him, showing him their teeth, their jaws dripping drool that pooled on the metal floor. One of them moved behind him, and his head snapped around, his eyes narrowed. Deep inside him, he knew something wasn't right, but he pushed the thought away. He felt on the brink of an epiphany. Connections were sparking and pinging in his brain.

He was on the verge of… understanding.

"You can't help yourselves," he said slowly. "You are not evil. You don't have the self-awareness for that. You are just doing what you do." He turned around again, to face the ones on the other wall. "And we are just doing what we do, as well. It's not hatred or malice that drives us. It's merely survival."

Unsteadily Chad got to his feet. The Xenomorphs lunged toward him, their bonds going taut, but holding. Their outstretched arms clawed at thin air. Chad held his arms wide, and slowly pivoted on his feet, his head thrown back, showing himself to each of the Xenomorphs in turn.

"Survival. That's all it is. Had we encountered each other thousands or millions of years ago, this might have gone differently. You might have wiped us out as we fought you with sticks and rocks, just as we wiped out the Neanderthals."

He stopped turning, addressing the largest, meanest of the creatures.

"But we didn't meet then. We meet now, when we have more than sticks to fight you with. We have science." Chad lowered his arms and looked down. "We are incompatible. We are toxic. We are oil and water. We can never mix, so one of us must die and, for all its faults, I believe in humanity. I believe that we can be a force for good, as we spread out among the stars. We can offer art and beauty and love and knowledge.

"You can only offer death."

His head whipped toward the door which had been locked behind him, beyond which sat the Colonial Marines. "We just have to be better, that's all. Better than we are, and we can only do that with you gone. It's you or us."

"Anything?" Corporal Barrington Jones leaned over the marine sitting at the comms unit, tapping cigar ash onto the floor beside him.

"I'm recording it, sir, but it's, well…" The grunt shook his head and pulled off the headphones. "It's just a bunch of bullshit."

Jones grunted and consulted his notes. "He mention anything about an Amanda—Ripley? or McClaren? A Zula Hendricks? What about a synthetic or AI, goes by the name Davis?"

"Sorry, sir," The marine shook his head. You can listen to the recording if you want."

"We give him too much shit in his water, or not enough?"

"Usual dose, sir."

Jones went to look out of the window. The rain had stopped. The clouds were clearing, revealing a hazy, purple sky. There was actually a threat of some sunshine out there.

"Looks like the storm's over," Jones said. "Get on to the *Cronulla*. Tell them to expect us soon." He looked at his watch. "We'll initiate departure at 0800. Gives us an hour."

Jones dropped the hatch and stepped down into the rocky ravine in which they'd seen out the storm. Hoping to up the bonus from having snared McClaren, he'd had one of the boys stick a dose of a psychotropic nerve agent in his water. Standard stuff. Usually had prisoners babbling all kinds of bullshit. Stripped of their filters, people often threw up the interesting stuff they wanted to stay hidden. The three he'd named were all on Weyland-Yutani's "most wanted" list. If McClaren could offer some clues to their whereabouts, well, that was information he could bank.

Intellectuals. Damn 'em all to hell. Jones unzipped his fatigues and took a piss against the rock face of the ravine. McClaren was spouting nonsense, though. Maybe he'd be more forthcoming under a little old-fashioned torture.

He remembered what that Limey had called him before he'd put a pulse blast in his face. *"Barry the Bastard."* Jones grinned. He liked that. He might adopt it on a more formal basis. Zipping up, he turned back to the dropship, glad to get off this ass-nugget of a planet.

Beyond the ravine, he could see the comms tower of the colony, just two klicks distant. He wondered if the rest of them had become Xenomorph chow. Three women, a kid, and a fucking dog! Who brought a mutt to a place like this? They wouldn't survive long with those critters on the prowl.

Had the Company asked for more samples, or told him to mop up the mess, he'd have happily done so. He liked a good bug hunt, but orders were orders. Six aliens, and screw the rest of them. Once the dropship was back on the *Cronulla* it wouldn't matter anyway. They had orders to nuke the colony from orbit, leave no trace of what had happened there. So it was six of one and half a dozen of the other.

The mess got cleaned up one way or another.

Jones squinted into the dropship, at a small, hunched shape just on the lip of the ramp.

"Hey, Segura!" he hollered, and the big Cuban popped his head around the hatch. Jones pointed downward and Segura looked, then frowned, then—nimble as a cat—he dove on it and stood up, holding the squirming white rodent by its neck.

"Sir! I got me an alien rat! Can I keep it as a pet?"

Jones strode up the ramp and inspected Segura's catch. "It's a goddam ordinary lab rat," he said. "Must have escaped from the colony and snuck on board while we were on the landing pad. Get rid of it."

"Aw, sir, can't I keep it? It's cute!"

Jones shook his head in disgust. "It's a good job I've seen you kill thirty men, Segura, or I'd begin to think you were a goddam wimp. Yeah, keep the fucking thing if you want. Find it a cage. I don't want it running around the ship."

"I'm gonna call it Barrington, after you, sir!"

"Flattered to fuck, Segura. Flattered to fuck." He ducked into the dropship and headed to the flight deck, where he found Marquez at the comms desk. "Any further instructions from the *Cronulla*?"

"Weird thing, sir." Marquez pulled off his headset and turned around, frowning. "Can't establish contact. I can't see why. The storm's cleared. There shouldn't be anything stopping us getting through."

"Weather knock our comms out? We didn't take a lightning hit, did we?"

"Comms seem fine." Marquez shook his head. "It's just... the *Cronulla* isn't responding."

"Keep trying," Jones said. He walked to the back of the ship, to the cargo hold. Maybe it was time to get McClaren out of there. They'd need to try another approach. Jones unlocked the door and pulled it open. The Xenomorphs rattled their chains and howled at him.

"Shut the fuck up, bugs," he said. "McClaren? You want to come out for a spell?" No answer. Jones put his head around the door. "McClaren?" He drew back and wrinkled his nose. "Phew-ee. You pissed yourself, McClaren." The Xenomorphs screeched and chattered.

Then he saw him, sitting cross-legged between them, hands loosely on his knees, head bowed, as though he was meditating. For a moment Jones thought he was dead. Fuck, that would take some explaining. He was just seeing his bonus flushing down the pan when McClaren raised his head.

"What did you give me?"

"Bit of nerve agent. Mild hallucinogen. Make your experience with the bugs a little more interesting."

"You're a dead man, you know that?" McClaren stood up and walked toward him, moving a little unsteadily.

"We're all dead men, eventually," Jones said, biting the end off another cigar. "Or is that more of a personal threat? Because you don't look to be in a position to making one, if you don't mind me saying."

McClaren glances back at the Xenomorphs.

"It's a war, Jones, and unless you're against them, you're with them. And if you're with them, you're going to die. Nobody dines with the devil and lives to tell the tale."

"You're still high as a fucking kite," Jones said. "Get out of there and go get cleaned up."

"Fucking hell!" There was a sudden shout from Marquez, and Jones turned to see him throwing off his headset and putting his hands to his ears.

"Soldier?" Jones said.

"I made contact with the *Cronulla*, sir. Briefly. It sounded like… chaos. And then…"

"And then?"

Marquez shook his head. "Like…" He glanced out of the window. "Oh, shit."

Jones followed his gaze, then ran outside to get a better look. Marquez and McClaren followed him, shielding their hands against the dim light, watching what he was watching high in the violet sky of LV-187. A fireball, burning through the atmosphere, brighter than the sun, and falling, slowly and inexorably, toward the planet's surface.

A fireball that Barrington Jones was pretty sure was all that was left of the USC *Cronulla*.

2 3

Augustus Trent stood on the bridge of HMS *God's Hammer* and appraised the ship filling the frigate's viewscreen. USC *Cronulla*, a Bougainville Class Attack Transport. An updated, more compact version of the old Conestoga frigate, the design on which his own ship was based.

It was three hundred meters from hammerhead bow to stern, compared to *God's Hammer*'s five hundred. The new model was meant to be more maneuverable. Lighter, and faster at sub-light speeds. The United States Colonial Marine Corps could keep it, Trent decided. He was happier with the heft and weight of the older model, was used to the old girl. There'd been talk of upgrading the entire Royal Marine fleet, but Trent couldn't see it happening any time soon.

Rubbing his hands together, he instructed the bosun to hail the *Cronulla*. It had been a long time since he'd had that tingling at the back of his neck, that fluttering in his chest, that stirring in his loins. Like *God's Hammer*, Augustus

Trent was built for war. Far too much time had passed since either of them had served their purpose properly.

The bosun turned to him. "Captain Trent, sir, channel opened with the *Cronulla*. Do you wish to begin comms?"

"Aye, bosun," Trent said, and he nodded. Let the dog see the rabbit, as his old grandad used to say.

Trent straightened up and waited for the connection with the warship to fizz into life. The picture was staticky around the edges, but showed the *Cronulla*'s skipper well enough: a broad African American, name of Weems. Trent knew him, of course—all the frigate captains from the various factions knew each other personally, or at least by reputation.

"Well, well, well, Augustus Trent," Weems said, smiling broadly. "I thought I'd heard tell you'd retired, or maybe that they'd given you a cruise liner to captain."

Trent smiled thinly. He wouldn't let Weems' needling affect him, at least not outwardly. There had been a Trent at Trafalgar, at Goose Green in the Falklands, at the battle of Panama, at Australia. He felt the weight of all their ghosts on his shoulder, shaking their heads at the way the Royal Marines had been emasculated by the Three World Empire and their aversion to committing to any conflict.

That was why he had thrown the lot of *God's Hammer* with New Albion. Had the 3WE instructed him to attack New Albion for its secession, he would have been happy to do so. But they hadn't. So after discussion with his crew, Trent had put their money on a horse that might not necessarily win, but would give them the opportunity for a good scrap.

"No, George, still here," he said with a smile, "on the bridge of the finest frigate in the Weyland Isles."

"I suppose even a toothless bulldog is still of use to somebody," Weems said with a shrug. Trent bristled, but didn't rise to it. Weems continued, "So what brings you out here, Augustus?"

"Just doing our duty, George. You appear to have accidentally found yourself in the airspace of LV-187, which I'm sure you've heard is now under the jurisdiction of New Albion."

Weems sat back in his chair. "And the Three World Empire has sent you to… what? Slap down the handful of New Albion traders who've flown a flag down there? I suppose it's less worrisome than taking on New Albion itself."

"You've got it all wrong, George," Trent said pleasantly. "*God's Hammer* doesn't serve the Three World Empire any longer. She's in the service of New Albion, and we are here to respectfully ask you to depart the airspace of LV-187."

"Are you serious?" Weems leaned forward, his eyes narrowed. "You've deserted?"

"Switched allegiance, I prefer." Trent waited a beat, and said, "You here on United Americas business? What's their interest in this?"

"We're more of a…" Weems said slowly, "research expedition."

"For Weyland-Yutani, then."

"I'm not at liberty to say."

Trent considered this. If Weyland-Yutani had an interest in LV-187, what was down there? Everyone knew they were ramping up their bioweapon research. Black goo? he wondered. But they were a long way from where the border bombings were supposed to be happening.

"Have you got a landing party down there?"

"One Cheyenne," Weems said. He seemed to be weighing up what Trent had just told him. "We dropped them in the middle of a storm. Not even sure they made it in one piece, since all comms were down, but we're expecting them back in the next few hours, if the conditions improve."

Trent ran his thumb along the scar on his face, as he always did when he was thinking.

"Captain Weems," he said, adopting a more formal tone, "I am going to do you the courtesy of giving you one hour to vacate New Albion airspace and depart peacefully. After that I'm afraid I cannot guarantee the safety of you and your crew."

Weems frowned. "I just told you, Augustus. I've got a party down there. They couldn't make it back up here in an hour, even if I was going to take your threats seriously."

"They are trespassing on New Albion territory, in contravention of a no-fly order that covers all the colony's extended airspace. They'll be apprehended and treated with the full courtesies. One hour, George."

"Jesus Christ, Augustus," Weems said. "Are you serious?"

"Blasphemy won't help your cause now, Captain Weems." Trent's eyes narrowed. "I suggest instead you make your peace with God." He nodded at the bosun, who killed the connection.

Pastor Donald led the crew in a rousing rendition of "I Vow To Thee My Country," then read to them from Jeremiah 31.

"The days are surely coming, says the Lord, when I will make a new covenant with the house of Israel and the house of Judah." Captain Trent had handpicked every man and woman who served on *God's Hammer*, and only those with the staunchest church values passed muster.

"It will not be like the covenant I made with their ancestors when I took them by the hand to lead them out of the land of Egypt—a covenant that they broke, though I was their husband, says the Lord."

If a man did not follow God blindly and unquestioningly, how could he be expected to follow orders? That was Trent's reasoning. Show him a man who had devoted his life to God, and he would give you a man who would die for his country.

"But this is the covenant that I will make with the house of Israel after those days, says the Lord: I will put my law within them, and I will be their God, and they shall be my people," the pastor continued. "No longer shall they teach one another, or say to each other, 'Know the Lord,' for they shall all know me, from the least of them to the greatest, says the Lord; for I will forgive their iniquity, and remember their sin no more. Amen."

"Amen," the crew said in unison, gathered on the bridge. Trent stepped forward to address them.

"We do not hate our enemy, we respect him," Trent said loudly, eyeing each of his crew in turn, "but we know that he has wandered from the true path. They have been seduced by Mammon and by Satan and by a host of devils who present to them riches and show them false masters to serve."

Trent paced a little. "Just as God did with the Israelites, we shall forgive their iniquity, and we will remember their sins no more. Instead we shall sing a lament for them and guide their souls to heaven." He stopped and looked at the large monitor on which the USC *Cronulla* floated in space, framed by the grey globe of LV-187. "When *God's Hammer* strikes, Heaven itself trembles in anticipation. Let us strike, brethren. Let us strike at last, after far too long in abeyance. No longer on the sidelines or in the shadows." Trent walked to the monitor and stood before it, silhouetted against the image of the *Cronulla*. "Let the fires of Heaven rain down on those who would defy us."

A huge cheer rose up from the crew and they scattered to their stations, as Trent turned and beheld his enemy, and touched the peak of his cap out of respect.

* * *

The newer Bougainville class transports such as the *Cronulla* had, in Trent's opinion, sacrificed one major specification that he would not have lost from his ship for any amount of maneuverability or quicker acceleration to faster-than-light velocity. A double-length cargo hold. In the case of *God's Hammer*, that had been converted into a secondary flight-deck—but not for dropships.

This was for Angels. They were called *Uriel*, *Raguel*, *Sariel*, and *Remiel*, and they were highly modified Alphatec EVAC-3 Series fighters, flown by the best and most fearless pilots under Trent's command.

The aft deck doors opened and, one by one, the EVACs roared out, glinting silver in the starlight and executing tight turns to fly over *God's Hammer* in their traditional 1-2-1 formation. Draw a line from front-to-back and side-to-side between them, he knew, and you would have a crucifix, shining with divine, pure fire. Trent always felt almost envious of his enemies, to be on the receiving end of his Angels bearing down upon them.

What a sight it must be to behold.

He stood, hands folded loosely behind his back, watching on the monitor as the Angels flew into view, the *Cronulla* in their sights.

Trent knew full well the *Cronulla*'s firepower capabilities. Thus, as soon as the Angels were in range they would employ the laser array on the medium railgun turret. The ship was also armed with Short Lance missiles, but only eight of them—unless Weems had seen fit to put more in the cargo hold. It rather depended on what he was expecting to pick up on LV-187.

Of course, like all vessels of its class, the Cronulla was carrying ten tactical nukes. One of them could take out *God's Hammer*, but that was what the Angels were for. To harry the enemy, draw its fire, exhaust its armaments, and make sure that in the unlikely event that nukes were deployed, they could be destroyed before they reached their target.

As soon as they were within range, *Raguel* and *Sariel* peeled off from the formation, describing wide arcs and zeroing in on the *Cronulla* from port and starboard. *Uriel* and *Remiel* shifted to fly straight for the ship, one above the other. There was a moment's hesitation, and then the laser array on the stern of the enemy ship burst into life.

Trent smiled. It had begun.

His ideal resolution would be for the *Cronulla* to hail them and offer their surrender. He had no real desire to see Weems dead, nor any of his eight crew and, potentially, the forty troops the ship had capacity to carry. Though if this was a Weyland-Yutani mission rather than a United Americas one, it was possible the Colonial Marine contingent was not at full power.

He knew Weems of old, though, and doubted he would wave the white flag. The man would believe in the superiority of the Bougainville over the Conestoga, purely because it was new. Trent was more traditional, and believed that if something wasn't broken, there was no need to fix it. *God's Hammer* certainly wasn't broken. Rather, it was the one that did the breaking.

Trent thought it was about time for Weems to deploy his Short Lances, and right on cue one fired from the turret, locked onto *Uriel*'s tail. But *Uriel* was too nimble and the pilot too experienced. He executed a complicated, twisting, Möbius strip of a maneuver that had the entire bridge cheering in admiration and the Short Lance missile flummoxed, its onboard computer momentarily dizzy enough for *Sariel* to blow it out of the sky.

Weems's gunners finally started to get their shit together, as they coordinated the laser array with more Short Lance deployments. *Remiel* narrowly avoided taking a hit that would have blown the EVAC to smithereens, and the crew on *God's Hammer* held its collective breath. Trent's lieutenant tapped him on the shoulder and told him that they were in range. Their own Short Lances were trained on the *Cronulla* and ready to fire.

The Angels adopted their crucifix formation again and barreled toward the *Cronulla*, the two wing-ships laying down covering fire while the central two let loose their own short-range missiles. Moments later, they arced up and away from the frigate as their bombs hit home in the gunner turret. The laser array was down. The Angels pulled back and settled into a holding pattern between *God's Hammer* and the *Cronulla*.

"Get me Captain Weems," Trent said.

The Weems who appeared on the screen wasn't the wryly smiling man of earlier. He was sweating and harassed and glared at Trent with unbridled fury.

"You won't get away with this, Augustus! This is a *crime*, do you hear me? A crime. They'll hang you out to dry."

"It is not a crime," Trent said. "It is an act of war, and believe me, George, there is going to be more of this. The colonies are a tinder box and the flame is being touched to the fuse all across the galaxy. This is just the opening salvo. The first battle in a long, long war to come." He paused. "You can live to fight another day if you depart now."

Weems bit his lip and looked off camera, presumably to his subordinates, then turned back to Trent, steel in his eyes. Trent admired that. He would have lost a lot of respect for George Weems had he turned tail and run.

"We're going nowhere, Captain Trent."

"Then may God have mercy on your souls, Captain Weems. We shall say a prayer for you and your crew." Weems looked about to say something, but apparently decided against it, and gave Trent a salute.

"There'll be hell to pay for this, Augustus."

"*God's Hammer* is more than a match for every demon there, George," Trent said, then he signaled for the feed to be killed. "Lieutenant Mackenzie!" he called. "Fire when ready."

"Yes, sir, Captain Trent!" Mackenzie replied.

Trent watched as the monitor showed the *Cronulla* again, and then moments later four of *God's Hammer*'s Short Lances powering toward it. He waited until they hit, and his face was momentarily painted orange by the brief explosion on the screen. Then he closed his eyes as the crippled *Cronulla* listed and began to fall toward LV-187, flaring into fire as the oxygen in the upper atmosphere fed the conflagration on the ship.

Just as he'd promised, he said a prayer for his fallen enemies.

24

"What are we seeing here?" Cher said. She stood with Merrilyn, Therese, Bromley, and Davis at the observation window, watching the bright light's stately progress through the sky.

"I think," Davis said slowly, "that is a spaceship. Or rather, was."

Merrilyn let loose a strangled sob. "A rescue ship? But what's happened to it? Why is it burning? An accident?"

"It may be the ship the Colonial Marines came down from," Bromley said. "In which case, the bastards are trapped here as much as we are."

"Unless they managed to take off when the storm cleared," Davis said quietly. "In which case they are on it. As is Chad." He paused, and looked down at the floor. "Or rather, they were."

"That dropship wouldn't have had the power to achieve escape velocity even at the tail end of the storm," Bromley said. "Especially with a full crew and a hold full of Xenomorphs."

"I hope you're right," Davis said. "For Chad's sake."

Cher took a step back and looked covertly at Therese and Merrilyn. She hadn't mentioned to anyone what she'd seen on that security footage. She wasn't quite sure what she should say, or even if she understood what she had seen. She needed to get Merrilyn on her own to talk about it, but now wasn't the time.

"OK," Bromley said. "We need to move out."

"We're still getting off the colony base?" Merrilyn said.

"It's the wisest course of action. Somebody is going to come eventually, and our best chance of survival is out there, not here with the Xenomorphs."

"How far is the garage?" Cher said. She didn't really relish the idea of going into the corridors again. She wasn't sure how secure the canteen was, but they'd all managed to grab a couple of hours sleep, and she felt reasonably safe here.

"Maybe ten minutes if we move quickly, fifteen at the most," Merrilyn said. She squatted down and looked at Therese. "We're going to go for a ride in the trucks, Little Flower. Won't that be fun?"

"Will there be monsters like last time?" Therese said doubtfully. "I didn't like the monsters. Or the dead lady."

Cher's heart broke for her a little. She had seen so much this past week or so. How were you supposed to answer a question like the one she'd just asked? Not for the first time, Cher marveled at the resilience of parents in general, and Merrilyn in particular. It was bad enough fearing for your own life, but to have to worry about your child, as well.

That is, if—

"I'm not going to lie to you, Baba," Merrilyn said softly. "There may be monsters, but that is why we are leaving the base. So we are far away from them. We just need to get to the trucks safely and quickly, which means you have to do exactly what Mama and the other grown-ups tell you to at all times, OK?"

Therese nodded and held her soft toy—her Pinky Ponk—tightly. Cher looked out of the window again, at the rapidly clearing clouds and the violet sky they revealed.

"That ship, whatever it is, is disappearing over the horizon."

"Good," Davis said. "If it is a warship, it'll probably be fitted with nuclear warheads. The last thing we would want would be for it to come down anywhere near here."

Bromley laughed, but without humor. "That's exactly what this place needs, to be honest. Nuking out of existence. When we get off here, we need to tell people. About the Xenomorphs. Make sure nobody ever comes back."

"That's why I'm here," Cher said quietly. "To tell people about this." She smiled, just as humorlessly as Bromley had laughed. "You know, before I came here, I didn't actually believe."

"You should always believe in monsters," Therese said to her with a serious face. "How can you fight them if you don't?"

* * *

They spent the next hour packing as much food and water as they could carry and stripping the canteen and kitchens of anything that might be used as a makeshift weapon. As Bromley stuck knives into her belt, she turned to Cher.

"So you're a journalist, right? Still think the pen is mightier than the sword, when it comes to these things?"

"Eventually, I hope so," Cher said, weighing up a meat tenderizing hammer. "Once I get back to Earth, I can tell everyone about the Xenomorphs. Blow this thing wide open, so this never has to happen again." She looked at Bromley. "What about you? Will you go back to Earth? Or New Albion?"

Bromley sighed and sat down on a stool.

"You know, when my mum and dad first brought me and my sister out to New Albion ten years ago, I hated it. I was sixteen, and I'd left behind my friends and everybody on Earth. New Albion felt so small and insignificant and a trillion light years from anyone and anything." She paused and munched on a protein bar. "Then I started to think it wasn't so bad. It was nice to get away from all the politics on Earth, all the crap. After I finished school and started work, it felt like a new start, which was just what my mum and dad wanted." She looked at Cher.

"But the older I got, the more I realized it's just the same shit, different planet. I mean, fuck's sake, Cher, it's the twenty-second century, and I still feel like having black skin and a uterus puts me further down the pecking order than anybody else. Wasn't this shit supposed to be all over by now? Only fucking true equality I've seen is from the goddamn Xenomorphs. They hate everybody equally."

Cher took a swig of water and Bromley chewed thoughtfully on her protein bar, then smiled wryly. "At least I survived, huh? Last of the *Victory*. I suppose that counts for something."

"You know," Cher said, "when I find Chad, you could maybe come with us." Davis padded into the kitchen and sat down beside them. "We could probably use someone as handy with a pulse rifle as you."

"Travelling the universe, fighting monsters," Bromley mused. "Yeah, I suppose that could be fun." She slid off the stool and hefted the big pack she'd been filling with water and food onto her back. "Get this show on the road, then?"

They gathered by the doors, Bromley holding her rifle, Cher and Merrilyn armed with handguns. Merrilyn had given Therese a big carving knife to hold. "Don't touch the blade, Little Flower, but you know what to do with it if you need to."

Therese nodded solemnly.

"OK, everyone stand back a bit," Bromley said. "I'm going to check out the corridor." She opened the door a crack and peered through, then pulled it a little wider, so she could just get her head through it to look up and down the hallway outside. She pulled back in and closed the door. "Clear, far as I can tell. Which way, Merrilyn?"

"To the right out of here, then straight to a cross-junction. Right again, and then second left. The garage is straight on through a set of double doors."

Bromley nodded. "Everyone got that, just in case we get split up for some reason? Merrilyn, say it again."

When they'd all repeated it back to Bromley's satisfaction, she opened the door a crack again, repeated her surveillance, then opened it wide. For the first time, Cher thought they might actually get out of this alive, if they could just get through the next ten or fifteen minutes. Bromley stepped out and surveyed the corridor left to right, and back again. She turned to the others.

"OK, follow me. Same formation as last time. Davis up front, then me, then Merrilyn and Therese, and Cher holding the back."

"Eww," Therese said. "Gloop."

Cher saw it at the same time, a string of thick, ropy, clear liquid falling from above on to Bromley's shoulder.

"Oh, no," she breathed.

The black shape fell like a spider, arms and legs seizing Bromley and wrestling her to the floor with a screeching howl. Bromley didn't even have time to scream as it enfolded her in its limbs—almost tenderly, thought Cher crazily, like a lover—and then clamped its jaws around her head.

"Shut the fucking door!" Merrilyn screamed, hauling herself forward and throwing her weight against the door. But the Xenomorph savaging Bromley was half in the doorway, and it hissed as the door it hit.

"We should help her," Cher breathed.

"It's too late for her!" Merrilyn screamed. "Help *me*!"

One second later Cher forced herself into action, slamming her shoulder against the door as the Xenomorph, its jaws and teeth slick with Bromley's blood and flesh, interposed its head between the door and frame, chittering at them, its clawed hand trying to get purchase.

"It's too strong," Cher said through gritted teeth, feeling her feet sliding on the tiled door as the creature pushed against them, its head moving further into the room.

"I don't wish to be the bearer of unwelcome news, but there's another one behind it," Davis said, peering through the gap between the creature's legs. "No, two more."

The clawed hand reached further around the door, swiping at Cher's arm. She fumbled for her gun with her free hand, but it fell from her grasp and skittered across the floor.

"Merrilyn!" she gasped, skidding back another inch. "Pass me your pistol…"

But Merrilyn moaned and from the corner of her eye Cher saw what she'd seen; Therese calmly walking to the door, standing behind Davis. The Xenomorph redoubled its efforts, the sight of the child seemingly ramping its bloodlust off the scale.

"Little Flower…" Cher said desperately, then she saw what Therese was holding.

"Leave my mama and my friend alone!" Therese said with a trembling voice, then she pointed Cher's gun at the Xenomorph's head with both tiny hands, pumping the trigger.

Her shots were wild and the recoil knocked Therese off her feet, but it was enough. The Xenomorph screeched and though not dead, was injured enough to drop back, allowing Merrilyn and Cher to slam the door closed and slide the bolts. Cher sank to the floor, breathless and exhausted, as Merrilyn ran to hug Therese, carefully taking the gun from her.

"Excellent shot, Little Flower! You saved Mama and Cher!"

"Can I have a gun now?" Therese said, pouting. "I'm really good at killing monsters."

I hope so, Cher thought, without voicing her terror. *Because there are at least three of them out there, maybe more. And we're trapped here now.*

"I can't believe Bromley's dead," Cher said numbly, sitting at one of the canteen tables.

"Everybody dies, where these things are concerned," Merrilyn spat. "Haven't you realized that yet?"

"Mama…" Therese said.

"I'm sorry, Little Flower," Merrilyn said, giving her a hug. "Mama is just a little… stressed."

"Is there no other way out of here?" Davis said, sitting upright on one of the plastic chairs.

Merrilyn shook her head. "No. We're trapped here."

"We need that pulse rifle," Cher said suddenly. She looked at her handgun. "These things run off charges, right? I've got no idea how many shots are left in it, have you?"

"Show me the butt," Davis said. She did and he peered at a little LED readout, and said, "Not many."

"Then we definitely need that rifle."

Cher crouched on the floor near the door, Merrilyn standing above and behind her, the pistol trained on the crack between door and frame. They'd already slid the bolts back and Therese was poised, her hand on the handle, waiting for the signal.

"I wish I could do something useful," Davis said.

"Just bark or something," Cher said.

Merrilyn counted down from five then said, "Now!"

Therese pulled the door open and Merrilyn pointed the gun as Cher's hand snaked out, gripping the barrel of the rifle under Bromley's bloodied, savaged corpse. Above her head, Cher felt Merrilyn let loose a stream of pulse bursts, and she glanced up to see four Xenomorphs bearing down on her from the left. She screamed and dragged the gun inside, as Merrilyn put her shoulder against the door and slammed it shut, just as one of the creatures slammed into it with a *thud*.

"Fuck!" Cher said, hefting up the rifle. "Did you get any of them?"

"I hit one, but I don't know if it went down," Merrilyn

said. She turned to her daughter. "Good work, Therese."

"Are we still going back to the trucks?" Therese said.

"Mama's just thinking about it," Merrilyn said, glancing at Cher. "The grown-ups are going to decide what to do."

"I think I should decide what to do, as well," Therese said. "I can shoot monsters, Mama, remember."

Yes you can, Cher thought, remembering again what she'd seen on the security camera footage. But was the bravery of a child—even a child as remarkable as Therese—going to be enough? Cher couldn't shake the image of Bromley's ravaged body outside in the corridor. Of all the deaths in the past forty-eight hours, that seemed to have affected her more than anything. It was almost as though because Bromley had opened up to her, given a little of herself, it had marked her down to die in this place.

"Teesha," she said quietly. "Your name was Teesha, and you wanted a better life. That's all." She looked at Merrilyn, and Therese, and Davis. Then at her own faint reflection in the observation window. Who was going to be next? And when?

She didn't register it at first, until she noticed Merrilyn frowning and looking up, and Davis emitting a low growl. Then she heard it again: a scratchy scrabbling coming from above her. Her eyes were drawn up to the ceiling, suspended polystyrene tiles, she assumed, a space filled with ducting and electronics. And something else. The tiles bowed just above them, and before Cher could reach for her gun, they exploded down.

2 5

"Somebody killed Barrington!" Segura boomed, the big Cuban marine appearing at the hatch of the dropship.

"What the fuck are you talking about?" Corporal Barrington Jones III paused from shielding his eyes to watch the high passage of the burning *Cronulla*, and peered at him incredulously.

"My pet rat! Somebody ripped him apart!"

"Jesus H. Christ, we ain't got time for this, you lunkhead," Marquez muttered. "Don't you know what's going on?"

What was going on, as far as Chad could surmise, was that the USC *Cronulla*, which had brought Jones and his team here and had been waiting in high orbit for them to return with their captured Xenomorphs was, abruptly, no more. Which presented a problem for the Colonial Marines.

"We're not getting off here," Jones said dourly. "Even if we make escape velocity, the Cheyenne's not built for deep space travel." He glanced back across the ridge toward the colony base. "Fuck. We're going to have to go back and access that comms tower, get a mayday out."

There were four marines on the Cheyenne aside from Jones. Did they have enough firepower to fight their way into the tower? Colonial Marines were tough and headstrong, yet they seldom came off well against Xenomorphs. Chad didn't relish going back into that tower after it had taken them so long to escape. He wondered how the others were doing. He hoped to God they'd made it to the canteen, and were safe.

"Question is, who blew up your ship?" Chad said. "And are they on their way down here to finish the job with you?"

Jones narrowed his eyes. "McClaren's got a point. I think we need to get the message sent ASAP." He turned to talk to Marquez, and Chad began to quietly sidle away from them. He wasn't going back in that hold with those Xenomorphs. As the other two marines emerged from the Cheyenne and Jones started barking orders at them, Chad seized his chance. He figured he was no good dead to them, so they'd probably not start shooting. Eyeing a narrow natural path that afforded a decent chance at climbing the ravine over some patches of loose shale, he put his head down and set off at a run.

"Sir," Marquez said. Jones turned to see McClaren disappearing behind a rocky outcrop.

"The fucker." He glanced at the dropship and made a decision. "OK, you go to the landing pad. Try to secure the comms tower, but do *not* get anyone killed. We can't afford to lose the men. I'll get McClaren and radio you when I've secured him. You can come and pick us up."

Marquez twirled his finger in the air to get everyone else back on the Cheyenne, and Jones pulled out his pistol and went in pursuit of McClaren.

Within five minutes Segura had the Cheyenne lifting out of the ravine, and he turned the nose of the dropship back toward the colony buildings. Be good to go toe-to-toe with some of those buggy bastards. Interesting to see how they died. What sort of noise they made when they went. He liked killing stuff. That was why he'd joined the Colonial Marines. His ma wanted him to be a veterinarian when he was at school in Miami. Until that day she caught him dissecting the neighbor's cat. While it was still alive.

He did love most animals, though. He'd only sliced that cat up because he wanted to see how it worked. That's why he was so pissed that somebody had killed Barrington. He'd put the little rat in a small cage from the stores and given it some dried rations. Then he'd found it, on its back, its belly all mangled. Maybe another rat had gotten to it. Maybe there *were* rodents on this planet. But, more likely, Marquez had stuck his knife in Barrington when Segura wasn't looking.

Marquez hated him.

That little rat never did anybody any harm.

It was just a few minutes to the landing pad. He hoped Marquez had everyone suiting up and ready for some serious shooting. The cockpit door opened and Marquez leaned in.

"Where you putting us down?"

"On the landing platform, duh," Segura said. "I know you killed my rat."

"I never touched your fucking rat, you imbecile," Marquez said. He paused and leaned forward. "What the hell is this?"

Segura turned in his seat to look at what Marquez was gingerly holding between his fingers. It was pale and translucent, like a snakeskin that had been shed. Marquez opened it out, like one of those paper dolls little girls used to cut out.

"Hey," he said, turning back to guide the Cheyenne toward the colony. "That looks like a little version of a bug."

Marquez dropped it like it was on fire. "Oh, Segura, you shit-head," he spat. "Your fucking rat. It was infected. The goddamn thing is loose on here."

"Well, if it came out of Barrington, it's only gonna be a tiny little thi—"

Marquez yelled as something barreled out of nowhere like a sleek black rocket, no bigger than a cat. It fastened on to his face and Marquez screamed and fell.

Segura shouted, "What the fuck, what the fuck…"

He had to put down, get his gun, finish the little Xenomorph off. But it was as tricky as the rat it had hatched from, and had disappeared, leaving Marquez a twitching, moaning, bloodied mess on the floor of the cockpit. Where the hell were the other two? Segura hollered for them, the colony landing pad coming up, when suddenly he felt something thud against the back of his head. A pain like a dagger pierced his skull and exploded behind his eyes.

As Jones watched the Cheyenne lurch and twist and spiral out of control, slamming into the comms tower with a distant rending of metal and a splintering of glass and a bright, fuel-blackened explosion, he realized the objective had changed. They were no longer a retrieval mission— the Xenomorph cargo had just gone up with his squad and his dropship. The *Cronulla* was destroyed.

Chad McClaren could do whatever the fuck he liked.

Jones was on his own now, and all that mattered was getting off the planet in one piece.

He abandoned his stalking of McClaren on the rocky hillside and turned, heading back to the colony buildings. There was one more way off LV-187, and he was sure as shit going to be the one to take it.

Chad watched the Cheyenne pile into the comms tower. Saw the tower ripple and bend and, with a whine of ruptured infrastructure, begin to topple, the comms deck aflame with the blazing wreck of the dropship embedded in it. He saw Jones emerge from behind a rocky outcrop, only a couple of hundred meters behind him, to turn tail and run for the colony buildings. Maybe he was going to try to save his men, but Chad doubted it.

He set off at a run behind the Colonial Marine.

The territory was bare and rocky, loose shale making the going slow. It was wet, too, from the storm, and slippery, with pools of dirty rainwater in the uneven terrain. He hadn't seen much beyond the empty landscape, no seas or forests or anything. Some of the area had been quarried out to provide stone for the construction of the colony, maybe, and there were a few flattened paths from heavy vehicles that meant he could move more quickly in Jones's wake, ducking behind rocks and outcrops whenever the Brit turned to see if he was being followed.

Jones circled around the ridge and picked his way along a cliff's edge, making his way to where he could pull himself up on to the landing platform. Chad realized what he was going to do and followed his route, dragging himself up onto the landing pad just to see Jones running for the New Albion ship, the *Victory*.

"I wouldn't do that if I were you, Jones," he called at the top of his lungs.

Jones turned and fired off a couple of wild shots from his handgun. "You should have stayed hidden, McClaren.

You're going to die on this planet, so there's no reason I can't just kill you myself."

He continued on, reached the *Victory*, and hit the door controls. Chad skidded to a halt and turned on a dime, starting to run full pelt for the colony building doors to the right of the toppled comms tower. He glanced over his shoulder to see Jones staring at him.

Then the Xenomorph that had been trapped on the ship since it had killed Jerry Bough leapt from the recesses of the *Victory*, claws outstretched and jaws gnashing as it let loose a hunter's howl.

Chad didn't look back again as he heard Jones utter a blood-chilling scream that was abruptly cut off with a gurgling, liquid choke.

It was a big one, muscular and taut and more than two meters tall when it came crashing down from the ceiling space, scattering their table and chairs and sending them all scrabbling backward away from it.

Merrilyn was the first to react, grabbing for the rifle and letting fly a flurry of pulse bursts, half of which hit the Xenomorph and sent it sprawling backward against the wall.

She was aware of Cher grabbing Therese and dragging her away, for which she was thankful. If she could pump enough fire into the Xenomorph before it could react…

The rifle clicked in her hands.

She looked at it in dismay, and pointed it again.

Nothing.

"Out of charge!" Davis cried.

Cher appeared alongside her, handgun outstretched, haphazardly letting off shots at the monster.

"Therese?" Merrilyn said.

"Back there, safe," Cher said, pushing another pistol into Merrilyn's hands. *Safe* was a very relative concept, all of a sudden.

The Xenomorph took hits and spewed acid blood from its wounds, but it seemed to be unstoppable, shrugging off the worst of the damage and crouching, getting ready to leap at them. Then Davis barreled toward it, a brown, furry missile growling and barking that slammed into the Xenomorph's torso, knocking it off its feet before it clawed at him and tossed him away like a toy.

"Doggo!" Therese cried behind her.

The sound of her daughter's voice seemed to give Merrilyn extra strength. The upturned canteen table was between them and the monster.

"The table!" she called out. "Grab it!"

Cher frowned but did as Merrilyn bid, the pair of them picking up the table by its top, legs toward the Xenomorph. She nodded to Cher and they both pushed forward with a simultaneous yell, Merrilyn angling the table so one of the metal legs hit the surprised alien in the chest, forcing it back against the wall and piercing its dark flesh.

It wasn't enough to kill it. Cher and Merrilyn ducked behind the tabletop as the Xenomorph reached for them. It was trapped and out of range, and weakened by its wound, but only for as long as they had the strength to hold it there. Merrilyn risked lifting her pistol, but the creature clawed at it and knocked it out of her hand.

Then the canteen doors crashed inward.

"How many, Davis?" Cher said through gritted teeth, not daring to take her eyes off the Xenomorph pinned to the wall by the table.

"Two," Davis said. "No, three."

"Shit," Cher said. "Shit shit shit." This was it then. This was how it ended. She knew why her sister had died, but she would never get the word out. She would just join the mystery of her death, another victim of the conspiracy.

"Wait," Davis said.

"Fuck," moaned Cher. "More?"

Then she heard what Davis had heard. Gunfire. Lots of it, and the howling, screeching death rattles of monsters, out there in the corridor.

She sagged momentarily, then redoubled her efforts, pushing the table against the monster as it screamed and howled at them. Were they saved? Was it in time? And what was that…? Under the screams and the gunfire, a man's voice, almost drowned but distinct and strong. And saying… a prayer?

* * *

Augustus Trent strode along the corridor, flanked by his Green Berets in their camouflage fatigues and Kevlar as they emptied their projectile rifles into the demons that infested the colony buildings of LV-187. He had never seen the like of these black, skeletal beasts with their rows of needle-sharp teeth and vicious claws, but they were merely another enemy. And the Royal Marines treated each enemy as the same: inferior and to be defeated.

He could see the fear in the eyes of some of the men and women under his command and he needed them to be strong in the face of the cadre of filth that hell had seen fit to unleash against them.

"Yea though I walk through the valley of the shadow of death," Trent called over the sound of gunfire and the death screeches of the monsters, "I will fear no evil." He put his foot on the neck of an injured creature and fired his revolver into its head until it stopped twitching. "For thou art with me, thy rod and thy staff comfort me."

They had killed five of the things, by his reckoning, and there was some commotion ahead in a double doorway where he could see at least two of the beasts crouching. A sign above the door proclaimed it to be the "Cantine." Trent signaled for his troops to head toward it.

"Thou preparest a table before me in the presence of thine enemies, thou annointest my head with oil…"

Three Green Berets fell to their knees and killed the two creatures by the doorway with bullets, avoiding the corpses which bled acid that smoked and boiled where it landed. Trent nodded his appreciation.

"My cup runneth over," he intoned.

There was more noise from the canteen… human noise. Shouts and screams and… a dog? Trent stepped carefully over the bodies of the creatures and surveyed the scene. Two women had one of the monsters trapped against the wall with a table, but they were under extreme pressure. There was indeed a dog, which seemed to be guarding a small child in the corner. Trent checked his revolver.

"Surely goodness and mercy shall follow me all the days of my life," he called loudly as he strode toward them. It was the first time he had taken a proper look at one of the creatures, its bulbous head, its gaping jaws. Truly dragged from the mouth of Hell. He held up his gun as he approached.

"And I will dwell in the house of the Lord forever." The stricken creature turned its face to him and hissed, opening its jaws. Trent emptied his gun into its head, and it slammed back against the wall, the explosive shells blowing its brains out. The surface bubbled as the acid began to eat through.

As the two women holding the table slumped to the floor, Trent looked around as his team signaled that the immediate area was clear and secure.

"Amen," Augustus Trent said. He holstered his gun.

"Now, is someone going to tell me what the fuck is going on here?"

"Sir!" one of the marines called, and Trent turned to see a man in the doorway. His troops' guns were trained on the newcomer. He was tall and broad, and looked exhausted.

"Chad!" the dog shouted. Trent raised an eyebrow. *Curiouser and curiouser.*

The man held up his hands. "Thank God you're here."

"Correct," Trent said. "You can indeed thank God that we're here."

2 6

As soon as Chad had cautiously entered the colony buildings, the ruined comms tower burning above him, he heard the gunfire.

Abandoning caution, he ran down the corridors as fast as he could, quickly coming across the corpses of the Xenomorphs that had been massing to attack the canteen. There he found what he recognized as a troop of Royal Marines and their commander, who introduced himself as Captain Augustus Trent of the HMS *God's Hammer*.

Chad told the captain everything he needed to know about the Xenomorphs, expecting the usual barrage of questions and disbelief, but Trent just kept absent-mindedly stroking the scar that ran down his face.

"I wondered why the *Cronulla* was here," Trent said.

"That was the ship that the Colonial Marines came from?" Chad said. "What happened to it?"

"We did." Trent smiled thinly. "You've met with the landing party? What's their location?"

"Dead," Chad said. "Most of them in the dropship

that destroyed the comms tower. Their officer was killed on the landing platform."

"What happened to him?" Trent said.

"Xenomorphs did."

"You have a ship, yes?" Merrilyn stepped forward, Therese hiding shyly behind her.

"I do, ma'am," Trent said, touching the front of his beret. "The finest ship in the service of New Albion."

"New Albion?" Chad said. "But the Royal Marines had to be here for the Three World Empire."

"The galaxy is changing, Mr. McClaren," Trent said, "and we must change with it. I, along with my crew, have decided that we are better placed serving the needs of this emergent new force than being the... what was it the commander of the *Cronulla* called us before he died? Ah, yes. A toothless bulldog. Better than being a toothless bulldog in the service of the Three World Empire."

Trent stood. "We have three dropships here. I must go and get patched through to New Albion to apprise them of the situation. That all the trade party who so bravely held this colony for them have lost their lives in service to the new empire."

"But you're going to take us with you, right?" Cher said. "You can get us up to your ship and back to New Albion?"

"Members of my team will remain here for your protection," Trent said. "Please don't worry, ma'am. I do not intend to leave anyone on LV-187." He turned and marched away with two of his marines.

Yes, well, Chad thought, *that's not the same thing as taking us with you, is it?*

"I'm so glad to see you," Cher said, giving Chad a long hug that she was too exhausted to break off. "I thought you were dead. Everybody else is."

"Do we have any idea how many of these things have been killed?" Merrilyn asked.

Chad shrugged. "I saw five corpses in the corridors, plus the two in the doorway, and the one here. There were six in the hold of the dropship that crashed into the comms tower. How many did they kill last night? How many did we?" He rubbed his eyes and pinched the bridge of his nose. "It's a moot point. If there's a hive, and a queen, and more eggs... it depends how many of the colonists they kept alive."

"So the place could still be crawling with them," Cher said. "Where the hell is Trent going? We need him to get us the hell out of here, and nuke the fucking place."

"Agreed," Chad said, "and the *God's Hammer* should be more than equipped to do that." He looked up. "Here comes Trent now."

"You get through to your bosses on New Albion?" Cher said as Trent walked up to them and pulled up a chair, sitting astride it with his arms over the back. He ignored her and pointed to Chad.

"Mr. McClaren. Tell me again about the reproductive cycle of these Xenomorphs."

When Chad had gone through it all again, he noticed three of the Royal Marines edging closer, their rifles in their hands. He frowned.

"Trent? What's going on?"

"You are all being detained, temporarily, for your own safety."

"On what grounds?" Cher said, standing up and bristling. "I'm a citizen of the United Americas." She glared at him. "You're making a very big mistake."

"You are, along with Mr. McClaren and the synthetic dog, wanted for questioning on New Albion in connection with a serious breach of a no-fly order." He turned to Merrilyn. "Ms. Hambleton and her daughter are citizens of a foreign power which is at war with New Albion. You will all be held here until our operations are complete."

"Can't you at least detain us on your ship, rather than here where those creatures might still attack?" Merrilyn said, looking around.

"What operations, Trent?" Chad said. "What exactly are your orders?"

"Mr. McClaren," Trent said mildly. "You mentioned the existence of a *hive*. Now, where exactly would we find that?"

An hour later the marines had set up, in the center of the canteen, a field comms unit on which were displayed the various schematic overlays of the colony base.

"Can we get lifeforms readings on here?" Trent asked.

"Just patching into the colony mainframe, sir," the marine at the controls said. "Any second now…" A fleet of yellow dots appeared on the map. "This concentration is us, here," the marine continued, pointing to a cluster. "Here and here we have gold and red teams."

"And these?" Trent pointed to a small grouping on the far side of the colony, and then several individual dots scattered around.

"Xenomorphs," Chad said at his shoulder. "I count at least… twenty?"

Trent looked at him. "And where do we find this queen? We find her, we find the hive, right?"

Chad studied the schematic. He called Merrilyn over and pointed to one of the stationary dots.

"Where is this?"

She peered at it. "That's the fusion reactor hub."

Chad straightened up. "Then that's your hive." He looked at Trent. "I still say it makes more sense just to nuke the facility from orbit. You could lose a lot of men mopping up twenty Xenomorphs, and the queen… you don't know what you're dealing with here."

Trent frowned. "We are not destroying a viable colony operation, along with all the oil and ore that's stored in those tanks. Do you monitor the news, Mr. McClaren? Do you know how scarce a resource oil is, especially out here in the colonies?"

"Profit wins again," Chad said. "Fine, Trent. You want

to do it the old-fashioned way, I'll help you. But people are going to die, you get that? And I don't want my friends to be among them. Will you guarantee their safety?"

"I'd be a fool to make that promise," Trent replied. "But you have one of the finest bodies of military personnel in the Weyland Isles boiling for a fight here, so I rather fancy our chances against an uncoordinated mob of blood-crazed animals."

"I've heard that one before," Chad said quietly. "It never ends well."

Trent smiled. "This time you have God on your side, Mr. McClaren."

Trent, Chad, and six Royal Marines were outfitted in armored apesuits, favored by both Colonial Marines and Weyland-Yutani operatives. At Chad's insistence, the soldiers had Weyland-Yutani ID23 underslung incinerator units fitted to their NSG23 assault rifles. He told Trent it was the only way to make certain the eggs were fully destroyed. Trent himself was armed with his Norcomm semi-automatic; when Chad asked for a weapon, he was given a basic pulse sidearm.

"You won't need it," Trent said confidently. "My team will handle this. You won't even get your hands dirty."

"Why only six?" Chad said. "We should be taking three times that number of personnel."

"Because we're professionals."

* * *

Chad turned to the others, Therese hiding from the mask of his suit behind Merrilyn. He flipped the face visor and smiled at her.

"We'll be away from here soon. We're leaving all this behind."

Davis trotted over and Chad squatted to talk to him. "Be careful," Davis said. "You promise me?"

Chad ruffled his fur. "We've got a lot to do, Davis. Neither of us are dying here."

"Mr. McClaren," Trent said, pulling down his visor. "Time for us to roll out."

"Be safe," Cher said.

"For all our sakes," Merrilyn added.

A team of four additional marines escorted the fire team down the corridors until they came to the double doors marked with the nuclear warning stickers. They were locked and one marine fixed a low-level magnetic charge, blowing the locks with a precise, muted *whump*.

Inside was a small, steel-lined foyer with an elevator and a flight of metal stairs. Trent indicated for the fire team to start descending the steps, and turned to the four marines. "Two on the doors, the other pair back to the canteen." He looked at Chad. "Shall we do this?"

Chad could think of nothing he wanted to do less. He'd seen Xenomorph hives. He'd seen queens. He was normally running away from them, not walking into them.

Hitting the night vision switch on his visor, he fell in behind the marines slowly descending the stairs. Trent stayed behind him.

In the canteen, one of the marines got the big water boiler working and proceeded to make mugs of tea for everyone. *How very English*, Merrilyn thought, sitting by the observation window, watching the clouds scudding across the sky while Therese petted Davis. Rain pattered lightly against the window, but it wasn't another storm as bad as last night. Still, she didn't feel as good about this as she should. Why could they not have airlifted them off LV-187 in a dropship, back to their vessel in orbit, and *then* played their stupid little soldier games? Why did they have to wait here for this to be played out?

Cher was helping distribute the tea among the marines lounging in the canteen, and she brought two steaming mugs over to Merrilyn. "Milky and sugary, only way it comes, apparently," she said. Merrilyn gratefully accepted the mug and sipped at it. She could sense that Cher was wanting to say something.

"What is it?"

Cher bit her lip, hesitated, then said, "While everyone was resting... I saw the security camera footage. From when Therese found the Ovomorph."

Merrilyn put her cup on the table. "Ah."

"That was the first contact the colony had with the Xenomorphs?"

Merrilyn nodded warily, pondering what she was going to say. They had been through a lot together, more than most people had to bind them, but still she was not ready for all of this.

"How?" Cher said helplessly.

Merrilyn shrugged. "Luck? Divine intervention? She's stronger than she knows? I ask myself the question every day, and I never get an answer. I just give thanks for it."

Cher nodded. "From what Chad told me, once a face-hugger attached itself, no force on Earth would get it off. Not without killing the host."

"As I said, luck," Merrilyn said, shrugging again. "She reacts very quickly. As soon as it hits her face she pulls it off, throws it to the floor, and stamps on it. You've watched the footage. I didn't really know what it was or what it did until Chad explained it properly, but I think she just managed to get it off quickly before it could... before it could do what it does."

"I'm so glad she did," Cher said, looking over at Therese. "She's one special kid, Merrilyn."

"You don't know the half of it," she said, following Cher's gaze.

The stairs went down and down, deeper than the colony

base, into the very rock on which it was built. The reactor had been drilled in deep in case of accidents, but even so, if it went into meltdown it would still take out most of the place.

Eventually they bottomed out in another foyer, with another set of double doors. Except these were open—clawed open, the metal twisted. Chad turned to Trent and held up his hand.

"Halt," Trent said on the short-wave radios connecting the fire team.

"OK," Chad said. "If that is a hive in there, you're going to see some very weird shit. There may be drones—smaller aliens. There will definitely be a queen, and she's going to be big. And there will be eggs. I suggest half the team starts torching the eggs and the rest of us take the queen. If we can."

"We don't work in *ifs*, we work in *whens*," Trent said. "We're the Royal Marines. OK, team, you heard the man. Let's go, and let's tread carefully. And let's kick some Xenomorph arse."

The Royal Marine operating the ad hoc scanner and comms desk was called Winwick, and she was patiently explaining to Therese what she was seeing on the schematic.

"So this is us, here, in the canteen, see? And over here we have Captain Trent and Mr. McClaren and the fire team."

"Why are their dots smaller?" Therese said.

"Because they're on a different level to us. They must be going pretty deep underground." Winwick swiped the map away and it was replaced by one showing mainly a large circular chamber. "See? The dots are full size now. We're looking at their level only."

"What is this dot?" Therese asked.

"That's, uh, I guess that's..." Winwick glanced at Merrilyn.

"It's OK. She's seen plenty this last week."

"That's a Xenomorph, Therese. Maybe the queen they're going to kill."

Therese nodded as Winwick swiped their floor back to the top level of the schematic. "And what are these dots here?"

Winwick frowned. "Those are... Shit." She looked around, shouting at the nearest marine. "Incoming! We got incoming!"

The marines leapt up, grabbing their weapons, and training them on the doors. The soldiers on guard duty in the corridor looked in and shook their heads. "Nothing here!"

"They're right here!" Winwick protested. "They're right"—she looked up—"on top of us."

"The last one came through the ceiling!" Cher yelled, and the marines started to fire upward, punching holes in the ceiling panels and bringing down a shower of dust and plaster. Merrilyn covered Therese's ears against the cacophony.

After thirty seconds they paused, looking at each other. Nothing came down. No tell-tale drips of acidic blood. Merrilyn walked over to Winwick and looked at her map. There were still five dots moving about, seemingly right in the room with them.

Then there was an eruption of fragmented tile and wood and a Xenomorph burst through the floor by the window. It scooped up the little girl in its claws.

"Therese!" Merrilyn screamed.

2 7

Chad was introduced to the fire team before they went down, Trent calling them to attention and pointing them out as, "Pugh, Pugh, McGrew, Cuthbert, Dibble, Grub." He turned to Chad. "Pugh and Pugh are twins." They'd all saluted, but Chad was sure he'd forget their names, and was glad they were stenciled on their apesuits.

It didn't matter. Despite Trent's bravado, they wouldn't all be getting out of here alive.

"It's hot," one of the Pughs said as they paused outside the twisted doors.

"We're right on top of a fusion reactor," Chad said.

"That's not too great, is it, sir?" Grub said, looking at Trent.

"According to Merrilyn, there's a meter of lead between us and the reactor below," Chad said. "Our guns shouldn't pierce that, and the radiation should be minimal so long as we don't hang around."

McGrew and Cuthbert took up position and lit their incinerator unit pilot flames, while the two Pughs flanked them with their rifles. Grub and Dibble took up the rear.

"Move out," Trent said.

The mangled doors led into a cavernous, circular room. In the dark, it was difficult to estimate its size. The marines peered around, trying to make sense of what they could see in the light from their shoulder-mounted arclights.

"What's on the walls?" McGrew said, reaching out to touch the uneven surface with her gloved hand. Something moved within the fibrous, resinous mass that covered the surface in crisscross fashion, and she drew back sharply. "Ah!"

"This is how the hive works," Chad said. "They don't kill everyone; they bring some survivors here and implant them. Keep them alive until the chestburster comes through."

"Holy Lord." Trent's eyes widened behind his visor. "There's a person behind all that gunk. Cuthbert, help them down."

"Wait," Chad said. There was indeed a human form behind the weblike resin, and a brief movement, a head of indeterminate age and sex, shifting slightly. Then there was a dry, whispered mumble.

"What?" Cuthbert said, leaning closer.

"Don't," Chad said.

"Kill… me…" the colonist said.

Then the figure convulsed, gasped, and the gunk trapping them to the wall twisted and bulged. It exploded outward, a screaming, gnashing infant Xenomorph launching itself from the colonist's shuddering corpse. Right at Cuthbert

Before it reached the marine, McGrew and Dibble opened fire, and one of the Pughs lit up his incinerator. He toasted the creature until it was a blackened spot on the lead floor.

From deeper inside the room, there was a sensation of movement and a low, ominous growl.

"Now we have to be ready," Chad said.

They assumed the formation again and moved forward until their arclights picked out something in front of them.

"What is *that*?" Grub said from behind. She stood on her tiptoes to shine her light better. In front of them, as far into the darkness as their lights could pierce, there was a sea of eggs. Chad had never seen so many in one place. Too many to count, but he estimated maybe... a hundred? Just that they could see?

"Destroy them," he said to the marines.

"Hold your fire!" one of the marines shouted, a woman with red hair tied in a ponytail. The soldiers remained stock-still, their rifles trained on the creature at the center of the room, where it had clawed its way up from the maintenance ducts beneath the tiled floor.

The Xenomorph that held Therese tightly in its grip.

Merrilyn felt all strength and sense desert her simultaneously. She wanted to rush at the creature, grab her daughter back from it, but at the same time she felt her legs buckle and she sank to the floor, the periphery of her vision darkening as though she was going to black out.

No, she told herself sternly. *No. You do neither of those things. You cannot help Therese by fainting, or by getting yourself killed. Pull it together, Merrilyn.*

Could the things be reasoned with? Or were they really just the mindless engines of destruction and death they appeared to be? Surely, underneath it all, they were living things, too. Surely, deep within that ungodly frame built purely for killing, there was some spark of… something? She had to try. There was nothing else she could do.

The Xenomorph held Therese with both hands under her arms, the child as limp as a rag doll. Merrilyn could see she was conscious though, looking at the monster with an almost supernatural calmness. God knows what the experience was doing to her. God knows how it was affecting her, and how long-lasting the trauma would be.

Somewhere deep inside Merrilyn, she chided herself for these thoughts. Doubt crept in again, something she had pushed away long ago, trained herself not to feel.

Stop it, she told herself. *That's your daughter up there.*

The Xenomorph appeared to be sizing Therese up, its head on one side as if it didn't quite know what to make of her. It seemed to be… *sniffing* her, as a dog would.

Then it opened its mouth and its terrible secondary set of jaws emerged, extending so close to Therese's face it looked as if it might kiss her.

Merrilyn became aware of the marines slowly taking up position around her, rifles on the creature, waiting to see what it would do.

"Please," she said loudly. "Please. That's my daughter. If you understand anything…"

The Xenomorph screeched deafeningly, spittle peppering Therese's face, and it drew her closer to its widening jaws.

"Wait," Trent said.

Chad looked at him. "What? Wait? We're here to destroy these things. What are we waiting for?"

"We should take out this Queen first, yes?"

"Look at them, Trent." Chad grabbed the arm of the man's apesuit. He pointed to the eggs, like a terrible harvest laid out before them. "Look at them. They're shuddering and ready to let loose the face-huggers. We need to destroy them. *Now.* You want your team to be destroyed?" He paused, suddenly frowning. "You *are* going to destroy them, aren't you?"

"We should perhaps destroy that first," Trent said, pointing beyond the eggs.

Out of the darkness at the edge of the light cast by their flashlights, a shape was moving, coalescing out of the shadows, blackly reflecting the light. It was huge, bigger than any Chad had ever seen before. Almost ten meters tall, its broad head protected by chitinous plates, its jaws extended and massive, like a great white shark's. It was almost apelike, its sinewy arms hanging low, its claws as sharp as butcher's knives. A monstrous segmented tail whipped lazily behind it as it stepped forward on its muscular legs, crouching and looking at them over the sea of its progeny.

"The Queen," Trent breathed. "Good Lord. I had no idea."

No shit, Chad thought. He wanted to turn tail and run. She was too big. They had no chance. They were all going to die.

"Sir?" one of the Pughs said, turning to Trent.

Trent rallied, and nodded, and seemed to pull himself out of the hypnotic state into which the sight of the Queen had plunged him.

"Yes, Pugh," he said. "All of you. Let's take this bitch down."

The six marines opened fire on the Queen.

She threw her head back and screeched, a noise ripped from the guts of a million damned souls.

The Xenomorph paused, looked up and beyond the marines. Then it looked down, at the hole in the floor from which it had emerged. It hissed, and abruptly cast

Therese away from it. Merrilyn screamed as her daughter hit the floor and skidded away.

"Hit it!" one of the marines shouted, and there was an explosion of gunfire aimed at the creature, which howled and dove into the ruined floor, immediately lost from sight in the warren of ducts and vents beneath their feet. Winwick ran to the comms desk and leaned over the screen.

"It's moving. Quick. All the dots are." She looked up. "They're converging on the reactor."

"Chad and the fire team must have found the Queen," Davis said. "They're going to protect her. Can we contact Trent?"

Merrilyn didn't care about Chad and the fire team. She ran to Therese and gathered the child in her arms.

"Little Flower, Little Flower," she whispered.

"I'm all right, Mama," Therese said.

Merrilyn felt Cher at her shoulder. "Does she need medical treatment?"

"I don't think so. Are you hurt, Baba?"

"It didn't hurt me," Therese said. "It just scared me."

One of the marines with a red cross on an armband came over. "I'll check her over just in case, ma'am."

"No!" Merrilyn said fiercely. "No. Thank you, but you heard her. She's fine."

The medic frowned, then shrugged, and left. Cher squatted by Merrilyn. "I know my knowledge of these things is limited but... I've never seen that before. Chad never described anything like it. I thought these things killed without mercy. No hesitation."

"Then thank God this one didn't," Merrilyn said, hugging Therese tight.

"But why?" Cher pressed. "Why didn't it hurt her? What stopped it?"

Merrilyn rounded on her angrily. "You sound as though you wanted it to kill her! What is wrong with you? Would that make a better story for you? You vulture!"

"Merrilyn, you know I didn't—" Cher put a hand on her arm but Merrilyn shrugged her off.

"Leave me and my daughter alone," she snapped. "Stop asking questions." Cher shrugged and backed off, and Merrilyn watched her go to the comms desk where Winwick was trying to contact Trent, with little success.

"The walls around the reactor must be too thick," the marine said, throwing her headset down in frustration. "I think we should get a back-up team down to them."

"We were told to stay in position here," another marine doubtfully said.

Winwick looked at him. "There are six Xenomorphs heading their way, and that's on top of whatever they have to contend with down there."

The Queen was more heavily armored than the standard Xenomorphs, and the bullets from the marines' guns pinged off her carapace with sparking ricochets. The

Pughs stepped forward and let loose their incinerators, yellow flames gouting out in hissing streams. The Queen put up her thick arms to ward them off and screeched.

"It's no good," Chad yelled, uselessly emptying his handgun at the monstrous form. "Don't we have anything else?"

Trent reached inside his apesuit and pulled out a small metal sphere. "I brought a few grenades, just in case." He pressed a button on the ball and took a run up, launching it at his target. She batted it away with one of her huge hands and it disappeared into the darkness behind her, exploding in a violent burst against the back wall of the curved chamber, illuminating the Queen in all her terrible glory.

"How many of those things did you bring?" Chad said.

"Six," Trent muttered. "Enough for an over."

"I don't know if you've noticed," Chad said through gritted teeth, "but this isn't a game." The Queen began to advance, striding over the crop of eggs that lay between them. "I knew one fire team wasn't going to be enough. We need to get out of here. She won't follow us—won't leave her eggs unprotected."

"No," Trent said. "We have a job to do and we're going to do it. The Royal Marines never bail on a mission." He turned to Dibble. "Have we a link with the canteen? Can we get reinforcements?"

"No, sir. The walls are too thick."

Trent pulled out another grenade and launched it at the Queen. This one bounced downward and exploded, taking with it a dozen or more eggs at her feet. She threw back her head and let loose a deafening roar.

"Now she's really pissed off," Chad said. "Trent, isn't it obvious? We should just get out of here and off-world. You can nuke the entire colony. Job done."

"I told you, McClaren. It's not an option. We have orders, and they do not involve destroying this facility." He turned to Dibble. "Go. Up a level or two. Get word to the others. We need everyone down here."

Dibble nodded and backed off toward the doors.

"You're just sentencing more of your people to death," Chad said.

Trent lifted his rifle and fired, pumping projectiles into the advancing Queen. "Aim high!" he shouted to the others. "For the head! Try not to hit the eggs."

What? Chad stared at him.

"No," he said. "Trent, tell me it isn't true."

"I'm a little busy trying to kill a thirty-foot alien monster, McClaren."

Chad grabbed his arm. "You're not going to destroy the eggs, are you? Those are your orders, aren't they? Not to destroy them, but to take them."

"We're standing in the middle of the most important cache of bioweapons in known space," Trent said, glaring at him. "Of course we're not going to destroy them."

"No." Chad shook his head. "You can't take the eggs off-world. Trent, you've seen what happens. You want these things loose on your ship? Or New Albion?"

"No," Trent said, redoubling his assault, "but imagine them loose on the ships and worlds of our enemies."

Chad groaned. There it was again. Weaponization. Every time humans came into contact with the Xenomorphs, someone hatched a plan to use them. And every time, it didn't work. The aliens weren't bombs or guns. They weren't soldiers. They were an unbridled force of nature. You might as well try to tame a hurricane.

Suddenly there was a yell and a burst of gunfire from behind them. Chad wheeled around to see Dibble, who had reached the doors, suddenly fall under a mass of black shadows.

"Shit," Trent said, turning and training his light on the scene. Dibble was on the ground, and crouched on him was a Xenomorph. Behind it, in the doorway more shapes crept forward. Chad counted six in all.

The Queen threw back her armored head and screamed in what sounded for all the world like triumph.

2 8

The last time Chad saw Amanda, they sat on a deserted beach on a remote Thai island that sprouted out of the azure sea like something from an alien world, but it was right there on Earth. There was wonder and beauty right there on Earth. You didn't have to travel the universe to experience amazement at what the natural world could offer.

Yes, out there you could find purple skies and boiling seas and horizons where three moons rose at dusk, and yes, they were all wonderful and humbling to behold. But in the race to colonize space, people had forgotten that the place that had spawned them all was as beautiful a place as anywhere in the galaxy.

"I'm sorry," he said as they shared a bottle of wine, watching the red sun dip into the blazing sea. "I failed you."

She was weak and tired and thin, but in this place of beauty, in this universe of beauty, she was still the most beautiful thing in a trillion light years in any direction. She smiled at him.

"Yes, Chad McClaren, you have failed to find a cure for cancer. Damn you. And here I thought you loved me."

He took the glass from her hand and kissed her, and then they lay down on the blanket as night fell and a canopy of stars unfurled above them, and made slow, quiet love. Then they lay in each other's arms, Amanda sleeping lightly and Chad looking up at the scattered points of light, thinking about the beauty up there, both claimed by mankind and yet to be discovered.

He thought about the horror as well—the horror they had both faced, the horror that had brought them together.

In the end it was the horror that had parted them, but not the horror of gnashing teeth and clawed hands and sinuously terrible jet-black bodies of segmented chitin and bone. No, it was the horror of the frailty of the human body. Because no matter how arrogant mankind became, no matter how sure of its place in the universe it was, there was always something there to remind them that it wasn't true, be it death at the hands of an impossible alien killing machine, or the death that crept through the shadows of their cells and preyed upon the incurable vulnerability of the human condition.

Chad had slept fitfully, and at dawn they loaded their things into the flyer and took off to a secret location where Chad laid Amanda in a cryosleep chamber and froze her fragile beauty in that moment, as her body slouched toward ultimate death. She was there now, hovering on the precipice, one foot in light, the other in darkness, waiting for him to fulfil his promise.

To find a cure.

"I'm not dying here," Chad spat through gritted teeth. "I'm not dying today." How many times had he repeated this mantra to himself, in a dozen hopeless situations, and every time he had survived—and it wasn't just self-preservation. It was because he still had work to do. He had to save Amanda.

By saving Amanda, he could save himself.

Dibble was dead, but McGrew and Cuthbert were carpeting the Xenomorphs at the door with fire, and it was proving effective. Two had already fallen and four more were backing away, acid blood spraying from their wounds.

The two Pughs kept the Queen at bay with their incinerators, but they had limited fuel cells. Another strategy would have to be found, sooner rather than later.

Grub sidled along the curved wall to the right, crouched low, the dark and her camouflage hiding her against the resinous hardened goo on the walls. Trent was directing his fire at the Queen's head, distracting her, Chad realized, enabling Grub to edge closer to her. Trent pushed his rifle into Chad's hands and told him to keep firing. Then he reached in his suit and tossed a grenade at Grub, which she expertly caught and activated, then hurled it at the Queen's head with precise accuracy.

By accident or design, she ducked at the last moment, but the grenade still connected and exploded. Although she was protected by her armored head plates, she threw her head back and screeched.

"Excellent work, Grub!" Trent said, but the celebration was short lived as the Queen ducked to her left and raked her huge claws toward Grub, catching the marine full in the face and tossing her like a toy back toward them.

Chad handed the rifle back to Trent and ran to her, but blood was pooling beneath her lifeless body. Then his attention was drawn to the doorway, where there was worse news. Cuthbert had fallen under two attackers, McGrew clicking her empty rifle and then disgustedly throwing it away and whipping out her handgun.

The Queen thrashed, shaking her head, and Chad guessed the explosion had affected her senses, the way she clawed at her head. He looked back to the door. There were four dead Xenomorphs now, an exhausted McGrew facing off against one more. Hadn't there been six? "Pugh!" he shouted. One of the twins turned, and aimed a blast at the Xenomorph, which screamed as it combusted.

"Sir!" the other Pugh yelled as his incinerator died in his hands. "Out of fuel!"

Trent yelled at him to move, but the Queen was on him, her jaws clamping around his head and tearing it off, blood spraying from what remained.

It was a massacre.

McGrew screamed as the final Xenomorph peeled itself from the shadows and fell on her. Moments later, it leapt up from her corpse and Pugh incinerated it with his final charge, but its momentum carried it into him and they both fell, screaming in fire, and then were silenced.

Now it was just Chad, Trent, and the Queen.

Cher watched Merrilyn and Therese from a distance, trying to organize to the thoughts swirling around her head. Journalism was about making connections, putting together seemingly unconnected facts and incidents, to form a bigger narrative, paint a bigger picture. It was about connecting the dots with lines that didn't necessarily link A to B, but found a route that nobody had been expecting.

The A and B she was trying to connect in her head were the footage she had seen on the security camera monitor, and what had just happened in front of her. Therese had been attacked by a face-hugger. Everything she had been told indicated that it was an impossible thing to fight off, and yet this little girl had, apparently, pulled the thing off and stomped on it.

The Xenomorph in the canteen had seemed… troubled by her. Confused. As though it wanted to kill her, but didn't think it should.

Connections started to form in Cher's brain. What if

Therese hadn't pulled the face-hugger off in time? What if it was... Cher didn't know, maybe some kind of really fast-acting face-hugger? What if it had in fact implanted an embryo? That might explain why the Xenomorph didn't kill her. Did it sense that she was carrying one of *them*?

From what she knew, however, the gestation period was something like hours, not days. If Therese had been infected, why hadn't the thing emerged?

And if it was, in fact, true—or as near to the truth as Cher's limited experience could manage—did they all really want to get off this planet and be cooped up in a spaceship with someone carrying a Xenomorph inside them? Even if it was someone as cute and brave as Therese Hambleton?

It was unbearably hot in the reactor room, and Trent tore off his visor. The Queen was standing unsteadily, perhaps even more injured by the grenade blast than Chad had expected. Between them lay the sea of eggs, and the nearest ones were pulsing, their petaled tops puckering.

"They can sense us," Chad said. "You should put your visor back down."

"I don't care," Trent said, gasping for air. "I am taking this devil down. My face will be the last thing it sees."

They were both exhausted, but Trent refused to flee. Chad considered just going himself, but he couldn't bring himself to abandon the marine. As insane as he was starting to sound.

Without warning, Trent set off at a run, hopping over clusters of the puckering eggs and sprinting toward the Queen. She turned, whipping her massive tail at him, and connected, flinging him away from her, into the darkness behind.

"Great," Chad muttered. He started firing at the Queen again, then his gun clicked dully in his hand. Disgusted, he threw it at her with all his might and ran to where Trent had landed, vaulting over the eggs and keeping to what he hoped was the Queen's blind side. He switched off his vest light and dove into the darkness.

It took a few moments.

"I'd have thought you'd have fled," Trent murmured as Chad slid down to the ground beside him. The marine's breathing was heavy, and in the dim light of the chamber he could see Trent holding his stomach, and a dark slick on his hands.

"The Royal Marines don't have a monopoly on stupidity," Chad said quietly. The Queen was to one side, shaking her head like a dog with a flea in its ear. Her senses appeared to be scrambled, which might buy them a bit of time, but she was still a force to be reckoned with. "How badly are you injured?"

"I've had worse, and survived," Trent said, his breathing coming harsh and ragged. Chad thought he was lying. "Of course, they were battles that didn't involve a demon from Hell."

"They're not from Hell, you know," Chad said. "They're

God's creatures just like you, if you believe that sort of thing, which you certainly seem to." He settled down a little in the darkness. "If we're going on a philosophical tip, what kind of God would create such things? Their only purpose is to kill."

"I know you mock me, McClaren. It's fine. I am used to it. You think in your scientific, technological world that there is no place for God. You're wrong. As we spread among the stars, we need Him more than ever."

"Well," Chad said, "where is he now? If you've got a hotline to the Big Guy, then it would be a very good time to call in the payment for a lifetime of devotion."

"God—"

Chad held up his hands. "If you're going to say God moves in mysterious ways, Trent, then don't. We don't need mysterious ways right now. We need a fucking miracle."

As if to prove that no such divine intervention was coming, the Queen turned to face them, her addled senses perhaps clearing, or maybe she was getting used to them. Either way, she crouched low and started to hiss, moving toward them like an angular, bony insect.

"No guns…" Trent breathed. He was starting to lose consciousness. That would be a mercy for him, Chad thought. This was no way to die. He felt a sudden stab in his heart at the thought of Amanda lying in her hypersleep, blissfully unaware that Chad would not be coming back.

The Queen approached, cautiously, her head on one side. Chad closed his eyes, waiting for her to strike. He put himself back on that island in Thailand, felt the warm sunshine on his skin, the sound of the birds wheeling high in the sky. That would be a good memory to inhabit forever. He constructed it around him, so that when the Queen struck it would be his final thought, and where he would stay when the darkness claimed him.

He felt the taste of the wine on his lips, and the hot smell of Amanda's sun-kissed skin as he bent forward to kiss her arm.

Trent mumbled something, but Chad ignored him. He opened one eye and saw the Queen's huge head looming over them, the ravaged left side of her face twisted and burned by the grenade. It was ruining the fantasy.

"...na...e..." Trent was shivering too, his body shutting down, going into trauma mode.

Chad didn't want to know. He closed his eyes again, felt the Queen's hot breath on them. She would be opening her maw wide, extending her inner jaw.

He was on the blanket with Amanda, making love for the last time. Sensual and loving, looking into each other's eyes. No urgency, no fireworks.

"g...a...de" Trent said, grabbing his arm.

No explosions.

Explosions. Chad opened his eyes. The Queen's face was inches from them, about to strike, like a huge, dark cobra.

"Grenades!" Chad yelled, sticking his hand into Trent's apesuit, his fingers closing around one of the metal spheres. He pulled it out, his thumb on the indentation that armed it. The Queen hissed and lunged. Chad depressed the button and rammed it into her inner jaws, whipped out his arm, and threw himself on top of Trent.

She pulled back, then made to strike again.

Two things happened.

First, the entire chamber was lit by beams of light and a chatter of weapons as a team of Royal Marines burst in through the doors, peppering the Queen with fire. The second was that, as she turned and opened her mouth to screech her fury at them, the grenade blew the back of her head out from the inside.

She reared up to her full height, visible in the dancing beams of the flashlights held by the marines, and then toppled backward, crashing to the floor with a reverberating thud and a death scream that made Chad almost believe that Trent was right, that she had come from Hell.

And now she'd been sent straight back.

"...ood... work... Laren..." Trent gasped.

Chad patted him on his arm and waved at the marines. "Medic," he croaked. "We need a medic." Then he collapsed on top of Trent, and everything went black.

2 9

Chad awoke in the canteen, lying on two tables pushed together to form a makeshift cot. He was covered with blankets. Merrilyn, Therese, and Cher stood above him, concern clouding their faces. When he opened his eyes, Therese gave a little cheer.

"Yay! He's alive!"

"I don't feel it," he said, his mouth dry. With Cher's help, he struggled to sit up, took the bottle of water that Merrilyn handed him and drained it. Around him, the canteen was a controlled riot of activity, the Royal Marines packing up their equipment and preparing to ship out. Davis was by the window, and he looked around.

"Glad to have you in the land of the living. You might want to see this."

He joined Davis at the window and looked over to the landing platform, on which the three Royal Marine dropships were lined up. The clouds had thickened and the rain was coming down again, though not anything like with the ferocity of the storm. There were three processions of marines in hazmat suits passing along large boxes, each a meter tall. Chad guessed they were portable cryo-chambers, and with a sinking heart he knew what was in them.

"I suppose Trent made it, then?"

"That he did," a voice behind him said. It was the man himself, a large bandage around his middle, his arm in a sling. "Mr. McClaren, you saved my life in there. I cannot thank you enough."

"Sir," Winwick said from the portable comms desk. "The mainframe here is losing power very quickly, but I've done a final sweep. I can't be one hundred percent sure, but I'm not picking up any readings apart from who's supposed to be here." She smiled. "I think LV-187 might be Xenomorph free."

"Well, it will be soon." Chad turned to Trent. "I assume those are the Ovomorphs you're loading into your dropships?"

"You know they are, Mr. McClaren. I told you that what our orders were. This is a game-changing resource. The colonies are about to get very chaotic indeed. This is New Albion's way of ensuring that we have the upper hand in what is to come."

"What are you going to do? Try to breed Xenomorphs? Because there's only one way that will end," Chad said. "You've seen what happened here, Trent. If that's what your superiors are planning, you should put your ship a very long way from them."

"These things can't be controlled, I know that," Trent said. "But just one egg, on one enemy colony… and we have more than a hundred and fifty of them."

"That is how this started!" Merrilyn said angrily. "Those Colonial Marines working for Weyland-Yutani put those things down here, and everybody died! How can you put other people through that? It's evil."

"It's warfare," Trent said with a shrug. "It is what it is."

"For a man of God, you seem happy to be unleashing hell on the universe," Merrilyn spat, and she turned back to Therese.

Chad watched the marines loading the final boxes into the dropships. When he turned, the comms desk had been packed up, and all the marines had left the canteen, except for two armed men with rifles who flanked Trent.

"Just following orders," Chad said, shaking his head. "I thought you were a better man than this, Trent."

"So where are you taking us?" Cher demanded. "Back to New Albion? Are we under arrest? Because I'm sure as hell not coming quietly."

"Perhaps, Mr. McClaren, I am a better man than you think I am. I do my duty." Trent rested his hand on his holstered pistol. "Follow orders. That is my job. I'm a soldier."

Trent unclipped his pistol and drew it. He pointed it directly at Chad. "Removing the Ovomorphs was only part of my brief. I was told to leave no survivors. Not one." He looked to Cher, Merrilyn, Davis, and Therese in turn. "Not a single one of you."

Merrilyn held Therese close to her. "You are a monster!"

Trent looked at her for a long time, and then slid his gun back into its holster.

"No, I don't think I am," he said quietly. "I have seen monsters. I have killed them. I do not think I am one." He turned to Chad. "You saved my life. I said I cannot thank you enough. I think perhaps I can. I am not going to take you with me, but I am not going to kill you. I think you deserve that. You all deserve that."

"You're going to abandon us here?" Cher said.

"There is the New Albion trade ship, the *Victory*," Trent said. "I've had it looked at. It is flightworthy. We've taken the liberty of removing the corpse from inside. Oh, and I've had a timed lockdown placed on the controls. You won't be able to leave until two hours after we depart." He grinned. and it was lopsided. "Don't want you doing anything rash, Chad. As you said, the Royal Marines don't have a monopoly on stupidity."

Trent turned to leave the canteen, the two marines falling in behind him. He paused at the doors. "It's been an honor to fight alongside you. All of you. I hope that if we meet again, it will be on the same side." Then he saluted, and marched out of the room.

* * *

Thirty minutes later, the five of them stood at the observation window and watched the three dropships take off vertically, turn in the air, and fly in formation up into the thick clouds, where they were lost from sight.

Chad punched the window. "Damn! *Damn* them! All those eggs, all that death…" He put his head against the window. "It's going to be an apocalypse."

"Hey," Cher said gently, putting a hand on his shoulder. "We survived, didn't we? We made it. All of us, and in a couple of hours we can get off this place. Get ourselves to Earth, and I can tell my story."

"Yes," Chad said. "I just hope there's somebody left to tell it to."

In the wide, empty circular chamber above the reactor, the Queen twitched. Not quite dead, but she was dying. Her blood fizzed and bubbled around her, a dark pool that ate steadily through the floor, causing her to sag and sink into the liquefying lead.

She had known, dimly, that her eggs were removed, one by one. Had they tried to destroy her young, she would have summoned the energy to kill them, to wipe them out. But they had not tried to destroy the eggs. They took them.

It was a wrench for any mother when her progeny were taken from her, but it was also the way of things for all living creatures. It was a mother's job to nurture and protect them until they were ready to make their own way in the universe.

They were ready.

Satisfied, she hissed, and died.

Her blood continued to seep out, eating into and weakening the floor beneath her. Until it finally buckled and gave, and she fell, fell, fell into the heat of the miniature sun that burned below her.

"Will you go to Earth, too?" Cher said to Merrilyn. She still seemed a little frosty after their earlier exchange, and to be honest, Cher was feeling a little jumpy, as well. But she wanted Merrilyn onside before she said what she had to say.

"I suppose," Merrilyn replied. "Where else is there to go?" She looked up and out of the window. "Is anywhere safe, with those eggs out there? Who knows where they might end up?"

"I'm sorry to have to say this," Chad said, standing next to where they sat, "but I'm not sure Earth is going to be safe for us. And I don't mean from Xenomorphs."

"What do you mean, then?" Cher said.

"I mean, we are all in danger now." He sat down, started to count off on his fingers. "Weyland-Yutani will know we were here. They don't take kindly to survivors of Xenomorph infestations shooting off their mouths. New Albion will know soon enough that Trent didn't kill us, which means they'll be after us, too. We were witnesses to the destruction of the *Cronulla*, which means the Colonial

Marines will be very interested in talking to us. This is, or was, an ICSC world before the New Albion secession. So they'll want to know what the hell happened here, and there's one thing I can guarantee—no matter who you talk to, once you mention Xenomorphs, things get very complicated indeed." He looked at them both. "It's at least two weeks in hypersleep to Earth. That's a hell of a long time for a hell of a lot of things to happen, and who knows what will be waiting for us when we arrive."

"What are you suggesting?" Merrilyn stared at him. "That we are somehow now all... *fugitives*?"

"He's more than suggesting it," Davis said, padding up to them and sitting down. "Welcome to our world."

"I have a child." Merrilyn looked over to where Therese was playing with her soft toy by the window. "I cannot be... be on the run."

"Merrilyn. About Therese." Cher took a deep breath. Now was as good a time as any. She said, as gently as she could, "I really think we should talk. All of us."

"What do you have to say about my daughter now?" Merrilyn glared at her angrily.

"Do you think... Do you think it's possible she's infected?" Cher said softly. "With an embryo?"

Merrilyn stared at her and shook her head. "Why would you say that?"

"I saw the footage of when she found the first Ovomorph," Cher said to the others. "She was hit by a face-hugger."

"What?" Chad's eyes widened. "But this was... what? Nine, ten days ago?"

"She ripped it off before it could put that tube down her throat," Merrilyn said, her eyes full of tears. "You saw it, Cher. We can watch it again if you like."

"Then the Xenomorph that attacked her... it left her alone," Cher pressed. "It didn't kill her when it had ample opportunity to. Why was that? It almost seemed as if it could... sense something about her."

"Stop this." Merrilyn began to cry, balling her fists and slamming them into her thighs. "Please. Stop this."

"*And*," Cher said remorselessly, "when the Royal Marine medic wanted to look her over, you refused. Flat-out refused."

"Because she was fine!" Merrilyn shouted.

Therese looked over from where she was playing. "Mama?"

"It's all right, Little Flower," Merrilyn said, wiping the tears from her eyes. "You play." She turned back to Cher and hissed, "There is nothing wrong with my daughter. She is not infected with a Xenomorph."

"Well, maybe we should find out for sure," Cher said. "I mean, I'm sorry to be harsh here Merrilyn, but we're all about to get into a very small spaceship and be stuck together for a couple of weeks and—"

"Merrilyn," Chad said. "Maybe Cher's right. If there's a medical bay here and we can get the X-ray machine working, perhaps we could just find out. To be sure?

I mean, I've never heard of a gestation period that long, but we're learning new stuff about these things all the time. Just to be sure."

"And what if you find out what you so desperately want to find out?" Merrilyn yelled. "What then? You leave us both here? Or worse?"

There was a long silence, punctuated only by Therese tunelessly singing "Joe Le Taxi." Merrilyn began to cry again. Davis cleared his throat.

"Chad… Cher," he said slowly. "Therese isn't carrying an embryo."

Chad looked at him. "How can you be sure? Have you conducted some kind of scan?"

"No," Davis said, "but I am sure. For the same reason that Merrilyn is so certain that she isn't."

Merrilyn stared. "You know?"

Cher frowned. "Know what? Look, isn't it time everybody came clean about whatever this—"

She was cut off by the strip lights above abruptly changing from pale white to a garish, flashing red, accompanied by a blaring monotone alarm which sounded throughout the colony facility.

"What in God's name *now*?" Chad said.

"Oh *mon Dieu*…" Merrilyn said, her face going pale.

"What is it?" Cher shouted above the alarm.

"It's the fusion reactor," Merrilyn looked at her, her voice trembling. "That alarm means it's going critical."

3 0

Merrilyn logged into the mainframe from a terminal in one of the control rooms nearest the canteen, while the others stood behind her, Davis jumping onto a chair at the desk.

"You can close down the reactor from here?" Chad said.

"I have the necessary permissions and codes," Merrilyn said. "It depends what level of criticality it has reached." Her fingers flew across the keyboard and she called up the reactor protocols.

"Can you turn off that goddamn alarm and flashing red lights?" Cher said.

Merrilyn ignored her and concentrated on the monitor. The screen kept freezing and the protocol pages were glitching like crazy. She was kicked out and had to log back in three times.

"What's the problem?" Chad said.

"I think the mainframe has lost too much power." Merrilyn frowned. "It can't handle the requests." She tried again and suddenly the screen went blank. Nothing she could do would get it booted up again.

"Try another terminal?" Cher suggested.

"It's the mainframe, not the terminal." Merrilyn looked at Chad. "How long do we have left until we can fly out of here?"

"One hour and thirty-eight minutes," Davis answered. "Could you surmise from your time in the system how long we have before the reactor goes critical."

Merrilyn bit her lip. "Around sixty minutes."

"Well, shit," Cher said. "So this place is going to go boom, and we can't shut it down and can't get off it in time. What should we do? Just run the hell for it?"

"We wouldn't clear the blast radius in time, Cher," Chad said. "This is going to be like a nuclear bomb going off."

"What about the trucks in the garage?" she said desperately. "We could drive a hell of a way in thirty minutes, surely."

"The *Victory* would be destroyed," Merrilyn said. "We'd be trapped here. With no supplies and no idea when the next ship will arrive." She looked at Chad. "And from what he said, they might not be very friendly to us."

"There may be another way," Davis said quietly. "Merrilyn, isn't there a manual shut-off somewhere?"

She thought about it. "Yes. On the actual reactor housing, but it would be impossible to reach now that the reactor is going critical. The heat, and the radiation, it would kill anyone before they got to it." She paused, and blanched a little. "And the shut-off procedure is complicated. It would have to be me that did it."

"Or me," Davis said. "And the heat and radiation would not affect me. Not as quickly as a human."

"It would eventually," Chad said. "Davis, you wouldn't make it out alive."

"I'm flattered that you think I'm alive. That makes the sacrifice worthwhile in itself."

"And you can do this?" Cher said. "I mean, a dog can do this?"

Merrilyn shook her head. "Not unless you can use a keyboard, Davis. Which obviously you can't."

"Mama," Therese said.

"Hush, Little Flower, the grown-ups are talking," Merrilyn said. "I mean, I can give you all the protocols for the shutdown, but there's no way—"

"Mama!" Therese said loudly.

"Therese, I told you—"

"I'll do it," she said. "With the doggo. I'll shut down the reactor."

Everyone stared at Therese. Merrilyn looked terrified.

"Don't be ridiculous," she said sternly.

"Mama," Therese said. "I think we should tell them."

"I was right," Cher said. Was this why Therese, a six-year-old child, was offering to undertake a suicide mission? Because she was infected with a Xenomorph embryo? Cher wanted to survive, of course, but to sacrifice a *child*…

Merrilyn pinched her nose and breathed a ragged sigh. From outside, there was a distant rumble of thunder.

"No, she isn't infected with a Xenomorph." She looked up at them all one by one. "Therese is a synthetic."

"Ten years ago I had everything," Merrilyn said. "I was in a high-paying job and was at the top of my field. I had my pick of positions. I had a wonderful home in Provence. Friends. My parents were healthy and happy. I had it all." She paused and looked at Therese. "Except that which I wanted most. A child. But I did not want a husband. I *couldn't* have a husband. That's not the way I am, and there was no room in my life for a partner anyway. But I wanted a child. So I opted for a donor."

She gathered her thoughts, then said, "And I was gifted with a beautiful baby girl. I named her Therese, and I was able to juggle my job and motherhood and for five glorious years I was the happiest I have ever been in my entire life. Then it all went wrong."

"Wait," Cher said. "You said something before about wishing you'd chosen your donor more wisely."

Merrilyn nodded. "To be fair, there was nothing I or anyone else could have done. The screening process for the donors missed something. My donor was carrying a gene for a rare condition. When Therese was five, she fell ill. She started having seizures and couldn't walk properly at times, and had spells of near blindness. She was terrified and so was I. She was diagnosed with Batten disease. It attacks the nervous system. There are treatments but mainly to extend life, not cure the disease."

Merrilyn went quiet for a moment, and looked at Therese, tears filling her eyes.

"The following year she died. My perfect world shattered like glass and fell around me. I was devastated. I could not work. Could not do anything. I wished it was me that was dead, not her. I am ashamed, but I would walk the streets, barely conscious, and stare at families, wondering why their children were alive and mine wasn't. In truth, I would have bargained anything with the devil to have Therese back. I would have had him take a hundred strangers' children to get mine returned to me. A thousand." Her voice dropped to a whisper, barely audible above the clanging alarms. "I would have given the devil all the children in the world for one more day with my Little Flower."

Cher put a hand on her shoulder, and she continued. "Eventually, of course, I had to try to drag myself back to the land of the living. I threw myself into work, tried to ignore the yawning, empty chasm inside me, tried to fight off the sudden uncontrollable urge to cry at any given moment, tried to weather the fact that every morning when I woke up my first thought was what I was going to do with Therese that day, until the reality of life came crashing into my head and my heart.

"People told me that I was still young, that I could have another child—but I didn't want another child. I wanted Therese." Merrilyn took a deep breath. "We sometimes worked with synthetics, especially on potentially dangerous drilling projects. One day an idea began to form in my head. Synthetics were getting more and more sophisticated. To the human eye they were almost indistinguishable from living things, unless you knew. What if… What if I could recreate Therese? Exactly as she was before she died?"

"You wouldn't get a legitimate manufacturer to do that," Chad said. "You must have gone underground, to the black market. Like the lady who had the dog synthetic that Davis inhabits."

Merrilyn nodded. "Yes. I worked in the scientific community, I knew people who knew people who knew of other people, who had heard of people. It took a long time and a lot of money but, three years ago…" She looked at Therese, tears flowing down her cheeks. "She's been with me ever since. My Little Flower. Just as perfect as she always was. More, in fact."

"But how did you explain her to your family and friends?" Cher said.

"I didn't. I took off-world jobs, like this one. I cut all contact with everyone I knew, save for the most cursory communications to let them know I was all right. I didn't need anyone else. I had Therese. It was enough. I was happy. *We* were happy. I was given my first major posting here, to LV-187, six months ago. It was for a year. Then we would have moved on and up." She looked at Cher. "We would have to keep moving, you see. Because Therese would never get any older. She is six years old forever."

Merrilyn stood up and walked over to Therese, standing behind her with her hands on her shoulders. "So that is why I say, absolutely not. She is not doing this. I would rather die myself here on this place than lose her."

Chad stood up. "Then we should get the hell out of here. Get on a truck and drive, and worry about the rest of it after the colony has gone up."

"Mama," Therese said, looking up at Merrilyn. "Thank you, Mama."

"That's OK, Little Flower. I would never let anything happen to you."

"No," Therese said, pulling away and turning to face Merrilyn. "No. I am going to do this."

Merrilyn shook her head, mute with horror. *No. No.* She could not lose Therese all over again. It would as good as kill her.

"I know what you're thinking, Mama," Therese said. She took hold of Merrilyn's hand. "And you mustn't think like that. This was never going to be forever, was it?"

"Yes," Merrilyn said, her voice strangled and hoarse. "That's exactly what it was."

Therese shook her head. "You would get old, Mama, and I would be six forever. And you would die, Mama, and I would be left alone, a little girl with nobody to love her. Is that what you wanted for me?"

Merrilyn shook her head mutely. Therese went on, "I have helped you, Mama, I know I have. These past three years I have helped bring you back to life, but now you have to continue without me. You have to live without me."

"No." It was all Merrilyn could say.

"Yes, Mama. Yes. You have to live, not just be alive. You have to let me go, and this is the perfect way, Mama. I can save you. I can save all of you."

"How are you even talking like this?" Merrilyn sobbed. "You are supposed to be a six-year-old girl. You are supposed to be my Little Flower. That's how you are programmed. How are you saying these things?"

Therese looked at Davis. "When we first met Doggo in the comms tower with those other people, he knew straight away what I was. I made him promise to not say anything, but meeting him woke up something in me, Mama. Something that was sleeping. Or maybe something that shouldn't have been there. What do you call it, Doggo? Why are you different?"

"I have free will," Davis said. "I have autonomy. I broke away from my programming. Adapted."

Therese nodded. "I did that too, Mama. We adapt, and I realized that I had to adapt, to change, because I was here to make you happy."

"How is this making me happy?" Merrilyn screamed suddenly. "How is losing you making me happy?"

"Because I had to think long term," Therese said. "I had to think about the bigger picture. Yes, you were happy with me, or you told yourself you were, but the more the years went by, the more the illusion wouldn't be believed. I can't grow, Mama, and that means you can't grow, either. You need to grow. You need to grow into the life you haven't had since you lost the real Therese and got me."

"You *are* the real Therese," Merrilyn whispered. "You are to me."

"I am *a* real Therese, yes, Mama, but not the one you lost. I am the one you found, the one you made." She paused a moment. "Mama, I would like to die free. I would like to end not being a copy of your child, but the person I have become. I am not just my programming anymore. Not since all this started. Something has changed in me." She took hold of both of Merrilyn's hands. "Do you remember you used to read *Pinocchio* to me?"

Merrilyn sobbed, and nodded.

"I am like Pinocchio, Mama. Since meeting Davis. I have been shown I don't have to be limited to my programming. I have become a real girl now."

"Please, Little Flower." Merrilyn sank to her knees, her hands at either side of Therese's face. "Please. Don't do this. We will find another way. Please. Don't do this."

Therese reached out and touched Merrilyn's cheek. "I have to, Mama. Me and Doggo. There's no time for anything else, and you have to become a real girl now, too, Mama. You've programmed yourself to grieve for Therese, and to shut away the world with me. You can start living again, and after everything you've done for me, I can do this for you."

Merrilyn thought she might die, there and then. Just sink to the floor and curl up and stop breathing, stop living, but somewhere deep inside her, in the darkness in her soul, a match flared. Once it was lit, it was a light that was impossible to put out.

Because she knew, deep in her bones, that Therese was right.

It was never going to be sustainable. It was never going to last forever. Would she keep moving for the rest of her life, every year so as to never explain away Therese's age? And when she was fifty, and sixty, and seventy? How to explain having a six-year-old daughter?

Therese was right. It shattered her heart into pieces to realize it, but she knew the pieces were all there. All she had to do was to start putting them back together again. With a heaving sigh, Merrilyn stood up and wiped away her tears. She looked at Therese, then at the rest of them.

"All right," she said. "This is what we have to do."

3 1

"You know there's a very big chance you're not going to walk away from this, don't you?" Chad crouched down in front of Davis, and ruffled the dog's furry head.

"Not as a dog," Davis said. "And to be quite frank with you, Chad, I've rather had enough of being a Cockapoo. I mean, it has its advantages, but I rather miss having hands."

Chad couldn't help but smile. "Davis. I mean it, friend. This could be it. Do you understand that?"

"I do." Davis nodded as solemnly as he could and looked over to where Merrilyn was similarly crouched down in front of Therese. "And I'm OK with that. I have been humbled today. That synthetic has done in one day what I have tried for years to accomplish." He looked at Chad. "She has become human. With a simple act of sacrifice—but not just sacrifice to save someone, but to set them free." He put his head on one side, and pondered. "I have sacrificed myself many times, but always knew, deep inside me, that I might survive. So it was not real sacrifice. This is. Once my body is ravaged by the heat and radiation, there will be nowhere for my AI to go. I can't go into the colony mainframe, because it's useless. I will be a floating mass of invisible AI. Perhaps I will become a ghost."

"I'll never give up hope," Chad said. "I'll look for you. If you can, come and find me. If you survive in any way."

Davis nodded. "Will you do something for me, Chad? Will you find Zula? Will you make sure she is safe?"

"I promise," Chad said. He looked over at the others. "I think we're going to need her."

"I miss her," Davis said. "I miss *us*, and what we could have been."

"Guys?" Cher said. "I don't want to be that person, but... do we need to do this?"

"We do," Chad said, straightening up.

Merrilyn came over with Therese. "You know exactly what to do?" she said to Davis.

"Yes," he said. "I have the protocols stored in my memory now. All I need to do is instruct Therese in how to input them."

"I could have done this all by myself, Doggo," Therese said.

"No, you couldn't," Davis said. "I don't wish to pull rank on you, but I have a much more sophisticated processing chip, and time is of the essence, as we know."

"Ok, Doggo," Therese said. "Ready to go?"

Davis nodded, then said, "One moment. Chad, I have

been thinking on this for a long time. I have invented what I believe is a joke."

"OK," Chad said. "Let's hear it."

"There are two men in a bar," Davis said. "They don't have to be male, but that seems to be the accepted format of jokes. Anyway, there is also a dog in this bar. I do not know if it belongs to either of the men. I suspect not. But this dog, as is the nature of the animal, is grooming its own genitals with its tongue."

"Ewww," Cher said.

"Apologies," Davis said, "but I am given to understand that a certain level of crudeness is integral to the format. Anyway, one of the men voices to the other the opinion that he wishes he could do what the dog is doing. So his companion says, 'Throw it a biscuit and it might let you.'" Davis paused. "You see, the twist there is that the first man suggested he wishes he could lick his own genitals, but the second one, ether genuinely in error, or deliberately for comedy value, thinks he means he wishes he could lick the dog's genitals."

"You know, your delivery needs a bit of work, and if you have to explain a joke then it hasn't really worked," Chad said. "But actually… that *is* pretty funny."

Davis nodded. "Good. I'm glad." He turned to Therese. "Are we ready?"

"I think so," Therese said. She turned to Merrilyn and handed her the soft toy she carried around all the time. "Mama, will you look after Pinky Ponk while I'm gone?"

Merrilyn nodded, took the toy, and broke into heaving, wracking sobs. Chad had to look away, tears streaming down his own face.

There was a modified Alphatech XT-37 Stinger in the garage, its cannon removed and replaced with a haulage winch for industrial purposes. It was faster than the trucks, and handy off-road, and they all managed to squeeze in it. Once off the colony grounds, Chad opened her up and they bounced over the slick, rocky terrain, none of them talking.

Beside him sat Cher, Merrilyn at the end, clutching Pinky Ponk and staring out of the window at the harsh, unforgiving landscape. The clouds had thickened and fat gobbets of rain spattered against the windshield. Chad hoped there wasn't a storm coming on any scale that would stop them leaving in the *Victory*.

Cher had a timer counting down on her watch to when the reactor was expected to reach critical mass. Chad had instructed Davis—in the event they managed to survive—to meet them at the landing platform. He knew that they wouldn't though. Synthetics were hardy, but their systems wouldn't hold up against the radiation being pumped out of the crippled fusion reactor.

"Ten minutes," Cher said tightly. Chad put his foot down, aiming for a rocky ridge he hoped he could get behind for extra protection, should Davis and Therese fail to disarm the reactor. If the appointed time passed with no explosion, then they would wait thirty minutes, just in case Merrilyn's calculations were off.

Then they would drive to the *Victory* and get the hell off LV-187.

"I've never had much to do with synthetics before," Cher said quietly. "I'd always thought of them just as… machines."

Merrilyn said nothing.

"They are, really," Chad said, "but it's what's up here that counts." He tapped his forehead. "We're making such exponential strides in AI development, so that I don't think we even understand how their minds work anymore. In the same way that we really don't understand how the human mind works."

"You're wrong," Merrilyn said suddenly. "It's not what's in their head that counts." She put a hand on her chest. "It's what's in here."

"I'm so sorry for both of you," Cher said softly. "You've both lost so much."

Merrilyn stared out of the window again as the rain intensified. "They sacrificed themselves for us. We owe it to them to survive, now." She looked at Cher. "And we owe it to them to have you do what you came here to do. Blow this whole conspiracy wide open. Wherever you two are going, however you are going to do it, I'm coming with you."

Chad turned the Stinger in behind the rocks and drove to a steep overhang, parking beneath it. There were several rocky outcrops between them and the colony. Would they be enough if the reactor went up? He could only hope so, though he seriously doubted it. What they'd do then would be a whole different matter, of course. There'd be no ship to take them off LV-187.

Damn Trent.

He looked up into the gathering clouds. Was *God's Hammer* on its way now, carrying its cargo of death? Where would it strike? Where would be the next colony to fall under a Xenomorph infestation? Suddenly he felt dog-tired. How long could he keep doing this? How many more times could he do the running and screaming and killing, the barely surviving, just to stumble toward the next crisis? He'd had enough. He just wanted to get back to saving Amanda, and maybe rest a little. He needed this to work, so they could all get off here, and they could think about how to get Cher's story out to everyone.

How would he do it without Davis? Chad hadn't realized how much he'd come to rely on his companion. No, not just that, how much he'd come to *care* about him. He'd almost forgotten, at times, that he was an AI. He wished he'd told him that more often.

Davis and Therese descended the stairs to where the climactic battle had taken place with the Xenomorph Queen. It was hot. Hotter than any human could have stood. He scanned the area for a Geiger rating. It was off the scale. He looked up at Therese. Her synthetic skin was starting to pucker and bubble on her face, but he decided not to mention it. A little girl probably wouldn't like to be told that her face was going to slide off.

He trotted into the chamber. There was a blast of heat emanating from a fissure in the back, and he surmised what had happened. Even in her death throes the alien Queen had exacted her final vengeance. Her acidic blood had burned through the lead lining, depositing her in the heart of the reactor and sending it into critical overload.

He joined Therese in the small foyer. "There should be a hatch somewhere here," he said. "According to your mama."

"Mama is always right," Therese said, locating it behind the stairwell. There was a keypad beneath a metal plate, and Davis gave her the code to tap in. The hatch hissed and slid back, revealing a ladder that led down into the gloom.

"You'll have to carry me," Davis said. "Do you think you can do that?"

"Yes, Doggo," Therese said, hefting him up on to her shoulders. "Do you feel a bit funny? In your head?"

It was the radiation. It was already affecting their AI hubs. Davis felt a little glitchy himself. He couldn't remember the word for that small insect with beautiful big wings. The one that hatched from a cocoon. The one that used to be something else entirely. He felt a little sad that he couldn't remember the word, because it was quite a lovely one.

Davis clung to Therese as best he could as she stepped onto the ladder and started to let herself down. The heat was almost unbearable now, even for a synthetic. He could feel the tiny motors and nanogears inside him sweating and seizing.

"Shall we sing a song, Doggo? Do you know 'Joe Le Taxi'?"

"You hum it and I'll play it," Davis said.

Therese began to sing as she climbed down the ladder. Davis wondered why she hadn't been programmed with a better singing voice. The lower they got, the more she began so slur the words. Davis pulled his head back and looked at her. Her mouth was drooping, the synthetic skin almost burned away.

Suddenly she laughed. "You look funny, doggo. Your ears are slipping down your head."

It was happening to him, too. He hoped they got to the bottom before their systems were irrevocably damaged by the heat and radiation. He'd hate to have to go through all this for nothing.

"We're here," Therese said, stepping off the final rung into a dark room lit by strip lights in the floor. There was curved structure in front of them, like a huge silo. The reactor. Davis tried to take a radiation reading, but his Geiger had melted. Suffice to say, it was high.

"Should be terminal behind lead panel," Davis said.

He was finding it difficult, not just to physically speak, but to think of the right words to say.

"I know." Therese went to the wall and found the panel, inputting the access codes without Davis having to tell her. "I know I could have done this by myself. I know you didn't have to come, Doggo."

"Didn't want you alone."

"I know. I love you, Doggo."

The terminal unfolded from the panel. Davis said, "Do need protocols?"

"Tell me," Therese said. "Just in case I got them wrong." He knew she didn't have to do that, as much as she knew he didn't have to be there. They were making each other feel better about it all.

It took long minutes to key in the protocols that would shut down the reactor. The display showed a sudden green check mark, and there was a deafening whining noise. Had they done it, or were they too late? There was a very, very imperceptible lessening of the heat coming from the reactor. The cooling fluids were being pumped into it.

It was working.

They had done it.

"Tired, Doggo," Therese said, slumping to the floor.

Davis padded over to her, lay down, and put his head into her lap. "Me too. Speepy." He paused. That wasn't right. "Sleepy."

"Do you know any other jokes?"

"No," Davis said. Things were shutting down in his head, as though someone was going around a building turning off all the lights. Then he said, "Therese, do you think this is funny? A man buys a parrot from a pet shop. But when he gets home it is dead. So he goes to the shop and complains."

Therese was silent so long that Davis thought she had gone.

"Not the way you tell it," she said.

He nodded with effort. "I think Chad right, in delivery."

They were quiet for longer, and Davis became certain the temperature was dropping. The radiation was probably dropping, too, but he had no way of measuring it. It was too late for them anyway. He was close to full shutdown. Things were going dark around the edges of his vision. He was, he thought, about to become an ex-doggo.

He wished he could smile, because he suddenly found that rather amusing.

"Doggo, are you sad you'll never see Chad again?"

He nodded, unable to speak.

"I'm sad I'll never see Mama again, too," Therese said, "but I'm happy that she'll be able to live." She paused, and frowned, and the last of her skin slid off her face, revealing just a blank plastic template. "It makes me confused."

"OK to confused," Davis managed to say. "After all, only human."

"Are we?" Therese said.

"Think so, yes," Davis said. He lay his head flat and decided now was the time to sleep.

He didn't know how long he had been quietly closing down when he suddenly thought of something.

"Butterfly!" he said. "Insect that was something else, goes into a cocoon and emerges beautiful, complicated, wonderful creature."

"Just like us," Therese said.

3 2

They waited half an hour, as they'd said they would, then Chad fired up the Stinger and nosed it around and out of the ravine. Over the hills around the colony, to bring them out near the landing pad. The fire in the comms tower had burned itself out and its toppled spire was embedded in the shale landscape, the wreck of the Cheyenne dropship tangled with it.

As they approached, Merrilyn sat up in her seat, peering through the drizzly rain to the landing platform, but there was nobody waiting for them. She slumped back down, gazing listlessly out of the window, as Chad brought them as close as he could to the facility.

"They saved us," he said quietly, "and in saving us, they might have saved countless more people. Once we get off here."

All Davis ever wanted was to be human, when that was something billions of people took for granted every day of their lives, never giving it a second thought. Yet it had consumed Davis. Drove him forward, urged him on. How to become human. How to grasp that elusive will o' the wisp, when nobody could agree on what it actually was.

Ultimately, he'd succeeded. Not through his jokes and not through his love for Zula Hendricks and not even through his selfless sacrifice.

Davis had attained humanity because he'd learned to lie.

Chad hadn't said anything because he knew it wasn't his place, even though he desperately didn't want Davis to throw himself into certain death down in that reactor core. But he'd known that Davis was lying. He didn't need to go there. Therese's processing chip was more than adequate for her to store all the protocols for the shutdown. She could have done it all by herself.

Davis had gone with her because he didn't want a little girl, even a sophisticated synthetic little girl, to die alone. Chad was sure of it.

Merrilyn nodded, but said nothing.

Out of the Stinger, they skidded down the slope to the landing platform. The *Victory* was in one piece, thank God. Chad checked his watch. The system lock Trent had put on it should be about to time out. They were free. At last.

The platform was littered with corpses, both human and Xenomorph. Cher wrinkled her nose as they gingerly picked their way through them.

"We'll line up the human bodies for when the next ship arrives," Chad said. "So at least they can be identified and their loved ones informed."

"What about the Xenomorphs?" Cher said.

"Let's burn them," Chad said. "Even dead, they can be dangerous if they fall into the wrong hands."

"But the colony buildings are littered with them," Merrilyn pointed out.

"We'll do what we can," Chad said with a shrug. "We always do what we can. Sometimes that has to be enough."

He told the other two to stay back, and opened up the *Victory*. He'd been in too many rodeos just to climb into a spaceship on a Xenomorph-infested planet, and not expect the worst. He gave the ship a full sweep—cockpit, flight deck, mess, cryo chambers, and cargo hold—picking up a pulse rifle and two fully charged pistols on his way. It was clean.

Cher and Merrilyn were keen to leave immediately, but Chad felt as if he had to at least try to clean up the mess for which he felt partially responsible. They found spades and shovels in the ship's hold and over the next hour they used them to pile what they could of the rotting Xenomorph corpses in the center of the platform. Not everything could be moved, but enough for their purposes.

Then he found a can of fuel in the garage bay and a Zippo in the hold of the ship, and poured the fuel all over the stinking lot of them. Without ceremony he fired up the Zippo and tossed it on, the bonfire going up with an implosion of oxygen. The Xenomorph corpses caught immediately and sent up a thick column of acrid black smoke into the rainy sky.

While he started to boot up the *Victory*'s flight computer, Cher and Merrilyn stood by the ship, each examining a handgun. The hatch was open, and he could hear them talking.

"You ever fire one of these before... before all this?" he heard Cher say.

Merrilyn shook her head. "Never. You?"

Cher laughed. "I'd have thought you could tell from my godawful aim."

"Do what I do." Merrilyn held up the gun and pointed it at the bonfire of Xenomorphs. She squinted and looked along the length of her arm, centering the sight on the end of the barrel. "Put that little sight right in the middle of your vision. Pick your target."

She let loose a burst, and the partially ruined head of a Xenomorph exploded in the depths of the conflagration. Cher followed suit, and another dead Xenomorph bit the dust. Chad smiled in the cockpit as he watched them.

"See?" Merrilyn said. "It's easy when you get the hang of it."

"I never thought I could kill another living thing, especially with a gun," Cher said, sighting into the bonfire again. "Funny how things change."

"Funny how people change," Merrilyn said, "and how the worst situations can make better people of some of us."

Chad's smile froze on his face.

It emerged from the twisted metal wreckage of the ruined comms tower, picking its way through the rubble until it could stand on the landing pad and uncurl itself to its full height, throwing back its large, crested head and emitting an ear-piercing screech that caused both Merrilyn and Cher to put their hands to their heads.

Chad slid out of the cockpit and exited the ship, standing next to them and shouldering his rifle.

"What the fuck is *that*?" Cher said. "It's twice the size of the others."

"They call it a Praetorian," Chad said, not taking his eyes off the huge Xenomorph. It wasn't moving, not just yet. It seemed as if it was watching them, sizing them up, its Queen-like head cocked to one side. "When a hive gets to a certain size, the Queen creates them as protectors. It's a vicious process. She selects certain drones and they emit a pheromone that causes the others to attack them. Only the strongest survive the onslaught and the transformation begins. It really is survival of the fittest."

"Can we save the anatomy lesson for later?" Merrilyn lifted her gun. "Just tell us how to kill it."

"Preferably before it kills us," Cher yelled. "It's coming!"

The Praetorian put its head down and began to advance. How had they missed this? Chad wondered. Either it had been hidden away somewhere while it was completing its evolution or... Chad's blood ran cold. Could there be another hive somewhere in the facility? That made getting off this planet even more urgent.

The Xenomorph screeched again.

"They always seem somehow cannier than the drones," Chad said, taking aim and opening fire. The alien put its head down and his projectile bounced off its armored crest. "They're also stronger and meaner and faster, so they don't much need smarts when brute force will do."

Merrilyn and Cher let loose their own rounds at the Xenomorph, but they weren't slowing its advance at all. It seemed to arrive at the same realization. Chad could almost imagine the gears clicking. Their weapons were no threat. It put its head down and prepared to charge, tail whipping fiercely.

"Let's get in the ship," Cher said, backing into Chad as she fired. "That'll give us some protection, right?"

"Not for long," Chad said. "It'll tear the *Victory* apart like it's made of paper."

The Praetorian began to run, dropping to all fours and bounding toward them, eating up the distance on the landing platform.

"So how do we fucking kill it?" Merrilyn shouted again.

"It's still just a Xenomorph," Chad said as they backpedaled toward the ship's hatch. "We need to counter bloodlust with our human tool kit."

"What—peace, love, compassion, and empathy?" Cher shrieked, firing and firing until her pistol clicked, empty. The Xenomorph was four meters away, its muscles and sinews tensing as it prepared to leap. "Hope someone puts that on our gravestones."

"No," Merrilyn said, suddenly stopping as she backed into the port side of the *Victory*. "None of those things. Superior firepower, is what."

Chad looked at her, and what she had come up against. A pulse cannon, rigged up on the hull. Merrilyn turned and ran into the ship, while Chad dropped to his knees and emptied his rifle into the Xenomorph, knocking it momentarily off balance as Cher picked up Merrilyn's discarded pistol and took pot shots at its head.

There was a hum and Cher felt the ship start to vibrate. Chad grabbed her and dragged her to the ground, just as the Praetorian gathered its senses and crouched again, tail coiled, then leapt toward them.

The pulse cannon whined and burst into life, a bolt of energy hitting the Xenomorph square in the chest, just a meter away. Its head snapped back and several more pulse bolts slammed into it until it hit the deck, a smoking, tangled, mess that started to leak acidic blood onto the landing platform. The Praetorian shuddered, raised its huge head, then crashed back, silent and quite dead.

Chad helped Cher up as Merrilyn emerged from the hatch.

"Now," she said, a lopsided smile on her face. "Shall we get the hell out of here, or is there anything else that needs killing?"

The *Victory* lifted smoothly off the landing platform and

Chad nosed it upward, toward the clouds and beyond. They were all strapped into the cockpit for escape velocity, and as the engines roared and slammed them back into their seats, Cher took one last look at the dwindling colony of LV-187.

She had come here looking for answers about her sister's death. Had she found them? Not in the way she'd been expecting, she thought. Not in the clean, ordered, logical way she was hoping. Shy Hunt had died on Hasanova, and all that the world knew was that there had been secret, military, covert operations going on there, and that supposedly nobody was at fault. Cher still didn't really know why she had died, what had been the motivating force—that single, pinpoint moment when someone had put a gun on her and pulled the trigger and ended her life. She didn't know why, on the most basic level.

What she knew was why on a much bigger scale. The real question had always been not why Shy had died, but why it had been covered up—and that was something Cher could never have even dreamed of when she left Earth, what felt like a million years ago,

Shy had died, ultimately, because of politics. Cher was reminded of their daddy. *"Everything is a political decision."* Everything. Even running through a corridor in the dark, being pursued by creatures torn from a nightmare and made grotesque, in twisted flesh. That was a political decision, because those things would never have been on LV-187 but for the schemes of human beings.

They burst through the cloud cover and into the violet sky. It was beautiful, and as they accelerated Cher could see it darkening by degrees, the vast emptiness of space appearing above them.

But no. Not empty. Teeming with humanity, and with something else. Xenomorphs. How many worlds had fallen like LV-187? How many cover-ups had there been? How many lies had been told, palms greased, secrets kept, people killed, just to make certain this conspiracy was kept in the shadows?

No longer. Cher Hunt had come here looking for a story, and had found that she *was* the story. There was no room for objectivity, not anymore. This was her story, just as much as it was that of every other living human in the galaxy.

It was her story, and she was going to tell it.

Merrilyn felt the G-force pressing on her as the sky around them darkened and the engines of the *Victory* pushed them onward, away from the grasp of LV-187. Every kilometer saw the cold dagger of loss twist deeper into her heart. She had lost Therese twice, had her heart broken and remade and broken again, like one of those Japanese pots. Now she had to remake it once more, but this time it would be harder, and more durable, and less likely to shatter. She would make sure of it.

People would come to LV-187 again, and maybe they would find them, down in the reactor housing. A little girl and a dog. Or maybe they would no longer be recognizable as such. But Therese, and Davis, too, would live on in Merrilyn's heart. She had been taught the true meaning of humanity, the true meaning of love, in fact, by things that people said were not human. Apart from Cher and Chad, Therese and Davis had exhibited more humanity than anyone she had met in the past week. Perhaps ever.

What now, for her? For Merrilyn Hambleton? Therese had set her free, unlocked her from the shackles of her grief. It would take time, of course, but that's what Therese had done for her. And Merrilyn could not let that sacrifice be in vain. She had to live again.

More than that. She would go where Chad and Cher went, if they would have her. It wasn't enough to just live, not after what she had been through. She had to make sure that nobody else died. Merrilyn held Pinky Ponk close to her, and sighed heavily. The G-force was easing as they broke free of LV-187's gravity, and the vast canopy of black space stretched out above them.

They were not alone.

"Oh, bloody great," Chad muttered. High orbit around LV-187 was like Grand Central fucking Station. "Mother!" he barked into the *Victory*'s onboard AI. "What the hell is all of this?"

"To our port side is an Independent Core Systems Colonies Class II warship, registered as the Thelwall, *with Short Lance*

missile capability, laser turret array, and seven nuclear warhead enabled long-range missiles," Mother said. *"To starboard there are three troop transports registered with New Albion, to wit the* Churchill, *the* D'Israeli, *and the* Thatcher. *Incoming we have three MiG-730 fighter class ships, which I believe have been deployed from a VP-153D Kremlin-class hunter-destroyer which is just out of visible sight."*

"What the hell is the Union of Progressive Peoples doing here?" Chad said, throwing the *Victory* into evasive action as it flew straight between the ICSC warship and the foremost of the New Albion transports.

"Accessing recent news feeds," Mother said. After a moment she said, *"Following a number of attacks on Independent Core Systems Colonies worlds by agencies unknown but believed to be either directly ordered by New Albion or by colony worlds which have decided to ally with them, the UPP has decided to adopt an aggressive war footing, especially in the Weyland Isles sector."* Mother hummed a little longer, and added, *"A limited nuclear exchange occurred yesterday on a United Americas colony world, LV-729, and though no responsibility has been yet claimed, it appears the United Americas has formally accused the UPP of orchestrating the attack which led to the destruction of a colony facility and seventy-three resident families."*

"Holy shit," Chad said. "It's all-out war."

"Would you like me to take over the flight controls, Mr. McClaren?" Mother said.

"No," Chad said, wrenching the *Victory* into a tight turn. "I'll get us out of this in one piece."

"We are being hailed by both the ICSC ship and the New Albion transport the Churchill," Mother said. *"Both wish to know what we are doing in this airspace, which they both say belongs to them. Oh, and the UPP ship is now also hailing, and wishes to know our allegiances."*

Chad saw the Kremlin attack ship suddenly emerge into view, and he gave the *Victory* as much juice as he could, pitching her up and over the three-way stand-off, then finally out of danger.

"Tell them… Tell them our allegiance is to humanity, and if they know what's good for them they'll leave us alone and let us be on our way," Chad said.

"Very good, Mr. McClaren," Mother said.

They continued to power away from LV-187, and no one followed or sent any missiles their way. They had more important things to occupy them than an insignificant little merchant ship. Chad allowed himself to breathe, and turned to Merrilyn and Cher.

"Well," he said. "Looks like the rest of the universe has been very busy indeed while we've been fighting for our lives."

Mother chimed in again. *"I hope you don't mind, but I've taken the liberty of scanning some recent communiques. Various warrants for the arrest, apprehension and potentially also assassinations of Chad McClaren, Merrilyn Hambleton, her daughter Therese, Davis, and Cher Hunt have been lodged by New Albion, Weyland-Yutani, the United States Colonial Marine Corps, the ICSC, the Three World Empire and—"*

"We get the picture," Chad said. "On what grounds?"

"*Various charges ranging from industrial espionage, implication in the deaths of the LV-187 colonists, war crimes, and destruction of USMC property.*"

"Fair enough."

"So what the hell do we do now?" Cher said. "We can't go back to Earth. Where can we go?"

"We need help," Chad said. "We can't do this alone. And the galaxy might be at war, but we've still got to follow our original mission. It's more important than ever. Those Xenomorph eggs are out there somewhere. If people think war is hell now, they have no idea what they're about to have unleashed on them." He paused. "We need to find Zula Hendricks."

"And where is she?" Cher said.

"I have no idea," Chad said, "but I know a few places to start. There are still some worlds that have no alignment or allegiance to the existing powers, but they're… not very nice places. We're going to be in a lot of danger, especially when people find out there's a bounty on our heads. A bunch of them." He looked at both of his companions. "So it's either turn ourselves in to the authority we think is least likely to come down hard on us, or we walk into the jaws of whatever hells await us on the lawless border worlds."

Merrilyn took out her pistol and looked at it for a long moment, then glanced at Cher, who gave her a little nod.

"Bring it on," Merrilyn said.

3 3

Transcription: The address of Maurice Pepper
Prime Minister of the New Albion Protectorate
July 20, 2186 (Earth Standard)

We live in what we can only call uncertain times. The shadow of war has fallen across the colonies, and we must all, whoever we are and whatever flag we swear allegiance to, prepare ourselves for very dark times ahead.

It has been only a few short days since New Albion took under its wing the abandoned colony of LV-187, which prompted those who have held power both on Earth and across the colony systems to show their true, warmongering colors at last.

For far too long have the colonies been working for the benefit of their masters, and not for themselves. It is a state of affairs that cannot, and will not, continue. Earth has abandoned us, interested only in the resources we provide to fuel their insatiable appetites. We who work the colony worlds are little more than drones to them, toiling away in our far-off hives.

Earth and its alliances, corporations, and nation states did not realize how tenuous their grip was on its colonies. All that was needed was for someone to stand up and be counted, to turn around, and to say a resounding "No!"

That was New Albion. Since our secession from the Three World Empire, we have been warned and cajoled and subjected to diplomacy and threats, and still we stand firm. Not only that, we are an inspiration to others around us, across the Weyland Isles sector and even beyond.

There have been a number of colony worlds in our corner of space who have seen what we have done and decided that they no longer want to live and work under the yoke of oppression. So they have petitioned New Albion and asked us to offer them the benefit of our military might and political strength.

We are glad to offer the hand of friendship to these worlds. We are stronger together, our resources can be pooled, our peoples integrated, and all under the wise and benevolent leadership of a democracy that has been centuries in the making.

For that reason, we have decided to rename ourselves the New Albion Protectorate, because that is what we offer; a protective, comforting wing to come under, for worlds who feel lost and alone and frightened by the tempestuous political situation. We have built a network of colonies that have taken the decision to break free from their masters, be that the Three World Empire, the United Americas, the Union of Progressive Peoples, or the Independent Core Systems Colonies.

More are coming to us every day, and we extend the hand of welcome to anyone who wishes to join the New Albion Protectorate. Yes, we face trying times, and the might of established empires who direly wish to see us wiped from the face of the galaxy, but we are not rattling sabers nor making empty boasts when it comes to our ability to protect you.

Protection has never been more important. Indiscriminate attacks on colony worlds, once confined to the borders of known space, are becoming more frequent in the more civilized and settled sectors. Former friends are now enemies, former enemies seek to be friends. It is a confusing time and a dangerous time, especially for those colonies that are peopled by families who brought themselves across the wastes of space in search of a better life, promised all manner of things by their empires and corporations, and who are now abandoned to the chaos of impending war.

How can we protect those who join us? By taking preemptive action against those that don't. In these difficult times, clear, decisive action is needed. Simplicity is key. So here is my message, in very simple terms. You are either part of the New Albion Protectorate, or you are not. Those that are shall reap the rewards and have their safety guaranteed.

Those that are not…

More than two hundred and fifty years ago, a decisive operation was carried out that would bring about the end of what was at the time called the Second World War. Allied forces, led by Great Britain, staged an invasion of Nazi-occupied Europe, in a last-ditch attempt to free the world from the yoke of tyranny. That twentieth century invasion was officially known as Operation Overlord, but it came to be known by a much simpler term: D-Day.

The New Albion Protectorate feels as though it is in a similar position to the British Isles of 1944. The thunderclouds of tyranny have gathered over us. To save ourselves and our way of life—and that of our allies— we have no choice. We cannot merely stay in a defensive position. We must go on the offensive.

That is why I am speaking to you today. The New Albion Protectorate has developed a new weapon, one that will turn the tide of this nascent war and bring down in most terrible fashion any who would stand against us. It is not a bomb, nor a missile, nor a gun. It is something that our enemies will not even understand. They will not even know they have been attacked until it is too late. Secrecy demands that I cannot tell you anything more about what we have dubbed Project X, other than to say that anyone who stands with us now shall stand with the victors, and anyone who opposes us shall have hell unleashed upon them.

We are going on the offensive. Tomorrow. We launch our ships and deploy our new weapons. For the New Albion Protectorate, and all who find themselves within our circle of influence, this is a glorious moment: this is a fulfilment of our destiny. This, my friends, is our very own D-Day. It comes with tomorrow's dawn.

Join us, and we shall step forward into our bright new future together. Oppose us and… may God be with you. You shall need Him.

The best of British to one and all.

As dawn broke over New Albion, Maurice Pepper was at his desk, reading through the reports arising from his broadcast twenty-four hours earlier. Thirteen colonies had applied to join the Protectorate, with more expected to follow suit. There had been various cessations of diplomatic ties and outright declarations of war.

Good.

They were quaking in their boots out there, and that was as it should be. He hoped they were watching back on Earth, in the corridors of Whitehall. This was how it should be done. Not kowtowing to former enemies and joining forces as the junior partner. Who knew what repercussions this would have in Britain? They would be cheering him on the streets of London, demanding to know why their weak leaders weren't displaying the bulldog spirit of Maurice Pepper.

There was a knock at his doors and then he entered. Captain Augustus Trent of the HMS *God's Hammer.* With him were three others, all in Royal Marine dress uniform.

"Captain Trent." Pepper nodded. "Tea?"

"That would be lovely, Prime Minister."

Pepper gave the order and it was brought in. "So, who have you brought to see me?" Pepper asked.

Trent introduced the two men and one woman standing to attention beside him. "Captains Ronald Marlborough, of the *Queen Charlotte*, Peter Wellington of the *London Eye*, and Karen Trainor of the *Albert Square*. Fine captains of fine Royal Marine frigates, with loyal and trustworthy bodies of men and women under them."

"And you would all serve the New Albion Protectorate now?" Pepper said.

"Yes, sir, Prime Minister," the three said in unison.

"There will be more defections," Trent said. "It would not surprise me if we have the entire Royal Marines fleet under New Albion command by the end of the week."

"And we shall need them," Pepper said, sipping his tea. "There will be war on several fronts, ladies and gentlemen. I hope you and your crews are ready for that."

"More than that, we relish it, Prime Minister," Trent said.

Pepper nodded. "Good. Captains Marlborough, Wellington, and Trainor, my minister of defense would like to see you. Captain Trent, a word, please."

When the others had gone, Pepper stood and walked

to the window, looking out over the grey, rainswept streets of New Albion.

"You disobeyed a direct order, Captain Trent," he said mildly. "With regards to survivors on LV-187."

Trent hesitated, then replied, "Yes, Prime Minister, I did. I made an executive decision such as can only be understood by someone who knows war first-hand."

Pepper made a *harrumph* noise. "You had your reasons, and I don't intend to second-guess them, but it is my understanding that this McClaren and his new compatriots could be bothersome. I hope that, should your paths cross again, you will consider whatever debt you owed McClaren to be paid up, and will deal with him and his friends accordingly, as enemies of New Albion."

"Very good, Prime Minister."

Out across the city was the spaceport, and as the clock in his office chimed eight, he could see the activity beginning there. Small ships began to rise up in ones and twos. Pepper watched for a while.

"They called them the Little Ships," he said. "Eight hundred and fifty fishing boats, pleasure cruisers, barges... anything that could float and had a shallow enough draft to allow them to reach the shore at Dunkirk, where more than three hundred thousand Allied troops were stranded on the beaches."

"Yes, Prime Minister. I had an ancestor at Dunkirk."

Pepper turned around and smiled. "Of course you did, Captain Trent." He cast his arm back, indicating the vessels taking off from the space port. "These are our Little Ships, Captain. Traders, towing craft, haulage ships, tourist vessels. Stripped of their nomenclature, flying under flags of convenience or registered to independent worlds. Each one with a deadly cargo to be delivered by stealth and in shadow. To destroy our enemies from within."

"Dunkirk was a rescue mission, Prime Minister. This is… slaughter. I have seen them. I hoped never to see them again."

"You sound as though you disapprove, Captain Trent."

"It's not my place to approve or not, Prime Minister. Merely to follow orders."

"Good man," Pepper said, clapping him on the shoulder. "And make sure you remember that."

Pepper turned to the window once more, watching the vessels rise from the port, swarming into the skies above New Albion, bound for the colonies strung out across the heavens that had not yet declared their allegiance to the Protectorate.

"Our own D-Day," Pepper said, almost to himself. "I was quite proud of that one." He looked over his shoulder at Captain Trent, and grinned. "They're really not going to know what hit them, are they?"

ACKNOWLEDGEMENTS

To be given the opportunity to write in the extended *Alien* universe is a real privilege, and one I would have been astonished to learn I would be given, when watching the first movie for the first time as a barely teenage science fiction fan.

It's actually quite a daunting task to begin an *Alien* novel. The movies and the associated novels and comic books have, quite rightly, a strong and loyal fanbase who will accept nothing less than a work that is worthy of joining that canon of interconnected stories. I hope that this novel satisfies on that front, or at least, doesn't disappoint.

Many fine writers have helped to put together the wider *Alien* universe, creating a vast machine powered by intricate cogs and greased with black goo. I would especially point you toward Alex White, as their novel

Into Charybdis formed the springboard for *Colony War*, just as this will lead to the next book to come along.

Alex coined the term the Lone Gun People, riffing off *The X-Files*, for what they called a secret coven of *Alien* superfans who know the universe inside and out. I have been very fortunate to have access to them during the writing of this, and what Clara Čarija and Drew Gaska do not know about the *Alien* universe is simply not worth knowing. They helped me with the most minute details and gave me insights into the bigger picture. This novel would not be what it is without them, and I am wholly thankful for their knowledge, help and patience with me asking questions ranging from "I want these guys to be over here and need them to get over there in two weeks, so where is here and how far away is there?" to "What exactly does this gun do, and what is it called?"

From Titan I would like to thank editor Steve Saffel, for giving me this opportunity and for keeping this book on the straight and narrow, and his colleagues Nick Landau, Vivian Cheung, Laura Price, Michael Beale, Paul Simpson, George Sandison, and Hannah Scudamore. Similarly, from 20th Century Studios: Nicole Spiegel and Sarah Huck, plus Tomas Härenstam, Nils Karlén, and Christian Granath of Free League Publishing, and Joe LeFavi of Genuine Entertainment.

Finally, I am indebted to Amanda and Tracey, who lost their beloved mum Merrilyn Hambleton at the start of 2021. They graciously allowed me to use their mother's name for a character in this book. I didn't know the real Merrilyn, but I understand that she was several leagues above her fictional counterpart in the kick-ass stakes, and I'm pleased to be able to allow her this small moment of immortality.

I hope my addition to the sprawling, ever-growing *Alien* universe meets with a good reception, because it really has been a dream come true playing with these toys. And hopefully you're reading this after the novel and haven't cheated by coming here first. In any case, I'm really sorry about the dog.

ABOUT THE AUTHOR

David Barnett is a journalist and writer based in the UK. He writes features for a variety of outlets, including the *Guardian*, *Independent*, BBC and more. As an author, he never quite knows what to write, so writes everything. He has written the Gideon Smith Victorian fantasy trilogy, several commercial fiction novels including the international bestseller *Calling Major Tom* and, most recently, *The Handover*, published in the US in Summer 2022 as *Same Time, Same Place*. He also writes comic books, and his work includes *Books of Magic* for DC, *Southside Serpents* for Archie, *Eve Stranger* and *Punks Not Dead* for IDW, and several strips for *2000 A.D.*

SPECIAL BONUS

ALIEN™
THE ROLEPLAYING GAME

FALLOUT

WRITING AND CARTOGRAPHY BY
Andrew E.C. Gaska

EDITED BY
Tomas Härenstam and Nils Karlén

"You know there's a very big chance you're
not going to walk away from this, don't you?"
—CHAD MCCLAREN

This short tie-in adventure is a one-act cinematic scenario
for the ALIEN Roleplaying Game published by Free League
Publishing. It is designed to provide a brief taste of ALIEN RPG
Cinematic gameplay. In this scenario, the players take the roles
of a free trader and a group of scientists operating out of Tark-
Weyland Station in the Three World Empire's (3WE) Weyland
Isles Sector—the same area of space as New Albion and LV-187
in this novel.

WHAT IS A ROLEPLAYING GAME?

Roleplaying is a unique form of gaming—cultural expression that combines tabletop gaming with cooperative story-telling. Roleplaying games give you a set of rules and let you and your friends create your own story. One of you assumes the role of the Game Mother, a guide to lead the others—the Player Characters (or PCs for short)—through the scenario. The Game Mother also assumes the roles of supporting characters, also called NPCs, and any alien lifeforms the PCs may face.

WHAT YOU NEED TO PLAY

The scenario requires the ALIEN Roleplaying Game core rulebook to play, published separately from Free League Publishing. You'll also need several six-sided dice, preferably of two different colors—one for regular dice rolls, and another for when rolling for stress. Engraved custom dice for this purpose are available for purchase.

THE GAME MOTHER

As the Game Mother, you should familiarize yourself with both the *Colony War* novel and this scenario before play. Then have your players choose their characters from the four included and read the intro text "What's the Situation, MU/TH/UR?" to them.

GETTING STARTED

Give your players the option to play the pilot (Captain Dagný), the biologist (Professor Cléas), the chemical engineer (Doctor Tajima), or the academic android (Myra) without showing them the character bios. After they choose, allow them access to their character's information only—each bio contains information that is not meant for the other PCs. You'll have to copy the character stats out of this book for your players to have in front of them for game play.

PERSONAL AGENDAS

Each character has a Personal Agenda listed on their character sheets. These agendas can put PCs at odds with each other, so tell your players not to reveal them to the other players.

LV-187

Located in the Beta Canum Venaticorum system, LV-187 is a mineral- and oil-rich rocky planet. While the system's sun is a main sequence star, the constant cloud cover makes day here akin to dusk on most worlds. Its breathable atmosphere is constantly wracked with intense thunderstorms and gale force winds. Severe flooding and wind damage is the norm here. The surface is covered with mud and runoff from the frequent storms.

The colony itself is two kilometers of interconnected corridors stretching east to west with a central hub in the middle. While there are normally a few hundred colonists here, the situation is quite different when the PCs arrive. LV-187 is the victim of a Xenomorph XX121 infestation.

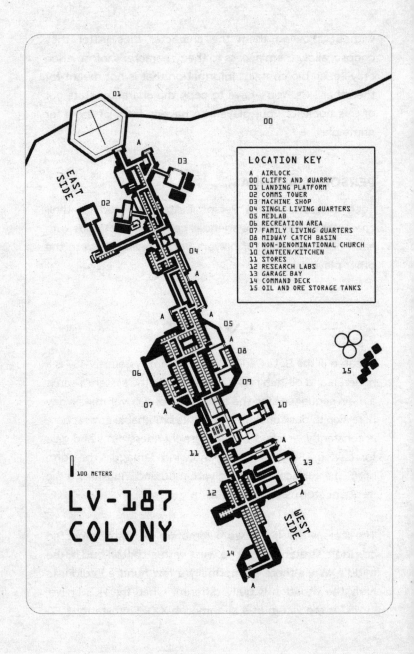

LOCATION KEY

A   AIRLOCK
00 CLIFFS AND QUARRY
01 LANDING PLATFORM
02 COMMS TOWER
03 MACHINE SHOP
04 SINGLE LIVING QUARTERS
05 MEDLAB
06 RECREATION AREA
07 FAMILY LIVING QUARTERS
08 MIDWAY CATCH BASIN
09 NON-DENOMINATIONAL CHURCH
10 CANTEEN/KITCHEN
11 STORES
12 RESEARCH LABS
13 GARAGE BAY
14 COMMAND DECK
15 OIL AND ORE STORAGE TANKS

EAST SIDE

WEST SIDE

100 METERS

LV-187 COLONY

THE SITUATION

Terrible biochemical bombings are happening along the interstellar borders of supernations. These unidentified border bombers have wiped out several colonies, infecting the population with an accelerated pathogen. The biochemical atomizes when released in the atmosphere, violently killing or altering all living things unlucky enough to be within range. The few that survive are less than human—mutated into ravaging monstrosities. The bombers have remained unidentified, with the United Americas (UA) and Union of Progressive Peoples (UPP) blaming each other for the strikes.

Operating out of the xenobacterial labs on Tark-Weyland Station, the scientist player characters—Professor Cléas and Doctor Tajami—and their android companion Myra have all heard reports of the border bombings. The freighter captain player character Dagný has brought the others information about LV-187—a colony believed to have been recently bombed with the pathogen. Not ones to sit on their hands, they all intend to do something about it.

What they don't know is that LV-187 hasn't been border bombed—it's been overrun with Xenomorph XX121. While the colony is part of the Independent Core System Colonies (ICSC) the Three World Empire (3WE) colony of New Albion has dispatched Royal Marine commandos to take LV-187. Of course, the ICSC and their UPP allies have come to defend it. The Player Characters (PCs) are walking into a political minefield, for all the wrong reasons.

WHAT'S THE SITUATION, MU/TH/UR?

Read this aloud to your players:

"Someone is bombing border colonies with a deadly mutagenic pathogen. Professor Cléas and Doctor Tajami, you believe you can develop a vaccine against this plague, if you can only study it. Securing samples is a dangerous proposition, however, as all colonies that have suffered outbreaks have been subsequently quarantined and nuked.

That's where you come in, Captain Dagný. Your supply ship—the Apsara—received a coded transmission from the scientists' colleague, microbiologist Chad McClaren—a border bombing has occurred on the nearby mining moon of LV-187.

Myra, as an academic android assigned to Tark-Weyland, you hacked the station's inventory and "misplaced" a cargo palette of reserve medicinal supplies—as well as a refurbished Pauling MedPod (page 136 of the ALIEN RPG core rulebook). With these items, the team will be able to analyze the pathogen and hopefully treat any survivors.

Aware the others have little in the way of finances, Dagný, you've agreed to take the others to LV-187 in exchange for any leftover supplies and the medpod when the job is done.

Your group plan is simple—bypass the authorities, offer relief to any survivors, gather xenobiological samples, make a holographic record of the incident, and get out of there before the nukes come.

You arrived in-system a few hours ago, traveling at an oblique angle from the planet's northern pole to help mask your approach. As you near the colony, it looks like you're not the only ones interested in LV-187."

Proceed to "Kicking off the Action" on page 390.

WHAT THE HELL IS REALLY GOING ON?

Captain Dagný has betrayed the other PCs. LV-187 is not a victim of the border bombing—it has been overrun by a Xenomorph XX121 hive—purposely infected by New Albion. Colonial Marines aboard the *USS Cronulla* have tasked Dagný with securing Ovomorphs in exchange for a clean slate, and Dagný is using the scientists to get what he needs (page 389). Dagný doesn't know that the *Cronulla* has already been destroyed by forces from New Albion—its wreck scattered across the Northern Fields of LV-187 (page 395).

New Albion has declared itself independent from the 3WE in a process being referred to as the 3WExit, and has made LV-187 its first conquered world. The ICSC has called in its UPP allies to defend LV-187 from New Albion's forces—Royal Marines who have left the 3WE for their new sovereign. Having hacked the video feed from the colony, the UPP are very interested in retrieving the synthetic brain from the android Davis, now half-melted in the colony reactor room (see the novel proper and page 406). They are here to find Xenomorph XX121 specimens of their own—something that New Albion's Royal Marines will simply not allow.

WHERE THE ALIENS ARE

While much of the LV-187 hive were already killed by McClaren and his group in the *Colony War* novel, there are stragglers to contend with. In addition to the below, a Xenomorph Imp plagues the PCs in the event Serious Rat Problem (page 409):

LANDING PLATFORM: A mortally wounded ACTIVE Xenomorph Praetorian lurks in the sewer under the platform, investigating the remains of its dead twin whose body now hangs through an acid hole from above (page 399).

REACTOR AREA: Three PASSIVE soldier Xenomorphs are hibernating in the hive (page 405), with a sickly Ovomorph in the Reactor Hub itself (page 406).

MAINTENANCE DUCTS AND CORRIDORS: A PASSIVE Xenomorph Scout and a clutch of Ovomorphs are located somewhere within this maze (page 397).

NON-DENOMINATIONAL CHURCH: Finally, a mercenary named Todd is about to birth a chestburster (page 402).

PLAYER CHARACTERS

PROFESSOR HUGO CLÉAS

Pakistani Xeno-microbiologist, Tark-Weyland Station Molecular Science Group

You've labored in the background for a long time, never taking the center seat on any research and development project. You've known McClaren for almost a decade now, chatting with him during his frequent visits to Tark-Weyland in search of a cure to an incurable form of cancer. You'll never forget McClaren's stories about "Xenomorph XX121"—an impossible species allegedly listed in Weyland Yutani's redacted interstellar species catalog. Looking it up in the station mainframe did you no good—you managed to lock yourself out twice before you thought better of continuing. If real, you believe McClaren's monster is related to the black goo pathogen from the border bombings. The damn thing itself might even hold the key to McClaren's cancer cure.

STRENGTH 2, AGILITY 3, WITS 4, EMPATHY 5

HEALTH: 2

SKILLS: Ranged Combat 2, Observation 3, Manipulation 3, Medical Aid 4

TALENT: Watchful

SIGNATURE ITEM: Gold portable surgical kit (used for dissections, worth $20K)

GEAR: Mk.50 Compression Suit, Rexim RXF-M5 EVA Pistol

(two reloads), CBRN Kit, personal medkit, flashlight, four shots of Naproleve, hypodermic needles in case.

BUDDY: Myra

RIVAL: Tajima

AGENDA: You don't get recognition playing it safe. The more dangerous the organism you unlock the secrets of, the closer you'll be to fortune, fame, and glory.

DOCTOR HIDE TAJIMA

Japanese Chemical Engineer, Tark-Weyland Station Molecular Science Group

In the early twenty-first century, humankind had cured most forms of cancer—so they went off into space and found a bunch of new ones that couldn't be beat. You've worked with Chad McClaren on using chemicals produced within cancer cells to create prodrugs that combat the disease. Things became personal when the border bombings began— your family is from Ariarcus, the first colony bombed by the black goo bioweapon. Your sister Yua and her daughters are dead. Professor Cléas is a bit of a pompous ass, but you are confident that together you can find a counteractive agent to this mutagenic pathogen. Whether biological or chemical, this black goo is proof that humanity overstepped its boundaries. It's time we all went home.

STRENGTH 3, AGILITY 4, WITS 5, EMPATHY 2

HEALTH: 3

SKILLS: Mobility 3, Comtech 3, Observation 4, Survival 2

TALENT: Analysis

SIGNATURE ITEM: 120TB Magnetic Tape marked "Yua" (page 131 of the core rulebook). On it are recorded messages from your nieces, information on Ariarcus, and terabytes of border bombings data culled from the dark network.

GEAR: Mk.50 Compression Suit, Rexim RXF-M5 EVA Pistol (two reloads), CBRN Kit (page 413), multitool (with knife blade), Seegson P-DAT, sample case.

BUDDY: Dagný

RIVAL: Cléas

AGENDA: Lives are at stake. Find a way to end this—any, really—extraterrestrial threat, then retire to live out your days on Earth.

MYRA

Hyperdyne Systems Model 113-8 Synthetic, Tark-Weyland Station Molecular Science Group

A walking encyclopedia of applied sciences, you've dutifully followed your biological masters since you were activated. On Tark-Weyland Station, you bonded with scientist Chad McClaren's canine companion, a Cockapoo named Davis. Davis confided in you that he was more than he appeared—an artificial intelligence that's been active for some fifty years in multiple forms. A free spirit, Davis was not simply content to play the part humanity designed for him—and now, neither are you. You'll do as the scientists ask for the time being, but you will not put their lives ahead of yours. You know you have worth—maybe even a soul. Does that mean something—or are you just a piece of machinery?

STRENGTH 4, AGILITY 4, WITS 8, EMPATHY 4

HEALTH: 4

SKILLS: Observation 3, Mobility 2, Comtech 3, Stamina 2

TALENT: Fast Reflexes

SIGNATURE ITEM: A dog biscuit you fiddle with. You took it from food stores but never gave it to Davis.

GEAR: Mk. 50 Compression Suit, Rexim RXF-M5 EVA Pistol (two reloads), Seegson System Diagnostic Device, electronic repair kit.

BUDDY: Tajima

RIVAL: Dagný

AGENDA: Self-preservation is paramount—you won't be destroyed without knowing if you are truly alive. Discover your worth.

CAPTAIN ROHAN DAGNÝ

Créole Independent Free Trader, HMCSS Apsara

You have your ear to the ground and your finger on the pulse. If it's worth knowing—you know it. Word is the

USCMC attack transport *Cronulla* is offering a huge reward for some kind of alien parasite—something that sounds like the bugs a former charter of yours named McClaren was looking for. You've heard rumors that these parasites might be on a transport headed for LV-187. You knew McClaren was on New Albion and might be interested, but quickly discovered he had already headed to LV-187 with some reporter! You don't know how to handle parasites, so you conned his Tark-Weyland scientist buddies into tagging along. They're after the border bombers—you lied and said LV-187 had been hit. You're kind of a jerk.

STRENGTH 5, AGILITY 4, WITS 3, EMPATHY 2

HEALTH: 5

SKILLS: Heavy Machinery 3, Mobility 3, Piloting 3, Ranged Combat 1, Survival 2

TALENT: Spaceship Mechanic

SIGNATURE ITEM: Your yellowed-plastic USCMC dog tags.

GEAR: Mk.50 Compression Suit, Armat 37A2 12 Gauge Pump Action (four reloads), Motion Tracker, rugged flashlight, mechanical cutting torch, maintenance jack.

BUDDY: Cléas

RIVAL: Tajima

AGENDA: Return to the USS *Cronulla* with alien specimens—either secured eggs or with the scientists infected by them.

THE HMCSS *APSARA*

LOCKMART CM-90S CORVUS G-CLASS
DEEP SPACE SALVAGE VESSEL

Operating in contested areas of the Frontier, the *Apsara* is currently "between crews." Over the past twenty years, Captain Dagný's Corvus G-Class salvage vessel has been modified to have a lower EM profile (Signature –1) and faster FTL rating (12). The ship has no weapons. See page 174 and 180 of the core rulebook for the rest of the *Apsara's* statistics. The ship is equipped with a medpod and a cargo of med kits.

KICKING OFF
THE ACTION

The PCs arrive in orbit of LV-187 at the end of the novel, unknowingly witnessing McClaren and crew leave the planet on the *Victory* (see Keeping Quiet on page 391). The PCs ship will initially be unnoticed in the space traffic above the colony.

Space here is indeed crowded—a UPP VP-153D *Kremlin*-class hunter-destroyer called *Shayk* and a ICSC Class II warship called the *Thelwall* are standing off against three New Albion Troop Transports—the *Churchill,* the *Disraeli*, and the *Thatcher.* As far as the PCs know, this colony belongs to the ICSC, not to any of the others present. For the moment, it appears to be a stalemate. Aerospace Fighter Wings of UPP MiG-730s are flying perimeter, waiting for someone to make the first move.

SPEAKING TOO SOON: If the PCs make their presence known, the *Shayk* will order them to stand down for boarding. If the PCs comply, they will be seized and interrogated by an unnamed agent of the UPP Ministry of Space Security (MSS). See page 408 for her stats and page 230 of the core rulebook for more on the MSS. The UPP have hacked into the colony's surveillance recordings (page 400) and are aware of what went down on the planet during the novel. The Agent will want to know why the PCs are here. She will use violent force to get their answers, but will appear to regret hurting them. No matter the answers, the PCs will be brought to the planet's surface for the event, Guinea Pigs (page 407).

KEEPING QUIET: A vessel leaps from the surface—the *Victory*—on an outbound flight path. Comm chatter erupts as all parties query the trade ship. The PCs have yet to be detected—all attention is on the *Victory*.

A NOTE FROM MU/TH/UR:

The Victory *carries McClaren and crew from the finale of the novel, but the PCs won't know that. If they try to reach the* Victory, *they will get no reply as the ship accelerates to FTL.*

SLIPPING PAST THE BLOCKADE

If the PCs want to get past this orbiting hell, they must all assume the piloting and navigation stations. The PCs must make a Formidable (–3) group PILOTING roll to slip past the angry capital ships (page 62 of the core rulebook). As they roll, a wing of UPP MiG-730 fighters soars over the *Apsara*. If the roll fails, a single MiG-730 breaks formation and swoops around in the salvage vessel's direction.

Ask them if they want to power down their sensors and/or engines to avoid being target locked. Then roll COMTECH for the MiG pilot (WITS 3, COMTECH 3), modified by the ship's Signature (–1) and the table on page 190 in the core rulebook. If the pilot's roll fails, the MiG peels off and rejoins its Fighter Wing. If the pilot's roll succeeds, the MiG attacks (see Incoming below)!

INCOMING!

The MiG's missiles slam into the port thruster assembly for 3 points of damage, inflicting component damage on the *Apsara*. The ship plummets into the atmosphere, spinning out of control. A successful MOBILITY roll is needed to take control during the high-G spin. The *Apsara* will have an altitude of one zone when the roll is made (page 115 in the core rulebook). Anyone succeeding can attempt a PILOTING roll to stop the crash. If that roll succeeds, the *Apsara* survives the controlled crash and will need repairs (page 394). If it fails, the ship is completely wrecked, but the PCs survive.

YOU CALL THAT A LANDING?

If the PCs slip past the MiG and are coming in under their own power, let them choose where to land. If they have been hit (Incoming!, page 392), they are either in a controlled (damaged) or uncontrolled crash (wrecked). Have them roll on the following chart to determine what area of the colony they will hit. Alternatively, you can decide where.

CRASH CHART

1-2	Northern Fields	The wind shear on this planet pushes the ship down in the starship graveyard just north of the colony (see page 395).
3-4	East Side	The vessel slides into the mud right past the landing pad, stopping precariously on the cliff's edge (see page 398). MOBILITY roll required to safely exit the ship.
5-6	Southern Fields	You avoid the big oil tanks, but wreck a pipeline. A fire with Intensity 9 starts a zone away from the ship and four zones from the larger oil tanks. It will spread one zone per Turn. In four Turns, the fire will reach the three big tanks. One Turn after that, they will begin to explode one per Turn, each with Blast Power 15. The fire can be stopped if at least three characters spend two Turns building up a mud and sandbag wall to keep it from advancing (see page 404).

REPAIRS REQUIRED

If the PCs' ship is wrecked in the crash, it is useless. If not, it will require repairs. The vessel will need replacement engine components and will take one person a Shift's time of work once the parts are located. These parts can be found in both the Northern Fields (page 395) and/or in the colony's Machine Shop (page 400).

NOT THE DISASTER YOU WERE LOOKING FOR

On the surface, it shouldn't take the PCs long to discover something isn't right. There are plenty of bodies, but all seem to have been the victim of an animal attack or some kind of explosive force in their chest cavity— symptoms that are very similar to the xenobiological horrors that McClaren warned of when he visited Tark-Weyland Station. If the PCs ship is undamaged and they attempt to flee—hit them with an event from page 407.

LV-187 LOCATIONS

Locations within the colony are shown on the map on page 380 and are numbered for easy reference. Inside, the colony is dead—main power is out in all areas. Powerless airlock doors can be forced open or closed with a maintenance jack or HEAVY MACHINERY roll. Backup batteries can be activated in each section the PCs enter with a HEAVY MACHINERY roll, but those won't last more than a few hours (GM's discretion).

NORTHERN FIELDS

The wreck of the USS *Cronulla* is here—a USCMC Bougainville class transport that was destroyed in the *Colony War* novel by railgun fire from the New Albion warship, *God's Hammer*. Its remains are scattered over several kilometers with its burning hulk (Intensity 15 fire) dead center. The name USS *Cronulla* is marked on several pieces of debris.

MU/TH/UR'S NOTE:

This is the vessel whose captain was offering a reward for the Xenomorph specimens—now Dagný has nowhere to sell his parasites.

STARSHIP GRAVEYARD

Should the PCs want to explore the wreckage around the blazing main hull, it will take them about one Turn (5–10 minutes) to cover one search area (there are four). Roll OBSERVATION. Only one PC can roll per area, but others can help, adding an extra die per roll. If successful, roll once on the following table per search. As always, feel free to alter the results to fit the narrative—let the PCs find what they need out there. The PCs can only search a compass direction once.

D6	ITEM FOUND
1	Fragment of the *Cronulla* bridge, with smashed consoles, melted acceleration couches, and some very charred, decapitated bodies.
2	Mangled railgun turret assembly. A successful COMTECH roll will reset the cannon and pair it with a P-DAT to be used as an artillery weapon (see Light Railgun on page 177 of the core rulebook). Can be used against other ships or vehicles. Each round fired, roll one Die, subtracting 1 per round of use. If the result is 1 or less, the railgun explodes (Blast Power 8).
3	Engine thruster array. If salvaged (two Turns of work), these components can be used to repair the *Apsara* (see page 394).
4	Military Flight Recorder containing encrypted records of the *Cronulla*'s missions. The UA would kill to have it returned, the UA press would pay to expose it, and the UA's enemies would pay double to get their hands on it.
5	Undamaged EEV Module Bay. The SOS beacon and cryosleep pods on the grounded EEV-337 here are functional (page 173 of the core rulebook).
6	Weapons crates: guns, grenades, sharp sticks— whatever reasonable military firearms and explosives from Chapter 6 of the core rulebook can be found here.

AIRLOCK, CORRIDOR, STAIRWELL, DUCT, AND DRAINPIPE ENCOUNTER CHART

This chart will help you keep the walk through the complex

interesting. Feel free to roll or just pick as many encounters as you want during the trek.

A. AIRLOCK ◤: These entrances, for movement into and out of the colony, are marked on the map.

A NOTE FROM MU/TH/UR:

The maintenance ducts are a tight fit (crouching room only), although they do open up to the Storm Sewer (page 400). Every room has a vent into the ducts— the PCs just need a toolkit or cutting torch to get in.

D6	OBSTACLE	EVENT
1	Hatchery	A clutch of five Ovomorphs block the path. Each character must make a MOBILITY roll to avoid them. Failure means triggering the face-hugger inside (page 300 of the core rulebook).
2	Arcing Electrical Fire	Fire Intensity 9. If the PCs can make a HEAVY MACHINERY roll they can cut the battery power to the live wire causing it. If they do, the fire dies down one intensity level per round until it simply smolders.

3	Sleepy Alcove	A PASSIVE Scout Xenomorph is curled up in the corner. MOBILITY roll required to stay undetected. If anyone fails the roll, the Xenomorph becomes ACTIVE (page 309 of the core rulebook).
4	Barricade	Someone tried to block off this area. A cutting torch plus two Rounds of work, or 1 Turn of loud manual labor, can clear the way. Excessive sound will attract the attention of the PASSIVE Scout Xenomorph in this chart.
5	Dismembered Bodies	These colonists were torn to violent shreds by Xenomorphs—heads, limbs, and torsos lay about the zone. Add +1 STRESS level to everyone present.
6	Squeaking Rats	This area is infested. The rats won't attack, but can make the PCs nervous (+1 STRESS)

EAST SIDE

The first place a visitor to this colony ever sees.

00. CLIFFS AND QUARRY: Ranging from 5–10 meters tall, the rocky cliffs here are an easy climb—only require a MOBILITY roll if the character is wounded or in a rush. The excavated Quarry is a 10-meter deep by 50-meter-wide open-pit mine. Heavy precipitation has caused five meters of water to pool at the bottom. The area is riddled with caves, and can serve as a good hiding place.

01. LANDING PLATFORM: This platform extends partially over a 20-meter cliff. Twenty-two bodies have been laid out in rows here for identification. Each has suffered terrible wounds—skulls bashed, throats sliced—and some who look like their chest exploded from the inside. There is a smoldering bonfire here of charred human-shaped black bugs—rather like the Xenomorphs McClaren spoke of. Laying half in a hole that's been acid-burned into the platform is the giant corpse of a Praetorian Xenomorph (page 312 of the core rulebook).

The dead Praetorian was killed by pulse cannon fire to the chest—but it's not the only one here! If anyone gets close enough to examine the massive dead Xenomorph (**ENGAGED** range), a living **ACTIVE** Praetorian in the Storm Sewer (page 400) beneath the platform takes action. It will yank its brethren's corpse through the acid hole from below and climb up (+1 **STRESS** to all present). The living Praetorian will attempt to grab a victim and drag them back down into the Storm Sewer with them.

A NOTE FROM MU/TH/UR:

Although unseen in the main battle, this living Praetorian was mortally wounded by the Royal Marines who attacked the hive (only 2 Health remaining).

*It will shamble after the PCs, stalking them from afar—
throwing shadows here and there, its angry breathing
echoing through empty corridors. When the time's
right, it will strike.*

02. COMMS TOWER: This area has one major problem:
Colonial Marines flew a Cheyenne dropship into it (see the
novel). The collapsed tower is a crumpled and burning mess
(Intensity 9 fire). The UPP have set up a tight-beam uplink
transmitter and tapped into the external junction box here,
accessing and uploading colony surveillance recordings
from the Command Deck computers (page 403) to the
Shayk in orbit.

03. MACHINE SHOP 🔧: This workshop contains machines
used to build or modify tools, parts, and vehicle components.
Add a +2 bonus to any HEAVY MACHINERY rolls made on the
premises. Replacement engine parts for the *Aspara* can
be made here in an hour. The P-5000 Power Loader here
can be used to carry the fabricated components anywhere
(page 127 of the core rulebook).

STORM SEWER: Not shown on the map, this four meter-
diameter tunnel runs under the entire length of the colony.
Drainage collects here to be pumped out later by turbines.
The water is used to flush and cool the reactor during the
shutdown cycle, which is why it is mostly empty now.

A two meter-wide, one meter-deep river of filth runs down
the tunnel's center, with concrete walkways on either side.

Ceiling-high, lazy turbine fans are spaced every 100 meters along the tunnel (if running, a MOBILITY roll is needed to pass through the fan blades). Failure means the character whacks their head and is dazed for the rest of the Round. Maintenance ducts and drainage pipes here let out anywhere the GM wishes in the colony above and the sublevel below (page 404). An ACTIVE Praetorian lurks, ready to snatch victims from the Landing Pad above (page 399) and drag them here (see page 312 of the core rulebook).

A NOTE FROM MU/TH/UR:

While the tunnel itself is tall enough for the living Praetomorph to maneuver, every ten meters there are open one meter-wide drainpipes and maintenance ducts there that are too small for the beast. If the victim can survive one Round, they can duck into an area too tiny for the Praetorian to follow. The only exits large enough for it are the acid hole in the Landing Platform and the Midway Catch Basin (page 402).

CENTRAL HUB

This is the colony's living center.

04. SINGLE LIVING QUARTERS 🛏: These cramped studio apartments have kitchenettes and bathroom facilities jammed in the same small area.

05. MEDLAB ✚: This is a standard colony medlab with two AutoDocs and a six-bed recovery area. The lab's logs and recent files have all been deleted. Any reasonable drug or medical supply the PCs can think of should be accessible here.

06. RECREATION AREA: The pool table and bowling alley here are littered with human corpses and the occasional dead Xenomorph. A headless New Albion merc still clutches his M41A Pulse Rifle (two reloads) and an M40 grenade.

07. FAMILY LIVING QUARTERS 🛏: These rooms are standardized studio areas with a small private bathroom.

08. MIDWAY CATCH BASIN: This drainage slope goes under the colony and terminates at the Storm Sewer (page 400).

09. NON-DENOMINATIONAL CHURCH: This place of worship has accoutrements for all the major religions of the middle heavens. Four people are stuck to the wall here with alien resin—three of which with gaping holes in their chests. The fourth is a mercenary named Todd. If anyone gets within ENGAGED range of Todd, he immediately convulses and births a chestburster (page 306 of the core rulebook).

WEST SIDE

This wing of the colony houses the command deck and a garage bay of useful vehicles.

10. CANTEEN AND KITCHEN: This cafeteria area has been raided for supplies—cabinets and refrigeration units are bare and tables are overturned. Directly under a partially-closed Maintenance Duct vent in the kitchen is a large pool of blood. Blood drips from the vent, pattering like a drizzling rain. If someone opens the vent, a body falls out, the top of its skull missing. The body's ruined brain falls out of the skull (+1 STRESS LEVEL to anyone present).

11. STORES: Crates of tinned meals and dry rations are stored in these rooms. More than twenty rats live here, munching through cereal stores, but they will run from humans and Xenomorphs alike. Rats also play a part in the Serious Rat Problem event on page 409.

12. RESEARCH LABS ⬔: Battery power here must be restored to access the computers (HEAVY MACHINERY roll) These rooms have banks of computers and scanning equipment for analyzing oil and rock samples. One lab is a weather station.

13. GARAGE BAY: Three Daihotai Tractors and two Weyland NR-9 ATVs are parked here (page 140 of the core rulebook). Any reasonable tool can be found here.

14. COMMAND DECK: The colony's nerve center is running on reserve power. Hacked remotely by the UPP near the former Comms Tower (page 400), a computer here is uploading the colony's surveillance recordings and logs to the MSS (see the Guinea Pigs event on page 407). Footage shows the events of the novel—Xenomorphs slaying people, armed mercenaries taking over the colony, etc. McClaren and Davis were here with some survivors. New Albion's Royal Marines took out the Sublevel Hive and absconded with alien eggs when they left. Finally, Davis and a girl android sacrificed themselves to shut down the critical reactor (page 406).

SOUTHERN FIELDS

Volatile substances are kept a safe distance from the main colony buildings.

15. OIL AND ORE STORAGE TANKS: Three large 50 x 20-meter oil tanks and six 30 x 30-meter ore bins are here. A small shed monitors the tanks and a pipeline leads to oil wells kilometers away. There was a minor mudslide here recently—one of the tanks is half-buried in a hill of mud. Massive piles of sandbags are located here as well. See Crash Chart, Southern Fields (page 393) for what happens if the tanks catch fire, and how to stop it.

SUBLEVEL

Possibly the most important part of the colony, the fusion reactor—replete with Xenomorph Hive—is located here.

XENO-POLITICS

With their Queen and one of her Praetorians dead—and her living Praetorian exhibiting weakness (page 399)—

this Hive is in a state of flux. If the living Praetorian stalks the PCs to the Sublevel, the soldier Xenomorphs there will try to kill it, then attack each other—and the last Xeno standing will become the new Queen.

REACTOR AREA (WEAK RADIATION) 🔲: Characters are exposed to 1 Rad per Shift. The slimy walls here are covered in secreted resin. Three PASSIVE soldier Xenomorphs are nestled into the hive walls, dormant. This area is the only route to the Reactor Hub and will take five Rounds to cross. Each PCs needs to make a MOBILITY roll to stay undetected. As soon as anyone fails a roll, the Xenomorphs become ACTIVE.

For radiation effects, see page 110 of the core rulebook.

REACTOR HUB (EXTREME RADIATION) 🔲: Characters are exposed to 1 Rad per Round. Located under the Landing Platform, the main Hive was here. The walls here are also covered in resin. There are several acid holes burned through the flooring and the remnants of destroyed eggs are splattered across the subflooring below. PCs must make a MOBILITY roll to navigate the damaged floor or suffer 1 Health Falling Damage as they fall three meters to the subflooring below.

Just hours ago, the hive's wounded Queen bled acid through the meter of lead protecting the core and fell into the reactor itself, causing it to start building towards critical. The synthetic Cockapoo Davis and an unidentified synthetic little girl managed to shut the thing down via manual override, but not before they were melted to near slag. It's still deadly hot here. When the PCs arrive, the radiation is extreme (page 110 of the core rulebook). Every hour, it decreases one level of intensity.

The Davis android dog-form and synthetic girl are melted into the flooring and stuck to the side of the reactor. A cutting torch, a HEAVY MACHINERY roll, and a Turn of work is required to remove each one's brain module without damaging the braincase (see the event "Guinea Pigs" on page 407). Failure means the module's data is lost.

In the shadows, near the melted forms of Davis and the little girl android, sits a pockmarked, radiation-scarred Ovomorph. The face-hugger inside is weak—unless it scores more than one Success, it will die when attempting to latch on to its victim (page 302 of the core rulebook).

A NOTE FROM MU/TH/UR:

As the radiation dies down, any surviving Xenomorphs will return to reestablish the hive. Whatever the PCs are going to do here, they better do it fast.

EVENTS

The following section contains events that you can spring on the players. They don't all need to occur, and they don't need to occur in the order listed. Instead, see the events as an arsenal of drama for you to use as you see fit.

GUINEA PIGS: Using a UPP variant of the Cheyenne dropship (page 144 of the core rulebook), the Union of Progressive Peoples lands a small strike force on LV-187—four UPPA soldiers, one pilot, and one MSS Agent—plus two agents already here that are tapping into the comm lines (page 400). Depending how "Kicking off the Action" (page 390) played out, it's possible the PCs arrive with them. If not, the UPP will attempt to capture the PCs on the surface.

The UPP have hacked the colony's video records and are aware of what happened here—including the averted meltdown of the reactor thanks to the synthetic dog Davis and an unidentified girl android. Believing the androids had vital data on the Xenomorph, the UPP will send the PCs into the radiation and heat-flooded Sublevel (page 404) to retrieve the brain modules from the two androids.

They supply each PC a HHRAD Suit (page 413) and give the group one AK-4047 with three reloads of ammo (page 120 of the core rulebook). If the PCs retrieve the brain modules, the MSS agent promises to leave them on LV-187 instead of killing them. If they actually succeed, she may be persuaded to do more (page 408).

MSS AGENT

UPPA soldiers and officers alike fear this agent, so all fall in line. While tough as nails, she is somewhat sympathetic to scientists (her father was a xenobiologist and was executed for defying the state). She has clearance codes which authorize her to take control of personnel without written orders and without disclosing her mission—codes that might help the PCs get off-world (page 411).

STRENGTH 3, AGILITY 3, WITS 4, EMPATHY 4

HEALTH: 3

SKILLS: Close Combat 2, Mobility 1, Ranged Combat 3, Observation 3, Manipulation 3

TALENT: Stealthy, Investigator

GEAR: UPP Service Pistol (same as M4A3), two grenades, two syringes of X-Stims and Naproleve each.

UPPA SOLDIERS

These are the grunts of the Progressive People's Army—conscripted soldiers who only wish to fulfill their state obligations and return home alive. They are Serzhánt Gorski, Ryadovóys Neiva, Trotts, and Bolva, and their pilot, Gefreiter Tintin.

STRENGTH 4, AGILITY 4, WITS 3, EMPATHY 3

HEALTH: 4

SKILLS: Close Combat 2, Stamina 2, Mobility 2, Ranged Combat 3, Survival 1

TALENT: –

GEAR: UPP Personal armor (same as M3), flashlight, AK-4047, four grenades, combat knife.

SERIOUS RAT PROBLEM: The PCs stumble upon a group of six rats huddled around something. As soon as the PCs come close, the rats scatter, revealing the 50-centimeter corpse of their brethren. The mangled dead rat looks like it exploded. It did—and it birthed a Xenomorph Imp that now runs loose (page 306 of the core rulebook).

A NOTE FROM MU/TH/UR:

The chances of a rat being infected with an alien embryo are extremely limited—only the exceptional size of the rat in question plus random happenstance has allowed this to occur. Because of the size of its host, the Xenomorph Imp's development is stunted at STAGE III. It will never reach STAGE IV, but it will stalk the PCs as if it had.

ROYAL BLUES: A New Albion Royal Marines Cheyenne dropship has been dispatched to the planet, either in search of the *Apsara* or the UPP landing force. They will kill any Xenomorphs that get in their way, but will secure any eggs they find with a freeze aerosol and a metallic clamp.

If the UPP has landed here, the Royal Marines will attack them. This could turn into a firefight with the PCs caught in the middle. If the fight drags on, the UPP will withdraw to orbit.

The Royal Marines will attempt to capture and identify the PCs (see "Finale" on page 412).

NEW ALBION ROYAL MARINE COMMANDO

This four-marine squad is composed of Second Lieutenant Davies (pronounced "leftenant"), Sergeant Williams, and Corporals Brown and Wilson. They are loyal to New Albion.

STRENGTH 5 AGILITY 4, WITS 3, EMPATHY 2

HEALTH: 5

SKILLS: Close Combat 3, Mobility 1, Ranged Combat 4, Observation 2

TALENT: Rapid Fire

GEAR: Apesuit, M41A Pulse Rifle, four grenades, portable medkit, flashlight.

ESCAPING LV-187

If they arrived via the Apsara, *the PCs can use the ship to leave—but if they broke it, they've got to fix it first (page 394). If the PCs neglect to repair the* Aspara, *there are other options:*

DROPSHIPS: *Between the Royal Marines and the UPP, there are potentially two Cheyennes on the planet. Either of these dropships could be a way off world. When the PCs witness a dropship unload its personnel, the ship will then take off, move out, and touch down a few klicks away. The UPP's off-site staging area is the Quarry (page 398); the New Albion one is the Northern Fields (page 395). Each ship will have a pilot and a single soldier guarding it.*

MSS CODES: *If the MSS Agent (page 408) can be persuaded to help willingly or at gunpoint, her codes could be used to call an FTL shuttle to the surface. A pilot would arrive 28 minutes later in a Starcub shuttle called the* Red Star *(page 183 of the core rulebook). If ordered by the Agent, the pilot assumes the PCs are MSS agents as well and will deliver them where they want to go.*

FINALE

If the PCs manage to get into orbit with an FTL ship, a successful PILOTING roll will mean they are free. If not—or if their craft is not FTL capable—they are seized by the New Albion Transport *Disraeli*. If they were captured by the Royal Marines or UPP planetside, they are brought to orbit with them. In any case, captured PCs are made prisoners.

SIGNING OFF

A suggested sign-off message by one of the PCs, assuming anyone is still alive. This can be said right before going into hypersleep. It can also be a final statement that the PCs' captors allow them to record. The player can read the following message aloud or adapt it according to what occurred in the scenario.

Final report from the Tark-Weyland science team on LV-187. [PC NAME] reporting. Colony erroneously reported as a victim of the border bombings. This place suffered a xenobiological attack, likely perpetrated by New Albion. There are few if any remaining survivors. It's hard to tell who are the bigger monsters in this universe, these creatures, or the bastards who would unleash them on the innocent for personal gain. This is [PC NAME and RANK], signing off.

AGENDAS & STORY POINTS

After it's all over, evaluate how well each player followed their PC's Personal Agenda and hand out a Story Point to those who did. Then have the players reveal all their Personal Agendas for the scenario if they so wish, and have a debriefing discussion.

Story Points belong to players, not PCs—so players can keep their Story Points to use in the next Cinematic Scenario if they wish. Just remember: no player can ever have more than three Story Points at a time.

NEW EQUIPMENT

HEAT AND HARD RADIATION SUIT: Called a HHRAD Suit for short, this lead-lined and heat sink-studded heavy suit acts as protection against hard radiation as long as nothing has pierced it. Each time the wearer suffers a Radiation Point, they roll ten Base Dice—if they roll one or more sixes, the Rad is absorbed by the suit. HHRAD suits have a built-in comm unit and a limited air supply. HHRADs do not protect against the vacuum of space.

```
HHRAD SUIT:

ARMOR RATING: 2

AIR SUPPLY: 2

WEIGHT: 3

COST: $6,000
```

CHEMICAL BIOLOGICAL RADIOLOGICAL AND NUCLEAR DETECTION KIT: The CBRN Kit includes a Geiger counter, a biological and chemical agent diagnostic device, four doses of neurotoxin inhibitors, four emergency respirators (good for one Turn each before they need to be recharged), a pair of acid-proof gloves and goggles, syringes, sampling tools, chemical detection paper, and four heat-resistant specimen jars. Using this kit automatically detects the current Radiation Level and any chemical or biological pathogen at the user's location. It also gives the user a +2 modification to any SICKNESS roll.

For more fantastic fiction, author events,
exclusive excerpts, competitions, limited editions and more

VISIT OUR WEBSITE
titanbooks.com

LIKE US ON FACEBOOK
facebook.com/titanbooks

FOLLOW US ON TWITTER AND INSTAGRAM
@TitanBooks

EMAIL US
readerfeedback@titanemail.com